The STHORY of TWO WIMMIN named KALYANI and DAKSHAYANI

The STHORY of TWO WIMMIN named KALYANI and DAKSHAYANI

R. Rajasree

Translated by DEVIKA J.

PENGUIN

An imprint of Penguin Random House

HAMISH HAMILTON

USA | Canada | UK | Ireland | Australia
New Zealand | India | South Africa | China

Hamish Hamilton is part of the Penguin Random House group of companies
whose addresses can be found at global.penguinrandomhouse.com

Published by Penguin Random House India Pvt. Ltd
4th Floor, Capital Tower 1, MG Road,
Gurugram 122 002, Haryana, India

Originally published as *Kalyaniyum Dakshaayaniyennum Peraaya Randu
Sthreekalute Kata* by Mathrubhumi Books 2019
First published in Hamish Hamilton by Penguin Random House India 2022

Copyright © R. Rajasree 2022
Translation copyright © Devika J. 2022

ISBN 9780670096909

Typeset in Adobe Garamond Pro by Manipal Technologies Limited, Manipal
Printed at Replika Press Pvt. Ltd, India

www.penguin.co.in

Translator's Note

'If the writing is *really* rooted in its language and culture, it is impossible to translate,' announced a friend triumphantly as he gifted me a copy of R. Rajasree's *Kalyaniyum Dakshayaniyum Ennu Peraaya Randu Sthreekalute Kata*. The book was by then a roaring bestseller in Malayalam, also feted for its success on social media. Rajasree had posted it chapter by chapter on Facebook first, where its readership swelled hugely. *Kalyaniyum . . .* is part of a larger trend in Malayalam literature: the novel has increasingly become a medium of questioning dominant, hegemonic, standard Malayalam—as a language, culture and history. Malayalam literature now tries to strip away Malayalam's/Kerala's singularity by giving voice to the diversity of the spoken word as uttered in different parts of Kerala, by shining a light on the microsites of culture and power, and on unseen pasts and presents smothered by the grand narrative of Kerala. The gift of the novel was a challenge to me.

Of course, most translators including me, are used to having some version of the Sapir-Whorf hypothesis thrown at them all the time, so this did not scare me too much as I have always have quoted Walter Benjamin's splendid 'The Task of the Translator' back at them. However, this gift was offered at a time when I was mulling over taking a long break from translating, bothered as I was by the direction that translation from Malayalam into English (at least) was taking, in a highly competitive, market-driven literary-cultural atmosphere. I knew that things had changed tremendously from the time I had started as a translator—translations from Malayalam are now neither few nor invisible. Yet some features of this success trouble me, especially because many of the texts chosen for translation had indeed posed defiant questions to mainstream Malayalam—they use the spoken word of particular regions in Kerala not as a mere embellishment but as a way of including much of that which standard Malayalam has always excluded as language and culture. Many of these experiments, including Rajasree's, have been brilliant successes in both the literary market and in (the rapidly shrinking space of) Malayalam literary criticism. That such success is more important now than ever before as a criterion by which literary texts are taken up for translation, has disturbed me for some time. But more than that, I worry about the manner of their translation.

I am certain that the intentions of the translators are spotless. Yet I cannot help asking myself several mutually-linked questions: what happens when the regional spoken word is simply absorbed into the translator's English, which, more often than not, is trimmed and polished with the unseen reader—the global reader of literary writing in English—in mind? Is the cursory acknowledgment of the spoken word's unique world through retaining some of its words and phrases in the text sufficient? Is it not that such a practice is necessary, but surely insufficient in a context in which Malayalam literature abounds with the challenge to the dominant, standard language that erases the words and worlds of the local spoken tongue? Especially when translating literary work in which tribal languages are used, translators usually turn to speakers of those languages for help. In that case, should not the latter be also acknowledged among the translators? The dilemma that these questions shape collectively is not a minor one for sure. Because there is no denying that the reader of Malayalam texts in translation is the global reader of literary writing in English, who occupies a certain (privileged) layer of the language. Yet, the translator from Malayalam can hardly excuse themselves from the context in which they have to deal lovingly with not just one but multiple source languages/worlds in a single text. This challenge that we face is not merely a curious coincidence but has arisen at an important political-historical moment in Malayalam literature.

As a historian, I worry that we may erase this moment if we do not take the challenge seriously. The fact that we are translating from regional languages/spoken words into a powerful, global language cannot be forgotten. If the latter is to be transformed by the former, this multiplicity of sources has to be taken seriously; and the historical moment of its rise to relevance has to be properly countenanced. Importantly, as a translator and feminist, I have argued that by translating anti-patriarchal writing in Malayalam to English, I seek to preserve the political charge of these writings from the debilitating 'taming' exercises of Malayalam literary circles. In order to be true to myself, therefore, I cannot turn away from these questions.

Rajasree's novel made all these questions jump up in my mind with urgency, like never before. For a key pivot of her story is the simmering conflict expressed as unfolding in and between two spoken forms of Malayalam—of the extreme north, where the protagonists Kalyani and Dakshayani claim roots, and of a southern region known locally as Onaattukara where Dakshayani's husband's roots are. These two Malayalams are vehicles for very different imaginations of the economy, family, society and morality. They are both patriarchal, but in noticeably different ways. The standard Malayalam and the academic style of reflection are used mainly by the teller of Kalyani's and Dakshayani's story (or by a few others who share her middle-class world fully or partially) who makes herself transparent, inserting herself into the novel as more than just the narrator—or it is the cows, beings that enjoy a fairly large measure of objective distance from human hustle, that engage in such reflection among themselves. It must be clear by now that the older, familiar practice of sprinkling the text translated into

Standard English liberally with words and phrases, or adding these first and then their translation in Standard English, cannot work for Rajasree's novel.

So I set myself the task of nuancing the translation to contain the echoes of these spoken Malayalams, in mainly two ways. One way I chose—and this for the spoken Malayalam of North Kerala— was to follow the sound of the spoken word and take some features that I noticed into the translation, like the frequent dropping of vowel sounds and the substitution of bilabial consonants and the pronounciation-style that blends words together, as well as the manner in which people there speak English ('bekk' for 'back', for instance). This was done as mainly a hearer of these sounds; I am certainly no expert in acoustic phonetics! The other way was to rely upon the manner in which English is spoken locally in the southern parts of Kerala (not 'girls' but 'gerls' and so on), and this was for the spoken Malayalam of the south. Of course, these rules could not be followed thoroughly and unfailingly, because meanings of words could alter entirely with some changes. The central consideration was that the spoken Malayalam should echo in the variant of English; the faithful adherence to (admittedly self-set) rules was given up wherever it hampered this.

Rajasree's novel is a delight, to say the least, and I discovered to my great joy its serendipitous reverberations in other feminist experiments in novel-writing in the country, most recently, the Geetanjali Shree's Booker-Prize-winning (2022) *Tomb of Sand*, in its irreverence and linguistic play, as well as the focus on the luminosity of women's mutual ties. It opens a fascinating door into the intimate lives and struggles of rural women in the 1960s and after, and the storytelling could well claim to be 'wimminist'. That is, it offers itself to the Malayalam literary public defiantly, challenging the innumerable misogynist representations of women in high-brow, low-brow and middle-brow Malayalam literature, and whatever has been tucked in between those. It bypasses mainstream literary aesthetics and opens up new worlds of lived beauty using the metaphors from the speech of the feisty rural women of North Kerala/North Malabar, and the irreverent laughter from the younger, anti-patriarchal imagination arisen in Kerala's present. The late twentieth-century History of north Malabar, as well as the very local 'histhory', unfold in the background, but does not overwhelm these unique lives. The narration bears a striking resemblance to a long braid—it is the braiding together of the stories of the lives and loves of Kalyani and Dakshayani. These strands are composed of an astonishing range of characters: human beings from the north and south, snakes, rat and dog, cows, minor deities in temples, vampire-like *yakshi*s who suck men's blood, cashew groves—all woven together into a tale told by the teller, a middle-class, educated young woman struggling to take control of her own life, a minor Scheherazade telling stories to protect herself from mind-police and family authorities. No woman, the story tells us, is allowed to belong to where she is born. And yet women denied roots hold hands across generations, social divides, share lives, and are energized by the strength that flows through these connections. Viewed from another angle, this is a radiant map of women's hands holding each other across places and generations, set in the larger history of the politics and cultures of Kerala's north and south. The story makes no false promises, though: it sees the times change and bonds loosen, but shines with optimism. For the minefields of patriarchy may be omnipresent and ever-changing, but women still hold hands and skip over and beyond them.

Devika J.

1

Kalyaniyechi: 'Wha'yuh doin', al'bent ober? Yuh puttin' lime on tha betel leaves?'

Me: 'I am writing on the phone, Kalyaniyechi. To put up an FB post.'(Her name is Kalyani but because she is older than me and like a sister, I call her 'echi', Kalyaniyechi.)

Kalyaniyechi: 'Abou' wha'?'

Me: 'About men.'

Kalyaniyechi: 'For thath matther, wha'yuh know o' men, eh? Whattcclod o'dirt they are?'

Me: 'I can write what little I know?'

Kalyaniyechi: 'Tell me wha'yuh write, uh, lemme see.'

Me: 'It is about the men that I have met. Some are such braggarts, so full of themselves . . . bad enough to make you gag. They scare me!'

Kalyaniyechi: 'Ah-true! Dis-gusthing ith is! I ha' to tell one of 'em—betther'n this, flash yer goods, uh, lifth up yer *mundu* an' show! Unn-bear'bl'-*appa*!'

Me: 'Then there's the type that wants life to be all fun and games, but simply can't enjoy themselves. For many reasons. And so they get all judge-y, sneaky, and spread tales . . .'.'

Kalyaniyechi: 'Lon'time bekk I whack'd uh feller on tha nekkid open groun' . I wa' carrying tha bundle of firewoo' dow' tha hill, an' . . . afther thath he wenth around telling eberyone one

thath I'm into *thath other* kin' of bissness—of fucking—thath wa'
his job.'

Me: 'There are some men, nice guys, but scared shitless of
people. Living and dying in one thought—what will *others* think,
what will *people* think? They will not dare to take even a hand held
out to them.'

Kalyaniyechi: Wha'ss tha use of gettin' uh man whoose all
limp an' lank—lik' sum sorry bannana peel? Wha's tha good o'ith?

Me: 'But others are first-rate predators. Dedicated to the hunt.
They know that an animal can be hunted only once. This sort of men
is, like Sakunthala said in the story: 'the well overgrown with grass.'

Kalyaniyechi: '*Mole*, my dear, hardd to see thos! Yuh kno' only
whe' yuh ge'bburned! And sumtimes yuh findd out too late. No
use. Wha' to say, eccept tha' we shud grab tha faces of th' wimmin
who runnafter them an' rub'em on tha groun'.'

Me: 'And then there men who are constantly at war . . .
Rub them on the wrong side, and they swoop on generations of
'enemies'—not just of the past, but of the future too.'

Kalyaniyechi: 'Thos'ar' tha simpl'tons, tha poor suckers! Tha
ones whoo got killt in tha kings' *mamankam* war, in their lasth
birth! Suicid'squa'mmen!'

Me: 'But some do catch on. They won't preach about things
they don't know. And because they can laugh, they also respect
women. If you are troubled, they notice—and come over to sit
quietly by your side. I like them, Kalyaniyechi.'

Kalyaniyechi: '*Uyish*! *Entappa*! Iffo'lly I couldggeth one of
thathkkind in my nexth birth! Mebbe he has no trade, mebbe no
tools—an' no Tool, an' can't screw either—I'd hab him happpily!'

Me: [scandalized] Kalyaniechi . . .!!!!

2

Kalyaniyechi: 'Bhere yuh hurryin' off to, early in tha mornin'?'

Me: 'To see if all this can be set right.'

Kalyaniyechi: 'Wha'?'

Me: 'All this mess.'

Kalyaniyechi: 'Is there summone who can make ith all righth ou' there?'

Me: 'Apparently yes, people who have studied such things.'

Kalyaniyechi: '*Uyi*! So sum hab stharte' sthudying how to set righth oth'r pipple's libes?'

Me: 'Also, there's pressure from home—that I should meet him.'

Kalyaniyechi: 'So yuh lookin' to libe lik' he say, frommnnow?'

Me: 'I don't know. Might as well try to live like he says for some time.'

Kalyaniyechi: 'How long yuh hab to libe like in tha piece o' paper he writ'?'

Me: 'Six months.'

Kalyaniyechi: 'By thenn yuh'll push outtha one growin' in yer belly?'

Me: 'Um. Yeah.'

Kalyaniyechi: 'So won' he hab to writ'tha piece o' paper againtthen?'

Me: 'Yes, he will have to.'

Kalyaniyechi: 'Yuh didn' tell 'im which month yuh wer' in when he wrot'thath for lasth six months?'

Me: 'No.'

Kalyaniyechi: 'If yuh can't 'gree bith yer man, why'd yuh packupp anddgo to his place firssofall, for wha' loaddof bullshith?'

Me: 'Helplessness, Kalyaniyechi, a woman's helplessness.'

Kalyaniyechi: 'Elplessn'ss? Whatttha 'ell is thath? *Bhere* is thath'? In tha womin's bum?

Me: [shocked] 'Kalyaniyechi!'

Kalyaniyechi: 'Wha'?!'

Me: 'The family's honour. My little girl's future.'

Kalyaniyechi: So *yuh* don't hab tha two o' those—tha 'onour and tha futur'?'

Me: . . . [speechless]

Kalyaniyechi: 'So, is eberythin' okay now?'

Me: 'Yes.'

Kalyaniyechi: 'Thennn why iss yer face an' eyes all puffy?'

Me: 'Nothing .Just—nothing.'

Kalyaniyechi: 'Yer face an' eyes shou' be all swoll'n like thiss, uh?'

Me: 'Shouldn't they be?'

Kalyaniyechi: 'Wha . . . '?!'

Me: 'What does it matter if my face and eyes are swollen, Kalyaniyechi? Who's losing anything?'

Kalyaniyechi: 'Lik' our Bhagavathy Muchilottamma say, *kottilaathu kunhambu, kaikottilil kunhi*—yer man's in tha bed, yer babie's in yer arms! Wha' mor' yuh bant?'

Me: 'So that'll do for a woman, right?'

Kalyaniyechi: 'No. A womin needs more—a womin needs t'bbe spunky an' sthrong. She needs to keep tha hair on her head from fallin'. An' yuh musth be such thath no matther how old yuh mebbe, men musth sneak a lookit yuh.'

Me: 'I don't think all that's going to work anymore.'

Kalyaniyechi: 'Why's thath?'

Me: 'Kalyaniyechi, you know nothing of gender politics and body politics, *linga-rashtreeyam*, Kalyaniyechi, *linga-rashtreeyam* . . .'

Kalyaniyechi: '*Linga* . . . thath means tha dick! Tha *raasthreeyam* of tha DICK???? [swearing hard] Pha! Indee'! Ah-I'll scalp yuh prope', yuh li'l bulb of pus, *kurippe*!'

3

At first look, you'd mistake Dr Narayanamurthy's house for a temple. There was no doorbell to be seen; instead there hung a large brass bell. As you entered the yard, on one side, there was a shiny blue pond. In the middle of it stood a statuette, of a man and woman embracing. When you stepped into the front of the house, lined tastefully with plants, you'd surely feel that the world that you had lived in until then was but an illusion. This appointment, however, had been secured through recommendations by influential folk who could get anything done north or south, anywhere. Father's face was dark and grim from the thought that no matter how pretty the setting was, we were there for something utterly dishonourable. Mother lowered her face, weighed down by an inscrutable and ancient guilt. Vinayan held our daughter as though he bore the entire responsibility of preserving our family. She tried her best to wriggle down and began to whimper and weep when she couldn't.

'Did you notice the name, Aaccha? Murthy. A Pattar Brahmin. Merit seat for sure! Nowadays when I go to the hospital I make sure to check if there's a second name so that we know the caste. This is a good doctor. That's why I insisted that you try to get his appointment.'

Father looked uneasily at his son-in-law's face and managed a smile. Just when our daughter began to make a fuss, wanting to

6

ring the bell, the door opened and a woman clad in an apron let us in.

We sat in the spacious veranda, waiting, not knowing who would call us and when. The lamps that hung on the artificial ceiling above were evenly-spaced. I could see many closed, well-barred rooms from there. The sudden thought that they may be prisons for souls made me shudder. It was exactly then that the door of the north-side room swung open and Dr Narayanamurthy stepped out. His eyes conducted a general survey and gestured to all in our group except me. They went into one of the inner rooms. I knew what they were probably telling him now. I could also guess what he would tell me. He was the third person we were meeting for a solution to the same problem. After a long wait, I was finally summoned.

'Be sure to tell the doctor everything—everything. When you get out, your mind must be clean. From tomorrow, it's going to be a new life. For our family,' Vinayan said, making way for me as I entered the room.

'Can you draw?'

Narayanamurthy asked me when I sat facing him. He held out a piece of paper and a pen.

'What should I draw?'

'Anything. Anything you like.'

I was reluctant. Generally, I am shy when another person watches me. He who was going to read me from whatever I drew was probably aware of this. So I glanced at him diffidently.

'It can be whatever. Just draw. Be brave.'

I took the pen and put it to the paper; and managed to draw the picture of a beautiful-enough woman. He peered at me from above the rim of his glasses. It was irritating. I struggled to ignore the look.

'What did you draw?'

He was making me talk about something that was clearly in his sight; anyone would have been irked by that.

'Tell me, what did you draw? It's important.'

'A woman.'

'Okay, a woman. What is she doing?'

'She is sitting.'

'How? Is she doing something?'

'No. She's just sitting.'

Narayanamurthy put away the picture in his file.

'Shall I say something?'

I felt the stab of an unjustified fear. The fear that someone may concoct yet another sleazy tale about you, no matter how hard you try to ignore them, is not a minor thing.

'Your self-confidence is low. You haven't drawn this woman's feet.'

All the women I drew as a schoolgirl had feet; only that both feet would be turned in the same direction. When I grew up some more, the women's feet pointed to different directions. By the time I was convinced that a middle path was appropriate when it came to women's feet, I had stopped drawing.

I did not tell him that. Instead, I said:

'Isn't it nicer to conceal a sari-clad woman's feet? If it were some other dress, I would surely have drawn them. And besides, what about the flowers, the ornaments, and the other adornments that I did not draw just because you were watching me, Doctor? I don't think it is correct to draw inferences about anyone from such exercises as these.'

Narayanamurthy smiled.

'I know that you have not drawn many things that you probably saw in your mind. But I have the clues that I need from what you have drawn. Can you really say that what I just told you is untrue?'

I did not deny it. I had no reason to do so, did I? Because it was true.

The first-round win had boosted his confidence. Now he had the upper hand. It is easy for a self-confident person to gain mastery over another who has none. That is how it is in all relationships—

personal, work, official. Things might be look fine, like they are moving without a hitch. From the outside, it might even look quite pretty. Narayanamurthy probably thought that it was easy to control me now. But does he know that techniques like the drawing exercise that he used to subdue me, have been discredited decades back and relegated to the pages of history books? Anyway, I mentioned to him an article that had appeared in the *Medical Daily Bulletin* that argued something to this effect. That was the only way I could escape the power he would perhaps hold over me.

'You must realize the absurdity of trying to use a technique that was last updated in 1969 to analyse a person,' I said. 'That is the first thing. Secondly, there will definitely be a subjective reading in any interpretation (I used the English words—'subjective reading' and 'interpretation'). Therefore it may be proper for us to rethink the validity of such observations. And there are researchers actually doing the rethinking.'

Narayanamurthy seemed somewhat crestfallen now. I decided to let him know clearly that I had no intention to please.

'Can we reflect on why a person is always thought of as belonging to some social group? Why can't we stop classifying her according to warts or wrinkles, whatever? Why not look at each person as a unique entity, like they were separate and free countries?'

Narayanamurthy studied me closely.

'I was told that the two earlier counselling experiences irritated you.'

This angered me, though the anger was not directed at him.

'That wasn't counselling, that was threatening! That children of separated parents will end up as criminals; that they will be ill-treated in rescue homes for children in conflict with the law; that I must reverse my decision to avoid this catastrophe . . . I threw my bag once at someone who made these threats. I'd have been ashamed if I didn't.'

'Don't let it bother you. Some people try the easy route. Forgive them. It's hard to reform them, and no one's going to be fully reformed. I can only say that there are specific circumstances which shape people, and people will be what they are. And there is something to be said for your criticism of these tests. But they become necessary because our time is valuable, mine and yours. Having to relate very personal experiences to someone you meet for the first time is like having to get naked before a stranger. You can just talk about things you are comfortable with. I will listen. Stories, experience, whatever . . . Maybe when you tell stories, you may feel closer to me and open your mind? My job is not to judge the person sitting in front of me. Don't worry.'

Narayanamurthy closed his pen and put the file inside his desk. He took off his spectacles, wiped them and put them back on his nose.

'First of all, I have nothing to talk about, really,' I said. 'Whining endlessly about my life has only demolished my sense of dignity. The stories I tell you may have nothing to do with my life. And if it does, that may be entirely coincidental.'

'That's ok. Relationships are things we make, between living things and incidents, between stories and life.'

4

It is said that Kalyaniyechi had a friend named Dakshayani. They both studied only till Class 3. Dakshayani had stepped firmly out into the world from the classroom after bestowing upon the male teacher who had lifted her skirt and pinched her thigh the exemplary blessing, 'Rot in 'ell, yuh sonofabitch'.

Kalyaniyechi also walked out of the classroom offering moral support. And then they both grew up munching on the tender grain ripening in the fields, going to see the gods of their land dance the *Kaliyattams* in the sacred groves, carrying bundles and working in fields, farming vegetables, carrying loads of stones, and so on. A big *purushan*—a man—or as they say around here, a *puruvan*—an important fellow—a man with lots of *koppu*—valuable stuff, that is—came asking to marry Kalyaniyechi. In the meantime, Dakshayani began to work in a plywood factory nearby. She knew how to help with birthing, and that brought some extra cash also. Some farming, enough of cashew nuts even though you could sell that only once a year—all that was saving which she invested in the monthly group-savings, the *kuri*. One of those days, she got married to a chap from the southern parts—from Kollam—who was in the business of selling nails in Madras (as Chennai was called then). This husband would arrive at her house early in the morning of the first Saturday of each month and leave by Sunday evening. The wife, overcome by the generosity that sprung from the fount of her love, would tenderly present before him her everything, including Income from Other Sources. Invariably, after his Saturday night lecture and the cultural activities that followed, the husband would demand full-disclosure of income—Income Tax Form 16, like the Government of India—from his wife. No idea how it started, but that was how it came to be. When the man was off to Madras at sharp 3 p.m. on Sunday, Dakshayani would resemble a cashew tree post-harvest. Soon she suspected that something was amiss.

The months passed thus.

All these months, Dakshayani had an income, but not a paisa in hand. When she managed to save some money, she prayed, May he not come! And the other way round when he came: let no money arrive now. The zing began to vanish and loneliness began to set in. She soon began to feel that a big financial institution, mainly interested in monetary transactions, hell-bent on extracting penal interest from her eternally, had entered her life and was now lying on top of her. The hours he spent with her were banking hours, actually, and when they were over, the accounting would start. It drained her. So, naturally, it was not long before the vendor of nails reached the conclusion that his wife became stiff and log-like at 10.30 p.m. on the Saturdays he arrived because she was romping around with Narayanan of Nisha Talkies, Kunhikkannan of K.P. Motors, Thomas of Mary Hill Produce Merchants Ltd. and the Gulf-returned Ayamutti'kka.

5

In the early months of their marriage, Dakshayani would ache with sadness whenever Nailsvendor set off for Madras. She would finish all her chores quickly and early on Saturday before he reached so that she could spend more time with him. She had learned, for his sake, to drink strong, nearly bitter tea and eat southern-style fish curry with thickened gravy. Dakshayani's mother was quite surprised when she found the southern-style spiced butter-milk—the pulissery, that is—idling away in the round-bottomed pot, bereft of cooked vegetables in it. She blurted out: 'Wha's thissmess yuh hab cook'd?' 'Amma, yuh don' touch ith, ith'ss for him,' she would come flying. Dakshayani, as time passed, devoted herself to scrubbing the stains off the kitchen floor on the days he came. The exit poll reports read this as evidence for the fact that Dakshayani's tongue had gone missing and that she was actually subdued—all due to the inimitable skill of her puruvan, her Man. Dakshayani's cheeks felt swollen from not laughing for so long.

The divergence of policy approaches towards capital preferred by Nailsvendor and Dakshayani began to reflect quite accurately in the bedroom. There was absolutely no congruence between need and production. Mutual exchange, enterprise and negotiation were cut by nearly fifty percent. Like it happens in alliances built with just impending elections in mind despite intense ideological disagreements, fatal divisions began to appear just before the

13

merger. With the accusation that all this was solely because of
the ineptitude of the minor partner in the alliance, Dakshayani
began to unravel. When it gets really tight, women have the ability
to draw their minds out of their bodies and fling it beyond body
and bed. The mind needs to be taken back and put in only at
day-break when you are up again. If such a move would let the
alliance survive—then let it, she contemplated, and articulated
that sacrifice in a few crisp and succinct words: 'Leth them damn
termitths tak'ith, bloody'ell!'

6

Dakshayani started her cooking on the next Saturday with a sambar made from fried coconut scrapings and spices ground to a fine paste and thinned to make some gravy. She also made a fish curry in which the sardines experienced an intense identity crisis when subjected to southern-style cooking—as they slowly swirled in a paste of fresh coconut mixed with tamarind juice. The round pot that once held the southern-style pulissery was washed and firmly inverted on the kitchen shelf.

She didn't forget to add a pinch of cumin to the curry. Nailsvendor got through dinner picturing in his mind the southern-style gravy of fried coconut with spices and vegetables—the theeyal—when he tasted Dakshayani's sambar—and the pulissery of the south when he ate the fish curry. He managed to finish dinner somehow and retired to the bedroom; Dakshayani laughed silently. All undocumented struggles begin from the kitchen. At night, she thrust her sharp nails into Nailsvendor's back and thwarted a start-up that he had begun to seed. It was painful; he threw her a look of disbelief. But that very moment, she faked extreme interest. And so got away with it. Wonder if Nailsvendor noticed that she had deliberately overturned the boat? Dakshayani waited with bated breath for the moment when he would get up totally undeterred by this Leg-Before-Wicket at the very first ball (it was, after all, like a game of cricket!) and call her to discuss family affairs. When he suggested that he could wind up the business in Madras and begin one here, she asked eagerly—'Bhere? Here?' With limitless contempt, he declared that this place of hers was no place at all; that he was not like the motherfuckers who lived in their wife-houses. Women have no native place; if you need it so badly, you may claim the native place of the fellow who married you.

The dinner had got him all riled, Dakshayani realized.

'Leth me thinkkif I shud come frommhere. Thi' is my place?'

It struck her that a quarrel might be useful now. What starts to smoke should blow up.

Leave it—give me the cash, he gestured, suppressing his ire and holding out his hand.

'For fucking WHA'? An' owing yuh WHA'?'

The little girl who'd run out of the classroom shouting 'Rot in 'ell, yuh sonofabitch', sat inside her and complained. But Dakshayani did not utter a word. Her grip on the last note inside her little purse was somewhat firmer. Nailsvendor grabbed that one too and began to make that peculiar hiss he made when he counted notes carefully, fingers wet with saliva.

Dakshayani stared at the dark outside the window, gritted her teeth and cursed: 'Leth tha cobra geth thi' *kaattukaalana*, this dreadfulogre!'

Reduced to penury this time, Dakshayani's throat ached with helplessness. And there was a very immediate and exact reason for that.

7

Normally, a cow does not interfere in the family affairs of human beings. But Kettil Govindettan's cow did put its head into Dakshayani's affairs. Dakshayani had asked him for a calf when it gave birth. Though she later forgot that request, Govindettan and the cow remembered. Govindettan had decided to give up rearing cows. It would be a relief for both Govindettan and the cow if she could go to Dakshayani's. One day, when she was coming back from the factory, Govindettan reminded her.

'*Uyi!*' she recollected anxiously. Yes. She had promised the old man. But at that time there was money from a chitty savings coming. Now she had none.

The cow and Govindettan looked at her with hope. On an impulse, she told them that she would pay him the next week. But the next moment she baulked inwardly, not knowing why she made that promise.

'Going there today ithself?' Govindettan asked the cow. No, she nodded.

'Then take 'er afther yuh pay,' he said to Dakshayani.

Her mind was in a twist till she reached home. She was the girl who bought herself the gold-and-black-bead chain she so loved with money earned from carrying bundles and farming vegetables with Kalyaniyechi. It was she who got the front of the house neatly laid with pebbles and the well re-dug. Such a girl now looked like a raw mango fallen and yellowing. There was now an auditor auditing her all the time. Her life was now largely in numbers and sums!! The issue now however, was not a cow—but a promise. The struggle was between a promise and counting the paisa.

Goat, cow, cat, dog—Dakshayani was fond of them all. She spoke to all of them in their tongues. When Dakshayani was a child, her mother used to have a cow. The day it fell, fully pregnant, into the ditch that was dug for the canal and died, she wailed: 'Neber! Neber will hab a cow here'ggain!' When Dakshayani told her about the cow, her eyes grew moist from that memory.

'Then ggeth ith. Goyindan's cow's good', she said.

Dakshayani needed that assurance. They had just sold the coconuts and coconut-palm fronds. She borrowed that money from Amma; and decided that she wasn't letting Nailsvendor collect his monthly moolah the next time. And as an early hint, told him of it when he was at it on top of her, at 10.33 p.m. sharp on the first Saturday of the Malayalam month of Kumbham. 'I inthend to geth a cow', she said clearly, when he was clambering back and was nearly on dry ground from his usual act. But he was distracted— full of delight when he counted more cash than usual that night, and remarked, 'Oh so youw haave caashu, lo..ots of caashu'!

'Won' gibb yuh anny cash nexth month, okay? Hab promis'd Goyindettan, an' borrow'd tha sum from Amma,' she told him.

'Loanu from Amma? Why d'yore Amma need money, *edi*?' He dismissed her, rolling the dismissal out in his southern drawl. 'Why shudd women keep yany money withu them? Maarried ones won'tu. Why do oldu people needu caashu?'

When she heard him say 'caashu, caashu', Dakshayani remembered the sound that she had heard in the serpent-grove once—when she had crept in there to pick the *jadaa*-flower. She pulled her arm away uneasily when his cold hand fell on it as he bid goodbye.

When he disappeared from eyeshot, she turned around and looked at the house, relieved. How pleasant it is to have one's own home and a native place too.

At the same time, in a cowshed in another house nearby, Govindettan was rubbing the cow's neck and comforting her: 'I'll commebby ebery mornin'. . . ith's clos', really clos' . . . '

But, upsetting the hopes of the cow, Govindettan, Amma and Dakshayani, Nailsvendor extracted his usual tax (or interest) payment. Dakshayani did not need a cow now; she did not consult him before promising Govindettan; the word of women, since they do not have the Adam's apple, is worthless; Govindettan who believed her was a cheapo sort of guy; Dakshayani's family is out to squeeze money from her; any new purchase must be made only for the new house he would be building down south, in Kollam; he would get a really healthy cow from the Thamarakkulam market; it will speak southern-style Malayalam—he informed Dakshayani of such matters. Dakshayani was shattered, seeing the prospect of her credibility and integrity crashing before the eyes of Govindettan, Amma and the cow. Just like in the war shown in the Ramayana serial on TV, there comes a powerful arrow, and the arrow that was waiting for it suddenly melted and disappeared. Govindettan's cow melted and disappeared in Nailsvendor's presence.

Dakshayani recalled the resident of the serpent-grove many times. This was the incident that prompted her to entreat the darkness outside tearfully—let there be an Encounter between Nailsvendor and Him.

8

Dakshayani did not go to the factory on Monday. She cleaned up the old cowshed, which was being used to store firewood; swept it clean, burned all the dirt in a corner of the yard. The cowshed that had become a junk house for all the unwanted stuff in the house after her wedding looked bright and clean now. She caught the scent of her own place and of herself in the old stuff that she moved from there. The place she shared with Kalyaniyechi, which belonged to many other women too.

The men from the south came to this northern place in which abounded endless cashew gardens, small factories and small sandstone quarries. Among them were those who came to build the irrigation canal; to do the cement-plastering on buildings; and to teach in the private schools. Many of them wed local women—Sarasu and Vimala and Sarojini—and turned into northerners. But there was something that just did not mix—like coarse shavings of the over-dry *tondan* coconut, which will simply not blend into the curry no matter how fine you grind it. Most people were unable to overcome those words, looks and feelings that made them feel reluctant to go over to the southerners for a chat; something stopped the people of the north from building relationships with them. Also, there was a saying going around—that it was more possible to trust that feared resident of the serpent-grove who stopped you when you sneaked in there to pick the jadaa-flowers, than the southerner. (No easy thing, really, to become part of a

people's folklore by just showing your true colours). Still, many
did not return to the south; but many of those who *did* go back
home did not return. Though some of these men had actually
sneaked off after having enabled live cultural confluence between
the north and the south through their dalliances with young girls,
no one went looking for them. Let them suffer, the local young
men thought—let them suffer. Yes, let these women, who jumped
at the very first chance to seduce fellows from nowhere, suffer.
They were somewhat more compassionate towards unmarried
women who were stuck in a corner of the house because of a bad
horoscope or terrible family circumstances; the locals took pity on
them and cursed the southerners who had betrayed such women.

There was general agreement, in principle, that a tiny group of
two or three, including Dakshayani, had managed to marry decent
southerners. Women married to southerners, but who did not fall in
this group stayed put at home and were generally voiceless. They had
little to do except visit the homes of relatives to toil on wedding eves
or to care for the old and children and women who had just given
birth; their relatives left them at home when they went to other
places. Come election time, and they would be given lifts in jeeps to
reach polling booths. Such women met each other in the verandas
of hospitals, temple festival grounds and wedding celebrations.
They passed each other glances that only they could sieve and
clarify. *Echi, Mema, Mootha, Elemma, Balyamma*—they withered
into these kinship names; they crept silently in kitchen corners,
spreading on soot-smeared kitchen walls. Their legs shivered and
faces went white at the sight of Dakshayani. In turn, when she saw
them, Dakshayani remembered the word that Acchooty Mash(ter)
had tried to make them write in class three: *swaat-anthryam*.

"Anth' of *chanthi*', he yelled, twirling his cane—from so
many years back in time. Swaat-anthryam—that meant 'freedom'
('Freedo-m', that is—with an 'm' like in 'bum'). Little Dakshayani
had thrust her tongue into the gap of her gums where the teeth
were missing and tried to say 'anth', only to fail over and over.

That evening, Govindettan brought the cow to Dakshayani's home. Though it was an old cowshed, the cow liked it. She stepped in, taking over as its complete and sole authority, turning to summon her calf inside. Then shaking her head she bid goodbye to Govindettan; tasted the rice gruel in the bucket and pronounced her approval: good, it is parboiled rice. Govindettan entrusted the end of her rope to Dakshayani.

'If yuh nee' sumthing, I'll come.' He took the money, put it in his waist pouch and walked away.

Dakshayani kept inside an old purse the little yellow book in which she wrote down the sums that were reduced with each repayment. That very night, she hid it inside the clothes-box and moved it to Amma's room. The annoyance of having to hide in one's own place was evident in the way she moved. That one has to run miles away from the very person with whom one had shared one's body, all that one had, is pathetic indeed—whatever the reason for it may be. No woman, or man, in this world deserves it. She gagged on the memory of her girlhood in which she tied up in a piece of cloth the little gold bought from her labour in the vegetable farms and lifting loads, hid it in a rice jar; and then went around looking for a safe place to keep it.

'Amme, bhere do I keeppthiss? In tha westh-side room or tha inne' room? What if a thief comes?'

' Oh, Justh keeppith summebhere!! Whi' robber's going to tak' yer half or quarte' sobereign of goldd?'

'Ssh! Don'ttalk of goldd loudl . . .'

Now Dakshayani was in need of a place to hide herself; she had to run away. She seemed to be shrinking and shrinking into just a silhouette each moment.

'Wha'thiss? Batthering down tha whhole house?' Amma stood open-mouthed, seeing Dakshayani rush about.

'Leth ith break, if ith breaks,' said she.

9

Only after Nailsvendor opened the door and entered the room did Dakshayani notice that his face looked rather grim and bloated. Usually, he entered the home-scene after a nap and bath. He would come in seeking his morning tea, Dakshayani by his side. Today, he did the exact opposite, coming straight in and sitting on the wooden chair by the small sit-out next to the main door.

To Dakshayani's weak-voiced query whether she should bring the tea, he gave no answer. When his gaze reached the yard, her feet began to feel clammy. She escaped into the kitchen. As she paced the kitchen like a snake trapped in a smoke-filled hole, a raucous discussion on the topic 'The Status of Dakshayanis in the Lives of Nailvendors' was breaking out inside her. What could be the worst, she calculated. When you carry a load you've got to balance it properly on the banana-frond *theriya* mat you wear on your head. That's a skill. If you place the load properly you can walk with your hands free. But if it isn't properly placed, the theriya will unwind and the load will tip. That's shameful. It was better to lower the load then. If you decide to do that, you are saved the bother of staring at the long road ahead and don't have to worry about how you'd cover it all. Everyone knows that once you've taken the load on, you can't stop walking. The weight will press hard on your neck. And you must walk as fast and as steadily as you can, before you feel the weight. Once you put it down, you can stand or sit for a little while.

If there's no load on your head, why walk at all?

Dakshayani squatted on the north-side step of the sit-out and bit her nails wildly. It was into that scene that Govindettan, Damuettan, and Achootty Mash entered. Damuettan is Dakshayani's older brother. He stayed a fence away. He whispered to Amma that Nailsvendor had stopped there on his way here and asked him to come to the house urgently. He thought something was wrong because he had called him *Aliya*—brother-in-law that means—and added, 'Yowu may gettu two peeple you trustu well'. But Damuettan had got Govindettan and Achootty Mash to come anyway. He scolded his wife who had dumped the dishes she was washing and rushed to the house after him: 'Go'way! Look ath 'er, running 'ere!'

'Wha'? Wha'?' Dakshayani's mother sounded frantic.

After a few moments of indecision, Dakshayani was summoned to the inner veranda of her house to be tried.

That was the first trial Dakshayani had ever faced in her life. In the movies she had watched in Nisha Talkies with Kalyaniyechi sitting in the middle of all those musty smells rising from the of damp clothes of fellow-movie-watchers, there used to be court scenes sometimes. In all of them the accused had a lawyer, even if that lawyer was meant to fail. But Dakshayani had no lawyer. No woman who faces trial in her own home has a lawyer. In the few minutes in which she realized that she was both lawyer and accused, Dakshayani studied her case. When she raised her head to look, Damuettan's head was bowed. Govindettan was unable to conceal his nervousness at having got himself into such an awkward situation. He kept expressing regret meekly. Achootty Mash, as was his wont, was trying to find out which side was stronger. She realized that all three were flustered by the severe tone of voice that came from the wooden chair.

'I waandu to know howu tha caashu fo-r buying this cowwu was gottu.'

Nailsvendor's voice rose.

'Ah bu'thath. . .she's bee' . . . going to th' ffacthory to wor' . . .' Damuettan tried to justify his sister rather weakly, sounding more like the poor helpless brother.

'No, no, no-tt - att—aall- thaat. I know howu. She haas no money. I taike h-er caashu correttly leaving j-est enuff fo-r he-r esspences. Aa-nd thennu whennu I askd, she tried to tellu, she go-tt it from h-er Amma. I knew, yit waas aall ye bunchu of lies. If I don'du understand thiss, I mustu be ye foolu!'

Dakshayani's mother began to say something, but held herself back.

'I toldu he-r, don'tu buy that cowwu.After aall I yyaamm he-r cunt-hair-fellow of a hussbannd? You say, she mustu obey me o-r naatt?'

'She musthobey,' said Dakshayani's mother.

'Yess, wha' else?' Damuettan said.

'She musthobey,' Govindettan joined them.

'She shuddobey,' Achootty Mash sealed it.

Nailsvendor got up from the chair delighted that he had won three-fourths of the case, and closed his fingers.

'So two-three thingsu nowwu. Firstu, I waantu know who gaive he-r tha caashu to buy tha cowwu. Two, no cowwu allowwed here. Three, stoppu going to tha faa'tory, stoppu sellingg cashew nutsu.'

No one uttered a word. In that absolute silence, the shrill trumpet of Travancore—the south of Kerala—sounded high above north Malabar.

Further, two lessons were learned by all present:

First: the truth is that each individual is a nation of some sort. Given the right time, the right moment, they will either turn themselves into independent nations, or remain mere vassals. They may become friends or turn into foes. They will unknot and converge as priorities change.

Secondly: each human is like the snail that carries its own house. One could say that they keep carrying their own place wherever they may go. Taste and distaste, sights, feelings; all of these are shaped and seen within those boundaries.

10

Dakshayani folded her arms and leaned on the pillar. The moment she heard Nailsvendor's Three Commandments, her mind cleared.

In the middle, Govindettan realized that his cow was the root of all this trouble.

'Yuh don' ttbother abou' tha cow', said he, 'I'll pay you tha money bekk and take her bith me. Thaths all I can say?'

Dakshayani looked at him sternly.

'Dakshoo, you tell'him abou' tha money—whateber ith may be. Wher' yuh go' ith from?'

Damuettan looked at his sister, exhausted. He lowered his head when she returned the look. Achootty Mash shifted in his seat. Nailsvendor felt a strange apprehension. He knew perfectly well that if what he expected fell from Dakshayani's mouth, then there would be no one there who would be so felled as he. The estimated number of lovers attributed to Dakshayani passed through his mind. Actually, he knew just their names. Dakshayani herself had submitted to him veritable oil paintings of each of those men—a headslapper of a mistake, she realized regretfully.

Be that as it may, everyone waited with bated breath to know who had given her the capital to purchase the cow. But when Malabar was readying to fall at Travancore's feet in the event that she indeed had slipped somehow, Dakshayani said, in most ordinary tones:

'Wha's upp bith yuh all? Damuetta, ith's a loan from tha Society!'

The relief that Nailsvendor experienced when none of the names that he'd thought up appeared, was not small at all. What if she had mentioned one? What figure would a batsman cut, standing stunned on the crease, foolishly dangling his bat well after he was declared out? But often, it is the batsman who outlives the threat of getting out and manages to play on who poses a real danger to the opposing team. As though reminding others of this, he got up, shaking his whole body.

'Thaar! Thaar youw hear h-er. Thissu waasu to maike h-er say thiss. Buyingg ye cow through loanu! Whenn I toldu h-er nott too . . .aar youer wivesu like this? They do whenn you tell them no-ttu to?'

'Ayyo, nothin' of thath kin' . . .'Achootty Mash said.

'Won' do, Govindettan said, reluctantly.

'No.' Damuettan sounded firm.

'Will youw doo yit, if yit were youw, Amma?'

Nailsvendor tightened the screw further.

'No', she murmured. With this, Achootty Mash stood up and declared to the assembly in general.

'She knows she di'wrong. See her face? Leth thi' end here. Dakshayani is going to understhand. If her husban' don' like ith, no needdto rear tha cow.' He turned to Dakshayani, 'Can'ttyuh go bith him, girl?

Then, turning to Nailsvendor, he said, 'If yuh can, tak'er alon' bith yuh?'

No one responded. If your panchayat's done, then I'd like some water, the cow mooed from the yard. Coming suddenly to his senses, Nailsvendor snapped: 'Youfellow—*Eeyaallu*—givv that caashu aand taike yaway tha cow.' 'Taike tha caashu and pay off tha loanu', he told Dakshayani.

Who's this 'Youfellow', this *Ee-yaal*, wondered Govindettan, and when he realized that it meant him, he felt an undying enmity to that word.

Amma, Achootty Mash, and Damuettan partook of the same feeling, though not in the same measure.

Suddenly, Dakshayani's voice rose sharp and shrill, like a copper pot crashing on the floor.

'Don'ttyuh touch tha cow, Goyindetta. . . . ! Thath's the cow *I* bought frommyuh, paying tha money yuh ask'd! If I gotta loan, I'll earn tha money slogging for ith and pay ith bekk. Dakshayani won'ttccome to yuh.'

Achootty Mash pointed his finger at her and scolded:

'Dakshayani, sith down. Dakshayani, don'ttalk.'

Dakshayani bristled from top to toe.

'*Yuh* keeppquieth, Mashe! Thi' is nottyer u-school! Thi' is my house!'

Achootty Mash looked stricken, speechless.

Nailsvendor grew uneasy at the three-fourth part-victory slipping from his hands. He left the gallery and re-entered the fray, confronting Dakshayani.

'Tha caashu fo-r tha cowwu—*nee enne vahichathaalyo*—youw tookku me fo-r ye ride eh?'

Dakshayani didn't get what he was hinting at first. So she was a bit bemused. But the moment after it struck her, she knew that it was shitty slime. A sound that was somewhere between Ee and Oo escaped her involuntarily.

'*Choppa*! Stinkin' rottin' dick!'

She gnashed her teeth. That word was totally foreign to the Travancorean, our Nailsvendor. He thought she was expressing regret. Ego doubly engorged, he advanced towards her. The two economic systems stood facing each other. They brushed against each other and the sparks flew.

'How a-rre youw going to pay tha loanu? Howw? Howw? Youw say?'

'So wha'? So wha'?'

With supreme contempt, Dakshayani raised herself on her big toes and faced him.

'Bith toil! Bith my sweath an' toil. . .hear thath? Bith toil! No' eben five paisha fer yuh from now!'

Dakshayani abandoned the respectful *ingal* for the disrespectful *nee*.

Her voice rose. But the words came out in a rasp.

'*Dee*', Nailsvendor screeched, invoking the utterly disrespectful *edi*. But his voice went all squeaky and that queered the pitch. Dakshayani would not be quelled. She was still calling him *nee*.

'Or, why shud I pay yuh money month afther month? He comes on Sathurdays. Wha' for? Justh to fuck?'

She said that half to him and half to the assembly. The veins on her neck rose.

'Whe' he leabes on Sunday, he takes away one 'undred if I hab ith, or two 'undred, if thath's wha' I hab. For wha'? Ooh! Starbin' gruel? Am I gibin' him tha money to fuck me? For *thath*? Ah, thenn I cud gibe ith to summone who ca' do ith well?'

As the entire universe bowed low to her in salutation, Dakshayani shook her hair open, tied it up again and strode towards the kitchen area. Amma, Damuettan, and his wife who were crowding the door, instantly parted and made way. She gulped down a full glass of cold water. And crossing the kitchen door, walked straight out; tossing off all burdens, swinging her arms. She passed by the platform around the erinjhi tree and stepped on the panchayat road. She met many people she knew and they asked her all sorts of things. Dakshayani did not want to interrupt the breeze that blew on her face by even moving her lips faintly. When she walked by the paddy field, she pulled off a bunch of unripe grains and held it in her hand. She bent down to gather some of the *njaaval*—jamun-fruit that lay scattered under the tree in the Upper-Primary School yard. Dakshayani walked on the narrow path that turned toward Kalyaniyechi's house, soaked with the scent of the kammunist-*paccha* leaves and lantana flowers.

(Kalyaniyechi, I haven't forgotten you. We will meet soon, be ye-easy! Dakshayani is standing in the path leading to your house. For now, hold a hand out to her.)

11

Kalyaniyechi was busy with coconut-plucking, collecting coconut-leaf fronds and clearing the wild. Dakshayani's hair was a tangled mess with bits of twigs and leaves sticking in it; she smelled of kammunist-*paccha* leaves and lantana. Though she was very fond of that scent, Kalyaniyechi turned her face away. Dakshayani stuck out her tongue stained purple with the juice of the njaaval fruit. Kalyaniyechi pretended not to see.

What to do now?

Kalyaniyechi, I called to her. If you don't call her, I'll be stuck. You have to make a decision about Dakshayani who is standing right in front of you at this moment.

'Don' *yuh* say a thing!!!' snapped Kalyaniyechi; she threw the machete she was holding at the *kanjhiram* tree.

'Yuh mak' me speak here an' there, lik' a cat gettin' tha head an' tail of tha fish yuh cut! Hab yuh eber tol' any of my sthories fully? Cann yuh fin' summone bith so many sthories, lik' me, in all thi' place? Yuh hab beennable to tell Dakshyani's sthory blow by blow, but who tol' yuh her sthory firsth? Me, righth? Is my sthory bith her, or tha othe' bay roun'?'

If I don't tell Kalyaniyechi's story now, Dakshayani will have to wait forever outside the house. Kalyaniyechi must talk to Dakshayani, take her hand, and invite her in. Offer her food—she's had just a cup of water, as you know. Already, Nailsvendor must have left on the first transport available; Achootty Mash

31

and Damuettan must have parted quietly without looking at each other; and Dakshyani's Amma must have thought, let the hussy go to hell. She had already shared with her daughter-in-law, Damuettan's wife, the worry that Dakshayani may meet with the same fate as as that other hussy, of the Erath house, Yasoda, whose southerner husband seems to have disappeared without a trace. Meanwhile, the cow tilted her head in utter disgust at all this, cussing to herself about these human beings being a bunch of sores, and trying to expel the black ant in her nose with a sneeze. Govindettan sighed—'*Uyyentane*. . . Ah my dear . . .' And went home. There's no point at all in Dakshayani returning there at the moment. But Kalyaniyechi is right. The story which began in her name is thrumming around Dakshyani now, who could bear that?

'Kalyaniyechi, the problem is that as long as I call you 'big sister'—Kalyani*yechi*—my storytelling won't work. You two are the same age, but I am not calling her Dakshayaniyechi, am I? I called her by her name, right? Now, that's nicer. I can tell your story only then.'

Kalyaniyechi moved two feet forward as though convinced.

'So yuh wan' to call me 'Kalyani'?'

'Yes, that's necessary.'

'Yuh'll call me 'she', 'her'—bith no resspect, yuh'll callmme *oll*?'

'Well, that's a habit, Kalyaniyechi.'

'Wil' yuh geth used to thath?'

'No. I'll change back to normal in between. But even the two of us shouldn't notice that.'

'Alrighth', then. Bu' if yuh don' tell ith righth, *I'll* be telling my sthory.'

'Agreed.'

'Ah, justh waith a momen', leth me ask—'Hey, hows *yer* puruvan doin'? Bhere's he now?'

'He's at Kollam.'

'Thath's very good!'

'What's good, Kalyaniyechi?'

'Leth thath be. Now yuh betther sthart my sthory—if yuh bant me to geth tha womin sthicking ou' tha purpl' tongue in tha fron' of my house and scaring pipple ou'tthere, to come inside 'ere. Yuh 're to call me 'Kalyani', righth? So call. Leth me hear.'

'So—shall I start?'

'Make ith quickk.'

So I started:

'No one around here was surprised that a fellow with lots of koppu—valuable stuff, that is—married Kalyani and took her away. They knew that a girl like her deserved such good luck.'

'How does that sound?' I looked at Kalyani(echi).

She was busy addressing Dakshayani.

'*Uyi*! Lookithyuh! Eh? *Paccilakkaattilacchi*! Tha Gree' leaffwench? Yuh smellin' o' lantana? Twigs an' grass in yer hair? From where di' yuh rush'ere'? Here, come, drink sum col' ricepporridge?'

'Ooh, sum koppu-fellow's womin! An' offerin' col'pporridge? Putton sum tea, will yuh?'

Dakshayani laughed loudly as she climbed the steps of Kalyani's house.

12

Kalyani's wedding was on a Thursday. A Jeep-full arrived from Koppu-man's house at her doorstep at seven in the morning. There was a whole panchayat of females in it. And: one basket full of jasmine; one of assorted flowers; a suitcase with Vanaja (Koppu-man's younger sister) carrying it; the first Ammayi (wife of senior uncle); the second Ammayi (wife of junior uncle); Aappan's wife (wife of father's brother); her daughter-in-law; the local fashion designer Thankamaniyechi; three grandmothers—who were in no shape to push and shove in the wedding party that would soon follow; six children in the range between the *bilimbi* fruit (little-finger-length) and the (medium-sized) guava; Pappy who never missed a single movie (Pappy was a special invitee to all weddings in the locality as she was the local beauty consultant); four women neighbours who simply couldn't be left out (north, south, east and west-side neighbours). And they all came out (in that order) through the back of a Jeep. They stepped on the tiny path that led to the house where the Jeep could not go, when someone jumped off its overhead carrier and yelled: 'Don'! Tha 'oroscopes haben'th bee' tied togethe'!'

Four senior men got down from the front seat of the jeep and walked towards the house.

On the veranda, Kalyani's and Koppu-man's horoscopes were tied together. Usually that would be done at the betrothal but there had been no betrothal.

When Koppu-man first saw her, Kalyani was pounding rice on the stone. Her body was swaying rhythmically, from her hair that fell lushly to her hips like the flowers of the drumstick tree, down to the hem of her skirt. She raised her face beaded with sweat and told the visitors, 'Pleas' sith down, I'll cal' Amma', and Koppu-man decided that second: This girl will do. The wedding was to be on the 12th of the Malayalam month of Meenam, in March-April. No one was to proffer any opinion.

He decided there itself to tell his brother Lakshmanan in Dubai to bring a Dubai-style gold-threaded sari when he came for the wedding. He had noticed Kuttyali's bride Nabisa wear one of those at their wedding in Valapattanam.

Once the horoscope-tying business was done, the oldsters called in the platoon of females.

'C'mmon-e, leth's geth tha bride ready soo'!' The women stepped inside the door decisively through the shower of rosewater produced by a troop of children standing on both sides shaking the sprinklers with all their strength.

Kalyani stood inside the bedroom looking rather meek. That's how it was to be. In postcolonial times, this troop which arrived to prepare the bride would be referred to as the 'advance party'. It is composed of women closely related to the bridegroom. The marks they give her are crucial. The new bride's score-sheet's opening; pay heed! If the girl was used to wearing a round bindi on her forehead, they may replace it with a long one. The man likes it that way, they'll say. They may pull the girl's hair back and tie it up so that her face looks like an egg. That too, is the man's wish. This is the day in which the self-expression of the eyebrow pencil reaches its zenith. The bride herself might be surprised to find out that she did indeed have such eyebrows. If the advance party is one that believes in democracy, it will allow some privacy for the bride to change into the panties, bra, and underskirt brought by the groom's party. Generally, that does not happen; there are thorny diplomatic issues here. Every country needs keen-eyed spies and

agents. Their sightings might be of great value later. (There's the
story of how a bridegroom was spared the status of the sire of
some notknownchap's kid because a sharp-eyed member of the
advance party espied a white scar on the girl's belly!) Only that
when the girl wriggles nervously into the new clothes, the eyes of
the advance party should, in theory, be on the tea, the bananas and
the sweetmeats—*pettiyappams* and *karayappams.*

At that delicate moment in which the blouse looked as though
it fitted yet was unfitted, Thankamaniyechi would leap up.

'Lethmmelookk? Nottloose?'

'Bhere's ith? Lethmmelookk?' That was the Ammayi.

'Lethmmelookk? Bhere's ith?' That was Vanaja. Koppu-
man's sister.

The blouse was stitched under her supervision. The new
Dubai-panty that Lakshmanan had brought from Dubai felt
prickly. Kalyani doesn't wear that sort of underwear normally. But
the wedding day isn't normal.

'No' bbad!' certified Pappy, taking in the sight of Kalyani's
front side clad in a sandal-coloured, high-necked, short-sleeved
blouse. The Dubai-saree, the colour of boiled eggs adorned with
gold lines and black paisley design, covered Kalyani.

Thankamaniyechi's hand touched Kalyani's underbelly as it
thrust a set of sari-pleats through her underskirt; her eyes scanned
Kalyani's face.

'Yuh don' feel tickly?'

She asked loudly.

'Litthle bith, yes,' agreed Kalyani as if she just remembered.

Her hair was covered with a whole basket of jasmine flowers.
Kalyani's mother who had come into the bedroom in between to
get something was promptly shooed away by the advance party.
No one should enter the room where the bride was being prepared.
Keep your brass lamps and *kindi* pitchers elsewhere.

In between, Kalyani's Ammayi infiltrated the space and
handed over the gold jewellery to the advance party. Three bangles

of half a sovereign of gold each lost shape by the time they were thrust up Kalyani's sturdy forearms. Pappy tied a necklace of thin gold leaves above the black beads-and-gold chain on her neck and stretched out her hand asking, 'Mor' chains?'

'No, thath's all,' Kalyani shook her head.

Then someone burst in and said, '*Baa, baa*, come, come, do tha resth afther tha ceremony'!

Someone thrust a tray with a garland into Kalyani's hands. She made her way towards the wedding pavilion—the pandal—with some of the wedding party walking ahead of her. On the way she heard them talk of the Koppu-man she had secured and her great good fortune. Suddenly, she wanted to see her mother. Remembering that she would anyway see her mother's feet when they showered the rice on her in the pandal, she controlled herself. She caught a glimpse of Dakshayani while stepping out to go to the pandal. Kalyani felt that a heavy load was on her head now. Seeing the bride enter the pandal, the women who didn't get a chance to join the advance party sniggered loudly, as usual, 'Oo did 'er makeup? Usselesss! Awwffuul. Desthroy'd tha girll'! In the commotion, Koppu-man tied the *taara*-chain with the marriage-locket around Kalyani's neck. The sight of that chain made her happy. She had planned to buy one of those after the vegetable farming season that year. Some desires are like misfortunes—they seek you out in a milling crowd when you least expect it. You won't be ready for them to come true. If only there was an advance warning, you'd think, you could have prepared better. Whether it was for joy or for sorrow, Kalyani nearly touched the chain once more when someone handed her a thin flower garland, which she placed around Koppu-man's neck.

And thus Kalyani became the Koppu-man's wife and left her place in the world, her land, her desham (for the time).

13

Seeing the jeep come up through the cashew garden, Cheyikkutty arranged the gold *kasavu*-bordered upper cloth on her shoulder in the one-shoulder style. She picked up the brass lamp and stepped into the front of the house. 'Sthop tha silly game,' she scolded her eldest daughter who was sulking and fretting. Nalini was weeping over her exclusion from the advance party—just because her man had less koppu, she was sure. She had no role at all in fixing the marriage; she *had* to be included in this at least! Determined to stay pig-headed, she didn't go to the wedding even. Her husband had gone on the luggage carrier of the advance party's Jeep.

Seeing her still teary-eyed, Cheyikkutty lost her cool.

'Uh! I'll knoc' yer tooth down, yuh pusthule of pesthilenc'! So *thath*'s yer problem? Yuh banted to be pushing and shoving bith tha forty pipple in thath Jeep? Tell me yer probl'm bith Narayanan, can' yuh be bith him for his big day? Eberhheard a sisther no'ggoing to her broth'rs wedding? *Sthopp rightthere*! I'll gibe ith to yuh in good'ttime! I'm not slappin'yyer face onnll' becos they're comin'nnow!'

The flame in the lamp she was holding shuddered in fright.

Now, you must pardon what follows: a historical and cultural analysis of (a) the advance party, and (b) the panty. Please do cooperate. In general, the Dubai-panty remained just an object of curiosity. Brides who were gifted those along with their wedding sarees would wash, dry, and lock the thingy forever inside the

38

clothes-box. Kalyani of this story, too, did exactly that. How that rose-coloured panty, shiny as a baby's cheek, which was chosen and bought actually by the younger brother of her bridegroom, came to occupy a key position in Kalyani's life is another story. It will be told, but we have some more time before. The old folk thought that this piece of clothing was even more obscene than nakedness. The high-born snobs found it a bit too hard to take. Those days there was a joke that went around houses where a wedding was on—about a Muslim chap who went to see a girl to marry (thinking that he was) wearing fancy underwear. The foibles and follies of this gentleman who was keen that his bride-to-be should catch a teeny glimpse at least of this prized inner attire *some* way or the other caused much mirth among women. They shared it with their peers, spicing it up real nice. Such jokes began to circulate more widely only after 1992. That was also the year from which the numbers of sweetmeat parcels reaching the neighbours during Id began to register a sharp fall . . .

It was also the year in which the advance party began to include the post of the Beautician. The Beautician figured for the first time in the advance party that arrived from the town to Thankamaniyechi's daughter's wedding. In the early days, the presence of the Beautician did not alter the veto power of the advance party, or its internal power structure. The Beautician was, at this time, like the Governor in a democracy. She needed to just sign the dotted line; but the signature had value. As for the advance party, though the policy decisions were still made by it, its discourse shifted from orders to be implemented to mere observations made sitting on the bed in the bride's room. But it was the local beauty consultants who suffered a crippling blow. Throwing the survival of local beauty consultants into utter jeopardy, the Beautician gained power, step by step. Power in the advance party was of a decentralized nature: Thankamaniyechi to drape the sari; Pappy for hairstyling; Vanaja for the face, and so on. The Beautician concentrated all these roles in herself, at least

in practice. The minor partners who were continually complaining
of poor representation in the coalition behind advance-party
formation found great relief in the Beautician's arrival. But this is
in the future, and so quite irrelevant to Nalini's predicament, and
so over to Cheyikkutty—sorry for the interruption.

Cheyikkutty handed over the lit lamp to her son's womin. She
instantly amended someone's instruction to carry it carefully, with
the flame still burning, to the bedroom:

'No' to tha bedroo', here on tha beranda.'

Koppu-man's house stooped to peek at Kalyani. After a little
while, Kalyani decided that nothing special had happened to her,
and that she wasn't more tired than she usually was after returning
from the Muchilottu Bhagawathi's *Kaliyattam* festival; nothing
that couldn't be solved with some good physical labour. And so
though she generally detested kitchen work, she went to join
the male gang that was busy cleaning and returning the utensils
borrowed from the neighbours for the wedding feast.

Needing a hand to drag the huge *vattalam*-vessel, to the well-
side, Kalyani went and stood in front of Lakshmanan.

'*Uyyi*, oh my, yuh? *Ingalaa*?' He asked, respectfully.

'Why? Tha *vattalam* won' come off tha groun' if ith's me?'

'No, pleas . . .'

'Leth's see?'

'Won'.'

'Wil'.'

The *vattalam* reached the well-side.

'No' bbad, no' bbad!' Lakshmanan complimented her.

'Alrighth,' smiled Kalyani.

14

It was nearly nightfall. Once she had a refreshing bath, Kalyani felt that the world was beautiful again. She looked tenderly at all the five wedding garments washed and hung to dry. Don't hang up the panty where people may see it, instructed Cheyikkutty in a whisper.

'An' no' justh thath. Don' hang anny clothes of girls outtin tha yard afther ebenin'. If yuh do thath, yer babie's arms an' legs wil' geth twisthed. Jus' remember to geth them inside.'

Kalyani nodded in agreement. Cheyikkutty had a few other things to ask her. She drew her daughter-in-law to the spot near the grinding stone.

'He didn' leth any of us wimmin come and see yuh. Shud hab ask'd yuh then ithsel'. Thath's alrighth,' she lowered her voice.

Cheyikkutty asked about a tactically vital top secret in the most formal language she could muster.

'Yer monthlies are reg'lar, righth?'

Oh, so this was the deadly secret, Kalyani had a good laugh in her mind.

'Ye', mines bery reg'lar,' she said, with pride.

'Does thath cloth sthink a lott when yuh wash ith?'

Cheyikkuty asked with high seriousness. Kalyani remembered instantly what she had heard at home, that her would-be mother-in-law was the daughter of a vaidyan, a healer.

'No.'

'Sthains thath don'ggo eben if yuh scrub 'ard?'

'Does ith blee' a lot?'

'Ye',' Kalyani admitted.

Cheyikkutty sighed.

'Thath's alrighth'. Now yuh don' hab to carry loads, uh? Here
we hab tha hibiscus flower in fron' of tha 'ouse. Pic' five buds in
tha mornin' an' grind tha leaf in tha water lefth ober from washing
rice, drink. Afther yuh can hab rice gruel or anythin' yuh feelllike.
Till yuh are full. There's no limith to wha' yuh can eath in thiss
house, alrighth?'

Her eyes which had forgotten to well when she left her own
home suddenly remembered to do so.

'Lethith bbe, Amma, yes', she said, nodding.

'Also, don' walk aroun' tha yard whe' it geths dark bith yer hair
down. Don' forgeth, we have tha Gulikan 'ere, and Chonnamma
too—spiriths! Tha other one 'ere losth her mind because
Chonnamma go' in her. She jumped all over tha yard here, so we'd
to senth her away. . .ah an'way thath one was a *thullicchi*—bery
jitthery womin—for sur' . . .' Cheyikkutty stopped momentarily.

Kalyani did not ask who this 'other one' here, that high-strung
woman Cheyikkutty referred to *thullicchi*, was.

'Yuh beren' toldd?'

She looked circumspectly at her daughter-in-law's face.
No one had told her. Even if they had, neither Kalyani nor her
family would have thought much of it. It is so much better to
have a Koppu-man from one's own place instead of growing stiff
and stringy in a corner of one's home, or getting hitched with
strangers from goodness knows where to live in homes where they
keep a tab on every morsel. No one thought it a problem that he
had brought a woman before; Kalyani too. If you can't swallow
something, what else to do but spit it out? That's better than going
round and round this whole long life like a snake that swallowed
its tail. Kalyani's mother herself was her father's second bride. Did
anything go wrong because of that? And besides, anyone would

want to give Kalyani's Koppu-man the glad eye. Seeing such a worthy chap so busy and rushed all the time made Kalyani sad.

'Poormman!'

Inside the bedroom, there was a narrow wooden cot with a cotton mattress and a white polyester bed-sheet with a print of red flowers. A small wooden almirah held Koppu-man's and Lakshmanan's clothes. In the corner, a clothesline ran from window to window. The shirt and mundu that Koppu-man had worn for the wedding lay in a heap on it, utterly exhausted.

When Kalyani had come into the bedroom earlier to change into home clothes, Vanaja had accompanied her, as was the custom. She seemed disgusted by the sight of Kalyani's rough, unmanageable locks.

'So bristhly . . . lik' coconu' fibre!'

'Neber yuh bother,' said Kalyani. 'Thath's on my head, leth' ith bbe.'

Kalyani dismissed Vanaja's submission with a twitch of the corner of her mouth. Though a little flustered, Vanaja did not retreat. She helped Kalyani take off her ornaments and said, in a very ordinary way:

'Ith was on thi' bery cot thath our father die'. Di' yuh see another' one in tha insid' beranda? Tha mahagony? Thath's bhere our gran'dad died.'

Kalyani felt a slight tremor within. She cast a hostile look at the cot.

'Wha'? Cots in yer 'ouse are for pipple to die on?'

In her own home she had slept everywhere, from the outer veranda to the kitchen steps. Her bed was a travelling one. A pillow, a mundu, and a sheet—that was opulence enough. Someone who had slept moving all over the house was now going to get a room of her own. At least, small part of that cot in there was to be hers.

Kalyani heard the Koppu-man snore gently.

'Lookk'ere . . .'

She called her husband.

'Yuh sleepin'?'

'Uh?'

Koppu-man jerked awake.

'Yuh fel' asleep?'

'Yea, could'n sthay up, fel' asleep.' He said that without looking at Kalyani's face.

'She was no' well from tha beg'ning?'

'Who?'

She did not have to say. He knew who.

'Ah! Don' know. Ith was such a fr'nzy. Chonnamma got her, they say.'

Kalyani was quiet. In the silence, Koppu-man's snore sounded again.

'Look 'ere . . .'

'Yuh sleep, alrighth? Leth's see if weccan go to tha movies tomorro'?'

'Oh!! Soo early in tha morning? Al-readdy?' She could not hide her scorn.

'Bhere?'

'To cinema?'

'Uh?'

'No, justh . . . to know if I hab to be up early . . .' Kalyani's mind murmured involuntarily as she curled up on the cot's edge to sleep.

15

Lakshmanan was busy building a second cowshed. There was some undergrowth to tame. The *karamullu* bushes and the *kattuchekki* and *uppila* thickets were competing there with each other. Also, wee boulders lay flat on their backs all around, staring at the sky. They had to be dislodged with a pickaxe and removed physically. The ground could be prepared only after. The sandstone bricks, wooden stakes, the areca palm trunk, and the tiles were in a corner of the yard. Cow dung had to be brought from the other cowshed and smeared on the floor. For the charcoal, you just needed to cut open a battery and mix. Usually you needed to do that for the inside of the house, but not for the cowshed. But all this requires is two more pairs of hands. The two who had agreed to come copped out. This wasn't easy like he'd thought.

'Don' bother bith thath if yuh can' fin' a hand to 'elp,' said Cheyikkutty rather glumly. 'Mebbe try afther sum time.'

'Yuh go on. I'll 'elp.'

Cheyikkutty and Lakshmanan turned to find Kalyani in the yard with a towel wrapped tight around her head.

'Yuh?' Cheyikkutty sounded baffled. 'Yuh pu' tha pot on to cook tha rice?'

In reply, she pointed to the filled water pots.

'An' I had drawn water from tha well. An' hab scrap'd tha coconu' and clean'd tha fish.'

That annoyed Cheyikkutty. 'So thath means tha work in tha house is all done?' She asked.

Just as she disliked housework, Kalyani also disliked loaded questions. If someone gave her clear instructions, she'd do it all. But she wasn't game for any weighing up and divvying.

'Thath work won' geth ober so soon,' she muttered, bending down to take the baskets and the pickaxe.

'Wha' can *ingal* do an'way?' Lakshmanan asked, using the respectful 'you' again. He was helpless.

'Leth mme see if I can' fin' summone.'

'Leth mme try. Wha' if it'll be of sum 'elp?'

She strode ahead.

When Cheyikkutty came out of the kitchen once the rice and fish curry were done, the weeds and bushes were cleared and the place was clean. Kalyani scooped up the pieces of rock into the basket, raised it on her head and asked Lakshmanan where the boundary of their yard was. He laughed.

'Yuh won' see any suc' thing—justh put ith unde' tha *jathi* tree.'

As Cheyikkutty watched, the baskets filled and emptied and the place where the baby rocks had lain was now level. Because the pickaxe fell insistently, the land began to yield. Dust and tiny bits of rock flecked Kalyani's hair and face and breasts.

'Kalyani, sthay clear of tha sharp edge of thath pickaxe,' Cheyikkutty couldn't help saying that. So hassled was she—that she sat down one moment only to jump up the next. She darted from kitchen to the yard and back in dreadful haste. Seeing her daughter-in-law take short, quick paces with the stones for the foundation of the cowshed on her head, she slapped her own head.

'*Uyyentappa*! Ennuff! Won' there be a mornin' tomorro'? Why tha hurry?'

'Yea, yea, there'll be,' Kalyani licked off the sweat that was flowing down her nose and lowered the basket. Cheyikkutty ran up to her.

When she was mixing some rock salt in the rice gruel, Koppuman came looking for Kalyani.

'Bhere's she, Amme?'

'At tha new cowshe'.'

'Ammo!! Wha's she doing there?'

'Musthbe watching?' She sounded sardonic.

Cheyikkutty took them some of the rice gruel.

'Enuf now . . . ith needs justh'a bith mor' work, afther all?'

Lakshmanan stopped working.

Kalyani gathered up the tools and took them to the firewood storeroom. She pulled off the dusty dark-coloured towel from her head and put it on the washing stone. Drawing a full bucket of water at a single pull from deep in the well, she poured it over her head. When the water ran bubbling through her locks, she pulled off a bunch of leaves from the hibiscus shrub nearby, rubbed them hard on the stone, squeezed the thick green juice out and smeared it on her head. When she lowered the bucket into the well again, Lakshmanan held out his hand and said, 'Gibe me tha rope . . .'.

He filled the big aluminum bucket with water and sat down on the washing stone.

'Is there a pond 'ere?' She suddenly asked.

'Yea. Bu' ith's bery' deep. Yuh can swim?'

Lakshmanan got up suddenly as if he had remembered something.

'Yuh don' go there at thi' hour. . .womin don' . . .' said he, and then, to Cheyikkutty, 'Amme, justh gibe me thath towel? Leth mme go to tha pond'.

Kalyani wanted to kill Lakshmanan who didn't tell her before that they indeed had a pond.

Cheyikkutty was changing the sheet on the cotton mattress in the bedroom when Kalyani went in.

'Amme, do we hab a mat an' a blanketh?'

'Wha'? Mat an' blanketh? For wha'?' Cheyikkutty looked at her questioningly.

'To sleep bith my arms an' legs sthretch'd ou', Amme. There's no space on tha cot.'

Though she tried, Cheyikkutty couldn't help laughing.

'I 'ad to sleep o' tha cot too . . .after *moopper*—my man—pass'd. . .tha chillren' insisthed!'

Kalyani stepped inside the bedroom with the mat Cheyikkutty gave her. Koppu-man was on the cot, lying on his side. She opened the mat on the floor, shook the musty-smelling blanket and covered the mat with it. Then she stretched out on it and exhaled loudly.

'Yuh wan' a pillow?' Koppu-man asked her suddenly.

Kalyani turned her neck to look at him.

'*Ingal* bant to come sleep 'ere?'

'No, *ppaa*! No' used to ith!'

'Th's is 'ow yuh starth getthing used?'

'Tel' me if yuh wan' tha pillow. I fee' sleepy.'

'*Baynda*—no—yuh sleep.'

Kalyani turned on her side.

Suddenly, out of the blue, she was gripped with the desire to open the window and take a look at the half-finished cowshed.

16

Kalyani discovered that the work outside the house was never-ending. Cutting the grass, untying the cow and tying it back again, bathing it, milking it, carrying the cow dung, plucking the cashew, chopping dried coconut, sunning it, growing the vegetables—all of this kept her busy. Except for the fact that sweeping the house, drawing water from the well, and scraping the coconut were included in the Annexure, the kitchen did not bother her at all. She would sit down for lunch along with Cheyi's two sons, her work done or in the middle of whatever she was doing. Cheyi would serve her also, heaping the rice on her plate.

'Befor' ith was enuf to heap two serbings on a plathe, now ith is three,' Cheyikkutty would say when she pressed each serving into the copper plates. The curry would still be bobbing on the rice, refusing to trickle in. If any of her daughters who came over to ask for something saw this and pulled a face, Cheyikkutty would give them an earful.

'Her toilin' isn't sumthing ordnery! Yuh justh finish tha bissness yuh came for an' clear out, alrighth?'

'How's yer son's womin, Cheyiechi?' The women who couldn't make it to the wedding asked.

'Won' come annyybhere near tha kitch'n, bu' neber hab I seen a womin toil like 'er outside, justh unn-bbeliev'ble!'

Cheyikkutty submitted the monthly report on Kalyani. 'Ah . . .thaath's ith . . .' The women gaped and then comforted her.

'Neber min', we need thath kin' of workin' too . Yuh don' hab to bother abou' thath now? When yuh look for a bride for Lachanan, yuh musth geth one who's good in tha kitchin!'

'Thath way yuh'll hab both!'

The history of wives of four sons in the same house specializing in specific areas is not at all of a distant past. Outsiders were envious of the division of labour among women of this desham. People here had shared the same home until they began to perceive their own interests as more important. They would divide work among them according to their likes. They spent their leisure hours telling tales about stuff happening in the neighborhood and picking the lice off each other's heads. Now, it will be grossly unjust if I don't say a few words about lice-picking. It is highly structured by *aachaaram*, or custom; regulated by an unwritten set of rules, hallowed tradition. If the louse tries sincerely, it is said, it can cross seven heads in a single day. Lice-picking should never be done sitting on a step or during the evening hours. Or God will find the dead lice floating on his nightly glass of milk! Another rule decrees that no lice taken from one head should be put back on it, or on another's. Normally, women engrossed in the massacre of head-lice are left undisturbed by men unless things are really dire. There's also the rule that if you spot a louse anywhere, even on the head of a sworn enemy, you must pick and dispatch it. People who refuse such obligations can be dropped quite legitimately from the guest lists for feasts given at births and deaths. Even great ideological struggles could come to a peaceable end, between nails with a *kiru-kiru* sound. The louse would leave the earth with a truly sincere hiss, completely satisfied. The very sight of women sitting beside each other, and picking each other's lice like similes strung in a row and pleated together, is poetry itself. What I was going to tell you is this: not a single louse on Cheyikkutty's head had to die at Kalyani's hands. For this Kalyani relied on Cheyikkutty's daughters who lived in the same family yard.

'Whath abou' yer son's womin, thath hot-headed *thullichi* wench, why don' yuh tell her to do thi'?'

The daughters tried to get her peeved.

'Becos, she workss lik' none of yuh! Nottoone of yuh can'mmatch her!!' Cheyikkutty would return the goal the next second.

When the lice-picking was proceeding in the veranda of Nalini's house, Kalyani walked around there with the long fruit-picking stick to pull down the cashew fruit, and a basket to gather them. Earlier, this was Cheyikkutty's postnoon chore. It was a pain—her neck would be strained, her shoulders and back would ache, her feet would inevitably get hurt and her hands would be stained by the black cashew juice. And on top of that, the red fire ants would fall in whole nests along with the leaves and the cashew apples. No saying where all they can bite you. They'll just scramble down your body all fired up by the prospect of biting you. Squeeze them to death between your fingers, and they leave behind a chilli scent. Below, the fallen leaves laugh and play, but step on them, and you'll sink right in. And even slip and slide down to the ground. Besides, there are the black ants and the teeny ants. The cashew apples heaped together after the nuts are extracted, bloat and stink. Hard to put up with that for long! To add to the stench, finally, people from around would come before it got light to take a dump in the yard. The pit-latrines had only started to make their appearance in homes. In the early days, people feared the intense loneliness of these latrines; they took refuge in the large properties of wealthy folk. The cashew tree does not require level ground. There are trenches in between two rows of trees facing each other. The soldiers of both friendly and enemy armies relied on signals sent via the rustling of leaves crushed underfoot for communication. Those who come to harvest the cashew apples had to necessarily develop the ability to sense human presence there. Else, it will be trouble. They should also learn to pick out that particular (faecal) smell from many odours, pleasant and otherwise. Anyway, Kalyani found it all very engrossing. On the journey in search of cashew apples, she would sing aloud everything she'd heard, from the *tottam* songs from the temple that she'd memorized, to cinema songs. Sometimes, she would also talk to herself.

'Don' geth tha cashew from tha tree near thath place.' Cheyikkutty called to her, pointing towards a trench.

'Leth Amma take ith.'

'Amma?' Kalyani was surprised.

'Thath's Chonnamma's *kottam*, on thath side—Her shrine. Yuh didn' see' tha chembaka tree? *Aada*, ober' there. Nebber take an'thing thath falls on Amma's groun'! As long as there's red soil there, Amma won' leth go. She's *bery* picky—won' leth yuh take eben a piece of sug'rcane from her yard'. *Kettina*? Yuh hear? Don' try to take nuts from 'er? Don' geth under 'er belly, eh?'

Before she raised the stick and began to pull at a bunch of cashew apples, Kalyani turned to look, almost without knowing. Will they all fall on the other side? She felt a tinge of worry at the feeling that the Chonnamma, the Red Lady—was standing on the boundary and keeping a sharp eye out for trespassers.

'*Daive* . . . Goo'ggod! Is ith troubl'?'

Kalyani lowered the stick, put it down, and began to gather the cashew apples. The heaps of apples reached right up to her knee. Cashew apples in green, yellow, red, and golden-red. She sat cross-legged on the ground, picked up each, pulled off each nut with a brusque twist, thereby beheading the apples mercilessly, and threw each nut into the basket. The reek of the apples grew stronger. She felt the chilli scent in her nose. As she watched, the cashew garden where sunlight did not fall even at high noon, turned a flaming red.

17

Because it seemed like there was no guarantee that she'd reach home no matter how fast she walked, Kalyani sat down and leaned on a tree. Her eyes were aflame from seeing all that red around her. She felt thirsty and bit hard into a cashew apple. When the sweet and chilli juice flowed down her chin and dripped down into the inside of her blouse, she felt a strange unease. Before she came down to harvest the cashew apples, she had gone into the bedroom to change her mundu. Her hair had come loose too; she meant to tie it up tightly. When she had changed into a blouse and lungi that were a nice dark blue (something that the cashew apple stains wouldn't ruin), Koppu-man entered. Seeing someone inside the room unexpectedly, he drew back with a start.

'Yuh there?'

When he saw that it was Kalyani, he came in again.

'Ooh, how scare' yuh were?' She teased. He smiled and sat down on the cot.

'Bhere's Amma?'

'At Naliniyechi's,' Kalyani said.

'Oh, thath's why I cudn' fin' 'er . . .yuh going to tha yard? Ok, thennggo.'

He was playing the big-hearted husband.

Kalyani remembered the movies she had watched with Dakshayani at Nisha Talkies. Those movies showed situations such as these, when the movie moms also went to the neighbour's.

How accurate her timing was, to come into the bedroom to change just now! Even the timing of her hair coming loose was perfect. In the confusion, Kalyani checked if she was wearing glass bangles. And regretted somewhat that they were missing. In at least a few movies she'd seen, this was the time when they inevitably broke. She hid the pleasurable sensation that emanated in waves from her lower belly at the thought, and looked at Koppu-man.

'If yer here, then whysshud I go to tha yard?'

Melting in such an impossible way that even the bedroom felt sure that she would never step into the yard ever again, Kalyani made that amorous move.

'Yuh go. I need to go an' meeth bith Avdur'kka. There are sum trees in tha garde' dow 'there thath nee' choppin'. Hab to go to Nilambur day afther' tomorro'. Oh, wha' . . . *paachilanne*!! Suc' a rush!'

Koppu-man's face was expressionless. He just said it.

'So yuh sthumbl'd in tha bustle and tha rush . . . tha *paachil* . . . and tumbl'd into doing a *mangalam* bith a womin? Gottmmarri'd justh lik' thath?'

Kalyani's real thoughts jumped out.

'Yuh cud say thath. I had cum to yer home justh to take a look at yuh . . . but when I saw yuh, I decid'd, I am taking 'er.'

Kalyani's love for Koppu-man boiled up and brimmed over. She moved closer to him, the closest she could. It'll do if my love for my man shines in my eyes and face, she thought in a wordless language. Won't he know when he sees? She needed a mirror to see it, but he did not.

But Koppu-man made her move aside, and going to the almirah, took a bag from it. He tilted his head sideways and said, 'Yuh go to tha yard then—hurry—ith is alrea'y late.

Kalyani was in a tricky spot now.

'I've bee' lookin' to ask yuh sumthing for sum time now,' she said.

She did not hide her annoyance. With astonishment and
dismay, she thought: how quickly had that love she'd felt for him
fizzled out and dried up! The string of love, any love, did not
stretch too well. It breaks so easily when stretched a bit more! And
later we wonder how we managed to get so far hanging on the
same fragile string.

Kalyani retained the respectful address: '*Ninga*'. 'Do yuh miss
'er a lot when yuh see me?

—*Ningakku ennekkanumbo ore ormayavunnunda?*'

She controlled her breath and asked the question about his
first womin, the one who was said to have turned mad, taken
over by Chonnamma. That was the explanation which she had
accepted since some days now. Is the womin who'd slept on the
bed here before me still present, even if unseen, she fretted. This
time too, he knew who she meant, but had to think for a moment
to find a reply. Inside the bedroom, there was nothing left of her.
Except for a bed sheet which she tore to pieces when Chonnamma
possessed her, there was no sign.

'Yuh remin' me o' wha' . . .?' As he turned to get out of the
room, Kalyani got on to the high step of the bedroom door and
barred his way with her body. She noticed that even though
he couldn't get out of the room without their faces and bodies
brushing against each other, there was nothing happening
between them that was at least natural (and of course, leave alone
something unnatural). Her body was surrounded, besieged, by
that knowledge which could not be translated into any of the
world's languages.

When Koppu-man left, she rushed out into the yard with the
fruit-picking stick and basket for some respite. No matter how far
she ran, the shame pursued her. *Sshe, sshe*—she kept spitting out
the bitterness in between.

Her whole body quivered in pain as though she had been
poisoned. Sitting on the ground, she leaned on the tree, stretched
her legs out.

'Daive, did oneo'ttha slithering sorth bithe me?' She asked herself.

No. There was nothing to be seen. The dry leaves were to be feared. In them live the denizens of the earth, who disappear in a flash—whose bite can sear your heart. Kalyani had seen them for herself. Sometimes the tip of a tail. Sometimes the markings of the body. The rustling of the leaves that matched the size and speed. That sound would persist for some time after the one who made it left. Poison is like fear; it spreads slowly to kill.

So tired was she that she lay down on the ground face up. The wedding saree of a colour like that of boiled eggs, with black paisley print and golden thread opened above her in the sky. Her eyes were closing.

'Wha's 'appened to yuh? *Ennaa ingakku?*'

Lakshmanan ran up to her, worried.

'Don' crush tha saree,' Kalyani mumbled.

'No.' His voice felt very close.

The next moment his face rose up between her and the sky, blocking her view. A bunch of ripe cashew apples scattered. Before she realized that half her body was in the heap of cashew apples, Lakshmanan's face disappeared from Kalyani's sight and the Dubai saree appeared once again in the sky. It's not just the smell of cashew-apples, Lakshmanan thought, a timeless scent was emanating from her body. As the moments passed, he sank into it; he felt breathless. Kalyani's hands slid around Lakshmanan's back and hair and yanked him close with a powerful movement. At some moment in between, her eyes moved towards the trees near the opposite trench. Was that womin who didn't let anyone take even a leaf from her land standing there, hiding herself from view? Kalyani heard innumerable slithering sounds from under the layers of leaves. She tried to keep count but soon gave up. Her hearing froze at their rustle. In the very last heaving of those sounds: the cashew trees, the Dubai saree, the heap of cashew apples, the reddish hue and Lakshmanan, all were rolled into a ball and it fell on her. She sank into the earth along with the dry leaves. The chilli scent blocked her nostrils. Her mouth was salty. The gentle taste of salt.

Kalyani got up and shook herself when Lakshmanan leapt up and left. It was almost dark. She tried to kick the rotten cashew apples back into a heap.

She brushed off the bits of dry leaves and soil from her elbow.

'Greathth cashewhharvest!' she said that—to no one in particular.

18

'Come 'ere, bhere did' yuh go?'

Kalyani appeared before Cheyikkutty who had come out to look for her; she looked like a fallen mango bruised from hitting a stone.

'I wa' going to come searchin',' she said, taking the basket from her. She noticed that the basket was rather light. Kalyani's face was swollen and her eyes, puffy.

'Yuh thripp'd ? Fel'down?'

That was always possible. If the basket fell on the ground forcefully, the nuts that leapt out at the chance would hide determinedly among the leaves. Then it required a rain for them to disguise themselves and raise their heads above the soil. No, Kalyani couldn't find them all no matter how carefully she searched. It's much better to look for something new than search for something fallen from one's hand and scattered all over. That's applicable to nuts, too.

'Can't . . .Amme, no' feeling good. . .loo's lik' a chill . . .'

Kalyani submitted her first leave application after entering her husband's house.

'Yuh shoul'nnot hab run off to tha yard? Narayanan's here? Culdn' yuh justh sthay 'ere?' Cheyikkutty went on scolding.

Kalyani did not answer. She wanted to take a bath. But she was too fatigued to draw water from the well. When she said she'd go to the pond, Cheyikkutty stopped her sternly.

'No goin'toppond-shond when tha darkness is fallin'!'

Kalyani sat dejected on the steps.

What to do!

'I'll be bekk soo' . . .' she tried to plead. Cheyikkutty would simply not allow. With sundown, all sorts gather in the yard. Cheyikkutty's mother, her father the healer, stillborn babies, many spirits of the slithering sort beaten to death, the restless ones who wander here and there—all of them together as big as a public meeting. And at that hour this girl, who's so ruddy that you'd think your finger will be stained if you touched her, wanting to go there to take a dip . . .!!

'Lachanaa . . .' She called out. 'C'mere.'

Lakshmanan felt worried seeing Kalyani stand burning up besides Amma. Kalyani too felt a bit flustered.

'Yuh draw her sum water from tha well? Says she can't do it.'

Lakshmanan took the rope. The buckets began to fill up.

'She says she can' do ith! Really! No' bbad! ' His look was taut.

The cold water fell on the top of her head and flowed down her body in irregular streams. Little nicks and cuts woke up here and there, ached and bawled for a brief while, and then fell asleep weeping.

'Thath's tha girl oo wen' jumping merril' tohharvest tha cashew. Look at 'er come bekk now, like a hen in shock!'

Cheyikkutty explained to her daughters.

No one said anything.

Would she have stepped into Chonnamma's yard? Did she take anything that she shouldn't have? If so, that bode ill. Cheyi had warned her in advance. The crazy wench might not have heard. But what to do if she just wasn't obeying?

When Kalyani returned from the bath, Cheyikkutty served her hot rice gruel with a bit of rock salt mixed in it. She stopped Kalyani when she tried to get up from the wooden stool. Taking some salt and mustard and chilli in her hand, Cheyikkutty curled her hand into a fist and moved it slowly over Kalyani's body, from top to toe, three times. Then she spit on the salt-chilli-mustard mix and threw it into the hearth. And found out that the scent that arose from the hearth was not that of chilli. She took another fistful of the same mix and moving the closed fist around Kalyani's breasts and belly and buttocks, threw it into the fire again. This time too, there was no scent of chilli. Cheyikkutty was helpless now. Most kinds of evil eye and evil tongue should have been resolved by now. But it didn't happen.

'Thi' is notttha evil eye,' she confirmed.

In the light of the hearth, Cheyikkutty saw a reddish hue spread on Kalyani's face.

'*Uyyintamme*! *Patticcha*! Did yuh take annyything of Amma's? *Thath's* tha thing—yer face looks so red! Now go to tha beddrroom and lie down, cober yersel' well. Don'come out. I'll send rice off'rings to tha kottam tomorro'.'

Cheyikkutty said that half to Kalyani and half to Chonnamma.

When Kalyani unrolled her mat in the bedroom, Cheyikkutty came in. She was going there after a long interval. She sniffed hard to catch the smell of the room. She suspected that there was there was a flash of red behind the almirah.

She opened the almirah and took out Lakshmanan's clothes.

'He may be goin' outttsummwhere,' She told herself. To Kalyani, she said, 'Yuh geth on thi' bed. Don' catch tha cold'.

Kalyani stretched on the bed, now its sole and complete authority. A torn bed sheet kept pricking her.

'Yuh cold?' Cheyikkutty asked.

Yes, her welling eyes said.

'Ah, why're crying fo' thath, my girl, mole? Ar' yuh scar'd?'

Yes, her nose trembled.

'Shal' I tell Narayanan to comm'ere?'

Kalyani said nothing.

19

Kalyani is leaning on the pillar near the half-wall of the veranda, ordered to do so by her two uncles—Valyammaman and Kunhammaman. Kunhammaman's whipping still stung her. The Kalyani who is sobbing and crying is all of nine years. Amma is sitting with her legs stretched out with a baby, Kalyani's youngest sister, lying there. She pays no attention to the whipping-scene, and is absorbed in feeding the little one ragi porridge. The porridge was browner than usual; it isn't to Kalyani's liking, but in between her sobs, she peeks into the bowl longingly. Amma will surely leave some of it after feeding the baby. Usually when she picks up the little babe and helps Amma up, Amma holds it out to her. Those leftovers were Kalyani's right. But it looks like no one's going to acknowledge that now.

Tha bigg battalam o' payasam
Thickkened at T'ichamabaram
For my babie's porr-i'-ge
In tha padanjhattini o' my house

Amma sings to the baby—but Kunhipennu is hollering and tearing the roof down with her bawling. Amma shovels the porridge into her mouth. A *shshoosh* sound, like water rapidly evaporating in a red-hot bronze *uruli*-vessel, rose when the crying and the ragi porridge and saliva and sheer bolshie combined. The baby is screaming with all its might, holding its breath; but nothing is coming out as voice.

'*Uyyentamme*! M' babie!'

Amma is terrified.

Seizing the moment in which Valyammaman and Kunhammaman were drawn towards that cry for help, Kalyani leaps into the yard and escapes.

If she admitted that it wasn't she but Dakshayani who had called Achootty Mash a sonofabitch, they would have granted her bail. Then the sole remaining charge would be that of running away from school. That would end when Valyammaman had a chat with Achootty Mash. (Both Valyammaman and Achootty Mash are Congress. When Gandhiji came to Payyanur, the two people who were with him constantly were Achootty Mash's father and Kalyani's grandfather.)

But Kalyani just couldn't stomach that. Not just because of her friendship with Dakshayani but also because she genuinely disliked school. Everyone except Kalyani insisted that she must be in school. A bright child. A quick learner. The school was very near her house. No issues about getting there or returning home. Most members in Kalyani's family had some schooling. On top of everything else, the local library is named after her grandfather. It was a girl from such a family who called her teacher choicest names and marched out of school.

' *Nkkane aada*! Sthop righththere!'

Kunhammaman jumps over the half-wall and is now in hot pursuit of Kalyani.

Despite the fact that she was still mulling over the distant prospect of leftovers of the ragi-porridge, Kalyani takes off. She jumps over the boundary of the yard and runs to Kaisumma's house.

'Kaisumma . . . thei' killin'mmee!'

Kaisumma comes running out of her house.

'Leav' her, *Appaa*!! Wha's thi'?'

Kunhammaman stops. Kalyani is now safely behind Kaisumma's back.

'Justhtwwaith till yuh geth bekk home, uh?' He growls at Kalyani.

Returning defeated, Kunhammaman warns Amma.

'Yer girl's going to growwuup an' be an awful harridan! . . . Yuh'd betther conthrol'er.'

The girl can't be scolded or beaten. Get her angry, and she'll storm out of the house. She'll hang back in some or other neighbours' place till sundown eating whatever they gave her. Then someone has to go around and yell for her. And given a chance, she'd happily be spending the night at some neighbour's.

'Tha imp!'

Valyammaman would blame his sister's laxity in disciplining Kalyani.

'Chill'en shud be rais'd by father an' mother togeth'r. Yuh can' do a thingg!! Thath's ith. Wretch'd brat, tha worsth kind!'

Kalyani sits on the half-wall of the veranda of Kaisumma's house and pants.

'Here, drinkktthiss.'

Kaisumma holds out the bowl to her.

'Ith's ragi porri'ge.'

She takes it. *Daivvve*!! The porridge is not at the bottom of the black-bordered metal bowl; it is almost full . . . with whitish porridge. Nice and sweet. She licks the bowl clean.

When it was past evening, Amma comes looking.

'Kalyani-yaa, eh—Kalyani-yaa . . . '

Shaking down everything that she had held back till then, Kalyani bawls.

'*Njaamborulla*! I'm nottcccoming! Yuh didn' come when Kunhammaman wa' beatin' me to a pulp? I am no' yer girl.'

'Yuh-*betther*-come . . .', Amma sounds furious.

'I won'ttcccome unthil yer two monsthers goaway from there.'

'Shuttupp!' Amma nearly roars. And tells Kaisumma, 'Justh loo' at her cheek?'

'Commeere NOW!!'

'*Njaamborulla* . . . I AM NOTTCCCOMING!!'

'Don' yuh thin' yer coming afther yer uncles leave!!'

When Amma goes back, Kalyani asks Kaisumma for a loan. If she didn't have cash, then some gold would do. She would sell it and go to Madras. Would work hard and live there. And that's when a really big Koppu-man would come and discover this astonishingly beautiful young girl. She would stride into this desham . . . as his wife, with a big flower placed sideways in her hairdo and riding a long-nosed car. By then these uncles would be bent and broken. The Congress would be extinct. And she wouldn't stay in that house no matter who pleaded and bathed her feet with their tears. Revenge! Kalyani gnashes her teeth.

'Lachuna, geth me my wool'n blanketh,' Cheyikkutty called, stepping out. She was feeling confident of finding the herbs she needed to make a concoction for Kalyani.

'Yuh musthbbe here. Ith's a chill an' feve'. Yuh sthay an' look afther her, I'm going to put on tha *kashaayam*.'

Lakshmanan covered Kalyani with the woolen blanket. Going close to her face, he said,

'Here, yuh don' be afrai', *inglu pedikkandatta*. I'm here'.

Kalyani wasn't afraid. She was spouting steam in the height of a fever. Soon she was being carried somewhere on a stream. Her eyes were overflowing even though they were closed; the tears streamed down her face. My limbs have come apart from my body, she felt sure. It was chilly. But the cold was felt by not her body but some other . . . the very thought made her shudder.

'Kalyani-yaa, yuh coming?'

She could hear Amma calling. 'I'l come ober there an' gibe you a gooddhhiding! Yuh are Chonnamma? To sthayawway when call'd bekk hom'?'

20

'*Paithale*...!'

Koolothamma called, her voice weighed down with sadness. She turned to look at *Vazhunnor*—the Lord of the Land—who stood some two feet away from her, hope blending with anxiety on her face. She kept knocking on the closed door.

'Paithale, my child, come, Acchan and Amma are here . . . To see our babie . . . *kunhi*'

Seeing that nothing stirred within, and that the door did not move, Koolothamma's heart quivered. Lowering the bronze vessel she carried on to the floor, she walked around the house. If only she would open the window a teeny bit, just a finger-width of gap!

'Paithale . . . '

Vazhunnor called to her, his tired voice filled with despair. Koolothamma came back after going round the house.

'Op'nd, spok'?' She asked.

Vazhunnor did not speak.

The bronze vessel had gone lukewarm. Koolothamma sat down near it and wept soundlessly.

'D'yuh nee' to be so stubbor', kunhi? D'yuh wan' to torment those who rais'd yuh bith tha barmth of thei' breasth?'

'I don' wan' to see anyyone.'

From behind the door came that sound, like a bronze vessel falling on the floor. Koolothamma jumped up. She flowed and spread like spilt milk.

'Th' washerwomin tol' me, my kunhi's blossom'd . . . go' her
monthlies . . .' Amma said. And then she asked:
Is my paithal grown strong an' hardy, lethmme see?
Is she now brighth and rosy, lethmme see?
Does her hair flow to her hips, lethmme see?'
Yes—was the reply:
'Yes, she's now sthrong an' hardy
Yes, she is now bright an' rosy
An' yes, her hair runs down to her hips.
'I came here a little girl, an' now I bloom'd.
Yuh know now.
Go. Now go.
I don' wan' to see annyyone.'
Vazhunnor noticed her words grow firmer. So did
Koolothamma and the entire retinue. Vazhunnor moved forward
and pressed his face to the door.
'Yuh're our sapling. Yuh musth marry and we musth habe a
greattccelebration! Yuh are our Heir, our Hope!! When our Great
House was dying, yuh were bor'. Now ith needs yuh, paithale.'
'Look' not for a match for me! I bant no husban', no babie!'
Sayin' thath I loithered an' sthrayed, didn't yuh beatmmedown?
Sayin' thath I didn't sthay in tha house, didn't yuh pushmmeout?
Sayin' thath I was soil'd an' foul, didn't yuh throwmmeout?
The paithal stood behind the door and counted each insult.
Koolothamma wept aloud.
'I got yuh afther praying to tha Holy One for whol' of forty-
one days! I didn' hab tha good luck to carry yuh—tha rice an'
flowers he bless'd was eathenbby a deer! Thoug' she bore yuh,
kunhi, di' I not come to yuh? Amma's brought you rice cook'd in
milk bith jagg'ry . . . my chil', please tak'tthi', ath leasth?'
'I need no mor' tha sweeth rice puddin' I cudn' get whe' I
wand'red in tha foresth hungry an' famish'd, oh Moth'r who
rais'd me!'

Seeing that paithal was unrelenting, Vazhunnor bent even lower.

'Each *jathi* is differ'nt, is ith no', kunhi? Yuh didn' obey whe' we tol' yuh not to mingle bith all tha jathis? Ar'nt yuh tha Vazhunnor's chil'? I hit yuh from tha rage then. Come bekk to us, bhere all we searched for yuh?'

Everyone heard the heavy tinkle of the silver anklets coming towards the door. Koolothamma and Vazhunnor waited hopefully for the door to open. When the sound ceased, they pricked up their ears.

I, born of a deer in tha wild,
An' rais'd by pipple, you!
What jathi for me?
I, help'd up by forest-folk
From tha dirt an'tha dusth
Bhere I lay,
What native place for me?
Losth in the foresth was I,
Thrown out of yer Illam—
Father Carpenter builth me a house
Mother Washerwomin gabe me tha cloth
When I bloom'ed red below
I'll be carried; I'll go on foot,
Now tha Warrior-Nambiar mus'salute me.
Yes, I will come out for thath.
Bu' neber bekk to yer Illam.
Thi' is my vow!'

The tears flowed from Koolothamma's eyes. They flowed down her breasts and belly that had never given birth, and dropped on the ground. They scalded the soil; the steam rose from there. Vazhunnor held her close and wept in his heart. They climbed into the palanquin. When it disappeared from sight, the door was opened.

A tall woman, the colour of wild honey, draped in a breast cloth of red silk, her thick, curly, brownish tresses falling in waves down her back, with a sharp nose and eyes that burned like coals, stepped out. She shone like a *murikku* tree in full bloom, the red flowers blazing. She kicked away the bronze vessel by the door. It flew to Kuttanad. Red rice sprouted and grew wherever the cooked rice in it scattered and fell. When her rage receded, she decided that she would not stay in a place seared by her mother's tears; off she flew like a bow from an arrow.

The soil—it continued to sear the heart of the Child of the Lords of the Land. Even in the far distance, the beat of the heart that had nurtured her did not let her live in peace. Even in the far corners of the world, a firm and warm lap rose up in her memory. She walked on till she reached a forest of palm trees. She pulled down one of the younger trees, bent it like a bow and held it tight. Then she let it go and in that force, she propelled herself towards one of the mature palm trees. And thus she became the protector of the earth and sky of the forest of the tall, stark, imposing *karimpana* palms. Then one day, the palm tree started shaking. It quivered as if it was taking blows on its trunk below. Quivering thus, it broke, turned in the air and fell hard on the ground with a loud wail. It was the Puthrveedu Soldier-Nair and his men. They had cut the palm to make some bows.

'Nothaleaf can moobe from bhere I am, yuh Nair!'

Soldier-Nair was not afraid of the heavy sound of the anklet and the rasping voice. He chopped the tree and made twelve bows and gave one to each of his men. But the twelfth bow, his own, he could not lift up from the ground. How heavy it was! Soldier-Nair heaved and heaved. But it would not move.

The gang of men pulled and pulled.

No. It wouldn't move.

'Don' try, yuh Nair, don'.'

A merciless mocking laugh flew above their heads.

'Wil' yuh take a sanctum, rice, flowers, worship? We need tha bows. We won' win annyy batthle bithout them, womin! You musth lethtthembe moobed! You musth geth up, not sith on tha bow! You musth leth us take ith! From now, we won' touc' yer land bithout asking.'

Soldier-Nair begged.

In response, a firm and deep hum was heard.

The bow could be picked up now. The murikku tree in full bloom stood among the karimpana palms looking at the bows being taken away.

'Who're yuh, Chonnamma? To sthayawway when call'd bekk hom'?'

'Amme . . .'

Kalyani's body shivered. It was drenched in sweat.

The fever was gone.

'If yuh hab taken sumthing from Chonnamma, justh gibe ith 'ere. I'l tak' ith bbekk.'

Lakshmanan whispered in Kalyani's ear.

'Won' gibe. If yuh wan', yuh can tak' ith from me, search me?'

A furtive smile gleamed on her parched lips.

21

'How long hab I bee' searchin'? Where's tha thin' yuh took from Chonnamma?'

Lakshmanan stroked Kalyani's ear. 'Is ith 'ere?'

He ran his fingers in the reddish curly hair.

''ere?'

No.

He peeped into her eyes.

''ere, mebbe?'

No no, fluttered the eyes.

Under the neck?

'No, fer sur', no.'

Between the breasts?

'Touchhthere, an' yuh'll learn a lesson!' The breasts leapt up.

''ere?'

He stroked her belly.

The fine hair on her belly trembled in fear.

'Oh . . . So ith is 'ere . . . eh?'

The search for stolen property had left Lakshmanan perplexed.

Kalyani presented herself before Cheyikkutty in the morning feeling fresh and invigorated. Like soil well-drained after the rains. Cheyikkutty surveyed her from top to toe.

'Yuh gabe us all a gooddsscare yestherda'! Wha' wasstha matter?'

Kalyani tried to recollect the events of yesterday.

'Lemme geth 'nother fisthfu' of mustar' and salt . . .' Cheyikkutty said.

She gathered all the stuff for the fistful to be waved around Kalyani's body—to do the *uzhiyal*. A fresh bunch of dry coconut fronds was thrust into the hearth. Once the waving part of the uzhiyal was complete, the fistful must be thrown there, and it should fall in exactly the middle. DO NOT stand around chatting away holding the fistful after the uzhiyal.

Kalyani sat on yesterday's wooden plank-stool.

The fistful of mustard and chilli and salt was waved all around her body with the sombre mystery of a sorcerer's ritual. This time the chilli smelt like chilli. The mustard and salt popped properly. Cheyikkutty was satisfied.

'Loo'! Yestherda' ith wa' sthinkin'. Didn' fee' lik' ith wa' chilli athall? Yuh go gallivanthing 'ere an' there, uh! Leav' yer hair op'n in tha ebening an'. . !'

Kalyani did not feel any resentment. She felt a deep affection for Cheyikkutty, and in the same measure, towards the whole world. She scraped the coconut and ground it with the same affection. Filled the water pots. But when she was about to step into the yard, Cheyikkutty caught hold of her.

'Where're yuh offtto?'

'Yestherda', couldn' geth many cashew-*andi* . . .' She cringed.

Cheyikkutty lost it completely.

'*Andi*! Nott tha *andi* but yer *kundi*, yer blasthed bum! Sthopp fidgetin' an' get going bith work *inside* o' thissplac', d'yuh hea'? Lookitth her wanderin' aboutt! Leth Narayanan be bekk . . . I've gott a lott to tellim. Early in tha mornin' tha husb'nd sneaks off sumwhere thru onesside, an' she slinks off thru tha oth'r!'

Kalyani stood petrified, stumped, as Cheyikkutty delivered the final judgment. It shattered her heart:

'From now, I'llggo to tha yard, nott yuh!'

Cheyikkutty's kitchen grimaced at Kalyani. The prospect of work that needed just sitting and bending drove her crazy. She

thrashed about inwardly like a dammed river. In the kitchen, you
didn't have to even stretch your arm properly. Didn't have to walk
long and well. As for lifting and carrying, just the weight of a
water pot. Kalyani was not used to it. She liked the work she did to
be seen. She was also used to getting paid for it. She did not want
to be going round and round the kitchen like cattle driving the oil
press. No one should be doing that sort of work. And if one did
do it, one should be paid.

This alternate policy document Kalyani had once presented
before her mother.

'Yea, yuh'll learn, yuh'll learn,' Amma had retorted angrily.

She peeped out again and again to see if Cheyikkutty was
returning.

'Esspet Amma olly by ebening,' said Lakshmanan.

'Afther yuh came she's been missin' her walkin' an' wanderin'.
She's goin' to be ramblin' all ober today! She's go' lotts of frien's on
tha oth'r side of tha kottam.'

Lakshmanan was lying on the half-wall of the veranda.
Finishing the chores, Kalyani came out there, sat down, leaned on
the wall, and stretched out her legs. She could hear Lakshmanan's
heaving breath. He was going to fall asleep, she thought.

'Don' roll in yer sleep and fall into tha yard,' she said.

'No'tthath side,' he replied, 'mebbe into tha veranda.'

He slipped off the half-wall and slid close to Kalyani.

'Bhere's tha sthuff?'

She shrugged her shoulders and asked a counter-question.

'Sthuff?'

'Thath yuh stole from Chonnamma?'

Lakshmanan pushed her to the ground.

'Won'ttggibb. If yuh cann, yuh finddith!' she said.

She unfolded herself before Lakshmanan. Now she was
the earth that held many secrets—Chonnamma's kottam, the
chempaka-tree forest, the grove of cashew trees, the broken well
said to be home to spirits which people avoided from fear, the

blooming murikku tree, the *paalmuthakku* vine, the thriving three-coloured *vellila* vines, the hanuman-crown flowers in layers of red, the *uppila* leaves. And she was also a scent you couldn't go back and smell again, or make again.

After he returned from ambling all over, she seized him with a single sweep and held him in the cage of her arms.

'Yuh gibb up?' She asked.

' I gibb up,' he admitted.

'Alrighth. So hear. Wh' shud I steal sumthin' frommy own yard?'

She pulled up Lakshmanan's sweat-drenched face.

'*Ninte parambaa?* . . . Iss ith yer yard?' ['Ingal' had vanished] He pressed his face in the hollow of her throat.

'Ummm.' She affirmed deeply. 'Why, isn' ith my yard?'

He didn't reply.

'Yuh wan' to see wha' I flick'd from *thissplace?*'

She scratched Lakshmanan who was dozing off.

'Uh-m.' He hummed absently.

'*Adu nee thanneyaado* . . . *Yuh*, tha' thing's *yuh*, Narayanan's broth'r Lachuna!'

'Indee . . . !!' He fought shy of admitting.

Lakshmanan's langour vanished quickly.

22

When Koppu-man returned, Cheyikkutty did not raise the matter with him right then. She had decided to tell her son to end once and for all his habit of leaving and returning without notice. Wasn't it proper that he told his family when he changed travel plans? That is, when he decided, initially, that he would be going off to Nilambur in two days—and then changed his mind abruptly and started at once?

Koppu-man did not go to her, either. He sat on the half-wall of the veranda, looking worn. Cheyikkutty who had readied herself to deliver a scolding, held herself back when she saw his face.

'Why's yer face so dim?'

No way can you expect the business to flourish just because you visit Nilambur once a month. For any business to put down roots, you've got to stay in that place for good. People who are not in constant touch with the lumber business cannot really understand its inner workings, no matter how much you explain it to them. And the climate in Nilambur was changing each day. Those who had come there once from the south for the lumber business and to farm were now the locals. Nilambur had a long history of giving way. The outsider *tampaans*, the lords who came from elsewhere, took away the land from the adivasis. The oldsters say that these lords brought with them the labourers they needed. From that day, everyone there was more or less a settler. But the southerners' arrival was somewhat more of an arrival compared to the others.

For them, survival and colonizing went hand-in-hand. The actual locals could only gape at the sorcery through which the land and the trees, all that had lived with them in perfect harmony till then, were now converted into cold cash. Once the competition evolved into tussles between the different groups of settlers, the locals huddled in the margins again.

Those who came to Nilambur from the north were another genus altogether. In all rivalries, they ended up defeated. Unsettled, many left the arena altogether. The original locals who bore a deep distrust and fear of the southerners, looked at the northerners with sympathy. These were men who could not rival the southerners in any way. Avukkar'kka lamented that Nilambur was like a tree decimated by parasites. Even if one didn't get to start something new, it was painful enough to witness a thriving business waste away like a salt-pot made of metal, he said. Either you give up everything and go back, or you get even deeper. But there was no guarantee of any real change. But what more could one do in the north, with just the negligible yearly income from the cashew and the coconut trees that were wasting away each year—was it wise to throw this away totally? What about the useless land up here in the north, full of boulders and abandoned wells and cashew trees and *kara*-thorn-bushes? Yes, there was some paddy land. But what was the use? Maybe the women can grow vegetables.

'Ah, *ellappa* . . .'

Cheyikkutty sighed as she heard him, chin on hand.

'Can't we justh gibb'up this chick'nfeed?' asked she.

This annoyed Koppu-man.

'I try to esplain so longg an' thi' is wha' you cud understhand?'

'You don'ggo showin'any nonsens' to those *chettanmaar*, alrigth? My fath'r has giben me enuf to lasth a life. Don' get yersel' killt by them for *my* sake, uh? If yer womin's needs can' bbe sathisfied with what we hab 'ere, then do wha' you like!'

Cheyikkutty said that with the pride that the woman of the family—she—would indeed inherit the family home.

By *chettanmaar*—literally 'big brothers', but actually referring to southie men—she meant the southerners in general.

Kalyani, who was listening quietly, felt a stab of pain. Her father was no more. She had no share in the family property. She simply did not have enough koppu. She would never be able to declare thus when she took Cheyikkutty's place one day.

'Oberthere south if there ar' three men in a 'ouse, they all come ober 'ere togeth'r. Eachhof 'em slice out thei' own-own land for themselves. Nothin' bithout hard cash!'

Summarizing the history of the migration from the south in three short sentences, Koppu-man sighed.

That reminded Kalyani of Dakshayani's Nailsvendor. 'My faamily, ouw-r faamily, faamily withu justu me, youw, aand ouw-r chillren'—apparently, he used to say. In that family, the only person from Dakshayani's desham would be Dakshayani herself. No one else was permitted. Dakshayani's attachments, bonds of love and friendship, the cow, the pooram festival, the vishu celebration, the Gods dancing the Kaliyattam—all these were to be kept out . Dakshayani was to be like a house lizard with its tail broken—so that he could make a family. His very mention of faamily made Dakshayani very uneasy, she had heard.

When Koppu-man mentioned the southerners carving out their own-own lands, she missed Dakshayani badly.

Koppu-man had some other things to say as well. And that information also came from Avukkar'kka.

It was about Lakshmanan. Avukkar'kka's younger brother had found it out. Nothing serious—not more than what many other young fellows around this place had done—Lakshmanan had never gone to Dubai. He went to Bombay, hung around there a bit, and came back. The goods that he brought back were Bombay-stuff. Though the news shook him somewhat, Koppu-man did not think that Lakshmanan's act was a big crime. But some weakness prevented him from bringing it up it in the presence of Cheyikkutty and Kalyani. Anyway, Lakshmanan will surely find out that there was talk about him on these lines when he went out. Or is he pretending not to know? Koppu-man decided that it was better that the new developments regarding the Dubai trip reached Lakshmanan in due course. Without him having to raise it at home. He simply could not hurt his brother.

Thinking that Koppu-man's face was dull because of his losses in the timber trade, Cheyikkutty and Kalyani tried to console him in their own ways.

'If one can' lifth ith up, then justh drop ith, come bekk, wha' else . . .?'

"Wha' if ith gets betther? Mebbe try onc' mor'?'

Cheyikkutty and Kalyani declared their all-time policy directions respectively.

When Lakshmanan came home that evening, Cheyikkutty described to him the losses that they had suffered. Kalyani noticed that the son was not really paying attention to his mother's words. He was drinking up his rice-porridge. But his mind was elsewhere. Kalyani felt that her heart was bursting, overfilled with scalding-hot steam.

'Wonde' wha'?' She asked herself.

Lakshmanan was standing under the tamarind tree looking thoughtful. Kalyani squatted near the well to wash the dishes.

'Wha'?'

She asked, truly sad.

'Wha'? Annythin' wrongg?'

'No, nothin',' replied Lakshmanan.

She remembered what Cheyikkutty had told her—he's the sort who won't open up his mind to anyone.

'He's always laughin', playin', bu' who knows wha's inside . . . ah?' Cheyikkutty had sighed.

Well, all people are a little like that.

Few are masters of their own minds, even. But Lakshmanan was two feet ahead of most people in his fickleness.

In her bedroom, making the bed, Kalyani ached inwardly for no reason. When he said 'no, nothin'', Lakshmanan shut her out of his secrets. He is banging the door in my face, she thought. But the realization that 'no, nothin'' was the apt phrase to use when one actually had stowed away a lot inside, dawned on her only later—when Lakshmanan waylaid Koppu-man on his way to the bedroom and told him, without actually looking at his face: 'I'd lik' to thinkkof gettin' married.'

23

If you consider the flow of this tale, you'd think that Lakshmanan had duped Kalyani—that thinking is pretty predictable. Not anybody's fault. The reply to such an attitude is this: life is not for those who can think only in a straight line. Similarly, those who think just the other way round—that the events described earlier in this book are inconsequential and amounted to merely three or four days in Kalyani's and Koppu-man's life, they too are prisoners of such straight-line-thinking. Or, this attitude is symptomatic of the stage-fright that I experience when I retell Kalyani's life right in front of her. Much of the detailing that may appear unnecessary to most readers became inevitable because Dakshayani is also present here as a listener. Others may not need certain details to fill some gaps in this retelling of Kalyani's life, but Dakshayani may need them. In some places, she needs no explanation, but others do need it. Taking both into consideration, Kalyani, Cheyikkutty, Koppu-man and Lakshmanan may have to live their lives rather quickly. Sometimes, even if it were for the sake of others, they may have to live those lives one more time. Haven't you seen aeroplanes circle the airport slowly, hover up there, loiter in the sky for some time, instead of landing? This is a bit like that. Only that these relivings may lack the original intensity. In any case, no experience is new. Experiences have always been around us, divided and distributed. The thing is that when they are concentrated on us personally, the nearness induces an intense jumpiness. And that could be because we actually like these experiences, or the exact reverse. That's the sole difference.

I am taking the freedom to say that if I have portrayed Lakshmanan here as a bad character, then that is the failing of my language and of your socialization. That Kalyaniyechi never thought of Lakshmanan as an edifice or pile that had to be dismantled from her life is a fact—attested by herself first, and then by me. I am not sure if he will reappear in her life again. If there are such moments, then I request you, please think of him as a good character, even if I forget to remind you. In fiction and in life, those who tell the tale tend to forget soon; that is, of course, not the case with those who listen to it.

And therefore, Kalyaniyechi admitted secretly that the words 'I'd lik' to thin' of gettin' married' bugged her for a long time like a cockroach stuck inside the ear.

Koppu-man had no issues at all about seeking a mangalam, a wedding, for his younger brother. But he should get into some gainful line of work before, he insisted. That's how Lakshmanan set off for Nilambur along with Avukkar'kka soon after the cashew nut season. Let him get somewhat steady. Then we'll look for a bride.

'Lemme see if I cannfindd one tha' stays put at home', decided Cheyikkutty. 'I can' standdthi' anymor'.' This was when Kalyani's careless fiddling around in the kitchen knocked down the mustard-seed pot.

So whad didshe thin'? Tha' she cud hab tha olde' broth'r an' tha younge' broth'r, both?

Did Lakshmanan leave for Nilambur out of the fear that people would come to know that he was a faux Dubai-man?

Got ith on justh three times, an' alread' tired of her?

Maybe because he didn't want Koppu-man to know of the relations he had with Kalyani?

Mebbe becos he thinks thath if he sthay'd there for mor' she'd geth toomuch attach'd an' wud not leth him go?

Did he calculate that he could help his brother in the trade, avoid creating problems in his family, and cover up the embarrassment of not achieving Dubai-man status?

Eee . . . 'ow cud he thinkkso?

Since my authority is not extensive enough to answer so many questions, and conceding the possibility that the questions may themselves be holding their answers within themselves, and because Lakshmanan is now leaving the house with some essentials packed in a box, over to Kalyani now, and apologies for the interruption!

Kalyani stood leaning on the wall of the veranda.

Koppu-man tried to heave up Lakshmanan's box. It didn't move.

'Don'hhurt yer bekk.' Though she said that, Kalyani just stood there watching.

Lakshmanan tried to hoist it up. It did not move.

'Wha' diddyuh sthuff in there?' Cheyikkutty's mouth fell open.

Avukkar'kka came over and tried to lift it.

'Justh tak' outt sum of tha sthuff. Yuh can take those nexth time . . . yuh aren' goin' to Dubai or sumw'ere.'

'No, sinc' ith's been brough' dow' . . .' Cheyikkutty stopped them.

'Stepp thisside . . .' Lakshmanan looked up hearing the raspy voice. It was Kalyani getting down into the yard.

'Holdd!'

Bending towards the box, she commanded Lakshmanan.

'Ithhwon' work.'

'Leth'ssee if ithwill.'

'Won'.'

'Will.'

'Won'.'

'Will.'

The box reached the Jeep.

As the Jeep got farther and farther away through the cashew garden, another red hibiscus flower that stood in the front-yard flushed redder still.

24

All the cashew nuts were sold. The coconut oil from the dried coconuts filled the cans spreading an aroma around. Pieces of wood laid down their lives in silence inside the kitchen-hearth. The rains started. The clouds covered the sky so closely that even Kalyani could do nothing other than stay indoors. But whenever the downpour eased a bit, she would slip out. She had managed to sweep up as much as she could of the fallen leaves in the cashew grove and make neat heaps of them. She checked if the cashew nuts that managed to slip beneath the leaves had germinated. When the frenzied rain hurled drops that hit the ground hard, like grains of sand, she would run back to the house. Koppu-man was at home too. When it was clear that the only possible chore left for the time being was that of conjugality, Kalyani decided, 'in thath case, leth thath 'appen'. In truth, it was only then that she was able to take a good look at Koppu-man. In the time that had lapsed in between, she had even forgotten that he slept on the cot in the bedroom. When it began to rain, she rolled up the mat, left it in a corner of the room, and sought her share of space on the cot. With his manner of lying down in such a way that they would not touch each other or turn over to face each other, that too in the cool season of rain, Koppu-man continued to be an unknown terrain for Kalyani.

'Ar' yuh 'fraid of me?'

Once when they had both woken up together, but rather rudely, she turned to her puruvan tenderly and asked.

'Why shud I be 'fraid?' He asked, 'Yer my womin.'

He defended himself in a low voice.

'The' shall I gibb yuh a kiss? Yuh'll tak'ith?' She touched her nose to his ears.

Koppu-man looked at her face. He noticed for the first time that there was a black beauty spot hiding under her lower lip. The fine down above her upper lip trembled as though caressed gently by the faint breeze. Then, because her brows seemed to hold the dark nests of many secrets, he withdrew his glance fearfully. Yet he could not help hugging the woman who lay facing him. With that, Kalyani gushed up and swept into him like water bursting out of a dam. Koppu-man was now trapped in an islet; he felt like a lone child whose house was inundated by the deluge. The waves rising all around suffocated him. The threat that the oar could be snatched from his hand any moment kept surfacing. What if he were sucked into some whirlpool, along with his canoe and the oar that he hugged with all his might? He could not haul himself up. The canoe capsized over his head. He had to push it aside to come up for a mouthful of air.

'If yuh can'ttdo ith, why di' yuh sthart all of this in tha firsth place . . . ?'

Pulling up her pillow and stuffing it under Koppu-man's head, Kalyani got up from the cot.

'Yuh go to sleep, tha's betther fo' yuh . . .' she said, 'Kee' yer head up a bith.'

Koppu-man thought that the heat gathering on the top of his head would keep swelling and that he would soon explode.

He suddenly caught hold of her arm.

'Yuh be 'ere. Lemme see if ith'll wor' . . .'

Kalyani did not feel like rejecting him outright. After all, that had been her policy all this while. Lower the bar for those who can't jump high. When they run up, jump and clear the bar, get the goose-bumps, and feel proud, you applaud. But the height that they *ought to* have covered would still stay up there, casting down a condescending smile.

Kalyani lay beside Koppu-man once again. This time she did not try to arouse him in any way. But Koppu-man was still intimidated by this knotty question posed in a language that he did not know. Very reluctantly, he pushed open his fingers and made an attempt to touch her body. The fingers took in a helicopter-view of her body from waist to forehead and withdrew. The philosophical dilemma about where Kalyani was to be touched seemed to be receding and finally, he touched her cheek.

'Yuh lik' my cheek tha besth?' She feigned innocence.

'Ruin'd ith, yuh womin!'

Koppu-man was annoyed. Her question, just when he had been . . .!

But she had by now assembled assorted nails—made of words and phrases—to drive into his ego. She took up the second one now.

'Wha'? Why shud I be quieth? Wha' yuh doin'? Gettin' out tha evil eye, waving tha mustar' seed an' chilli?'

Koppu-man turned his back to her on the bed quietly.

'Ah, lookk'ere . . .'

She shook him.

'Wha' am I to do?'

'Yuh do nothin',' he spat angrily. 'All yuh do is gad aboutt 'ere an' there. I hea' Amma murmurin', alrighth? Yuh seth off in tha mornin' an' come hom' at wha' hour? Yuh know thath Amma can'dd do all of tha housework?'

Kalyani got off the bed and tied her hair up. In a voice as cold as death, she accepted, very slowly, 'I know, Amma can't do *ith* all . . .'

Opening the window, she let the rain in. It fell on her face and breasts, leaving them speckled. The new cowshed outside was all wet and shivering in the rain; it looked at her helplessly. At that moment, Koppu-man came and stood behind her. He drew the scent of her hair into his nostrils.

'Wha'?'

She did not conceal her distaste; she turned away.

'Yuh smell nice,' he opened his nostrils.

'Smell wha'?' she asked.

'Lik' wet rupee notes. I lik' ith alott.'

Along with that last faltering line, he held her close.

When it was evident that he would not clear the qualifying round despite resources, experience, and luck coming together fortuitously, Kalyani kicked aside both the bedcover and Koppu-man. Spitting out an expletive sharp enough to cut him in two, she rose and left his bed forever.

'Go thro'wway yer thingy—ith'ss flagging lik' a soggy lamp wick! Bulb o' pesthilenc'!'

Pulling open the door of the bedroom forcefully and crossing its high step in a single stride, Kalyani walked towards the inner-veranda, smouldering like a wet, half-burned pyre. But she was suddenly jolted—seeing that the door from there to the outer veranda lay open—even in the middle of that heartache. Wisps of smoke were rising from the farther end of the half-wall of the outer veranda, and a distinct beedi scent spread from there.

'Who is there?' She took a step back even as she asked in a firm voice.

Just two more steps behind her was a little table on which lay a long torch. As Kalyani stepped back towards it without taking her eyes off the whorls of smoke, Cheyikkutty lit a match for the next beedi.

'*Uyyintappa*! Yuh, Amme! Wud've bee' quithe a sthory now!'

Kalyani lowered her voice.

'If I got a blow from yer han' ith'd all be pretty neat!' said Cheyikkutty, her hand flying to her head.

'Thissbbulb o' pesthilenc' hassno midnighth, no mornin'!' She murmured.

'Wha's tha matther 'ere,' Kalyani went up close.

'Nothin'. An ol' habith . . . couldn' sleep . . .'

Cheyikkutty said cryptically, in a voice that sounded very, very old.

Surrogates, so many! Humans are the masters of finding stand-ins—hapless, poverty-stricken proxies. What else is life but the search for substitutes?

Kalyani watched Cheyikkutty sit on the half-wall smoking a beedi and staring into the rain. Her heart welled. Her naked torso was covered with just an old mundu.

'*Paavam*,' she thought, 'poor thin', she mebbe old but won' she too hab her desires?'

Suddenly she remembered something.

'Amme, yuh've tha cash from selling tha cashew nuts? Can I hab ith now?' she asked.

'Cash, eh? Now? For wha'?' Cheyikkutty was surprised.

'Amme jus' gibb ith to me. I'll gibb ith bekk lat'r.'

'Ith's in tha box in tha south'n-side room, in tha corn'r. Be car'ful whe' yuh ope', don' lethththa lid fall on yer han' . . .'

The rain roared as it came down again.

Cheyikkutty returned to the swirls of smoke.

Kalyani went right back through the open door of the bedroom with a fistful of notes.

Koppu-man had not yet fallen asleep. A bedcover opened and folded itself before his eyes again and again. The one torn up by the woman who had whirled helplessly when Chonnamma got into her.

'Take thi' . . .ere . . . smellith . . .'

She held out the notes to him.

25

Cheyikkutty found Kalyani at the well-side at the crack of dawn, drawing up buckets of water and emptying them on her head in the pouring rain. She did not hear Cheyikkutty say 'wha' tha madn'ss'. Her movements were marked by a certain unquiet calm, the kind of which settles after a funeral. Emptying the last bucket on her head like she were completing some ritual, Kalyani left the bucket upturned on the well-side, and went soundlessly, wordlessly, with quiet footsteps, into the house. The water that ran down her body sank deep into the ground and impressed there the mark of Kalyani's life in that house till then. When she got into the bedroom, Koppu-man was leaving. He did not show her his face. She went in there and stood still for some moments. She remembered her wedding, from months back.

From the lowest shelf of the almirah, from below Koppu-man's and Lakshmanan's clothes, she pulled out the boiled-egg coloured Dubai sari with black paisley print and gold thread. She ran her fingers slowly on the Dubai panty. Like she was performing some really sacred ritual, she squeezed herself into it. The sari collapsed with sadness on her shoulder and breast. She tied the ends of her still-wet-and-dripping hair into a little knot. Then she looked for and found a small cloth-bundle made of a piece of mundu from the almirah. Vanaja had tied the gold bangles and chains in that bundle on the evening of her wedding day. All three bangles had broken when they were removed from her wrists. She wore the black-bead-and-gold chain around her neck with care. She removed the taara-chain from her neck and held it in her hand, looking at it for a moment. It was a pretty one, for sure. Never mind, she could get another one with two years of work. Then there was a necklace. 'Oh, tha neckless! All thath's lefth is to pu' thath' on!' She scolded herself, tied it up in the little bundle, and stuffed it inside her blouse. Crossing the door of the bedroom, she glanced back offhandedly. Did she see the reddish glow slip into the back-side of the almirah? Was there a woman hiding there whose laughter was falling all over the place even though she was trying to hold it back?

'I'mggoing bekk.'

Kalyani went up to Cheyikkutty and told her.

'Goin'? Wha' . . ?'

Cheyikkutty was clearly baffled.

But her mind told her this was no ordinary going bekk.

When Kalyani reached the sit-out, Koppu-man came opposite.

'I'mggoin' bekk . . .'

She told him in a calm voice. Then took his palm, opened it, and placed the taara-chain in it.

One of the Kalyani's chores was killing rats and mice caught in the mousetraps. Before she drowned the mouse, she would look at its face. And a dialogue would ensue between them, as follows:

'Yer tim's come, alrighth?'

'Bu', Kalyani, sum mor' days, pleas'?'

'If yer tim' is 'ere, wha' am I to do?'

'Hab got a piece of tapioca, Kalyani. Lemme gnaw ith a bith, please. An' then yuh can drown me, pleas', my goodggirl Kalyani?'

'I'm no' yer goodggirl Kalyani! Ha! Yer not getthin' to gnaw thath tapioca!'

'Don't, Kalyani, don' . . . kill . . . *nnaalum* . . .'

'No pleas-pees, no . . . nnaalum ok? Oh, weren' yuh gnawin' an' gnawin' away unde' tha tapioca root? Bhere's thath thing yuh were nibblin' . . ?'

'Alrighth, justh drownmme, Kalyani, I don' bant gnawin' nothin'.'

'Alrighth, 'ere goes.'

'Drown'd.'

'Dead.'

Before drowning and getting drowned, Subject and Object look at each other. That's natural law.

Koppu-man sat down on the half-wall quietly; sensing the seriousness of the situation, Cheyikkutty dashed out madly from inside the house.

'Don' yuh walkk a stepp more! Yuh try to go, I'll chop an' mince yer leg! Wha's got inta yuh, damn'd floozie! Tak' bekk thath leg of yers, goin' to yer death! Fuckin' whor'!'

She ran ahead of Kalyani and stood barring her way.

'If am a whore, thath's tha fault of yer son,' said Kalyani, without raising her voice.

I didn't mean that, Cheyikkutty was pained. She had no words now. Her eyes welled.

She had some legitimate suspicions. But the suspects were people who weren't in the frame of the living now. The wench who spent all her time till late in the evening in the cashew grove must have gone to both broken wells. Cheyikkutty's elder sister, her *Valyechi*, was in one of those. She jumped in there to her death after giving birth, for no reason. The reddish medicinal water for her postpartum bath was boiling outside. Her hair which was doused with oil was tied up on the top of her head. Her body was smeared with special medicinal unguents. Specially made by Achootty vaidyar for his daughter. Cheyikkutty was pounding the shoeflower leaves to shampoo her hair. On a mat laid on the veranda lay a male infant also smeared with oils, slipping off it. The breeze blew, the gentle sunlight spread, nothing was wrong. When Cheyikkutty set down the hot water in the bathing shed and got up, she saw her who had just given birth disappear into the well in a flash. What to do? Achootty vaidyar dug another well. That was all.

'Thath wa' a goodd *kerandu*, thath well. She took ith when she jump'd into ith.' He repeated, year after year.

Though she was now in the well, Valyechi did not forget the house. She'd peep in through the window now and then. She would come into the kitchen, move the pot covers, and check.

'Cheyi-ya . . . yuh fed tha babie tha muthaari?'

'Cheyi-ya . . . the mosquitho hasn' bitthen tha babie?'

'Cheyi-ya . . . why's tha babie bawlin'?'

'Cheyi-ya . . . I won' leth anyon' go easy!'

It's thath womin. Cheyikkutty was convinced. Was no good for life and so hopped in the well and now she's trying to light bonfires on other people's heads.

No, I won' leth go, eithe'. There's Chonnamma 'ere, the 'Pothy too. Leth'ssee! Those who stomped out of this place can't be allowed to fool around with the lives of those who are still here. Just carry on; walk the path you took.

She peered at Kalyani. Yes, need to pay attention.

One must never be angry with the Gods and the Departed. Their share must be given once a year inside the house. Or wherever they are.

'. . . whateber ith mebbe, we'll dea' bith ith . . . Don' mind me sayin' summthin' in anger . . . Yuh geth bekk in, Kalyani . . .'

She caught hold of her wrist.

'My girll, yuh shudn'ggo'way. If yuh go, Amma'll die of a brok'n heart.'

'Kalyani won' sthay 'ere anymor', Amme. Yuh senttawway one womin sayin' thath Chonnamma got her? Yuh can tell pipple thath Chonnamma got Kalyani too. Say tha' she wa' senttawway 'cause of thath.'

'Ah, thath's ith . . . yuh hab bee' taken by sumone. Wha'else? Yuh go in, leth's talk inside.'

'If Kalyani's benth on sum-thin', she's benth on ith, Amme. Is she goin' to go bekk in agai'?'

She took two steps forward.

The cows in the sheds old and new looked at her, stunned.

If you go who'll talk with us in our language, Kalyani? They asked, silently.

'Narayanaa . . . why yuh nott sayin' anythin'?'

Cheyikkutty left Kalyani and turned towards Koppu-man.

'If yer a man, Narayana, yuh shuddkknow how to keepp a womin unde' yer thumb. Thi' one's fallen off yer hand righth now . . . wha' good yuh ar', essept to be bawlin' lik' a cow in tha end? Tha infernal impp!'

Koppu-man was silent.

Kalyani laughed a rasping, merciless laugh and strode away without a second glance.

When she disappeared beyond the cashew grove, the rain fell in mighty torrents upon the desham.

26

The rain that fell on Kalyani's desham was also spraying the wooden window-seat of the south-bound train. When she thought of all that had happened in the short span of a few months, something hung heavy in Dakshayani's throat. She simply could not believe, still, that Nailsvendor was sitting by her side, brushing at her shoulder and arm as the train juddered and shook. She struggled not to turn her head towards him. Dakshayani had failed to foresee that no matter how strong its trunk may be, a tree will fall if its roots are weakened. That must be recorded as a crucial failure in her life.

One of the mistakes she made was to assess Nailsvendor from within her (limited) experience of the world, gathered from her job in the plywood factory, carrying bundles of fodder, birthing care, caring for cows, and cinema-watching. Her calculation that he could be pulverized by some biting words proved somewhat wrong. And when the cricket ball comes directly at you, whether it's a good one or not, you've to defend—what else to do since you have taken to the field? It is true that Dakshayani and all the witnesses, and Nailsvendor himself, thought that she had walloped Nailsvendor in the last ball of the over with a tremendous sixer. But the ball which flew amidst the deafening cheers was caught at the boundary. It took some time for Dakshayani to realize that her wicket had been taken. At that moment, Nailsvendor was seated surrounded by a select group of Dakshayani's relatives and crying his eyes out. Achootty Mash and Govindettan were present as special invitees. The sight of a fully-grown fellow sitting on the wooden chair in the inner veranda bawling about his faamily and his wife-u made Dakshayani nauseous. But the others were taken by that performance; they instantly formed a protective shield around him. The whole scene reminded her of the *oppana*-singing at Kaisumma's house on the eve of her daughter Nebisu's wedding. In the kitchen, Dakshayani's Amma and Damuettan's woman wiped their eyes with the edges of their mundus.

'Lookk at him soo . . . lovv'. . !'

Dakshyani's mother was so overcome, she swallowed the rest of the love.

'Yuhggott to be lucky to geth a puruvan so lovvin' . . . he isn' . . . lik' tha . . . oth'rs,' sobbed Damuettan's woman.

Ha! Her mother-in-law had a whole numbered list to counter that, but she decided that it was not yet time to pull it out; instead, she corralled her son's woman with a single pointed stare.

Meanwhile, Nailsvendor lamented:

'Yu tellu me whaat wraa-ngu I diddu! I haave olly luv-d he-r. Shouldn'tu we haave ye faamily? When yit ees ye faamily, yit means hussbandu, babies, ees yit nottu, *illiyo*? Will scoldu yif I see wraa-ngu. Doesu thatu meanu throw-ya-way? *Yeval*—thisswuman—will tell yuu thaat she yis biggu, but she yis justu ye foolu, justu ye foolu!! Shouldu I nottu checku yif she has faallen in-tu yany traappu? Shouldu I nottu checku yif some fellow yisn't tricking he-r aandu taiking the caashu? *Njaan pharthaavalyo*, am I nottu the hussbandu? Ees taiking cai-yar of the faamily something wraa-ngu?'

Each of his words was accepted by the audience as pearls of eternal wisdom. The word 'faamily' lay on the inner veranda of Dakshayani's house and kicked its baby-legs, tiny anklets tinkling. The audience realized that the faamily that Nailsvendor underscored was something very distant from what they knew and practised as family life.

Dakshayani stood in the kitchen's outer veranda, almost totally isolated now; seeing her there, the cow, which stood in the cowshed all alone, just like her, nodded, saying 'Yer netted, my girll, mole'. Even the best playmaker cannot withstand the combined strength of the entire opposite team and the gallery. It's easy to sit in the gallery and command, 'Take that catch, you sonofabitch!' But on this day, the whole world was arrayed against Dakshayani. Everyone has such days. Human beings do not live by reason alone. To the contrary, they may be sustained for long by the most laughable irrationalities. Meanwhile, the audience had reached the unanimous conclusion that Dakshayani suffered from nerviness as a result of not enjoying sufficient proximity to Nailsvendor.

Women who mangalam-ed—women who are married, that is—and then got shoved into a kitchen corner after the mangalam (like Dakshayani)—are distinct from never-mangalam-ed women who also end up as kitchen-corner-women. The former display a greater likelihood of generally losing it. Two instances were submitted as evidence for this assertion.

One: Sathy, the do-ughter of my math-ere's sister who livves justu to the *thekke* side of ouwer house, southu-facing. One day, she justu star-ttedu, oh, *phayangaram*, derrible, derrible, she haa-d ye frenu-zy aandu fit-u. Broke-u the tubelightu of the veranda! Peeple caught he-r aand tooku he-r to the exorcistu brahminu, Tirumeni of Kunnel. He tied ye thread on he-r but yit diddu no gooddu. Tirumeni saiddu she waas takennby one thousand spiritsu! She wudd nottu y-eat or drinku aand haad to be taiken to the Medical-Collegu. *Ariyavo?* Know whaatu the doctor there saiy? Bringu this g-erl's hussbandu nowwu! So they bringu. *Ippom entho parayaanaa?* Whaatu to say nowwu? *Aande*, thaar! Nowwu theye haavu two chill-rennu aand they haave built ye houseu too! Aall this ees justu, olly, this muchu . . .

Two: Our Uknni, of tha Kundathil hous'. She wa' goin' as sthiff as an ol' okra in tha corn'r bith no mangalam. Gott into a twisth bith a guy who cam' for tha' canal work, an' marri'd im. Betther than her becomin' a kitchin-corn'r womin, we thoughth. Afther two weeks he wenth off, sayin' tha' he wa' visithin' hom'. But nev'r turn'd up, no news. Bhere to searc' im outt? She wen' mad, didn'sshe? An' tha screamin' an' hollerin', tha'ssit. Now ever'y year she gets it two tim's, reg'l'rly!

Imagining a crazed Dakshayani smashing tubelights and burning down the house unable to suffer her separation from him, Nailsvendor sobbed.

'*Uyi*, don' cry, yuh . . . we'll mak' ith alrighth . . .'

Achooty Mash got up slowly from where he sat. This time he was smart enough to refrain from bossing Dakshayani around. If nothing else, he was a shrewd Congressman. Those days, the Congress ruled the whole of India! So what to say of this puny family problem! Achooty Mash set off to the kitchen seeking the support of the coalition partners. Their backing was vital in this matter. They were not to utter a word in support of Dakshayani. If they did, she may just grab it and climb right back up. If the puruvan orders, she should follow him. The man is willing to forgive the cheap things she shouted at him. The family (faamily) is the bigger thing for him. He's ready to take any insult for the fa(a)mily. Achooty Mash was successful in gaining their promise of support from the outside, without joining the government. Though the national leaders of the Congress at that time seemed oblivious to it, Achooty Mash knew well that taking over the leadership of a coalition and a government without winning the confidence of the smaller parties was suicidal. But his political acumen was not fated to leave his desham. Alas, the Congress still pays a price for this. Let it suffer. The stick ought to be in the hand of the guy who knows how to throw it. That's true for the family, and for politics, too. What's the use of the fellow who can't throw and just keeps holding on to the stick?

'Tha outhsider-typ's hab lefth so many youn' wimmin's lives
in a mess. When thissman wen'off thath day I neber thought he'd
comebbekk... but he cam'bbekk? Tha's because' he's a gooddman?'

Achooty Mash advised Amma and Damuettan: 'Yuh musth
tell er to subbmmith to 'im. When he's come to geth her bekk,
leavin' aside his bisness' an' eberythin', and cryin' an' all, yuh
shudn' kick him away.'

Later, when she thought of it, Dakshyani just could not see
how she ended up so powerless at that moment. Life, after all,
includes not just revolutions but also martyrdoms. Even the most
ardent revolutionaries have, at one moment or the other, fallen
prey to weakness.

Next day, early in the morning, stepping on the fallen leaves
in the front of the house and sounding like the rat-snake's
slither, Nailsvendor set out to catch the south-bound train with
Dakshayani following him.

'If you leave, with whom will I talk in your language,
Dakshayani?' The cow blew her nose.

From my limited knowledge, I'd say, the going doesn't look
good—she opined glumly.

Dakshayani's sadness grew heavier.

'Yitees aall ovver, *kettodi*, doo youw he-ear, *edi*? Youwer
jumbbing and praan-cing is aall ovver.' As they crossed the house-
front, Nailsvendor told Dakshayani, with a triumphant smile.

27

Though she had to put up with Nailsvendor, Dakshayani liked the journey. That was her first time on a train. Though land stretched out long and tube-like, no place was like a python with the same speckles all over its body—that much she gathered from the travel.

(The only desham-girl who had left the desham for elsewhere before Dakshyani was Nebisu, Kaisumma's daughter. But Dakshayani wouldn't have called it a journey. Nor would Kalyani, Kaisumma, or Nebisu. Nebisu's flight was like a desperate search for water when your throat burns from thirst. It was completely different. Therefore Nebisu shouldn't be dragged here.)

The south wasn't totally unfamiliar to Dakshayani. She remembered it from all the movies she had watched at Nisha Talkies with Kalyani. None of the characters in those movies talked in her tongue. But none of them were strangers to her, were they? How many times did she imagine herself to be one of them, with their polished, sharp talk, the tight, printed blouses from which protruded two conical missiles, and huge hairdos! She tried to think of her new life as such a transmogrification. From the pock-marked seats in front of the screen, right onto the screen for the moment—simple! Because she had accepted new tastes in food, eating wasn't much of a problem. Dakshayani knew that every place had its own ways and tongue. Like all the *theyyam*-gods had their own specific *thottam*-songs.

When Dakshayani stepped into Nailsvendor's house, the only person at home was Kunhippennu.

(Kunhippennu's story will be retold by Dakshayani to Kalyani at a particular moment with a specific intent. Since there's no permission to relate her story now, for the time being Kunhippennu will be just Kunhippennu.)

'*Alle*, ah! Look who-ees he-yer, Kunhippennu! Howw aare thinggs?'

That's how Dakshayani learned her name, when Nailsvendor made small-talk.

'Oh, justto givvu some milku, uh!'

She held up the pot.

'Whe-yer yis yeveryone?'

Nailsvendor peeked inside the house eagerly.

'Today ees the *kodiyettu*-festivalu at the Valiya(k)aavu temble, *allyo*? The *tamburatti*-princess yis coming he-yer fo-r some *nercha*-vow or sum-thing. Lo-ot of peeple haave go-ne from he-yer. Didn'tu he-r faamily rule us for ye ve-ry ve-ry longu time-u? Whennu she comesu so close-u, shuddu we nottu go yaand see he-r? Acchan and Amma wentu in the noonu-time-u itself.'

Kunhippennu presented these details with utmost devotion.

'Koppu!' swore Nailsvendor, clearly irritated. He then ordered Dakshayani. 'You go yand maike sum tea. Yevv-erything aafter thaatu.'

Dakshayani turned into a veritable tent of loathing as she went looking for the kitchen; just then, Nailsvendor's parents returned. For a few moments, no one spoke. All they knew about their son who seemed to have many sorts of dealings in lots of different places was that he was into selling nails in Malabar. He also made a few trips to Bangalore. That was for the clothes business. Then some minor usury. How to hang around here without solid cash? He told them about the tiny rooms in the rented line-housing in Malabar where four or five young men lived together for rent. Don't ask what happened if one of them caught the chickenpox!

They shared the kitchen and bathroom. He had to cook on his own. Hard to live like that for long! So when he told them that he was going to marry a good-looking girl from around there, they didn't feel like saying no. If they did object, he would simply leave them and go away. That was not wise. That would be a loss. He could stay in her house if he wanted. Apparently, only her mother stayed there besides her.

Nailsvendor's mother knew well that it was not wise at all to let her son slip from her hand. She had not seen Dakshayani before the wedding, and for that matter, after too. The wedding was attended by his father, two maternal uncles (their faces contorted with disgust) and two of his father's sisters (his *appachimaar*, that is). And a handful of his friends. The only bit of advice his mother had given her son then was, do not enter straight into the girl's house after the wedding, find a rented place for the time being at least. Mothers don't attend their sons' weddings, anyway. The custom is that they stay at home to give the new bride a lit lamp with which she was to enter her new home. Because of these reasons, Dakshayani's entry into Nailsvendor's life was not a matter of deep concern to his parents or the house. Dakshayani too knew that it would not be so. What left her confused was two deshams: Malabar, Madras.

Where exactly was the vending of nails taking place? The two deshams clashed inside her head. How were the boundaries formed? With what yardsticks?

Her classes in environment education began the next morning. Nailsvendor's mother pointed out the boundaries of their yard to her.

'Ovver the-yer is Villaasan's yaardu. He bo-ught thaat laandu aand hung himself! Why, nobody knowwsu. On the otheru sideu they aare *tandanmar*, coconut tree climb-ersu, low caste-u! On tha weste-rn side is ye pastor—he yis ye tenant, from sumwheyer! On the *kizhakkethu*—eastu-sideu ees the sister of ouwr *acchan*, my hussband. True, she yis my sister-in-laa.

But she yis a *phayankara* sorceressuu! Ye sneaky *Koodothrakkari*! Simbly phayankara! Fee-yarsommm-u! Youw shuddu nottu behaive like you did baack home! Don'tu knocku yeround these houses-u? Youw hear-u?'

'So there're no humans in thissplace'?' Dakshayani's mouth fell open.

It was just then that she noticed a cow in Villaasan's yard. Some luscious milk-vines were growing really close to where it stood, but the cow didn't touch them. Why?

She also noticed the barbed-wire fence forming the boundary between the two yards. Drawn between two slabs of granite. If the cow tried to reach the vines stretching its neck through the fence, the skin of its face would tear. She could poke her head through to reach the vines. But couldn't withdraw it without injury. That is the science of the wire fence. She had noticed such fences in all the yards on the way to Nalisvendor's house.

'Thi' is tha peshan aroun' 'ere?' (She meant to say 'fashion'.) She went close to the fence and asked the cow.

The cow did not reply. Why talk with a girl on the other side of the fence of a notknownchap, an *aaraan*?

'Ver' snootty, eh?'

Dakshayani bent down and plucked the milk-vine. It came off rather too easily. The soil was not firm at all. The roots never went very deep. But when you step on the ground, your foot would sink in the soil for sure. Back in her place, the soil was very firm. There were dark boulders there. And the *kaara*-thorn thickets. Those everyday sights now felt so dear, her heart ached. Dakshayani went near the fence and held out the vines to the cow.

''ere, eat. Yuh'll hab lo's of milk.'

'I don'd wandu the grassu frommu summbody yelse's fieldu. We havve innuff aand more-u yin ow-ur fieldu.'

The cow turned sharply and marched off.

Dakshayani felt foolish.

'*Uyyenttappa*!! Lookitt tha cow! So brash!'

'A-rre you plucking the graasu frommu ouwer yardu to feedu summbody yelse's cow? If you a-re so keenu, the-re aare two yin the cowsheddu he-yer,' Nailsvendor's mother called from behind her.

Nailsvendor who came in hearing that, said, ah she yis aafter aall ye cow-caring wuman, and threw her a pointed look. Dakshayani returned his look asking in her mind, so yuh dragg'd tha bothe' 'ere for thi'? But because she felt so ill at ease, as though a whole nest of fire-ants had fallen on her and they were running all over her body, she quickly got out of his eyeshot.

28

'Thees ees ouwer well. Yit nevver dries up. Yit doesn'tu haave to go downnu to the netherworlddu, like yin youwer plaice.'

Nailsvendor showed Dakshayani the well.

Dakshayani peered into the well. It was quite shallow, made of cement rings. Easy to descend into and get back from. The poor thing, it can't give you a weak reply even. Not even if you bend and holler into it loudly! She felt sorry for it.

'Ah is ith eben a well? *Ithellaam oru kerandaa*?' She frowned at Nailsvendor. That left him a little deflated.

'Howw is ouwer *naadu*? Like this plaice?' He tried to change the topic.

'For thath do yuh really hab yer ownnplac' at all?' She asked, innocently enough. 'Yer plac' is all inside tha 'ouse? Justh tha inside?'

Nailsvendor stomped back into the house. Dakshayani went back to the fence-side. She saw Nailsvendor's mother's sister-in-law, the phayankara-sorceress, coming towards her holding a leaf-packet.

She cut a pathetic figure—thin, emaciated, teeth jutting out of her mouth. According to her profile presented to Dakshayani by Nailsvendor's mother, a leaf-packet was perpetually in her hand. That's the deadly *koodothram*-packet, full of malevolent *bhasmam*—potent dust! She'll visit you for apparently no reason. Then, lulling you with her talk, creep to the well-side, and throw the dust into it. Only after the deed was done would she leave! The house is sure to be ruined soon after. There are many temples that actually specialize in such malevolent stuff. But our people don't go there much. We don't even utter the names of such deities if we can help it. The sorceress-sister-in-law is a regular visitor to such temples. All she wants is to witness is the utter ruin of her brother's family.

When she passed by, Dakshayani craned her neck to look. The sorceress grinned at her weakly.

'Howw aare thinggs, *koche*?'

Dakshayani shook her head to say, nothing special.

Why yuh no' comin' ober? That question welled up inside her and strained to pour out. Dakshayani had learned by then that she could not ask all questions to all women.

'Whaat wentu on attu the well-sideu? Saw *laval*—thatwuman— there withu yow-u? Didd she throw sum-thingu in the wellu?'

Nailsvendor's mother asked as she held her in a harsh stare.

Dakshayani wandered aimlessly inside and outside the house like a slow-burning bundle of cotton-wool. Her branches had been cut down. The money-box (she called it *alu*) which used to be full every month, had now died of starvation. She herself could not believe how her days dragged on without the bustle and laughter and the quarrels in the plywood factory. It is the tragedies that unfold silently, slowly, that are more fatal than those which upturn your life in a single day. It is truly like slow poisoning. If the antidote is not administered, then the poisoned person turns a bit more bluish each day, and finally dies. Not a soul around might notice—that's the beauty of it. Even the poisoned one may not notice it. Maybe the dog or cat or cow do notice, well and good then. Dakshayani missed her cow terribly. It was a very sensible, politically aware cow. Very perceptive of her circumstances as well. Quite downcast when Dakshayani left, too. When she remembered how her cow had stood still, struggling to subdue its surging sadness, shaking its ears, shooing off all sounds and staring into the distance, tears fell from her eyes.

That's when she suddenly woke up to the question, '. . . is no-won attu home-u?' She saw a dark-skinned man, a bit bent, stand there with a sheepish look on his face.

She turned to him and asked him to sit down. Ignoring the two chairs on the veranda, he sat on the floor and stretched his legs out towards the yard. When she learned that this was the Party member who had come visiting, the hum of the plywood factory came back to her ear. The waving tops of the red flags that rolled down the tiny path that led to the panchayat road visible from her house reddened her again. She could turn red in that way only at home. Dakshayani swelled inwardly with nostalgia. Though she mentioned a couple of times offering the visitor something to drink, they ignored her.

'Wha's up bith these creetures . . . won' they eben offe' a cup of water for tha thirsth?' She grumbled as she poured some buttermilk into a glass without taking anyone's permission. She took it to the veranda. When the guest left, Nailsvendor apprised Dakshayani of the following:

There are people who must be offered a drink of water and others who shouldn't be.

There are people who must be invited inside, and others who shouldn't be.

Those who know their place will sit where they must, others should be shown their place.

The recent visitor and the visitor's father too, will sit only where he just sat. That's because they know their place. Party membership etc. is secondary.

An image placed on a small wooden plank fixed above the top shelf in Nailsvendor's house gazed helplessly at Dakshayani. That was the picture of the legendary communist leader, Krishna Pillai—he too was a Nair, but not like these. He was a Nair who did the impossible—he had boldly rung the bells of the sanctum at the Guruvayoor temple, sending the Holinesses and the royalists there into paroxysms of caste-rage.

29

'Thaat felloww decidedu to go aand becommu *samaadi* on ye parrtikkularr day. Decidedu the plaice, aand wentu aand saat theyer, waitinggu. The disciplesu we-yer peering downn. But howwu? No waiyy! Samaadi waas justu nottu haappaninggu! Yevarybody got ti-yerd waitinggu, waitinggu. Ohh, this yis goingu to be ye biggu disgrace-u, thoughttu one of the disciplesu aand he took ye biggu coconuttu aand smaashude his headu aand killdu . . . isn'tu thaat yu-ver samaadi?'

Dakshayani peeped out—she was met with a huge burst of derisive laughter. Kunhippennu was standing near the veranda looking awkward. Nailsvendor's father was nearly choking on his mirth. His wife tittered along, mumbling in between some cautionary words—whyyu yowu say . . . suchu thingsu . . . As he followed his father's guffaw, Nailsvendor gestured to Dakshayani to laugh. Kunhippennu alternated between putting the milk-pot on the veranda and taking it back. Some more pressure, and even she may laugh—thought Dakshayani.

'They-yer, Kunhippennu ees haavinggu feelinggsu, listen, *ketto*?'

'*Pinne*! Oh, ree-yally? Don'd I know whaat aall feelinggsu commu to Kunhippennu?'

'Myy Goddu! Thiss man!'

Laughter. Dakshayani pulled her head back.

When Kunhippennu came over to the north-side of the house, Dakshayani asked, 'Wha' was thath, ober there?'

'Whaat to say, koche, my ge-rl? . . . Biggu itchu, whaat yelse?'
Kunhippennu did not conceal her annoyance.

'Iffu nothinggu elsu, he waas ye *siddhan*! Ye seer! Thaat waas
becose we saidd we aare goinggu to Varkala, fo-r the Samaadi day.
They don'ddu haave to salute-u, can'd they nottu insultu?'

This was about the annual Samadhi-day of Sree Narayana
Guru at Varkala who the lower caste people of Kerala venerate
for having led them out of the darkness of caste. He and his social
quest were, however, despised and derided by many of the Nairs—
secure in the power of their caste. They never let go of a single
chance to poke fun at the Guru. Devotees of Sree Narayana Guru,
especially the lower caste Ezhava people, congregated there on
this day every year.

Dakshayani did not speak. She had not yet got a sense of
things here. Kunhippennu kept grumbling—they had insulted
her. I am here only because there isn't another way, she said. Not a
good place for sure. Their mouths and hands are equally bad. The
milk-business was Chithrasenan's. He's been unwell after tripping
on the cow's rope; else she wouldn't have come.

Ah, anyway, who's going to come here? The old geezer is
almost in his grave and yet . . . no, better not say it. All you need
to do is walk around the place a bit and you'll surely hear the full
recitation of his virtue, the whole damn *konavathiyaaram*! Those
are nice histories, indeed. Each blighter in that bunch of bananas
is the same. So how's the pup going to find a wife from around
this place? The sluts who got themselves glued to the father were
rewarded with all sorts of nice things—from coconuts to gold.
There is historical evidence for this, but Kunhippennu was not
interested in digging it up.

'I will nevver comm he-yer,' Kunhippennu sniffed.

'I wi' come to yuh, alrighth?' Dakshayani consoled her.

That night, she told Nailsvendor that even if it was acchan,
he shouldn't have behaved like such a low-life with Kunhippennu.
Nailsvendor laughed rather too loudly at that. His laughter had

amplified somewhat after Dakshayani's arrival. Back at her place, he rarely laughed. Now his likes and dislikes had dismantled and rebuilt Dakshayani's home and place.

'*Tha dang felloww's hee-haww!*' thought Dakshayani. She was quite bitter.

Women know well that if you feel that your dislike for your man looked like it was going to swallow you whole, the wise thing to do is to swing right back and try to love him big. Dakshayani knows it well, too. But the temporary victories he secures in the middle may drive you crazy. That might persuade some women to turn the wheel towards the other direction. But Dakshayani's magical powers had died on Nailsvendor's turf.

Back home, Dakshayani could take the credit for some victories over Nailsvendor, because she was able to correctly anticipate some of his moves and stall them. She had him tied up so well that back there at her place, far from reaching the shore, he could not even row his canoe! But now that they were on his ground, her magical powers had vanished.

'Howw aare thinggsu, y-edi? Vaalue fo-r youwer caashu?' Nailsvendor gloated in a moment of triumph, as usual. In truth, Dakshayani had not yet understood that things had now irrevocably changed. She was merely observing as yet the new rules of the game that he was devising in this second episode of conjugal life. People of course will still feel hunger even after their dearest and nearest die. They still will reach for food even setting aside concerns about its taste. But Nailsvendor would snatch away the vessel from her hand just when she was going to flow with him. It would happen like this, roughly:

'Youw haave the luckku to sha-yre my beddu.'

His panting would fall on her ears and make her feel slimy. In the next instant, she would pull her mind out of her body and curse him inwardly—*damned sonofabitch*.

Nailsvendor had found some mantras to counter the schemes that Dakshayani had devised to defeat him. She realized within days that if he chanted those at crucial moments, his ticket to the next round was secure. The dash towards the goalpost after stopping her with the left leg!

'Ah, ok . . .'

She ran her hand on her forehead and felt a nail driven deep into it. Like the she-sprite, the yakshi, subdued by the exorcist, with a nail. How long she had carried it!

'Whaat youw say, y-edi? Vaalue fo-r youwer caashu?'

Nailsvendor panted. This time he made a small mistake.

He miscalculated: he thought that with a couple more of such reminders, Dakshayani would be defeated even more and that way, his victory would be all the more emphatic.

'Whe-yer iss youwer caashu, y-edi?'

'Whe-yer iss youwer cowwu, y-edi?'

With each question, he fell on her like a hoe breaking the ground.

'Whe-yer iss youwer Kalyani?'

Kalyani!

That was a historic moment. Like a bow the string of which was broken, Dakshayani straightened up. The nail in her forehead came loose and fell off.

A smirk twitched in the corner of her mouth as she asked Nailsvendor: 'Ah, hab bee' bantin' to ask fer long—Do yuh hab sum weaknes' in yer thingie? Oth'rwis' why yuh thrashin' aboutt' so muc'? Wha's thi' playin' aroun'?'

Nailsvendor's hand slipped from its grip high above. Dakshayani held back her laugh.

'Yuh kno' tha sawmill nea' our house?'

'Two youn' fellows cam' there to saw tha timbe'. Shoul' see how they load tha logs! How tha timbe' falls in two! Kno' how haardd ith is? Tha two geth five'undred a week as wages! Why don' yuh try thath? Sawin', sawin'? Whateber, I thin' ith's betther yuh don' try *thi' bisness* in bed anymor'.'

At that instant, the wheels of Nailsvendor's chariot were smothered in the sand. He was disarmed, the mantras had failed him.

There are clear instructions on how many times each mantra should be chanted. The practical possibilities are complex. Mantras are power-banks that may run out of charge any moment. If the letters are uttered wrong or get mixed up, they recoil on you. Never get into a battle trusting just the mantras. Nailsvendor's misfortune was that he had failed to understand this. He collapsed upon Dakshayani.

'Geth off my chesth, lemme breathe,' she said, without malice.

30

The Valya'avu temple was walking-distance from Nailsvendor's house. The princesses of the royal house of Travancore had come there from Thiruvananthapuram for the first day of the festival, when the festival-flag is raised. Nailsvendor's mother had already described them many times to Dakshayani. You must *actually* see them, to realize what the truly royal mien was. Just one look, you will know that this is royalty right before your eyes. They will come again. They wanted to see the *kuthiyottam*, but this is not the real one. The actual kuthiyottam is when young boys take a vow for many days and then have their cheeks pierced with small hooks. This is just some men singing praises of the Goddess and dancing.

'*Poorakkali*? Uh?' Dakshayani's eyes brightened at the memory of the local dance back in her desham. Men dancing with vim and vigour in a round, back home.

Her life was now a kitchen utensil, washed and left to dry mouth-down on the north-side kitchen pantry of Nailsvendor's house. The edges were completely mouldy. It needed to be warmed on a fire. The cobwebs and insect markings needed to be burned off. This was the chance to do that. She felt excited. A temple it is, then.

'When are we goin' to tha themple?' She asked Nailsvendor's mother.

'Mustu go,' she replied absently. There was a time when she went there regularly. But not anymore. Almost all sorts, the low-caste vermin too, now push and shove inside there. Wearing the sandal paste on their foreheads, all of them! Such conceit! You can't pray without someone brushing on you!

'Whaats the-y po-yint yin pushinngu aand shoviingu like thaat? Whaat fo-r, suchu pra-yyeru?'

But when these princesses arrive to watch the kuthiyottam, we must go. That is true *punyam*, sterling spiritual merit! The whole of this land was once their fa(a)mily property. All that you see here was created by them.

'Waasn't yit aall taiken from them by the gree-dy?' Nailsvendor's mother lamented.

Dakshayani did not listen. She did not harbour such attachments. She refused to be driven into any wall in Nailsvendor's house; she kept popping off and falling to the floor. In truth, she had no idea why he had brought her there. In just a few days, she had realized that her place in his life was absolutely insignificant. Maybe he did it almost instinctively, like the way one replaces a loose page fallen on the floor in an old account-book. But for that, he did not need Dakshayani, really. He did not have to tear her away from the capillaries of her desham. When the prospect of spending the rest of her life in Nailsvendor's house with no idea about why she should be there at all began to appear real in her mind, she was afraid. Where would her life find some flow again?

Taking a chance, she went over to Kunhippennu's house.

There were three cows there. They lifted their heads, glanced at her, let out a breath, and went back to munching the hay. Dakshayani stood before them for a little while with hope.

'Yuh won' tal'?'

'We aare yengagedu othe-rwise.'

'I hab look'd afther cows, too . . .'

'So whaat? Whaat shudu we do fo-r thaat?'

Dakshayani admitted defeat.

Kunhippennu did not seem too keen on going to the kuthiyottam.

'I haave to pre-payer the cotton seedu aand feedu fo-r the cowwsu, my ge-rl. Will haave to be baacku soonu by eveninggu . . . isn'tu the-yer someonnu he-yer who yisn't wellu?' She said, referring to Chithrasenan.

Noticing the disappointment on Dakshayani's face, Kunhippennu felt sad.

'The-yer is Ammachi at home-u, no?'

'Yuh come uh? Yuh come bekk early . . . I don' spea' muc' bith her . . . thath's why . . .'

Dakshayani did not try to get close to Nailsvendor's mother because she knew that the woman thought that she lacked the right feathers and markings of pedigree . . . she had already declared to her relatives that up north, if you just follow the tail of the caste-name, you'll be fooled . . . How then could Dakshayani speak with her?

'We didn'tu know! Whaat ye plaice!' She said of the north.

Really, the middle of nowhere! Not even decent vehicles around. Goodness knows how people live there.

When Dakshayani reached the temple along with Kunhippennu, the place was nearly full. The name 'kuthiyottam' sounded strange to her. The performance seemingly had nothing to do with *kuthu*—piercing—and *ottam*—running. She just stared emptily.

'Wha' upo' tha worlddis thiss?'

A group of men singing and stepping up and down with a lukewarm expression on their faces and with no passion or sense of belonging in their song. Not *Poorakkali* for sure. None of its heat or passion. But when she saw everyone—women and men—around her blend into it and enjoy, she felt doubtful of herself again. Different ways in different places, she consoled herself. Maybe the gods in this place like this sort of stuff; maybe the Goddess of this temple, too. Which woman doesn't like some men standing in a circle and dancing to her tune?

'Ah, leth them danc' . . .' She moved towards an empty place and sat down there. Instantly, an old man rushed to her and scolded, 'Sitting with yow-r bumm to Yakshiamma? Gettupp, go, koche!'

'Uyyentappa,' exclaimed Dakshayani, 'wha's thath?'

She leapt up. She had met some Yakshis in Nisha Talkies.

'Bheres tha yakshi?'

The old man craned his neck, pointing. 'Rightu he-yer.'

'Thi'?'

She pointed her finger at a big rock there.

'Whaatu, koche? Po-yinting youwer fingger?!' He shouted. '*Kollavallo*, nottu baadu! She will gr-aab youw-r fingger aand commu withu youw!'

Dakshayani pulled her hand back as though she was scalded.

The Yakshis she had seen in the movies at Nisha Talkies walked about at night, ready to seduce and sweetly kill men. They waylaid them, stopping them on their way and asking them for some lime-paste to chew some betel. Down south, everyone was familiar with the Yakshi; not so in the north. People in the north just could not stomach how such superhuman females could be made into adored deities by some, or how these women could even be your relative. They could not see it at all.

She stood there staring at the rock for some time. Is this rock that fair-skinned girl who left her hair open and asked sweetly in bookish language: please, do you have any lime-paste?

She saw bunches of black-coloured glass bangles heaped there. *A vow*, she told herself and calmed down. There were many small and big reddish marks on the rock, like bloodstains. *Wha' cud thath be?*

The Pala tree behind the temple was in full bloom. The abode of the Yakshi, according to the movies in Nisha Talkies. Its luminous white flowers gave off a piercing fragrance.

By evening, she was ready to return home. The drumming and singing had given her a severe headache. Kunhippennu must have left earlier. She could vaguely remember the way back. *Musth leabe before ith geths too dark*, she told herself. She was just getting familiar with the paths and lanes. They ran all over Nailsvendor's place infinitely. They made you walk and walk, only to lead you back to where you started from. She stepped out of the temple-yard slowly.

The scent of the blooming Pala followed her.

31

Dakshayani noticed the woman who was walking beside her only when she had passed the *chempaka* tree. She was fully pregnant—at least eight months gone. Her legs were swollen, eyes strained. Her belly should have been gently sloping earthward by now; the belly-button ought to have started gazing down at the earth. But no—it was still jutting out, not sloping. Wasn't the child coming out yet? The birth-carer in Dakshayani woke up.

'Why're yuh rushin' abou' at thi' lathe hour?' she asked.

Pregnant women ought not to be out at late hours. That's when the formless—the sprites—hang around. Some of them suck the juice out of pregnant women. Some of these slither on the ground; others fly. If you check in the morning, you'll find scratch marks all over the woman's body. They'd have sucked out the blood and the water, both. The infant will be thin and bow-legged, and you'll be lucky if it is alive. Pregnant women shouldn't go to temples either. If the Gods see pregnant women, they will rise up from their seats. That is so sad, to make them stand up, so why not just stay at home?

'There's no one at home,' said the pregnant woman. 'All those I have are right here. And no one lets me stay at home, either.'

'Ah, reallly!' Dakshyani said regretfully, thinking of the cruelty of people. Her new companion told her that she knew Nailsvendor's house and the way there. She was tired of waiting outside the temple; she wanted to pee. It would be good to have some company on the way back. Dakshayani too thought that—just that she remembered peeing only when the pregnant woman mentioned it. As far as the body was concerned, Dakshayani had reached a state of impassivity. In battles around the body, it made no difference whether she won or lost. It was all the same, whether they were directed towards the inner world or the outside. Pleasure and pain seemed to taste the same.

They stepped on the path; the darkness had begun to spread on it. Nailsvendor passed them with a group of men. He had been busy since morning, as an organizer of the kuthiyottam. The sandalwood paste on his forehead—laid so thick that it looked like a ridge—had dried and cracked and was beginning to come off in flakes. The blokes smelled of toddy. The breeze culled out just that scent and took it to Dakshayani. And she stored just that in her nostrils. How long it had been since she tasted some toddy! Govindettan used to bring them some of his toddy before he sold the rest to the toddy shop. It was a regular thing on the days in which the plywood factory was closed and she came back from loading stones. To be sitting on the half-wall of the veranda with your hair open after a nice bath with some toddy and clams—elambakka and coconut pieces cooked dry! Amma would frown but wouldn't object. She had not seen any elambakka at all since she came to Nailsvendor's house. Or any other favourite food. She had not relaxed like she used to—back then, when it rained, she would sit on the veranda's half-wall looking at it pour, munching rice crisps and coconut pieces mixed with jaggery. A whole ridge of land crumbled inside Dakshayani in the ceaseless thunderstorm within.

Seeing Nailsvendor and his friends go bonkers in the temple yard parallel to the kuthiyottam, the pregnant woman remarked, 'Now it's going to be a huge blackened-burnt mess here . . . That's how it is usually. They should be able to stand up straight, at least? Sometimes they fight, too!'

Dakshayani turned and looked at her.

'You are from the north?' she asked.

'You don't know the lanes and paths around here. Just walk ahead, I am with you,' the woman said, pointing out different places to Dakshayani as they walked on. She took in as much as she could in the growing darkness.

'Here, this is Villaasaan's property,' Dakshayani turned to look at where she pointed to. That was one of the boundaries of Nailsvendor's property; his mother had shown her. She could see it, but it looked like it was somewhat far. Oh, this girl seemed to know all the by-lanes and trails so well! A huge field opened up now in front of them. Dakshayani opened her nostrils and took in all of it. She was amazed to know that such a field existed here! But seeing the fully pregnant woman trudge and plod on the ridge of the field, her breath stopped.

'Pleas' tak' care! Ith'll be slipp'ry! *Baukalondaave!*'

The pregnant woman turned around without stopping and smiled.

Dakshayani could do nothing but follow. Isn't this wench walking a bit too fast? Why doesn't she slow down a bit? What if the cord goes around the baby's neck!

'Yuh pleas' wal' a bith slow'r, uh?' she reminded.

Though there was a woman walking ahead of her, the eerie, murky silence of the vast paddy field scared her a bit. It was scarier than the bushes back home in the dark.

'Do you know, your father broke someone's head with a blow from the handle of a machete . . . and then shoved him in the mud?' Asked the pregnant woman, suddenly.

Dakshayani's foot which was slipping into the mud was suddenly lifted and planted on the firm ground of the ridge.

'Wha'?!'

Her voice broke.

'Yes. People managed to pull him out alive. But he didn't live long. He had sucked in too much mud through his nose. The poor chap just got tired of the pain . . . One day he hung himself inside

his property. His woman had taken that route earlier . . . "Why
should I live anymore," he must've thought.'

'An' thenn?'

Dakshayani asked, swallowing weakly.

'Your husband's father escaped to Madras that very day . . . he
stayed there for very long. He couldn't come back, of course. He'd
have been murdered if he did! A murder is a murder after all, no
matter by whose hand it happens?'

Dakshayani stood petrified in the middle of the field.

'Don't be afraid. There are such stories everywhere. In all
places, in yours too. You just haven't noticed.'

The pregnant woman glanced at her and urged her to walk
faster. Night was nearly here. That's why she took a shortcut. To
walk slowly would be unwise.

Dakshayani moved her legs as fast as she could and followed
the woman, struggling to keep up.

They had crossed the field. Now there was a narrow trail with
lush grass on either side. The ground was soft; Dakshayani's foot
sank into it. She first thought of grabbing the pregnant woman's
hand and then reconsidered, feeling foolish.

*She has to drag hersel' summhow, and I am expcethin' her
pullmmeupp!'*

She suddenly felt ashamed at not having asked the pregnant
woman about her kith and kin and whereabouts. When did the
art of keeping people at a distance, on the other side of the fence,
sending them off with hard, matter-of-fact words, enter her
head—she wondered. The woman had shown her the way and
kept her company in the dark; taking help from someone and then
dismissing them was not Dakshayani's idea of culture. Must take
her home; share some food. Let her rest there a bit. She's walked
so far; her leg must feel even heavier now. There's lots of *njerinjhil*
growing here. If she doesn't have them in her house, must pluck
a whole bunch for her. If she'd just boil it and drink, the swelling
would disappear.

'An' . . . hey . . . listhen . . .' Dakshayani called. She thought that she had startled the woman.

'Leth us drin' sumthin' befor' yuh go? Yuh'll hab to make supper all by yerself at hom'?'

The pregnant woman stopped, panting, and pointed her finger. Dakshayani looked at where she pointed. Nailsvendor's house could be seen, sheathed in darkness. That a home might seem like an unwelcoming place was new to her. The more she saw the house, the more she felt the darkness seep in. She crossed the step with a heavy heart and turned around, calling to the woman, 'Com', com' inn.'

The pregnant woman still stood outside. She clung to the granite pillar of the wire-fence with one hand and held her belly up with the other. And she was bent with pain.

Dakshayani shrank back as though she had stepped on fire.

'Uyyentamme! Yuh can' . . !' She screamed and rushed to her, alarmed. She plucked the woman's hand from the pillar and held it close to her chest. The awful chill in that palm pierced right through her.

'Why iss ith so . . . col'?'

Dakshayani peered into her eyes. Her eyeballs were still.

'Yuh sith inside . . . lemme call sumon' . . .'

She took her in, sat her down on the floor of the veranda, and ran to the neighbour's.

'Pleas', please', come soo'. . . she's goin' to gibe birth righth' now!'

Kunhippennu knew most pregnant women around. She did not know of one who lived within walking distance. Who is this new one? She went with Dakshayani anyway. The woman was lying on her side on the veranda.

'See . . .' Dakshayani pointed.

'Where?'

Kunhippennu was stupefied.

'On tha floo', there . . .'

Kunhippennu was still stumped. Who was lying where?

Dakshayani ran up and gently made the woman lie on her back. The shiny belly was quivering.

'Goo'ggodd! Two of 'em?' Dakshayani placed her hand on the shiny skin.

'Yuh tell us bhere yer 'ouse is. We'll leth them know.'

She held the pregnant woman's head gently and tied her hair up in a knot.

'Tellus, bhere?'

The woman glanced at her, confused, and pointed towards the north. Dakshayani remembered that Nailsvendor's mother had told her that Villaasaan's property lay there.

'Thath's bhere her house is. Bhere in thath side?' Dakshayani asked Kunhippennu.

'Whaat's upp withu youw, koche?' Kunhippennu sounded rather abrupt. Dakshayani felt a rush of anger. What kind of humans, these? What greater reason do you need to get together? How can people be so totally selfish? When two lives hang on a thread, here they watch dully! She threw Kunhippennu a hard look.

'Doe' anyon' 'ere know her?' Dakshayani sounded helpless now.

'Yes, your father and others . . .' the woman's voice sounded as if it was withdrawing into the depths of a well.

'Koche, get up, go inside,' Kunhippennu grabbed Dakshayani's shoulder. Dakshayani felt unbearably riled. *I am done bith this womin*, she decided. She had never wanted to have anything to do with the inhuman sort.

'Don't get mad with her,' the pregnant one consoled, 'she can't see me.'

Dakshayani shuddered in body and soul. She shrank and became just a tiny dot.

32

The Brahmin Tantri of Kunnel was a great occultist, reportedly a friend of the legendary exorcist Kadamattathu Kathanaar, the priest of the Kadamattam Church. He had little connection with the living but there was no soul among the dead who did not submit to him. Most of the substantial trees in the yard of his homestead, his illam, had been granted to many troubled souls. Besides locals, there were also foreigners who the Tantri brought there. In the late evening, if you look at the illam-grounds from the paddy field, you'd notice a certain eerie iridescence. That's the ghostly glow of souls congregating. They are a varied sort, ranging from those covered with gold ornaments to those painted with mud. Locals and new arrivals lived together sharing an admirable democratic spirit. Among them were some who had entered retired life, satisfied with offerings of rice and flowers, and others whose blood still boiled and thirsted for action. Some needed spice in life and this they could not find much of in the premises of the Brahmin homestead. They needed to go out. These were relatively young sprites.

The Tantri of Kunnel wasn't a stodgy old chap. Only that he insisted on a Movement Register for those who needed to go out. They had to register their exit and return. All travels were to be completed and return registered before sunrise. The Tantri had prepared specific route maps for each and every resident. The Pei's path was different from that of Bhairavan's. The Yakshi could not take the path of the Rakshass. Anybody who encroached on the Yakshi's path could be instantly struck down. But the Maadan and Marutha were allowed to travel together. Those who had Sanskrit names were granted their separate leafy abodes in the homestead grounds. As long as their nails did not come loose, they were harmless. But the aforementioned group was certainly no bunch of sheep. They were capable of a range extending from peeping-tom-ery to bloody murder. When things got too wild, the Tantri got tough with them. But what use was that! Evil characters stay that way even if they are gods. When the Tantri's attention wandered, they would gang up together and indulge in nefarious activities. In truth, Kunnel Tantri was the true protector of the whole realm. But for him, this horde of sprites would have kept this place in thrall. The King himself had bestowed upon the Tantri the prized royal decorations of *pattum valayum*—silk and the royal bangle. He was granted the privilege of travelling in a palanquin. And if he so wished, he could have collected the taxes from the desham where his homestead stood. No one dared to flick even a piece of a coconut frond from his yard. If someone tried, then certain bodiless beings would reach their home even before them. What was the point of deliberately picking up the dotted slithering creature lying on the fence and wrapping it tight around your loins?

And so lived the Tantri and the denizens of his yard. The latter were all beggarly scoundrels of souls or minor deities or sprites, all shoved into the ranks of lowlifes of the netherworld, ready to throw themselves under the rolling wheels of the Tantri's magnificent occult-chariot. The Tantri used them. They got ground under those wheels into a nice, soft *guruthy*-consistency— one which also caused them to besmirch other people's lives.

Things were thus, when something happened. A Chettiar appeared.

This Chettiar, a chap who migrated here from Madurai, was surely not of Tantri's calibre, but could pull out an ace or two when it came to magic and the occult. He was a talented merchant. And of course, you probably know the mythical connection between Kollam and Madurai through that stubborn lady, Kannagi. And who was she? The wife of a man who was falsely accused of stealing and condemned to death by the Pandya king of Madurai. Her angry curse—flung at the king along with her torn-out breast caused the city to be burned down to ashes. The city of Kollam in Kerala had ample trade relations back then with Madurai. But there was an even stronger bond: in both places, Kannagi was widely worshipped. Thus there was a link that lay buried deep within the souls of the people of the two places, so the story wasn't just the bad-luck tale of some Tamil wench. Kannagi-ness was present, in the air.

Though an outsider, the Chettiar soon prospered in Kollam. His wife was a real knockout—when she swept past, even the earth would part. Her limbs shone splendidly; the sweet tinkle of opulence could be heard from everywhere on her body. The Chettiar was just big enough to fit in between the folds of her love handles, but they were in love, clearly, and were matched like sweet jaggery and crunchy coconut. She was skilled in the occult and magic. She was fond of toddy and the Chettiar was fond of her, and so it was said, he offered his respects to her every evening with toddy and song. The propitiatory singing and their loving babble could be heard even in the village on the far side! The villagers discovered her formidable occult powers absolutely by chance. This was when two wayward young fellows got drunk on toddy, and the drink fomented their curiosity: how did the Chettiar, who was barely half the size of this big female, manage to do it? They lay on their bellies in a coconut garden till evening and conjectured that the Chettiar on his wife's body must be somewhat like a rat running on a sack of rice. When a detailed discussion of the matter failed to yield a consensus, they decided to embark on empirical investigation—a visit to the field to observe the activity of interest at night. They crept up to the wall of the Chettiar's house which

was made of coconut-frond thatches and peeped in. They saw
the Chettiar untying the breast-cloth of his wife who seemed to
have fallen into a sweet stupor from the singing. The two breasts
which wore veritable crowns on their heads, stood regally upright,
blocking their view of the Chettiar. Suddenly, blood rushed into
the heads of the young peepsters. One of them went blind and
thus unable to register the sights beyond. The other fellow decided
to hang on for some more time. But where was the Chettiar? The
Tamil woman's sounds were copious. The observer rubbed his eyes
and peered further. The sight he saw rendered his ongoing life as
a human being null and void. The Chettiar was inside her vagina.
He had turned, all of himself was turned, into an instrument. He
was diving into her, from his head to toe, and rising up again. A
sound, like the squeal that escapes the body when life is torn out
of it, came out of the peepster's gullet. The blinded chap groped in
the dark unable to find his companion who had fallen insentient
on his back. (There is also a related story that the descendants of
these chaps, subsequent generations of peepsters, returned with
full force all over the world, in all lands, after a while).

Anyway, the terrible fate that befell the two youngsters became
a hot topic in the desham and the ruler of the desham referred
the issue to the Tantri for further action. The Tantri decided
to challenge the Chettiar to an occult duel. He however had to
concede defeat—the latter was well-prepared. But the Tantri did
not have to labour much to find out why he was humbled. It was
her. She who empowered her man each evening by dipping him
fully within her. The Tantri could not even imagine bestowing
such power even if he persisted for seven whole births. Then? On
the days she bled, the Chettiar used to sit beside her, touching
her body. Neither of them stepped out on those days. If the
Tantri tried to go over there to perform occult taking his chance
on these days, the guardian-deity of occult would slap him in the
face. And so he was, naturally, troubled. Finally, he summoned
all the sprites living in his homestead premises and outside for

help. The bodiless ones took the position that even though the Tantri was a class enemy, he deserved their support when faced with an external threat. This was not the time to take revenge for his nailing activities which had pinned them to some trees. And even if he had indeed nailed them to the trees, did he not feed and care for them?

'Yiss he nottu the fellow who gaive whennu he haad? Mustu helppu him in ta-imes of needu or ittu will be *thanthayillazhika*, the laick of ye faader,' they remarked collectively.

They sent two of their smartest to the Chettiar's house as a suicide squad. Because they remembered what had happened to the two youngsters before them, they guarded themselves against any potentially-dazzling sights. They were not, after all, much affected by human kicks and jollies. The Chettiar was preparing for his last dive that evening. Shutting their eyelids tight, both sprites caught hold of his weenie and were despatched with the same force to the inner-worlds of the Tamil lady. The two who had sacrificed their carefree lives in the Tantri's homestead for the welfare of the desham, now filled her womb. The womb grew full, with no space for even a strand of hair. The Tantri needed less than a moment to pull the Chettiar into his homestead grounds, fully alive. When the woman grasped the danger, she ran behind him there. The earth parted; her voluptuous body swayed; her anklets rang, but she could not save the Chettiar. He threw her a helpless glance from the *kanjhiram* tree, where he was nailed. If she did something stupid, the tree would be burned. All the nails would scorch and singe and the Chettiar would be charred soon. Did she want that to happen?

'No.'

'I will grant you a place here. Do not harm anyone else.'

The Tantri called from behind.

Who wants it! Snarling, she left that place. But the space between her jaws was stuffed with her own helplessness crumbling inside.

All this, of course, was about the first generation of the Tantris of Kunnummel (shortened now to Kunnel). The present Tantri was not so powerful. But Nailsvendor's mother thought that he was enough for this malady. Dakshayani had broken to pieces the tubelight on the veranda. It took a lot of effort to make her wear a piece of cloth above the waist. She claimed that she was pregnant. Now, all this could be forgiven, but what about the way she sat on the easy chair in the veranda, spouting the most unspeakable profanities—so filthy, no soap nor scent could wash them away—at the family and the locals?

'Diddu youw hea-yeru whaat she k . . .kkalled my son? *Cunntt-furr* . . . *Ma* . . . *y* . . . *ire* . . .' Nailsvendor's mother lowered her voice.

The father merely grunted.

33

Dakshayani was taken to the Tantri of Kunnel early at dawn one day. They had tied a black thread on her wrist, for temporary relief. Nailsvendor knew well that it would not do; that was just to hang on until they reached the Tantri. A tiny sliver of glass from the tube light had pierced Dakshayani's foot; it hurt her. Nailsvendor and his mother wouldn't let her bend down and pick it out. What if she ran away when they loosened their grip? Dakshayani was quite stupefied when she saw Kunnel Tantri, the punisher and protector of souls-come-loose. He was a small, thin, desiccated-looking man. He reminded Dakshayani of Govindettan. Except for his stoop, yes, Govindettan indeed.

'Wheres tha thoddy, Goyindetta?'

'Ith'ss gone sour.'

'Ith'll sour, I know. Yuh justh gibe ith to me righth now.'

'Yuh wan' tha sour thoddy?'

'Goyindetta, I'v' gone sour mysel'! And gone sthiffer and sthiffer lik' an overrip' okra! So why shudn' thath toddy be no' sour?'

'Yuh be quieth! Who sai' thath yuhr gone sour? Just yuh waith—yuh goin'e to geth a goodmman, a goodffellow!'

'Oh! Indee'! Hab yuh kepth one goodgoodchap in yer pocketh fer me? Justh sthoppkidding!'

'Here, tak' yer toddy. Show tha *bonie* here . . .leth me pour . . . don' glug ith all dow' ath onc', ok? Yer mangalam wi' happen in tha good thime!'

128

'Goyindetta, no, no . . .'

'Yuh'll see, there's goin' to be a man comin' fer yuh, and he's goin' to keep yuh unde' . . .'

'Keep me unde'? Wha' yuh thinkkof me? Am I deadd? A corpse? To be kepth unde'?'

'Yuh'll hab to sthay a bith unde', thath's fer sure. Ith'ss thathwway—if he's a gooddmman, then sthay a bith unde' him.'

'Thath's fin'—I willggo unde' then . . . bu' nottnnow, uh?'

'Give in!' The Kunnel Tantri suggested.

'Ddone! I'll do annything my Goyindettan tells me.'

Nailsvendor felt a sense of self-loathing when it struck him that Govindettan's name could have been added to the list of Dakshayani's lovers that he had drawn up at an earlier time. The oldster who went about everywhere led by his cow was a daily visitor to her house. The motherfucker. Nailsvendor had not noticed. No wonder she almost broke her rope insisting that they buy his cow. Should have given him a good slap on the sly when he went to invite him to be the mediator. Ah, should have made him spit blood, the motherfucking old geezer.

'Aafter this oldu maan, the mantra aand tantra aall will be go-ne,' said Kunhippennu ruefully about the declining standards of occult.' The younggu ones yin his illam aare gaallivaantin' yabout drungk aall the time-u, *allyo*? Nottu yeven living peeple listen to them, so how can tha Maadan aand tha Marutha cay-re?' She took some sacred ash that was tucked behind the doorframe and smeared it on Dakshayani's forehead, put the upper cloth back on Dakshayani's chest, gathered up her hair and tied it up on the crown of her head.

'Don'd go yeabout with youw-er ha-yir looseu.'

The pieces of broken tube-light and the obscenities, Dakshayani's handiwork, lay scattered all over Nailsvendor's house. Everyone, including him, stepped on them and got their feet bruised and hurt. They had an easy chair on the veranda. Nailsvendor and his father would lie there by turns. Their legs were always raised up and spread out on its extended arms of the

chair. Dakshayani had spied their inner secrets so many times
when she was sweeping the front yard. One, of course, she was
totally familiar with. The other was, a shrivelled thing with life's
very sap dried out. Both, however, produced equal amounts of
derision in Dakshayani.

'*Choppa!*'

She would hit the ground hardest with the broom as she went
off, still bent towards the ground.

'Aand nowwu, my sonnu will sit in thissu chai-yar!'

Nailsvendor would spout pride about his as-yet-unborn son.
'Whennu he sitsu on thiss chai-yar withu his legs paartted likeu
thissu, no oneu will saiy ye single we-rd, know thaat youw womun!'

Dakshayani was not convinced.

'If yer son siths on yer veranda showin' his weenie, why shud
oth'rs jumpp bith glee?'

After the sprite got into her, Dakshayani was constantly
aiming for that chair.

There was no saying when she would make a dash for it.
She'd sit, spreading her legs wide on the protruding long arms,
unabashed and firm. Uttering the choicest imprecations, letting
loose a free-flowing stream of expletives! That could happen
anytime, in front of anyone.

'Wha' THA FUCK are yuh fibbin' an' foolin' bith THA
SONOFABITCH?' barked Dakshayani, seeing Nailsvendor's
mother whisper something to his father, hurling at her the
shamefully disrespectful 'nee' for 'you'. They merely cringed
and stared.

'Wasn' ith yuh who strangl'd Billaasaan's daughthe' and threw her
in tha well? Wasn't ith yuh who hack'd down Billaasaan bith a knif?
Yuh devil of pesthilenc'! MAY YUH BURN! MAY YUH BURN!'
She cursed, flinging again and again the deadly insulting 'nee'.

She cursed again and again Nailsvendor's father to his face,
staring at him fixedly. He shivered in fright. This was from way
back! How did she find out?

'Where's yer son, thath BLACKGUARD, SCOUNTHREL, BLOODY ROGUE? Did yuh ask him if he eber learn'd to fuck hard enoug' to earn tha money he tak's?'

Nailsvendor suddenly appeared from behind his mother.

With supreme scorn, Dakshayani spat at him.

'Ah, he's come, tha useles' starbin' gruel! Why tha *pullaanhji* serpenth spar'd yuh till now? Is there no serpenth in thi' plac'? Or doesn' tha serpenth wan' to touc' yuh?! Huh?'

Nailsvendor had a hard time playing translator for his mother.

'Whaat yis this 'pullaanjhi', eda?'

'A cobra, amme . . .'

'Ayyo, my Naga-yakshi-amme . . . protecttussu!'

Though a veritable banshee when she sat on the chair, Dakshayani was not dangerous when she got off it. She would purse up her lips and immerse herself in housework. But she could return, anytime, to the chair on an impulse. That could be, literally, at any time: when she was grinding the cotton seeds, or taking a bath, or cleaning the slime of the *mushi*-fish caught fresh from the paddy-field, or rubbing the soaked clothes on the washing stone . . .

When she came to the veranda to sit in the easy chair, Nailsvendor was already sitting in it.

'GETHOFF tha chair thi' insthantt YUH OAF!'

Nailsvendor leapt up. Dakshayani strode there and lay on it. From there, she saw a demonstration. It was passing along the road on the other side of some wall. Only the waving tops of the red flags could be seen; they were all gathering in one place. The hum of the crowd was audible. A speech that rose from a low pitch towards the crescendo reverberated in her ear.

The plywood company had been shut for a while because softwood was not available. So for some time in the middle, she had worked in the sandstone quarry. Kalyani told her that the movie *Abhimaanam* was playing in Nisha Talkies. The moment she heard the song 'Darling, in this surge of my tears, let me confess

my wrongs . . .' she decided that she was watching it. Though she
had a headache hauling all that stone, if Dakshayani decided to see
a movie, she would definitely go. The better set of clothes and the
Cuticura talc were meant for that. On the way to Nisha Talkies,
they saw the demonstration. Many kinds of noises, voices, sounds –
they flowed together and blended into some mass meeting. On an
impulse, Dakshayani and Kalyani joined it. There was man on the
makeshift stage set up where the whole crowd flowed to. Kalyani
shared something that she had heard about him:

'He forgo' to eben' do a mangalam . . . they say . . . Now he's
bery weak . . . his wif' is twent'-six yea's youngge' . . !'

Dakshayani reeled.

'*Uyi*! . . . so wha' was her age whe' the' got marrie'?'

'Oh, twenty-two, saidd my young'r uncle.'

Kalyani knew more about the world than Dakshayani.
Dakshayani peered at the man they were talking about, the speaker
in the meeting. It was from the speeches here that Dakshayani
heard the word '*karuthal-thadangkal*'. She repeated it, taking in its
rhythm. '*Karuthal*' means care. '*Thadangkal*' means detention. So
karuthal-thadangkal means Caring Detention, Loving Detention.
At least that is what Dakshayani felt sure of and therefore she did
not feel the need to ask anyone. (If she had, she'd have known
that it had nothing to do with either love or care and that it meant
preventive detention). The man who uttered the word was A.K.
Gopalan, the legendary communist, the first person in India to be
kept in preventive detention!

It was on that very night that she shared with Govindettan
her apprehension of staying un-mangalam-ed and going sour and
stiff. After an interval, now the word returned to her with frills and
bows and all. The train that she had boarded with Nailsvendor
had also chanted to her, in steady rhythm, the very same word.
When the train sang it, she scraped the insides of her memory
trying to locate the rhythm. She now found it:

Kar'-thal- / thadan'-gkal

Kar'-thal- / thadan'-gkal
Kar'-thal- /thadan'-gkal . . .
Dakshayani stretched out flat on the easy chair and murmured:
Kar'-thal-thadan'-gkal
'Haa . . . *yish* . . . wha' fun!'
'Shaa . . all we taike tha che-yer yaway?' Nailsvendor asked.

34

Dakshayani was standing near the temple pond. It was surrounded on all four sides by screwpine bushes. Below the loose stone steps, a frog and rat snake seemed to be playing tag. If you moved a little bit forward, you could pluck a lotus. Dakshayani remembered that there was a scene like that in the movie *Sakunthala*. She hummed the old song: 'Whenttha pea-flow'r lines its eyes . . .' and waded into the water slowly.

'Dakshayani, a moment?'

Hearing a firm voice, Dakshayani turned around. She was standing above the steps of the pond. She held a leaf-packet and a bottle of what looked like rice water.

Her belly was still swollen. At first, Dakshayani felt a rush of anger but she controlled herself. No one can be blamed for all that had happened. Stuff happens, and when it happens, people are pushed into the lead randomly—Nailsvendor, sometimes, the cow at other times, and sometimes, Dakshayani herself.

'From bhere hab you shownupp now?' She asked the pregnant woman.

'That's not important. Please climb up here quickly, will you? If you fall into the water and die, I'll be blamed. Already, there's a story that I choked to death two curd-seller women underwater.'

Dakshayani took a good look at her, from top to toe.

'Did yuh do thath, really?' They were now on familiar terms, so Dakshyani spoke with her like a friend.

134

'For what?' She laughed. 'And why should I deny it if I did? Deny it to whom?'

'Humans are incredible! We non-humans are nowhere near you in the art of making up connections.'

The pregnant woman sat down on the ground with some difficulty. She placed the leaf-packet and bottle on the flat granite slab.

'I can't even sit down properly because of this blasted belly.'

Dakshayani went over and sat next to her.

'Wha's thi'?'

The woman opened the packet.

'Daive,' exclaimed Dakshayani totally elated, 'Elambakka! Clams!'

Clams, roasted slowly in coconut oil with coconut pieces, crushed dry chillies, button onions and curry leaves . . . they lay heaped on the banana leaf, looking absolutely inviting. Seeing that the heat of the chilli made Dakshayani nearly dance, the woman pushed the bottle towards her.

'Here, drink all you want. It is your Govindettan's toddy . . . Couldn't manage to get you the rain, but here's a glimpse of the paddy fields . . . that should hold you up for now?'

Time and space lay cleaved before Dakshayani like a wide canal. Govindettan's toddy, Amma's roasted clams, the rain from back home, the moonlight playing on the paddy fields . . .

Tears just flowed from Dakshayani's eyes and nose.

'If ith wa' poss'ble to go bekk hom' and come bekk so soo', I'd hab come too,' she blubbered. 'Wha' abou'mmy cow? Wha' did she say?'

'She didn't say anything, Dakshayani. She was lying down when I saw her. Her belly was full. Her eyes were welling and she couldn't even chew the cud, the poor thing. Your mother was squatting inside the cowshed with a lamp. Govindettan was running up and down between the two houses.' The woman's voice fell.

Dakshayani let out a loud wail of despair.

'Don't cry,' said the woman, 'Some things are like that. We can only stay nailed . . . immobile . . . we can see things . . . but beyond that . . . don't expect anything.'

'Alrighth, the',' Dakshayani said. The salt of her tears seeped into the clams in her mouth.

'Do you want to go back home, Dakshayani?' The woman asked, suddenly.

'Sabe me fromm'ere!' Dakshayani wept loudly again. Then ate the rest of the clams. Slurped the toddy and swallowed it. A frog leapt up from the water and fell right back into it.

Dakshyani was now in a mood for a song.

'I wan' neithe' puruvan no' tha mangalam. Ah, leth ithbbe, do yuh wan'to hea' me sin' a *tottam* song? Ith goes: *I'm no' tha one fer who a man come' askin'/ I'm no' tha one who wears tha fancy kaarola* . . . Yuh don' lik' my singin'? Yuh don' hab songs lik' thiss?'

The pregnant woman looked thoughtful.

'We too used to sing many songs. But I remember none of it now. It's all nailed to that *kanjhiram* tree. Even revenge is useless . . . What's the use of killing someone and taking revenge when you can't even sing . . .?'

'Kill who? Thath puny fella who loo's lik' an ugly lizar'?'

The wind tossed the pregnant woman's hair. It drew closer to Dakshayani, sending a streak of fear through her. Her lips dried up. The moonlight fell on the fields again.

'Dakshayani . . .' The woman called in her firm voice. 'You don't like him?'

Dakshayani's heady excitement dissipated instantly. She did not speak.

'Let me take a look at you. I'll decide for myself after that.'

She heard the woman's voice above the wind's hissing. Everything fell off her body, even the black thread around the waist.

After a few moments of silence, the woman spoke again.

'You'd better go back home . . . that's better for you.'

Dakshayani lowered her face.

'Look at your nipples. They ought to be rising at the mention of your man. All these years, they are still inverted . . . they haven't got beyond their edges even . . . They can't stand your man, clearly. Your bums are so cute! But when we talk of him, their cheeks don't quiver the faintest. You can't see your bum but I can see that it's never been squeezed tenderly, with love. A loved woman shows it in the faintest tickle, at least. Where is it? All I can see is a field encroached and ravaged . . . not the body of a woman!'

Dakshayani did not feel insulted. She was relieved that her body had not betrayed her.

'I thought I should help you. I am skilled in all sorts of tricks, but none of that is going to help you . . . or, you must start thinking of him as a soil rake or a spike to dehusk the coconuts—a tool, that is . . . which can be used and kept in a corner after.'

'No' poss'ble,' said Dakshayani. 'I'm a *Dakshayani*, afte' all. I'm tha Mercifu'.'

'So then, leave. There's going to be nothing at all between the two of you. But can you help me to give birth and empty this belly?'

'I hab neber see' a yakshi gibe birth . . . so can' onl' say I'll try . . . Lie dow' . . .'

'Like this?'

'Ope' yer thighs, rais' yer legs and planth yer feet on the ground . . .'

'Will you be afraid?' the Yakshi asked.

'Why shud I be afrai'?' Dakshayani replied coolly.

'Fine, then . . . Here goes . . .'

'Daive . . . !' Dakshayani exclaimed.

'What?'

'Nothin'. Justh thought, leth Him lend a handd—I called Him!'

'God? Which God is going to save me?'

'There's no god who won' hel' a pregnanth womin, in yer lan' or mine.'

'Dakshayani . . .'

'Yea?'

'What are you doing?'

'Whe' I firsth saw yuh, I thought, her belly's no' fall'n. Lemme press ith downnffirsth . . .'

'Hey, I'm hurting, alright?'

'Neber' min' . . . an' don'ttkick, huh? Becos if yuh do, my chin's gone foreber, my god *Muthappa*!'

'What's happening?'

'Yer belly's comin' down . . . Sha' I put my handdin there? Will yuh swallo' me? Lik' yuh swallow'd yer Chettiar?'

'No. I have to will it.'

'Alrighth, here goes . . .'

'Dakshayani, is this blood?'

'No, you little bulbb of pus, ith is yer water breakin''

'I'm going to be scared if I see blood.'

'*Uyish*! Firsth-class yakshi! Huh! Sum ghoul yuh ar'!'

'Dakshayani, my hips are breaking!'

'No, girll, yuh keepp lookin' at yer biggtoe . . . whe' tha skin on ith stharts breakin' . . . yuh'll 'hab giben birth!'

'You *koppe*, how am I to see my toe when this belly is so high?'

'Yuh musth be in pai' . . . neber min', ith'ss alrighth' . . !'

'Dakshayani, will it work? I can't make it . . .'

'Eh yuh bulb o' pesthilenc', if any womin gibin' birth said, hey, thi' is sooo eas', I can' do ith, thath very day tha roasthedd bean will sproutt!'

'True . . .'

'Alrighth, now push, push . . . let tha two devils come . . . ah, are yuh goin' to leav' 'em alon' once yuh get yer han's on them?'

'I'll decide later.'

'Hol' tha roots of thi' tree tighth . . . alrighth? The' push, push . . . oh, no good eben fer thath? Goo'ness knows wherefro' yuh come, yuh bulb o' pus!'

'Amme . . .mme . . .'

'Leth ith' come, leth ithi' come . . . if yuh sto' pushin', I'll kill yuh! Tha babie'll be trapp'd on tha way . . .'

'Baby! I'll kill it!'

'No' thath . . . fer tha babie to come ith musth lik' to come . . . now, be a goo'ggirl, geth ith done fasth . . .'

'Is it daybreak already, Dakshayani?'

'No, yuh three will be three by the'! I'm pullin' tha babie ou'!'

'Ahh . . .'

'Whatt 'hahhh'? There's anothere one lefth there'

'I don't think I can do anymore, Dakshayani.'

'The' go aroun' bith thi' thing in yer belly? Hol' yer legs firm, yuh awfu' imppp . . !'

'I'm shivering from the pain.'

'Ah, ith'ss all done! Yuh wan' to see yer babies?'

'No. Just put them next to me on either side and walk away. You should not turn back to look.'

'An' the'?'

'And then, nothing. Thank you, Dakshayani. You should not stay here anymore. Leave.'

Dakshayani's insides began to quiver as a terrible fear spread within.

In a single leap, she was outside the temple grounds. There, she stretched both arms towards the moonlight, examined her hands. Is the blood dripping?

'Do. Not. Turn to look.'

The firmest voice that she had ever heard until then pursued Dakshayani.

35

When Dakshayani reached her house, Kunhippennu was rubbing Chithrasenan's injured leg with medicinal oil. Seeing her, she leapt up in fright and rubbed her hands on her mundu.

'Wh . . . aat, koche? When diddu youw gettuppu? Whaat haappeneddu?'

Dakshayani's hair was a tangled mess, full of bits of leaves and dried grass. Her eyes were red and swollen. Her clothes were wet. They had set up a search party for her; someone had found her and taken her to Nailsvendor's house. She had fallen straight into the easy chair; so no one dared to ask her anything. One didn't know what all would jump out of her mouth! She reclined on it and slept off. These days, Dakshayani was outside all routines and cycles. That actually feels like a problem only at the very beginning. Once it becomes a regular thing, you become like a monkey missing its leap. Once you get out of a routine, it is hard to get back in, and even if you get back, you don't go round and round with the same force. You may treat the routine that you leave behind as the skin of a former birth that you shed, gave up— or you may simply forget it. As far as Dakshayani was concerned, an important chapter of her life was ending, whether she liked it or not. She stood before Kunhippennu feeling a void, like a book in which all that remained to be read was the index. She did not know how to describe in bookish language what had happened to her in life. She had no perfectly-formed losses or tragedies to point

140

to. On second thoughts, it is precisely such formlessness that is the greatest of human tragedies.

How would ith habbeen if ith were an'ther womin in my plac'? She had often thought.

'If olly youw caan taike yit baack to whe-yer-yever youw caughtt yit fromm aand throw yit the-yer!!' Nailsvendor's mother wouldn't have hit herself on the forehead, if that was the case.

Nailsvendor's father wouldn't have walked into the kitchen drunk, faltering, to grab both her boobs from behind. She wouldn't have snatched the burning piece of firewood from the hearth and thrust it towards his penis, yelling, 'I'll burnn yer balls, yuh sonofabitch'. Maybe the sprite itself wouldn't have entered her.

But each time, she still felt relieved that even the possibility of another woman in her place was just a possibility. Yet was she anything at all here? Not from around here, not of our caste— Nailsvendor had already declared about her and the shame that she had brought upon them. Well, that may be so. But was she anything at all to him minus these, something to be valued? Dakshayani's heart was constantly pained by the thought.

When a group of men came to meet Nailsvendor, she was lying on her side in the easy chair. She opened her eyes and looked at them in the morning sun. The visitors seemed scared stiff seeing her but they were jabbering away about something else. They all looked solemn. It was evident that they were about to go somewhere together.

'Don'du know whennu it will reachu here . . .' the party member who had come earlier and sat on the veranda said, his face bent low with sadness.

'Nottu su-ver if we caan see . . . haave bought summu flowe-rsu. Buttu thaat too we caan givvu olly if we are aible to see.' He whispered to Nailsvendor.

'They saiddu it comesu to Kollam at 12.30?' asked Nailsvendor. 'Thennu we are going to be laite anyway.'

'The olly consola-shun is thaat he wenttu seeing thaat womun lose the-ele-ctshun fullly, fullly.'

'How he suffer-ed in tha jayil!! He was beatun upp! Yessu, tha womun gone, consola-shun fo-r suver!'

'But it is nottu justu becaas he suffer-ed—nottu justu his pey-sonal thingg!'

'So whaat? When whole of India wha-llopped her, he-yer peeple threw yevvery-thingu attu the feetu of he-r supporte-rsu!'

'Ah, true thaatu! Yeeven thosu fellowsu mustu haave been shockk-du.'

People are going to gather in enormous numbers on both sides of the road, said Nailsvendor. The final procession with the body is going to be real slow. It is not going to reach at the stipulated time for sure. But better go and wait there, anyway.

They were talking about A.K. Gopalan's death and funeral, the passing of the Emergency, and Mrs Gandhi's electoral downfall. Rejoicing that the tyrant had been swept away by the election—even when Kerala voted Congress right back into power.

'Do we haave ye black-flaag?' The youngest in the group asked suddenly.

'Yessu.' Someone replied.

Then turning to Dakshayani who had curled up on the easy chair and was listening intently, he said angrily, forgetting that she was seated on that chair, 'Go yinside, youw *valaaye*! Dirty *valaa*! Look aat he-r sta-y-r-ing!'

Dakshayani's eyes glowed in fury. Something like the growl of an animal escaped her throat, a creature wounded and dying but which was poked and hurt again. Seeing her spring up, Nailsvendor and his gang cut and ran. But Dakshayani did not feel like cussing at that moment. Her claws were withdrawn. Like the dark scars that remain in a pot that was kept on the fire even after all the water has evaporated, the days that had passed had imprinted themselves inside her. She left the easy chair and got up.

'Who? Whaat haappened?'

Kunhippennu was removing the leaves and grass from Dakshayani's hair.

'Yit yis olly becos he can'd moove hissu leggu. Or thissu maan wuddu haave run to taike ye glimbse. To see the body on the wayy to Kannur.'

Chithrasenan sat with his head down, as if in a house of mourning. His swollen leg had him tied down.

'Women fromm youw-r plaice once beattu him up withu ye rice-pounding staaffu! Yes, youw-r peeple! Verry gooddu peeple . . .!"

He complained to Dakshayani, without raising his head, almost accusing her. He was remembering how women in Perlassery had once beaten up AK Gopalan. His passing seemed to amplify the memory. Dakshayani also lowered her head, as if taking the blame for such an incident if it did really happen. She itched to tell him that Perlassery was not the same place as Payyannur, but the neighbouring desham.

'No' fro' our plac' . . .' she tried to counter weakly. 'Hith bith a rice-pounde'? In ou' plac? *Our* wimmin? Hith 'im? *Uyi*!'

Chithrasenan sighed.

'You peeple don'd know gooddu fromu baadu. Youw peeple live yin the middle of nowwhere!'

'*Alle*!' Kunhippennu stepped in. 'Noww yis thissu fa-yir? Justu becos sum women sumwhe-yer diddu sum baadu thingsu, youw aare blaim-ing thisgge-rl?'

She took Dakshayani inside. She smeared the coconut oil heated with pepper and *thechi* flowers on her head and body, and carried into the bathing area some of the water she had heated up for Chithrasenan. Then she drew up cold water into the big brass vessel from the well.

'Koche, youw taike ye gooddu baathu . . . I will gettu you sum clothesu aafter,' she said gently.

Dakshayani sat on the stone inside the bathing area and poured some cold water from the vessel on her head. The cool water sank into her crown. One, two, three. At the third pour, she began to sob and cry. She did not know why, but she wept. Then she drank a cupful of the cool water. Steam rose up from her stomach. She watched the hot water splash on her body and roll off as if for the first time. She bathed her body with love and care, as though she were bathing a baby.

With this, Dakshayani's self-proclaimed Emergency ended.

Kunhippennu brought her some of her nicest clothes. Draping herself, she felt like a bride again. She began to feel renewed from each pore of her skin and so sat waiting eagerly as Kunhippennu served her hot rice gruel.

'Noww are youw feeling alrightu, koche? *Vallaazhikayonullallo?*'

Kunhippennu caressed her forehead.

'Youw mustu haave gottu better lastu nightu.'

Dakshayani shuddered in the memory of last night, but did not show her fear.

'Yuh hab sum money bith yuh?' Dakshayani asked Kunhippennu, sounding quite helpless.

Kunhippennu cast a sideways glance at Chithrasenan. He pretended not to hear.

'Why do youw needu caashu, koche?' Kunhippennu lowered her voice.

'I a'ways hab money. Ith fee's rea' bbad if I don' 'hab sum money. Cannyuh pleas' gibe me sum money justh to hol'?'

Kunhippennu looked at her face. Then without a word, went to the shelf where she kept the chilli and coriander, took out a bunch of notes and put it into her palm.

'Here . . .'

For a moment, Dakshayani wondered if she should hug Kunhippennu. But instead, she merely said 'I'm goin' now,' and went down the steps of her house. Nailsvendor's house stood behind them, still and menacing. If she turned around, she felt, some force of habit may drag her back there.

'Do not turn around to look.' Someone ordered her.

Crossing the *chempaka* tree, she cast a look towards the temple. Her heart beat hard. She remembered the two babies lying on either side of the mother. Why did she want them laid by her side, like that?

Deliberately drawing a heavy blanket over the memories of last night, Dakshayani walked and ran towards the road, and then the black flags blinded her. They flowed into the road from all over, forming a sea of black. Caught in the middle of it, she tried to make her way through it.

She sat on the wooden seat of the north-bound train. She had seen AKG's funeral procession sitting in the bus that took her to the railway station late at night. She thought of the dead man who would probably arrive in Kannur—home—along with her. He was coming another way, but their destination was the same—home. She might have seemed alone, but he was there, an invisible presence. That man who had spoken in a tired voice on that makeshift stage.

That journey felt good. She had forgotten that word:—*karuthal—thadangal*—on Nailsvendor's easy chair.

When the train reached Kannapuram Railway Station at dawn, she alighted as though from another life, breaking her shell. Seeing her, the paddy in the fields bent back with their hands on their chins, amazed. When she crossed the threshold and entered the yard of her house, there was the cow, standing there.

Its eyes opened wide as though delighted to see her so unexpectedly that morning.

'Dakshayani, look, I have another calf!'

The pretty little one went towards her mother, wobbling adorably.

'Look, this is Dakshayani,' the cow told her calf. She rolled her beautifully lined big black eyes and glanced at Dakshayani.

Dakshayani's eyes welled, too.

[At precisely the hour in which Dakshayani stepped on the Kannapuram Railway Station, a very important thing happened—the person who would retell the st(h)ories of Kalyani and Dakshayani most wonderfully, many years later, was born in a nursing home at Potheri. A st(h)ory is all very well, of course, but what about the teller? We have to put in a word for ourselves, right?]

36

The work of plastering the walls of Ayamutti'kka's new house was on, and Kalyani was supposed to join the workers there. It meant a fairly long spell of gainful labour, and mostly in the shade, too. Besides, Kalyani was not averse to heavy lifting. In the early days in which people began to realize that she would not be returning to Koppu-man's place, wherever she went to work, she had to get past a round of rapid-fire questions. Neither questions nor answers have ever bothered Kalyani. She handled it in the following manner:

Question: 'Why's ith yuh hab no' gain'd annyy weighth afther goin' to yer puruvan's plac'?'

Answer: 'If I go to my puruvan's plac', ith's he who'll pu' on weighth! An' thath yuh'r neber goin' to see, uh?'

Question: 'Why, yer ol' blouses still fitthin' yuh? He isn' manurin' them girlies bith his hands? They haven' grown?'

Answer: 'Ah, Kunhappetta, isn' ith tha truth thath yuh are manurin' thath *Yasodechi*'s breasths all tha time? Isn' thath why yer wife Januechi still wears her ol' blouses?'

Question: 'Whatt'appen'd? Yuh go' bor'd bith im or he go' bor'd bith yuh?'

Answer: 'I'm bor'd bith im, Rametta . . . Yea, yea, yuh geth bor'd afther sum tim', sure. Now I want to fin' summone lik' Sarojiniechi did—afther' she lefth yuh—bor'd, she's giben birth thwice!'

Not a single person who got mauled by the poison-tooth of Kalyani's retorts dared to step on her again. She carried in her head the entire database of the desham. That was the result of leading a richly discursive existence since Class 3. Kalyani's mother was no longer on talking terms with her. Her uncles, like she had fervently wished once, had gone bent with age; the Congress had been wiped out from the desham. One fine morning, Achootty Mash got up and found the whole desham had gone red and from that moment, he became a communist. He did have some theoretical dilemmas—actually, some wheezing—when Kerala honoured the Congress by handing it 20/20 in the elections even when Indira Gandhi lost in her own constituency. He wheezed, wondering from where the Congress had come back to clinch such a triumph. He calmed down only when his son Balan managed to convince him with a lot of difficulty that the survival of a certain politics did not always need an electoral victory.

'I know all of thath . . . yuh don' theach me how to theach . . .' He panted as he inhaled the steam. He had come face to face with Kalyani on the panchayat road. For a moment, he thought about persuading her to return to Koppu-man's home. When he was in the Congress, he wouldn't have hesitated. Now things were different. Two things were important. First, Kalyani may not remember that he was now a communist. Second, there is vagueness about the party's position on local issues that are not political. Anyway, he decided not to bring it up.

They were plastering Ayamutti'kka's kitchen on the day Kalyani realized that she could not lift up even a trivial basin-full of concrete. The masons finished up the concrete mixture in the basins pretty quickly. The filled basins she had to lift and carry lined up before her. The plasterers waited impatiently for her to bring more. The sand there was too pebbly; it had to be sieved. Pain shot down her leg from thigh to calf. She was now seeing double . . . two basins in the place of one. The plaster on the staircase was not yet dry, but she eased herself down on it.

'*Uyyi*, my god, *ente* daive!'

After she returned home and had a bath, Kalyani began a veritable *yaga* in front of the hearth, waving the chilli and mustard seeds around her body. Though there was dried prawns and coconut chammandi for dinner with rice gruel, it tasted terrible. In a sudden spark, she began to make some calculations, folding and unfolding her fingers. At the end of the adding and subtracting, she scolded herself, '*Nallayenne* . . .'

'Thi' is all thath I lacked . . . manny thanks!'

She turned towards the bedroom-side and bowed sarcastically. She tried to find Amma in the kitchen. But the moment she saw Kalyani's shadow, Amma went down the kitchen steps, crossed the north-side compound, and went off to Kaisumma's house. That's her usual thing these days.

'Wha' am I to do, my dea' god Muthappa?' Kalyani slapped herself on the head.

Then she remembered that the files of such matters are not handled by the office of Lord Muthappan; she called upon Goddesses Cherukunnamma and Muchilottamma. *No . . . no . . . thi' I can'tt do . . .* she flayed inwardly. Then, calming herself down, she thought for a while, and she too set off for what used to be Kaisumma's house. Kaisumma's husband's oldest brother stayed in the habitable part of the house with his family now. But he was not on good terms with Kaisummma. She now lived in the dilapidated outhouse-like projection at the back.

Hearing Kalyani call her, Kaisumma came out, looking like hopelessness itself in human form.

'Kaisumma, is my mother 'ere?'

'Yes, she's 'ere.'

'Thenn pleas' tell her to sthay there, she nee' no' come bekk.'

'Wha', Kalyani, what happen'd to yuh?'

'I'm knock'd up, Kaisumma . . . babe in my belly . . . cam' to justhttell yuh thath . . . Now I hab onl' yuh to tell'.'

Kaisumma said nothing. Her life was littered with many boxfuls of terrible sorrows, their lids off, mouths gaping open . . . all those sorrows were out there, flying around them, wings flapping . . . and so there was no point at all, trying to close those lids . . . it was then that Kalyani had appeared before her, drained and sad.

'I'm goin' . . .' Kalyani waited for a few moments looking at Kaismumma and then turned to go. She kicked out of her way the ripe tamarind that had fallen in their yard. She had nothing to do and so sat on the veranda with her legs stretched out. The cow dung plastered on the floor was coming off bit by bit. The floor needs another coat, she could see. Amma was still vexed. This is the girl who threw off her rich husband in a flash and jumped over the fence. Amma was not going to do anything for her or this crumbling house. Let both go to the seed.

'Yuh are NOT my daughther!' Amma had declared. 'Wha'yer uncles saidabbou' yuh whe' yuh were small ha' come true. Yuh've become a sham'less hussy! I hab not giben birth to somethin' lik' thi'.'

Lethith'bbe. Kalyani didn't take her curses seriously then. But her mind wasn't as firm now as it used to be. She needed a wall to lean on until she regained her strength.

When she stroked the floor again, more of the dried-up bits of cow dung came off. The smell of cowdung. A strange desire to taste it overtook her. She drooled; she could not help putting those bits into her mouth. The wound on the cow dung-plastered floor became bigger.

37

Though with some difficulty, Kalyani managed to pull down an unripe papaya from the papaya tree. De-skinning it lightly, she cut it up and stuffed as much of it into her mouth as she could. It tasted awful. She thought that her very guts would spew into her mouth. Throwing up nearly the whole world, she lay curled up and weak like a dead snake near the screw pine bushes at the fence.

'Justh' hopin' all tha bitther stuff'll wor'!'

Things were getting out of hand. The days dragged on as though boulders were tied to their legs. She had to labour, just to live.

She was good at carrying bundles and stones and vegetable farming. What she lacked was the little tricks that every village woman knew, like waving off the evil eye and killing the lice. What was the use! Kalyani's doors were locked, even if temporarily. She had to kick them open herself.

'Wha' if I go to see tha Mali of tha Hill?'

Tying her hair on top of her head, pulling herself up from where she lay fatigued, Kalyani began to think. That was the thing to do, she resolved—see the Mali, get it out of her womb. Decisions were never very difficult for Kalyani. Like they say, if your pocket is light, your heart is also light on the way because you don't worry about robbers stealing from you! The Mali—short for Malayi—has a little bit of everything: tribal people's magic, little tricks for easing birth, and for aborting it, too. For the Mali, this is

a minor thing, like twisting the deformed tomato off its stalk. She
has brought to the world so many, and despatched so many too!
She is life and death at the same time! If you smear the coconut
oil treated with her chants on the bellies of pregnant women, the
infant leaps from the womb just the way the seed of the jackfruit
slips smoothly out of the ripe fruit. She also has the nostrum to
turn back those who arrive without consent.

The Mali gave her small round pills. She was to grind one
each, mix it with water in a small earthen cup, and swallow the
resulting concoction in a single gulp every night. Drink it and lie
on your stomach for one whole night, she added. Next morning,
burn the mat on which you slept. She also prescribed some herbs
which had to be ground fine and applied inside. Breakfast was
to be of half-boiled eggs. Supper, of broken rice-gruel. Four or
five hibiscus buds were to be mashed fine in the residue collected
from washing rice, and this was to be drunk on an empty stomach
for two or three days. Slightly better-quality cloth than what was
normally use for the monthlies would have to be used. They were
to be burned for the first three or four days, not washed. No hard
labour should be attempted for two weeks.

Kalyani took the pill-packet from her. The path back from
the Mali's house was muddy. The tall grasses that grew lushly on
both sides brushed on her arms and scarred them. The Mali's dog
was sitting by her well with a totally inscrutable look on its face.
It stared pointedly at her. Kalyani hugged the packet to her chest
and increased her pace.

'Will ddis sore o' pesthilenc' chase an' bite me, goo'ggod?'

When she was about to turn, Kalyani took another look at the
dog. Its intense stare went straight through her heart.

'Wonde' wha' . . ?' An unfamiliar dread made her shiver.

Kalyani got back into her house through the kitchen door. She
hid the packet in her clothes-box soon after. The house before she
left to meet the Mali and the one she came back after felt like two
worlds. Something strange had got into her house. What could

it be? She felt anxious, restless. All around was deafening silence. Still, she wanted to see her mother.

'Wha's thisspplac'? A cemeth'ry?'

She pulled her hair, frustrated, and in the next second, started violently, seeing Cheyikkutty at the door.

'*Uyi*, yuh, Amma?'

The scene-book of her last birth opened in front of Kalyani. Cheyikkutty came towards her.

'Hows my girll doin'?'

Standing a childhood's distance away from her, Kalyani burst into loud weeping. Cheyikkutty's scolding was even louder.

'Here! Notgggoing to spare yuh, sthop crying, yuh pesky pus-fill'd sore! Lookit her holler lik' a cow! Bheres tha spunk thath made yuh jumpp tha fence thath day?'

Kalyani sobbed.

Cheyikkutty shouted.

'Sthopp yer sobbin'aan'weepin'!'

Kalyani stopped.

Cheyikkutty scrutinized her daughter-in-law.

'Wha'did yuh drinkkin tha mornin'?'

She did not reply. Cheyikkutty flared up again.

'Ith's so lat' afthe' mornin' an' . . .'

Cheyikkutty was thoughtful for a moment.

'Thath's alrighth, yuh geth ready to come bith me. If we sthart now we'll be hom' befor' ebenin' . . . the cow 'as to be brough'bback' . . .'

Cheyikkutty stepped out of the house in the full faith that Kalyani would follow.

'I'm . . . no' comin' . . . Amme, yuh go . . .' She said, mildly.

Cheyikkutty was totally surprised. Though was the gentlest of the tones Kalyani's voice could produce, both Cheyikkutty and her mother who had come in with a drink of water for Cheyikkutty, were shocked. Kalyani's mother put the cup down and started beating her breast. Then she lunged at Kalyani, slapped her, pulled her hair, pinched her cheeks hard, and threw her against the wall. Kalyani did not retaliate.

'Betther gethout an' leave soon, yuh dirty swine' . . . if yuh don', I'll kill yuh . . .' Kalyani's mother screamed. So loud that even Kaisumma rushed in, her face stiff and pale like paper.

'Whatshappenin'ere? Justh abou' tha whol' worl' can hear yuh screamin' and fightin',?

Cheyikkutty looked at Kalyani's mother.

'Sthoppith,' she said, 'she'll come.'

'I won' . . .' repeated Kalyani, not moving an inch. 'I can' . . .'

Kalyani's mother began to yell again.

'*Pha*, you *kaisaad*! Leav' NOW, quiethly! If no' . . .'

When she saw that Kalyani was unfazed, she began to threaten her.

'I'll jumpp into tha well . . . *yuh'll* see, yuh unhealin' festher of pesthilenc' . . . so yuh wan' to see me deadd, hangin' 'ere? I'll mak' yuh eat yer words . . . *Uyyi*, my dear Lord Muthappa, wha' am I to do? Yuh aren' my daughther . . .'

Then she testified before Cheyikkutty in a voice that sounded like the wind's rasp:

'Thi' pain inntha neck wasn' bornn to me . . .'

Cries and curses lay strewn in the inner veranda of the house like pieces of broken glass.

Cheyikkutty was at her wits' end seeing this ugliness. She announced coldly.

'I'm 'ere to see my daughther . . . I do NOT wan' to see yer drama.'

And then she turned again to Kalyani.

'Kalyani, justh come thisside. I need to thellyuh sumthin' . . .'

They stepped out.

38

'Kalyani . . .'

Cheyikkutty called.

'Yuh 'hab seenntha brok'n well in ou' yar'?'

Kalyani had not only seen it, she had also peeped into it. She admitted doing it.

'My older sisthe'—my *balyechi*—is inside ith.' Cheyikkutty said in a low voice. *Oh she is going to say thath thi' balyechi has got into me*, thought Kalyani.

'Sonnow Chonnamma's gone, ith's balyechi, huh?' She curled her lips. Cheyikkutty was unfazed. She dismissed the scorn; it is just a distraction when you are discussing serious things.

If it were Nalini or Vanaja, a quick, hard slap would have been in order. But this one was not easily reined, so Cheyikkutty held herself back. Besides, she had a small family secret to share with her son's womin. She had decided to reveal it only because she hoped against hope that it might help persuade Kalyani to return. The more usual thing for the woman who broke off and the man who did not step back in, was to go their own ways. They might migrate to some other island, spread roots around there, flower, bear fruit and wither, still distant from each other. Some such couples who parted ways may meet again years later at a temple festival or wedding celebration. They may exchange a smile or glance moist with memories.

'How'r things?'

'Nothin', *appa*—goo', goo'. Justh lik' thath.'

'Yuh'r chil'ren? How'r the' doin'?'

'All o' them in thei'ownn places . . . how'r things bith yuh?'

'Justh lik' thath! I saw yuh ath tha Akkarekkavu Theyyam at tha themple. Wa' too busy, the' . . . cudn' talk.'

'Is yer asthma betther?'

'How's ith to become betther?'

'Yer on med'cin's?'

'*Adelloondu*, yeah, they're allltthere.'

' . . . *enna*, the' lemme leav'.'

'Alrighth.'

These lives are light. They slip and slide, now moving closer to, now farther away from each other. They even knock on each other gently but without disturbing each other's whites and yolks. But Kalyani's and Koppu-man's lives hung a bit heavy in Cheyikkutty's mind. She had her reasons for that.

'Ith was our fath'r's *maruvon*—nephew—who marrie' balyechi. Those days all of us sthay'd in ou' house. We all grew up togethe', playin', fighthin', eberythin'. We libed justh nexth to eac' oth'r, afther all? There wa' no sayin' "thi' is mine, tha' is mine"—eberythin' was eberyon's! Our acchan was bery fon' of hi' maruvon. He gott *vaisshyar*'s bes' qual'thies, eberyon' sai'. He wasn' justh a relathibe', he was lik' acchan's son. Balyechi was his darlin' too. Bu' there's no rule tha' says thath onl' if yer love for summone is lackin' will yuh fall in love bith anoth'r! But balyechi justh cudn' see thath. She gabe birth to Narayanan an' then she got tha *eettupiranthu*—tha way yer mind beg'ns to sway afther yuh gibe birth. Acchan sai', eberythin' will be fine afther she took a gooddbath with lots of oil in her hair. Buttone day she justh leapth headlongg into tha well. Didn' we libe eben afte' thath? Yer Narayanan wa' justh three months old. When we took' her out o' tha well, balyechi was all swoll'n, like an acchi frog. Justh thinkin' o'thath mak's my heart poun'! I hugg'd her babe to my breasth, took him as my son. He was yellin' whe' they carrie' away his moth'r . . . Lachunan and he ar' tha ssame to me. I'm tellin' yuh thi' fromma mother's essperienc', Kalyani—in orde' to love, yuh don' need ith to be giben in writin' on a piec' o' paper. Sumtim's we get a shar' in sumthin' that isn't ours. Do yuh und'rsthand wha' Amma is sayin'?'

Kalyani slipped towards the floor. The old woman, with her breasts so fallen that they touched her belly. The upper cloth covering them. The mundu of white mul cloth on her waist. Her elongated ears, falling on both sides like swings. She stood before Kalyani like an old palm leaf manuscript with never-ending leaves.

'There's no winnin' or losin' in this, mole,' she said. 'We aren' playin' a game fo' thath. Justh lookin' to libe a life bithou' tears. Justh hab to do whateber we musth do fo' thath. Thath's tha righth thin' for us humans.'

Cheyikkutty left Kalyani out there and stepped into the house. Suddenly, as though remembering something, she turned and told her that Koppu-man was waiting in the outer veranda, and if she wasn't still going with them, she needed to tell only her. Thus Cheyikkutty put the ball completely in Kalyani's court and returned. Koppu-man sat impassively on the half-wall of the veranda.

Kalyani walked towards the veranda. She stood quietly for a little while behind Koppu-man, who sat facing the yard looking out. The present melted away from her eyes. Before she applied oil on herself for the bath, Cheyikkutty's older sister must have put her little son to her breast and fed him until his tiny tummy was full. And then she must have massaged him with oil, laid him on the mat, and gone to the side of the well. No matter how full, after the second pee, his little belly must have emptied. Infants so young need milk just enough to fill an areca-nut shell. By the time his mother rubbed the hibiscus-paste on her head, poured the hot medicinal water on her body, and came back feeling softly warm after her bath, Cheyikkutty would have bathed him too. Then it was time to suckle again, fall sweetly into slumber, and dream of naughty Kannan—little Krishna—come on tiptoe to pull Amma's nipple off his mouth. Still dreaming, he must have whimpered at the loss of the warm sweetness in his mouth. But the tragic truth is that not just the dreams of adults, but also of infants, may slip and tumble into the depths of a well anytime. No one can really help with the loss: irrespective of whether the dreamer is an adult or a child. By the time they got out Cheyikkutty's older sister who had become like a dead *acchi*-frog, her son must have peed at least two times. He was still not bathed. The little one must have thrashed about on the mat in his pee and the oil, screaming from hunger, drowsiness, irritation, the disruption of his routine—and plain sadness. Cheyi, watching her older sister leave, having nothing else to do, must have hugged his oily little body close to her breast. His wails, soggy with tears and saliva, must have crashed in waves against her breast and slowly waned. And in the distance of so many sobs and whimpers, he must have forgotten his mother. Even forgetfulness can be so cruel at times.

Kalyani moved back a couple of steps to make space for another woman. A second Kalyani stepped out from within her. This other woman was an unknown to the first Kalyani. She might do what Kalyani would never think of doing. This Kalyani could only watch her. The other Kalyani re-ran Koppu-man's babyhood sorrows in her head; she saw the sad little baby left alone by his mother; she melted. Right before this Kalyani's eyes, the other Kalyani let out a heartrending wail . . . '*Uyyi*! My babe!' and running towards Koppu-man, she hugged him tight from the back.

Kalyani felt embarrassed and angry.

'Ruin'd it! *Sollum kondu . . .*'

She tried to quell this Other, but the Kalyani who had got out of Kalyani remained unvanquished.

Her tears flowed down Koppu-man's cheek. The wail gradually subsided on Koppu-man's shoulder drenched in the fluids from her nose and mouth.

'Yer my babe, my gold'n one, my darlin' boy . . .'

Weeping and sniffing, she ran back into Kalyani. Then Kalyani, who was standing unmoving like a tree, also shook.

Weeping and smiling behind that veil of tears, Kalyani asked Koppu-man, 'Sha' I gibb yuh a kiss? Yuh'll tak'ith?'

39

On their return, it was Kalyani who entered the house first—the house which she had left of her own accord. Without the smallest grain of indecision or guilt, she went back a second time to Koppu-man's house, her mind quite sunny. The cows were waiting outside.

'We knew that you'd be back, Kalyani,' they said. 'That's how things are sometimes. Sometimes the game that pleases the gallery won't give you a win. Remember that through this strategic retreat, you've fixed the wheel of your native place—that had come loose and fallen off by the wayside when you marched back there! So take relief, but don't imagine that from now, things are going to be sweet and easy and you'll swallow it all like a mushy *poovan*-banana. If all girls who marry and leave bounce right back, won't local pride leave on the next ship? We too will have to take a share of that shame! You know that we are loyal creatures?'

Kalyani untied the cows and took them to the shed.

'Yuh'r *pai*—cow—an' yuh betther talk lik' pai-kind, ok? Thissort of fine talk yuh try bith Dakshayani! Bith me, yuh lie dow' righ'tthere in tha cowshe' and chew tha cud!'

She tied them mercilessly to the bamboo poles inside the cowshed.

Like before, Cheyikkutty kept her daughters at arm's length. She had told them that Kalyani had gone home for some time in her early pregnancy, but did not wish to pick and prise open

the events in Kalyani's and Koppu-man's life before anyone. She
feared, quite naturally, that if she told her daughters, they would
seize the chance to dig it up and make a mess. No matter how
close you may be, you have no business with another person's life.

'Yuh sleepin'?'

Kalyani asked Koppu-man. He thought she didn't have
enough space on the bed.

'No, wha's ith? Yuh ban' me to sleeppon tha floo'?'

He turned towards her.

'No, nothin',' she said.

'Yuh ban' to go pee? I'll come bith yuh.'

He got up.

'No, I don''

But he wasn't listening.

'Both'r!' She felt irritated. Koppu-man searched for the torch
and called her.

'Come, yuh can go pee.'

'Wha'ttha blazin' . . .' Though vexed, when Koppu-man
mentioned peeing a couple of times, Kalyani decided to go pee
anyway and got up from her bed.

The flash of red that used to bother her inside the bedroom
seemed to leave her untouched now. Except that the almirah that
also contained Lakshmanan's clothes reminded her fleetingly of
him, Kalyani was almost completely at ease now. But on the days
in which Cheyikkutty felt that Koppu-man should pay some more
attention to Kalyani, she did feel stifled.

Stepping out into the yard, Kalyani and Koppu-man spied
Cheyikkutty sitting on the half-wall of the veranda with the single
smouldering eye of the beedi. She usually sat watching the rain—
now it wasn't even drizzling. They were surprised. Can' sleepp a
wink, she complained. Too many different thoughts clouded her
mind when she tried to catch some sleep. She was seeing too many
people she ought not to have seen. They want to chat with her.
What right do people who left the world on their own whim have

to say anything about the lives of the living? Not knowing how to hide Kalyani's swelling belly from them, Cheyikkutty thrashed about in her mind. The dead who were still filled with the hunger for life may well bear deadly envy towards the unborn on their way here. Some of the former are leaving slither-marks on the soil. That is, the visible marks of the denizens of the earth which seemingly appear only to fulfill the task of dispatching the living to other worlds. These slithering ones have a sixth-sense connection with the departed ones. The former press their breasts to the soil and take in the heartbeats of the dead, some say. Cheyikkutty had been seeing two or three members of the slithering sort, lately.

'Don' go outt eben if ith is to pee.' She stopped her.

The night before, when Cheyikkutty lay restless and unable to sleep, she sensed movement near the window. When the scent of the medicinal oil, the hair oil, and the hibiscus-paste spread in the air, she sat up on her bed. She heard a sound like a pot dipping in the well water.

'Cheyiyaa . . .'

That is a call which she usually ignores. Usually she'd just say, 'Go'way, yuh', and go on doing whatever she was doing. This time, she could not. If you put your mind to it, you might persevere and actually overcome the world around you. But if the world around you rallies from the rout and manages a second coming, then you are going to be enfeebled for sure. Cheyikkutty knew that well.

'Cheyiyaa . . .'

'Yea, wha', balyechi?'

'Wha's bith my son?'

'No crow has peck'd him. He's alrighth'

'Yuh won' climbb an' grow on my son, know thath.'

'Oh, cudn' yuh hab clim'ed and grown on him? Di' summone tell you to play fasth an' loose bith yer life an' jumpp intho tha well?'

'Cheyiyaa . . . I won' le'ggo . . .'

'No, no, don' . . . hanggon tighth, alrighth?'

But Cheyi's peace of mind had vanished. That threat, 'I won' le'ggo', seemed to have multiplied into a hundred serpent-hoods over the years. Valyechi may not be alone. She must have been received by a whole community of serpents as she descended into the well. That's their land. Though they quickly move away when you meet them above the ground, that isn't how they greet you down below.

Cheyikkutty remembered that Kalyani had swept some decaying coconut fronds and dried-up areca-leaf sheaths into a corner of the yard and burned it all. She wanted to tell her to poke the heap about a bit before putting a match to it, but the curry started to burn and so she had to run back to the kitchen quickly. When she hurried back, the deed was done. Was it an ordinary fire? Did it not sear and burn rather too much? Wasn't there a strange crackling, like ghee splattering? The memory of an old tale made Cheyi shudder.

There was once a lady, a *pennungal*—a pregnant lady. The pennungal of the Nambyaam house. She once kindled all the dried up coconut fronds and sheaths when she cleaned her yard. A pregnant snake was hiding in one of those sheaths. It was trapped in the flames and died. The *pennungal* of the Nambyaam house gave birth before term. A baby girl. She grew, but could not get up on her legs. She would raise her head to look from the floor on which she crawled. And stick out her tongue. Just like a snake. Her second child was born with skin all scaly like a snake. The Nambiar of the Nambyaam house lost heart; he left her. The whole land was heartsick seeing the family suffer. What a calamity! Even though she didn't mean to do it, a wrong was done, and it was indeed wrong. Why did this happen? Those who sought a reason before the deities of the land were met with their lamentation: More than one life was lost in that fire. If you had given them a corner to curl up in, would they have coiled around the dried-up sheath of a coconut flower?

The people exchanged looks. Let them stay on either side of Chonnamma's kottam. The new generation of the victims of the fire accepted the compensation and slithered there.

'Do not make a fire, do not smoke the ground or step inside.'

Before disappearing into the tangle of vines in their new abode, they told the people of the desham.

Cheyikkutty shook awake Kalyani who was dozing away, not listening.

'Kalyani, tak' car' whe' yuh seth alighth tha leav's.'

'Kalyani, tak' car' whe' yuh mak' a fire.'

'Kalyani, don' go nea' tha well . . .'

40

Kalyani was sweeping the yard. Cheyikkutty followed her, looking keenly for any lines on the sand other than those from the broom. Irrespective of whether it was Kalyani or Cheyikkutty, the more they bent down holding the broom, the less sharp their gaze became. So they noticed Lakshmanan only after he had climbed up the steps. Kalyani stood up straight, hit the end of the broom with her left hand to even the broom-stick tips, and smiled at him.

'Yuh're early?'

His heart opened at his sister-in-law's lack of knowledge of the distance from Nilambur. Lakshmanan returned the smile.

'Lachanan's gone a bith brown'r!'

'It's all workk, *edathy*. Bu' yuh're fair'r.'

'Ah, she'll become fair'r, and yuh'll be brown'r—she doesn' do tha kinddofwwork yuh do?' Cheyikkutty intervened. Nowadays, all that Cheyikkutty said was a trifle loaded, Kalyani had begun to feel. Thinking for a moment, she bent down again with the broom.

She drew lines on the sand—maps, paths. *This* bayi *is tha road to Dachayani's Kollam . . . thi'* bayi *goes to Kaissumma's ol' house . . . all thi' goes to Lachanan's Nilambur . . .* the maps of many deshams opened up before her.

She was trying hard to sweep off the dry leaves fallen on her life and the deshams she had drawn on the sand. The grains of sand were falling stubbornly on her head and face. Because she had bent too low, the baby in her tummy, the little *kunhi*, protested.

'Enough,' it called out, 'I'm catching the soil's smell.'

Kalyani too caught a scent, of the Mali's medicine, hidden in the clothes-box inside the house.

'No, yuh go to slee'.'

She stood up straight. Koppu-man was standing on the veranda, looking at her. He came down into the yard slowly.

'Finish'd sweepin'?'

'Can' yuh see?' She panted.

'There's dry leabes in yer hair.'

He stretched out his hand to pick it off her hair but suddenly withdrew, as if remembering something.

'Why, if yuh pic' them out, will yer bangle fall off?' She burst out angrily.

Koppu-man straightened up quickly as though he were kicked in the back and started picking the dry leaves off her hair. He was dressed to go out.

'Bhere are yuh to?'

'Nee' to fin' a mangalam for him. He musth be marri'd soon. I hab to go to many oth'r plac's too. He's aroun' here now, for anythin' urgenth!'

Kalyani looked carefully at Koppu-man's face.

'Why're yuh grumblin'? Wha' am I to do, sitthin' here all day alon', gibin' up everythin' tha' brings sum money!'

Though Lakshmanan had indeed asked for a mangalam, nobody had really discussed the matter afterwards. Both Cheyikkutty and Koppu-man had felt guilty about it. Now that Lakshmanan was back, they thought that they should make amends. Lakshmanan had some strict conditions, too. Things had changed. No one was stuck in their family home anymore. Nowadays, everyone draws a clear boundary on whatever's rightfully theirs, don't they? This new fence was often invisible. But that did not mean it was made-up. That's how it is anywhere these days; these preferences didn't come up because of his move to Nilambur or his mingling with the southies. Whatever may be women's needs, the man can't do without family. He hatches in its warmth. It is upon this foundation that he erects all the pavilions of his triumph. Therefore, we need not be bewildered that Lakshmanan repeated his request for a mangalam during this visit too. When Koppu-man approached the gate, Cheyikkutty came opposite. She looked him up and down.

'Yuh'll be back by ebenin'?'

'No' sure.'

'*I am* sayin', be sure.' Cheyikkutty demanded firmly.

Koppu-man's face was averted as he walked away.

Lakshmanan walked about the yard all day. The cows raised their eyes to look at him. They were peeved. 'Kalyani's barely picked herself up . . .' They grouched and muttered. 'Now, go, break it all down! Really, you want to light your hearth loosening the rafters of this house and thrusting them in the fire, eh? *Really*? What to do if you *really* think that way?' They kept grumbling, grunting and kicking the ground, shaking their horns.

The yard looked unfamiliar to Lakshmanan. He'd seen only old, decaying stuff in the long years he had lived there. Now there were new things in every corner. There was the firewood, obediently smouldering in the hearth; the heap of dry leaves burning nice and controlled beside the yard. Kalyani, walking with her hair knotted high on her head, mundu tied up on her belly. All these looked new to him. Though Cheyi had declared that he would return by nightfall, Koppu-man did not come home. Cheyi was worried when he did not turn up. It made her scurry about the house aimlessly. She had told him to be home before late. Valyechi was sure to come at night. The bolts of the door were usually drawn shut when her son's presence in the bedroom was confirmed. The knowledge that Koppu-man did not follow any rule in his comings and goings did not console her. The memory of that call 'Cheyiyaa . . .' made her shiver inwardly. The only safe mantra in response to the question 'Bhere's my son?' was 'He's in here, quithessafe'.

'Di' my son tell yuh anythin'?'

The question that Cheyikkutty had sworn to keep in her throat broke free and escaped through her mouth.

Lakshmanan said that he would lie down on the veranda's half-wall till Koppu-man returned.

Way too long since one saw the stars above one's own yard!

41

In any story, the narrator enjoys some rights. Narrators are allowed to lead the characters on any course they choose and make them think and act in appropriate ways. If the characters are mainly inhabitants of the story, they will obey the narrator. But what to do when they are human beings? Hard to make them follow the narrator, then. Among human beings, it is rare to see people who wake up all of a sudden in the morning to take decisions that are then cast in stone. In fact, with humans, you can never be sure that decisions taken once will be followed through with absolute precision. Sometimes the right thing to do may manifest to a person only as they act.

Come to think of it, wouldn't it have been wiser for Koppu-man to let things drift? Things were moving smoothly for him after all? But no.

He stands on the veranda looking at Kalyani sweeping the yard. Then goes down to her and brushes off the bits of dry leaves from her hair. Says goodbye to her, his wife, telling her that he is going off to seek a bride for his younger brother. He was a busy man, of the type aroused or enthused only and only by cash. His Kalyani was beginning to see that, once again. Just because she called him her golden lad a couple of times, no Kalyani could be expected to chant the endearing words the whole year through. Human beings shake off the bonds of love when they are hurt constantly, when they are doused with venom, when they simply can't breathe, or when their hungers persist nevertheless. That's why he was unable to hate Kalyani who would laugh and pat it—his weenie—with her fingers gently when he faltered like someone who'd lost an oar in the middle of raging waters. She would ask teasingly, 'Wha's thi'? A deaddssnakeheadd?' 'Poo' littl' thin',' she'd say, pulling his mundu on top of it. '*Ummnaa* . . . babe,' she would coo to it endearingly, 'Now the thime fo' beddie-bed'. In return, he would caress her belly and ask sweetly, 'Wha'ssupp in there, *Ummnaachi*?' And then they would laugh together.

Laughter is the best blanket that you can possibly fling over your failures. There was absolutely no reason at all why Koppu-man, who had left the house after sharing a chuckle with Kalyani, should never have returned. It did not matter who did want or did not want him to return—the truth is that he never came back home. Maybe he left for Nilambur. Or got caught in some never-ending money-related business. Maybe he was procrastinating. Whatever the reason, he had disappeared from Kalyani's life.

'Di' yuh drin' sum wat'r?'

'Yer leg is sleepin'? Justh sthretc' ith ou' and pull tha litthl' fing'r.'

'Why're yuh slurpin' dow' tha dirt?'

'Yuh ban' to pee?'

'Why tak' so muc' throubl' to wash all thes' cloth's?'

'Don' yuh ban' to sleepp? Go to bed soonn.'

'Amme, will yuh sthopp scarin' her bith sthories of tha deadd?'

A whole basin-full of caring words that had elicited no response from Kalyani lay fallen and scattered on the floor of the house. She sat leaning on the kitchen steps, feeling weary and glum. She had a rough idea of the canal through which her life would flow if Koppu-man did not return. She had met many such women in her desham and here. Their men had come here from somewhere else, and had gone back after some time to wherever they came from.

But this is worse. Koppu-man had left his own place, his scene of grace, his own *tattakam*. Kalyani will have to pay a huge price. The concessions that Cheyikkutty or Lakshmanan may be granted will surely be not extended to her. No matter where she stayed—in her own desham or here—her hard times would end only when Koppu-man returned. Deshams always remember rejections, much more than the welcomes.

'Wha's thi'? Yuh've bee' sitthin' so lon'? Lookit'er sitthin' all tha thime? Why? Yuh bant tha babe's headd to go flath?'

Cheyikkutty carped.

Kalyani got up.

'Us'd to be runnin' all aroun' tha cashew garden an' tha vegethable fiel' lik' a cockroach! Now, look, sitthin' fer so lon'! I'm goin' to tell yer moth'r to come an' tak' yuh hom'. I can' beath yuh up here.'

Cheyikkutty threatened her. The word 'Amma' triggered Kalyani. A thousand bits of memory—of neglect—opened in her mind. She flew into a rage.

'Go to tha cashew garde'! Indee'! Thi' is tha resul' of goin' there!'

Cheyikkutty gritted her teeth and advanced menacingly towards her son's womin.

'Pha! Yuh *kaisaade*! Don'mmake me tal', yuh curs'd bulb o' pus! Wha'dd yuh thin', eh? Can' yuh see tha' tha resth of us libe here swallowin' our tongues?'

Kalyani could have just stayed silent. But the insinuation that she lived on someone's munificence drove her crazy. That she too had to swallow her tongue! People who have had to make sacrifices can always use that credit in quarrels. So she stood up to Cheyikkutty.

'Don' forgeth tha' sum pipple hab gain'd because' sum oth'rs have swallow'd thei' tongues!'

'How dar' yuh! Betther no' mak' me say sumthin' . . .'

'Ah, why don' yuh sing, eh? Sing, sing, go on! I'll sing tha resth . . .'

'Kalyani, bekk off now! Justh whe' I thin', ok, leththem fill thei' bellies, womin and babe, yuh go an'drag ith in bekk again. . . there was no nee'! No nee'!'

'Yea. Why'dd yuh drag me bekk here? To wash yer dishes' an' harvesth tha cashews and planth tha vegethabl's?'

'Thath yuh shud've ask'd yer puruvan! Nottmme! Di' I tell yuh to do all thath?'

'Puruvan! Don' make me say thin's, Amme.'

'Wha's wron' bith him, in yer eyes, eh? If he's not enuf fer yuh, go, crawl all ober aroun' here, sniff tha men!'

'*I'll* decid' bhere to go crawlin', alrighth, to all ober or here in tha 'ouse!'

'Sham'less hussy! Justh a *kaissad*! Yuh *tukkichi*!'

'Ah, womin, tellmme? Di' yer man brin' yuh hom', gibe yuh a fruit-pickin' sthaff, and tell yuh, go geth tha cashews an' di' he then sith inside tha bedroo' and starth chantin'? Is thath so?'

'Oh . . . mebbe thath's why yuh drobe my son away!'

'If yer son rannaway, tha's because he's JUSTH NOTTGGOOD!'

'So yuh hab yer eyes on sumone betther, eh?'

'Ah, yea. Mebbe. Wha' are yuh goin' to do?'

'No, THATH won' happenn, AGAIN, Kalyani. As long as Cheyikkutty's alibe, my two boys won' eath fro' tha sam' plathe! Don' thin' thath will happ'n!'

'*Uyyo*! Yer boys sith on yer lap an' eath thei' food! Thath's how one o' them got a weenie lik' a rott'n banana!'

'Curs'd wretch! Yuh'll burn to tha groun'! Tha serpenth's goin' to bithe yuh! There's Chonnamma in tha 'ouse, Chonnamma! Try takin' a blad' o' grass fro' here! Pha! Yuh cold sthinkin' rice gruel! Pphha!'

'Ah, I'm noth 'ere fer yer petthy paisa or kind'nness!'

The hedges on four sides ate up all their talk. Cheyikkutty made off for Nalini's house, forgetting even to throw the towel on her shoulder. Must ask Nalini's husband to find a mangalam for Lakshmanan. Love is all fine, but things have to be dealt with. Kalyani is a tree leaning more and more dangerously towards the roof.

42

Despite Nalini's persistent queries, Cheyikkutty did not tell her the details of the quarrel at home. She only shared her worry about her son's absence.

'It's lik' a drum beathin' in my ear',' she said.

'Wha' abou' yer son's womin there? Wha' does she say?'

'Wha' is she to say? Wha' s she to do if tha fellow justh ran away bith no eye or nose? Letthim gad about far or nea'!'

Nalini however declared that if her puruvan had set off like that, then Kalyani was surely responsible. Anyway, ever since she came, there's been no peace. If only Nalini had also been taken along with the advance party, none of this would have happened. Then you were all full of contempt for the koppu-less condition of Nalini's man. Now you need to get something done, and you remember Nalini's puruvan. So suffer.

'Thath's my man,' she said proudly, looking at Cheyikkutty. 'Why hasn' he run away frommme all thes' yea's? A womin musth hab tha qual'thies to holdd'im!'

'Alrighth, enuf,' said Cheyikkutty. 'Don' brag, uh? If he hasn' run away, thath's because he has nowhere to go. If he had, he'd be lon' gone.'

That shut her mouth. Nonetheless, she threw a vengeful look at the direction of the house. Kalyani was inside, of course.

Cheyikkutty did not feel like going home that day. There was that wench there, with her venomous tongue. It was hard to speak to her face. She would drain half of your energy. And on top, the other womin would climb up from the broken well asking, 'Bhere's my son?' Maybe she won't come over to Nalini's house. Cheyikkutty suddenly lit up with the hope of peaceful slumber for one night, undisturbed by the smell of medicinal oils and hibiscus paste. But something kept forcing her to get out of Nalini's house and go back. Cheyikkutty resisted it for a while. She sat on Nalini's veranda and looked towards her house. Grumbled first in a loud voice first and then feebly. She untied and tied her hair at least three times.

'Diddshe gibe me tha resspect lik' I was her puruvan's moth'r? Whattdid she mean by all thath she spew'd?'

She just couldn't bear it.

When Cheyikkutty got up to leave, Nalini scolded her.

'Isn' ith enuf thath she cuss'd yuh? Don'ggo today. Let tha man of thi' 'ouse come. We hab to geth a mangalam for Lakshmanan.'

'Nottthath . . .'

Cheyikkutty felt badly throttled.

'I'm feelin' bery worri'd sitthin' here . . .'

'If she's goin' to die bithou' seein' yuh, letther. Or whenn Lachunan's bekk, he'll come lookin' fo' amma. I'm no' sendin' yuh there otherbise. Or if yuh go, don' come bekk lookin' fo' us.' Nalini sounded quite fixed.

Her mention of Lakshmanan made Cheyikkutty feel uprooted. She knew that even if Koppu-man returned, Lakshmanan would not put in the effort to mend family bonds. Beyond a certain limit, he did not care for anyone. Otherwise he wouldn't have said about Koppu-man: 'Tha man who wen' bhere he bant'd will come bekk whe' he bants to'.

'Wha' am I to do, my Lord Muthappa?'

Then, as if in a flash of inspiration, she looked towards the side of Chonnamma's kottam.

'Yuh come ou' of thath kottam . . . and tak' a look at my 'ouse?' She told Chonnamma.

*No one should take a thing. Don't let them. All this is your wealth,
too. Outsiders shouldn't touch it.*

Swept away by the swift current of uncertainty, she grabbed
the clump of bushes on the bank.

'Till I go bekk, yuh shud look out fer myyhome . . .'

When Cheyikkutty made her submission, Chonnamma was
dozing. But she woke up, glided out of her kottam slowly, looked
around, and went back in.

*'Who's takin' anythin' here? I holddall thath's mine underfoo'. No
one can lifth ith up.'*

Lakshmanan raised himself on hands pressed down on the
floor on either side of Kalyani. Between them throbbed the space
of a tiny body. He measured that newly-formed distance between
Kalyani and him with his body.

'Ith's tha exacth measur'!'

Kalyani laughed.

'Now afther sum thime, *thath* sthick won' be enuf to measur'
ith, Narayanan's broth'r Lachuna . . .'

'Ah, thath's then, in tha futur'!'

Lakshmanan held his body up without touching her belly and
brought his face close to hers.

'Do yuh know sumthin'? A fello' who was bith me at Nilambur
toldmme. He's a southie. Crazy abou' templ's. There's no purana
he doesn' know. Yuh pregnanth womin shud hea' thi'.'

'Tell me.'

'Thes' fellows—Devas—they hab a masther. This masther
libed bith his olde' broth'r an' his womin. Thi' womin wa' sum
months gone. This masther had all sorths of feelin's for her.'

'All sorths of . . ?'

'Ah . . . am I not 'ere now habin' all sorths of feelin', Narayanan's
womin Kalyani?'

'Alrighth. Tell me tha resth.'

'So he grabb'd her whe' big broth'r wasn' home.'

'Greath'. An' then?'

'So whe' he tri'd to go in, tha babe inside scream'd, "No *Aappa*, Uncle! Theres no spac' here, not eben fo' me".'

'*Uyyi*, no'bbad!'

Kalyani lifted her arms and held up Lakshmanan's shoulders. 'Yuh're goin' to hurt holdin' yerself up lik' thi'. Come dow', go in, but' don' squas' my babie.' She licked off the drop of sweat that had reluctantly followed the story.

'Alrighth, now, tell me whatt'appen'd afther?'

'Thenn wha'? Whenn a man's thingie bants to come innthere, who cannssay there's no space, or if there's no renth receipt; or if ith's leas'd out . . ?'

'Weccann. We womin cann say.'

Kalyani said firmly. Acknowledging women's deadly powers of disarmament through a simple call from behind at decisive moments, Lakshmanan wiped off his passion and cast it away.

'Yuh cann. But I can'tt, and this masther, he too cudn't.'

'Thi' is yer sthory from Nilambur? Sthuff yerself!'

Kalyani tweaked Lakshmanan's nose.

'List'n, alrighth'? Tha babe kick'd outh tha sthick thath tha masther put in tha womb. Tha precious cum fell on tha groun'! Tha masther was bery angry! He gotallmmad an' curs'd tha babe, an' made him blindd!'

'Why diddyuh tell thi' sthory justh now?'

'Justh lik' thath . . . justh . . . Now tha babe mus' have been sthump'd . . . who's thi' comin' inside?'

'No. Narayanan's broth'r Lachuna, tha babe knows who's comin' . . .'

She dug a broad, straight channel in the sweat that spread from Lakshmanan's neck to waist. When he lay on his back beside her, she completed it, from forehead to toes.

'Wha's ith?'

He asked without opening his eyes.

'Measurin' Chonnamma's land? Yuh measurin' it?'

Kalyani's eyes flashed unusually.

43

Lakshmanan's wedding was also on a Thursday. Some guests did remember Koppu-man momentarily when the rice was thrown on the bridegroom, or when they saw Kalyani bustling about the house. And forgot him even sooner in the next wave of activity. Kalyani did not go anywhere near the room where Nalini was readying the suitcase to be taken to the bride's house by the advance party. Since Nalini had taken over power decisively, this time Vanaja went along with the rear-guard. Power and status slip away so easily! Cheyikkutty stayed back at home this time, too.

'D'yuh bant to go bith tha belly?'

Cheyikkutty asked Kalyani gently.

After the big quarrel, she rarely spoke to her. Conversation in the house was generally in hushed tones, even about matters related to Lakshmanan's marriage alliance. The latter discussions always dispersed before they reached Kalyani. All of them, even Lakshmanan, knew that she was not the one for such things, anyway. So she responded to Cheyikkutty's question with an expression-less 'I'm nottggoin'.'

Kalyani standing heartbroken near the room where the new bride's finery was being readied . . . Kalyani wiping her teary eyes in the bridegroom's presence . . . Kalyani crying her heart out in secret as the new bride entered the house . . . imagining Kalyani in all these ways could well make a fine drama, for sure, which may have a heart-wrenching effect on the listeners, who may even shed tears. But there's nothing that I can do. There's no warrant whatsoever to blow this up into a fine tear-jerker. The reason is simple. Kalyani didn't do any of the above.

The whole desham had agreed in theory that Kamala suited Lakshmanan really well. Most members of her family were pretty well-off, but her father was the best-endowed koppu-owner of the whole lot. From her babyhood, her father had been at Kamala's beck and call. There were no other heirs to the ragi-porridge that her mother made for her. She had many uncles, but they weren't in the Congress. These uncles never had to tie her to a pillar to give her a hiding. Above all, she studied till the seventh standard and passed the exam as well. She did not have a single friend who cussed at a teacher. And if she did indeed have one, Kamala would not have rested until this friend was produced as guilty before the teacher who was thus abused. She was a good, mild-mannered girl. Cheyikkutty had agreed to meet the local gods, grease their palms, load them with sweeteners, whatever, if the alliance worked out.

In the suitcase taken by the advance party, there was a sari with silver brocade design and a Dubai panty, specially imported for the occasion. Lakshmanan had chosen for her a gold chain known by her own name—Kamala—which was notorious for the way it kept turning the wrong side when worn. There was quite a furore at the backstage of the wedding because the shape of the bride's wedding-locket wasn't like the classic leaf-shaped *thaali* but more like the southie Christian *chettammaar*-style, the really small one—this has been recorded in history under the title 'Our *thaali* isn' nottlike thi". The photographer at Kamala's house snapped a picture of this conflict after he took a picture of the *thaali*; this constitutes an important primary source for historians. The rest of it remains scattered, hidden in the minds of many people as memories. Memories are not merely to be waved around to fan nostalgia from time to time. They are a wall on which some moments in history may be recorded. For instance:

'Didn' tha bus sthart runnin' thi' way afther Kamala-*kunhi*'s weddin'?'

Can't you see a bus come running through history, parting the desham in two, combing it neatly?

'Ith was fo' Kamala's mangalam thath I wenthout to geth a photographh tak'n. I goth a small album mad'. One bith thick black pag's an' butt'r-pap'r in bethwee' so thath tha picturss don' sthick. Thath was tha firsth album here.'

Did you notice the flashbulbs of memory aimed at history?

All the wedding photos were black-and-white. The photographer took photos of Lakshmanan, Kamala, Vanaja, Nalini, their respective puruvans, Kunhiramettan, the Jeep driver, who was also the Party local committee member, six children belonging to different families, all with their backs pressed against the Jeep that had been hired for the wedding. The photographer also cut out that part of the picture with Lakshmanan and Kamala in which she stood about a foot in front of him in her half-sleeved blouse and three necklaces and six Sheela bangles. It was to be turned into their wedding photo, to be mounted on the wall of the house. If Koppu-man came back, it would be on the wall of the house at Nilambur; if he didn't, it would stay on the wall here.

There was nice, rich, oil-soaked sambar for the feast because properly ripe coconuts were chosen, scraped, fried and ground well. The scent of the fresh virgin coconut oil refused to leave the fingers of the women who had gone to Kamala's house the night before the wedding to help prepare the feast—the oil asserted its presence for over three whole days after the wedding, they claimed. The bride shed many tears and sobbed aloud when she left for the groom's house. Onlookers were mightily satisfied. The Jeep carrying Lakshmanan bringing home such a Kamala came up through the cashew grove reminding everyone of another Thursday in the past. Cheyikkutty threw on her shoulder a new *torthu*-towel. Kalyani handed her the lit brass lamp. When Cheyikkutty took it from her, a few drops of hot oil fell off the wick and scalded her hand a little.

'*Ah, yuh shouldn' hab giben me tha lamp,*' thought Cheyikkutty. Kalyani was pregnant; what if she cursed Lakshmanan's womin? Reminding herself to wave Kamala in the evening to rid her of any evil eye, she held out the lit lamp to the new bride.

Kamala climbed up the steps of the house holding the lamp. Lakshmanan noticed that though she did not seem to be paying much attention, Kalyani was following Kamala's movements keenly and that her eyes were extraordinarily bright. He found himself, almost involuntarily, feeling desperate, seeking a place to hide Kamala. There was no place in the house, however, where Kalyani hadn't laid herself out on.

Kamala put the lamp down and told Nalini: 'Tha lam' is beryhheavy. Bery har' to lifth!'

She was taken into the bedroom by Cheyikkutty and Nalini. The almirah which had Lakshmanan's and Koppu-man's clothes was in there. The bedcover was of fresh white mul; there was a new blanket, too. Vanaja took Kalyani's mat and clothes-box out of the room and left it on the south side of the house.

Kalyani's going to go home for the delivery, anyway. Then the bedroom is going to be free, surely? There seemed to be no sign of Koppu-man. So wasn't it proper to let Lakshmanan and the new bride stay there? All gaps will be filled, knowingly or unknowingly. That was a boon that the earth had been granted, long back. That the hollowed parts would all be filled. There was no need to worry about the hollows that some people leave as they walk away. They are inevitably filled when life sediments.

This time, it was Nalini who helped Kamala take off her ornaments. She said she wasn't taking off the bangles. The sound of bangles jingling was heard for the very first time in the bedroom of Cheyikkutty's house.

'Leth pipple know thath there's a womin in 'ere,' said Nalini, caressing Kamala's bangle-adorned hands.

Kalyani was in the kitchen, preparing the food packets to be sent to the neighbours. She collected the empty dishes and put them all into the big *vattalam* vessel outside the kitchen. It had to be first carried to the well-side; then it had to be soaked and scrubbed. Was there someone to help? She came up from the never-ending flow of work to look around. Seeing no one available, she was about to drag it to the well by the handle, when she heard someone whisper in her ear: 'I'll 'elp . . .'

Kalyani turned to see Kamala. When did she come and stand behind Kalyani?

'Yuh? To lifth tha battalam?' Kalyani could not conceal her laughter. 'Go'way, go,' she said. 'Go try an' geth *ith* up—*thath* thing—which yuh can!'

44

Seeing Arjunan's face looking dull and lifeless, the Maharishis asked thus:

'Arjuna, why is your face so melancholy, why is your body so weary? Are you under Brahma's curse? Or did you copulate with menstruating women?'

Arjunan related to them his experience of terrible, pathetic failure. A fall that had awaited him at the end of a long series of victories.

'Gandhiva, which has been part of my body ever since I grew tall enough to handle a bow, has betrayed me. I could not lift it up at a moment of deep crisis. Why should I remain on this earth?'

The smallest cow in the herd rolled its eyes, unable to comprehend anything. The other two bovine ladies looked at each other and smiled.

What else but a story from the *Mahabharatha* to mark this moment?

'Look at these human beings! They are so prone to failure, even in things they may have been doing with complete ease.'

'Right you are. They don't have—what's the word in English—yes, consistency.'

'Alright, what's the rest of the tale?'

The oldest cow began to chew the cud of the tale again.

In the cowshed that could be seen from the window of the bedroom, three cows were telling stories, at night, unable to catch

183

a wink. The stories transformed themselves into shadows slipping and sliding in the faint light.

Lakshmanan stood near the window, listening. Clammy with sweat from top to toe, he threw a glance at Kamala who was on the cot, lying on her side. Yes, she could do that—she was at ease. It was he who had gone through the strange, unexpected, searing experience of losing esteem before his own eyes. Barely a few moments back, he had collapsed like a tree with its branches falling off one after the other, unable to muster even the courage to look at her. Though the circumstances in the bedroom were not very different, he had failed in this experiment. A player who was talented enough to win a match all on his own was returning to the pavilion in a test match, LBW-ed at the first ball of the first over. The screams of disbelief echoing from the gallery (within him) had pushed Lakshmanan from the heights of self-confidence to the scary depths of self-deprecation. The advantage that a failed player has, however, is that all those around would see him fail. Instead, what if his co-players did not realize that he had failed? And worse, what if his partner thought that this miserable performance was his career's best?

This was the heartrending situation that Lakshmanan now faced. Kamala was quite satisfied—she had accepted from the bottom of her heart that her virginity had vanished the moment he hugged her. And besides, he had also got on top of her. Nothing beyond that caught her attention. Like an experienced pole-vaulter, Lakshmanan had run up and vaulted over the bar with great confidence. But when he realized that the pole he had raised himself up on was stuffed with cotton, he fell pitifully to the ground. Like a kitten fallen in water, he was reduced in half, shivering. But Kamala did not notice. She had closed herself to such things and that wasn't so surprising. Oh, really! Do these people who climb the coconut tree ask it what it thought about the business of coconut-tree climbing? Leave that—do all these people that you see around ever ask the coconut tree before climbing it?

Sending a look of satisfaction at her clothes strewn on the floor, Kamala lay on her side, and told herself: 'I hab done wha' I was to do'. That is, what her aunt from Thalassery had advised her when she came away.

'Afther all of ith is done, moobe ober on yer side and lie quiethly. Don' jumppup an' run off lik' a conducthor in a bus!'

Lakshmanan opened the door of the bedroom and stepped out. When she suspected that his gaze may reach her, Kamala pulled the white bed sheet over her body. She felt proud of herself that she was following every bit of her aunt's advice even in all the confusion.

'Don' ggo nekkid thinkin' thath ith is yer husban' . . . thath kills tha feelin'.'

Kamala sincerely believed that the 'all' her aunt mentioned was done and that it had to be done just this way. She thanked Cherukunnamma—the Goddess of the Cherukunnu temple—for making sure that it all went well.

'Bhere yuh goin'? I'll be scar'd.'

She told him in a sad voice.

'I'm ober here. Yuh go to sleepp.'

He crossed the doorstep.

Soon, Kamala proved herself to be the queen of taste buds. She would keep remembering rather guiltily the massive loss of minerals that she caused Lakshmanan during sex.

'Will he wasthe away?' She thought to herself. What could she do to keep his strength?

After an interval, Cheyikkutty's kitchen came alive with the sounds of slow-frying and deep-frying.

'Edathyamme', she called. Kamala called Kalyani 'edathyamma' or older sister-in-law, and it was a respectful mode of address . . . 'Bhere is tha garlic? Crush a litthle garlic bethween yer fingers and put ith in tha fish curry, it tasthes real goodd.'

'Edathyamme, ith is goodd to fry sum coconu' in tha koottu-curry.'

'Edathyamme, will yuh see if tha drum-sthick's ready to be curri'd?'

'Edathyamme, fryin' some curr' leabes bith *kothambari* tasthes greath!'

'Edathyamme, I'm makin' some terakki rice boil'd in tha milk for 'im. Do yuh bant some?'

Kamala's priorities flew right over Kalyani's head.

'Who ar' yuh askin' abouth tha koottu-curry? Wha' curry fer those who won't come insid' tha 'ouse eber? Who's foreber sthayin' outsid'? Wha' terakki rice?' Cheyikkutty mocked.

Kalyani smelled the wild. She went out and looked around the yard. It was overgrown with bushes. The *kara*-thorn bushes and kanjhiram tree, the serpent-bushes and kammunist-paccha weeds which had not known the sharpness of Kalyani's machete, stood there with their heads up looking rather prideful. The wild had crept right up the back of the new cowshed. A chempaka tree from Chonnamma's kottam had grown right into the yard and showered the verdant greenery with a whole basket of red flowers. A freshly-fallen branch covered with flowers lay there. If planted, it would grow and thrive here, anywhere.

Kalyani was not thinking of clearing the wild. Let its scent be around here. She came back and sat down on the step of the kitchen.

Kamala, who had gone out saying, 'Please moobe a bith, edathyamme, I nee' to geth sum curry leabes', came running back, screaming in fright. Cheyikkutty, and Lakshmanan who was loitering around the veranda, rushed there hollering *ennane* . . .

'A snake! A bigggone!'

Kamala stammered.

'Bhere? In tha curry leabes bush?' Cheyikkutty interjected.

'On tha groun' . . . didn' leth me touc' tha curry lea' . . .'

Kamala shivered with fear and hid behind Lakshmanan.

He grabbed a stick and went over to the curry leaf bushes.

'Yuh all go inside.' He ordered the women.

Kalyani alone did not move. She remained sitting.

Lakshmanan searched carefully but could not find the chap who had scared Kamala so.

He was vexed.

'Tha blasthed snak' . . !'

'Yuh'll fin' nothin' there, Lachuna . . .'

He turned towards the rasping voice. And saw clearly the woman in soiled garments, her collar-bones sticking out, and strands of hair falling untidily out of the bun tied on top of her head. Her belly had now swollen so much, it reached her chest almost. It was sloping strongly towards the left side. Lakshmanan suddenly felt breathless; his lower belly ached.

He threw down the stick and went towards Kalyani. The sight of her made him feel the weight of something within— though it was lodged deep down somewhere and not really unbearable. He considered many things to say to her, but this was what he actually spoke:

'Whenn yuh reach yer home, yuh musth go to tha hospithal.'

His voice softened at the end of the sentence. Kalyani stared straight into his eyes.

'Wha's thi' sadn'ss on yer face? Sum-thing, eh? Wha'?' she asked.

'Nothin''

'I'm nottseein' yuh fer' tha firsth tim', Narayanan's broth'r Lachuna.'

'Nothin' . . . sumthin' sthrange . . . I'm remembering 'im . . . he's gon'ssolong . . . wonder bhere . . . We've bee' lookin' fer 'im but we can't find 'im . . .'

'Oh, thath's ith? I thougth . . . yuh wenth his way . . .'

Lakshmanan did not reply.

The bow that Chonnamma pressed down on the ground lay in his heart under the soil. His words were crushed beneath it.

To go in through the kitchen door, either Kalyani had to move a bit, or he had to step carefully past her. He made his way carefully through the door without disturbing her. His hand extended to hold the railings of the *njaali* brushed on top of Kalyani's head and lingered there for a few moments. As he went inside, somehow, Lakshmanan felt that his defeat was complete.

45

Kamala, who had gone out to bring in a fallen coconut, returned bleeding from both wrists. There was apparently a strange kind of thorn there. It was round-shaped, the seed of a plant which had the uncanny knack of dropping them on those who came near and wounding them. And you would bleed however lightly if it hit you. Kamala had bent down seeing the coconut; she did not see any thorn bush around. So wonder when it curved down towards her! Anyway, the sight of her son's womin bleeding made Cheyikkutty sad. This wasn't the first time, either. How many were the scars on her body! Her toenail had broken; her hair was falling off. On top of it all, the slithering ones leapt out of all sorts of holes and dens and scared her all the time! Kamala could not touch even the jasmine, even when it was in a wild fit of blooming—if she did, the slithering ones would hiss. The rope in the well would be covered with the *pamban*-ants which would quickly cover her from top to toe. All she could do was throw the bucket into the well and run inside the house.

'Ar' yuh crazy? Where's tha ants?'

Lakshmanan lashed out at her.

'Wha's thi' snake thath's scarin' justh yuh?'

'Where's tha' thornbbush? Can'tffind ith in tha yardd?'

Kamala glanced around and looked deflated.

'Sthop jumpin' on 'er,' said Cheyikkutty, looking thoughtful. All this was possible. She had seen such things happen earlier.

She pulled out memories stored away up on her mind's loft and searched through them. There was such a time in her life. Back then, the whole place used to scare Cheyikkutty. But she could not remember when exactly that was—whether it was after Valyechi jumped into the well, or if it was after her wedding. Even a raindrop would startle her then; Cheyikkutty had no desire to remember those times. But some things bind you not in their time. Their shackles click shut much later. You have to go back in time, seek them out, and put them in their place. Some riddles may be answered only that way. The truth is that even though it looks so swollen and fancy, this world of ours is actually made up of just a few things. When these things are shared by more and more, their sweep shrinks. This means that many people may have the same experience. That's why Cheyikkutty's experiences may be from another time but may still belong to Kamala.

The whole day, Cheyikkutty stayed aloof. She felt that a phase of her life which had been filled with warmth and tenderness was coming to an end. Kalyani was due to leave for her mother's house the next day. Cheyikkutty has not thought that her departure would affect her in any way. But now she felt that Kalyani had been in this house long before, even before her. That Kalyani had grown and spread even higher than the roof, beyond the touch of love and hatred, acceptance and rejection. The women who would take her back home were to arrive the next day. When she leaves with that cloth-bag and that firm gaze, Cheyikkutty's house would move back from the shade into the glare.

Where is Narayanan now? Is he alive? Cheyikkutty felt herself falter as the little wail in which the tears and saliva flowed together rang in her ears again. The tiny babe, slippery with the oil smeared on his body, slipped from her arms.

'*Uyyo*, my litthle gold'n one, *ente ponnunkatte . . !*'

Cheyikkutty struggled inwardly.

The unexpected thundershowers ruined her sleep completely. When she got up to close the window, there was Valyechi, standing in the rain outside. Usually, she banged at the window. This time she was silent, her stare directed inside the house. Anger and tears commingled in her eyes. Cheyikkutty shivered. Suddenly, she wanted to pee.

'Cheyiyaa . . . where's my son? Cheyiyaa . . . yuh gabe my son tha mango yer son tasthed and threw, didn' yuh?

Cheyiyaa . . . all thath our father Acchootty badiyar had . . . yuh thook all of ith . . . like a hen scratchin' and rakin' tha groun', keepin' tha worms unde' her claws . . .

Cheyiyaa . . . I won' leth ith go . . .'

Cheyikkutty tried to guess what Valyechi was hinting at. She was being accused of foraging through all that their father had left them, and keeping the best for herself, like a hen hiding the pickings of the day under her claws. What for? To give it all to her son alone.

Even the ones who hop in a well and return to stay among the living need to have some sense, thought Cheyikkutty, wryly.

'I neber thought of 'im as yer chil' or min'. It's yuh who thin' thath way.'

She felt the tears rising in her. Their eyes locked on each other's for some time; when Valyechi went off, Cheyikkutty actually wept, knowing that she was alone in this world. The beedis sent up curls of smoke in the veranda till day broke.

In the bedroom, Kamala lay next to Lakshmanan and sobbed aloud.

'Wha' an'ouse is thi'? Can'ttmmoobe aroun' anywhere 'ere. Can' ttouch anythin'. I am so scared! I thinkkof yuh, of wha' yuh'd do if I wenth away. Thath ith'll be a shame fer yuh. Or I'd habe tol' yuh to tak' me bekk to my 'ouse.'

She sniffed hard.

'Ar' yuh takin' Edathyamma's road, tomorro'?' Lakshmanan asked her quite seriously. Because she believed that making one's puruvan speak that way was shameful, Kamala swallowed the last of her sobs. No, she was not going Kalyani's way.

Kalyani left the next morning. The *kara-appams* and bananas and *petti-appams* and dosas sent by her family sat in the kitchen, turning stale.

'She us'd to eath tha bits of drie' cowdung fro' tha kitch'nn veranda. Tha's stopp'd now, I thin'.'

'Mak' sur' she isn' gulpin' dow' tha raw rice. Ith sthicks to tha womb lik' pasthe.'

'See thath she doesn' sith in one plac' all tha tim'. Tha babe's head will go flat.'

Suddenly, Cheyikkutty was assailed by the guilt that though she was a healer's daughter, she hadn't taken enough care of Kalyani. The additional moments one may gain in life are sometimes capable of exerting a pressure that could break the hitherto-steady hum of life. It doesn't matter what kind of life. Whether it was a happy life or a sad one or a neutral one, is irrelevant. The moments that intrude into a steady life as extra time may actually change its course. She didn't make it happen here.

'I'll com', uh? Mebbe Narayanan will com' to see tha babe. Justh see. My dea' girl, mole, yuh keepp Chonnamma in yer min' and go,' she said to Kalyani.

The cows smiled at Kalyani when she stepped out.

'It's just giving birth, Kalyani? But looks like you are off to a war or something! Anyway, it got inside you; it has to come out somehow? Go and be back soon. But when you return, who all . . . what all . . . we're not going to tell you any of that. It'd have been alright if it were just a story. But this is life, isn't it?'

Kamala stood in the inner veranda, her hair tied up. She did not dare to step out.

'Comm 'ere.'

Kalyani called to her.

'Wha'? Di' yuh forgeth summthin'?'

Kamala came out very reluctantly.

'Go brin' thath here.'

Kamala shuddered when she saw what Kalyani was pointing to—the broken branch of the chempaka tree full of blooms. Kamala decided that she wouldn't go over there even if she had to die. That's where the slithering sort hang around.

'Edathyamme, yuh ban' me dead?' She shrieked. Kalyani laughed like a bronze vessel rolling on the ground. Lakshmanan was in the bedroom; the peals of laughter pierced his ears.

'Yuh can go ober there, tak' ith, said Kalyani. 'No one's hangin' 'round there.'

She took the branch from Kamala.

'Yuh saw anythin'?'

'No.'

'Wer' there thorns there?'

'No.'

'Draw me a bucketh of wat'r from tha well?'

Kalyani washed her face with the cool water.

'Are tha pamban-ants on ith?'

'No.'

'Ah, thenn iths ober. Yuh don'ttbbe 'fraid. Tell Amma, too, nottto be scar'd.'

Kalyani walked on.

46

'To lose wickets from the striking end in the first fifteen overs when fielding restrictions are in place is shameful for any desham. Some balls may spin ravishingly in flight. Do not get overexcited. The result may be a pathetic return to the pavilion.'

So said the cow to her calf as she taught her how to extend her neck through the railings to nip at the fodder. Dakshayani was kneeling, stirring the rice gruel for the cows in the aluminium bucket. She shot the cow a sharp look. The cow ignored it, licked her calf's forehead, and directed her to keep eating with a nod of her head.

'Do you know what lies ahead, little one? Now that Dakshayani's and Kalyani's wickets have fallen in quick succession, the desham is going to be on the defensive. They are going to worry about more wickets falling.'

The calf pulled her head back from between the railings. She looked concerned.

'What else to do but keep shouting the slogan "Never defeated! Never defeated! Never in History, Ever defeated!"'

The cow cast a sidelong glance at Dakshayani. A fly alighted on her back and began to pester her. She despatched it to the netherworld with a single flick of her tail.

'Better eat up. If you don't, all you'll gain is the reputation of being a cow that won't eat grass.'

Mother and daughter began feeding. In between, the cow thrust her head into the gruel bucket and finding it inadequately stirred, flew into a rage.

'Why can't you stir it for me, Dakshayani? You haven't heard about the postpartum mummy's tummy? That which is always hungry?'

Dakshayani stirred the bucket vigorously.

'Really my dea', I didn' thin' thath by tha thime I rethurned, yuh too wud become so nasthy.' She was sad.

The cow felt a stab of guilt.

'Dakshayani, tell me, when does the mango seed grow hard? When the fruit is green or when it ripens?'

'Whe' ith rip'ns.'

She had no doubt.

'There is no cow that won't harden—firm up—after giving birth two times. I will be exactly like this from now on. If I start cooing to you, I won't have the time even to eat this grass, that's why.'

Dakshayani stood up. She remembered Kalyani. 'Wha's up bith Kalyani, I wond'r?'

The cow laughed so hard, the gruel went into her nose; she sneezed and blew her nose.

'Wha' yuh chuckling abou'?' asked Dakshayani, thoroughly irked. 'Di' summone danc' nekkid 'ere?'

'If you danced like that, wouldn't I be crying, Dakshayani?' The cow caught her breath. She continued: 'I laughed for two reasons. First, when I turned my face away from you for just a teeny moment, you sought Kalyani—that very instant. Just think, you humans—how frail are the explanations and reasons you create for relationships? And secondly, I can't help laughing when I see that now Kalyani is in a much worse shape than you. It's the same old pounding stone vs. drum comparison! The pounding stone beaten on one side complaining to the *maddalam*-drum beaten on both sides! What can be more fruitless?'

Dakshayani couldn't help thinking: 'No matther how much yuh may lov' ith, don' eber rais' an *educath'd* cow!' You just need to measure rice; why would you need a golden measuring-cup for that?

'Go and see her, don't delay.'

Dakshayani got up. She had known that Kalyani had come back home to give birth. And had decided to go meet her too. But the old village paths weren't so welcoming any more.

'Tha womin who threw off 'er puruvan and ranbback can' walk on me,' the Panchayat road seemed to be scowling.

'Don' yuh come an' sthand befor' us, Dakshayani,' the fields insisted, and the paddy plants seemed to be bowing lower and lower in shame at the sight of her. When she stretched out her hand to pull off some tender rice grains, the leaf blade grazed her finger. When she went to help with wedding feasts, the fried coconut on the grinding stone insisted stubbornly: 'I won' get groun' by tha womin who threw her husban' off!'

On her return, Dakshayani was learning that her birth-place, and much more, her own home, had become alien to her. It was as though she was being kicked into a bog and forced to remain buried in the mud. To stay in her own home, she needed the charity of someone who she felt utterly repelled by. And strangely enough, to belong to the home of her birth, she had to be first a part of this nasty man's home, and had to be known by his address! The muddy water gurgled in her throat, going glu-glu-glu.

The Dakshayani who had left Nailsvendor behind was strengthened and wounded at the same time by the general rejection that she faced everywhere. His loud-mouthed question— 'Whaat nayitive plaice does ye womun haave? Whaat home does she haave?' was now unfurling in front of her eyes. The house kept its eyes peeled for Dakshayani's secrets. Both house and desham were, at that very moment, finding and analyzing the data for the research thesis titled 'The Feelings of Nailsvendor and the Convictions of Dakshayani'.

Dakshayani was widely believed to have fallen now to the state of desertion that was the Great Fear, the veritable nightmare (of gettin' sthuck in tha kitchin-corn'r), of women of the desham since generations. Ah, slipped on wet cow dung and fell flat, they thought of her. She should have known better. Like a debt that simply refused to reach repaid status even if you paid double, the life she had left behind haunted Dakshayani.

'Wha' was wron' bith 'im? Didn' he sith on thi' *bery* chair, 'ere and cry outtlloud—sayin', my Dakshayani, my Dakshayani? He's a paavam, poormmild fellow. Di' he beath yuh? No, righth? Thenn eberythin' cann be forgiben.'

With each passing day, the outsider, Nailsvendor, shone like burnished gold and the insider, Dakshayani, grew dull and dirty. As the days passed, she even began to suspect if she indeed was the wrongdoer—if she had caused it all.

Dakshayani's southern sojourn lay exactly in the time between her two train journeys. She had no clue how she could have transformed, in that short interval, into a monster that threatened world peace itself. The venomous tails of looks and words wounded her in the beginning, and she flailed and writhed in pain. She even drew these poisoned darts into herself, directly and indirectly. They seared her throat and a baneful scar spread inside her throat.

But later, she hardened. So much so that that she could easily hurl the whole lot away. Like she didn't need a pot-holder to pick up a red-hot pan and toss out its scalding contents.

'Yea, I understhoodd!! Thath I'm a therribl' perso', alrighth, Govindetta. Yea. True thath. So whatt?'

The Dakshayani thus transformed set out to see Kalyani from her house—alone, poor, outcast. She stomped on the very spine of the Panchayat road that glowered at her, and finally reached Kalyani's house.

47

Kalyani was shearing the leaflets of coconut fronds, separating the green part from the mid-rib stick. The ritual of bringing home the pregnant daughter went its own way; Kalyani's mother sought the way to Kaisumma's rundown house. Puruvan and mother-in-law had come personally to take her back. Now she was back again like a bouncing rubber ball, and pregnant on top. All rituals to do with pregnancy rest on the expectation (and relief) that the girl who came to give birth will go away. Not to bring her over would be very shameful. That's the only reason they brought her back. Only because of that. As for Kalyani's mother, she always had a thousand excuses to pick fights with Kalyani.

'Didn' yuh seth fire to tha bery corne'-sthone of my life?'

'Didn' yuh knockkddown my milkpot?'

'Yuh're tha one who push'd my babe down?'

And she would add: 'I hab no daughther like thi',' and look daggers at Kalyani.

'I'm nott yer daughther!' Kalyani would return that look with matching force.

Amma's word 'my' referred to a world she had been excluded from, Kalyani knew that. It was that way, from childhood. Neither of them had bothered to find out why. It had just become a habit.

The house had become so decrepit, it was almost tumbling down. The two uncles never came that way. The baby sister who had screamed the house down on Amma's lap while drinking her muthari porridge had grown and become very smart; she knew how to stay inside the house. But she also knew that it was wiser to leave decaying houses; Kalyani thought that this wisdom came from the fact that her sister did have somewhere to go.

When she woke up that morning and was coming out, a coconut frond fell right there, telling her 'Kalyani, I'm fallin' on one side'. She decided to make a *machi*-broom out of it—an excellent tool to sweep the dry leaves on the ground and the cobwebs off the ceiling. So she was busy when Dakshayani appeared near the fence with the dry leaves and tiny twigs of the bushes sticking on her hair and face.

'Where yuh comin' from, bith all this sthuff? Yuh wer' aroun' 'ere? Whe' are yuh goin' bekk to yer place?'

'My plac'? Bhere?'

'To yer darlin' Nailsvendor's, bhere else! Yuh two are havin a goo'time blowin' hot- an'-col'? On-agai'-Off-again' sthill?'

When Dakshayani had nothing to say, Kalyani laughed.

'Yuh've become meek! So ith's true thath goin'away bith yer puruvan is good!'

'Yea. Yer belly's showin' tha good *yuh* got fromm thath!'

'Ah!' replied Kalyani, 'But Dacchaani, now, isn'thath kind of good yuh can eas'ly find eben *bithout* a puruvan?'

Dakshayani touched her belly. A very ordinary world throbbed inside it.

'I heard thath yuh're 'ere. I was goin' to come, bu' then put ith off . . . toda' I justh decid'd—lemme go to her quickly. I don' go anybhere . . . justh had enuf . . . Exxhausth'd.' Dakshayani sounded emotionally beaten, whisked, whipped when she reached the last word.

She looked intensely at Kalyani. It was the first time Kalyani heard the word 'exxhausth'd' fall from Dakshayani's mouth. Their friendship was a long one. But she remembered no regrets being shared. They had entered the waves of joy and sorrow unprejudiced, together. Now Dakshayani says she had enough, that she's exhausted! Enough of what? And what about Kalyani? Didn't she have enough?

'Why? Why d'yuh shutt tha door? Why shud yuh sthay inside?'

Dakshayani could simply not explain. She was as stuck as a weed-cutter that hit a stone and broke.

'Where's yer Amma?' asked Dakshayani.

'Gone to Kaisumma's 'ouse so thath she doesn' hab to see me.'

Kalyani, who'd thumped her puruvan and sent him running, laughed, as she said that to Dakshayani, who'd broken free from her puruvan and run back home.

But the two fell silent. Not because they had nothing to talk about. That kind of poverty they had never suffered. Deciding to get a life is like pulling a python out of its lair. If you do pull it out, it's going to lie right there, straightening its body, coiling, curling, scaring you and everybody else. There's no guarantee that it will go back into its hole. Kalyani and Dakshayani counted the markings on the uncoiled bodies of their lives as they lay before them, without exchanging a single word. The lashing of the waves inside you becomes audible when you are silent.

'Bhere di' he actuall' go? Wonde' if he's wanderin' summbhere . . . ?'

'Don'kknow. Leth 'im go an' come bekk afther seein' all those plac's. Lik' yuh wen' sighth-seein' and cam' back' righth 'ere.'

'I wen' sighth-seein'? I hab' seennno plac's. All I did was holddup his weenie. An' whateber cash I had is also gone. Yuh at leasth habe a babe. Wha' abou' me? I shud neber hab gone. I wen' there and wen' mad!'

'Lucky yuh are bekk 'ere now.'

'Tru' thath!!'

'Don'yuh bant 'im anymor'?'

Dakshayani remembered that she had heard the same concern in another language in a former birth. The woman who asked that question was full-bellied too; she stood in the temple ground, taking a good look at Dakshayani, separating grain and chaff.

'If 'e comes agai', will yuh go?'

The blood that had withdrawn now rushed into her.

'Wha' kin' of stharvin' gruel, uh? If sumone's so fondd of 'is thingie, leththem suck ith! I can'ttbe bother'd.'

Kalyani went up close to Dakshyani and touched her lightly. Her belly brushed against Dakshayani's body. The movement of a tiny leg inside gave Dakshayani goose bumps. She searched in the old leaves of memory. Was there something she needed to keep aside before she threw all of her memory into the river? As she examined each leaf, she grew redder and redder.

'Dachayani, hey loo' . . .' She looked where Kalyani pointed. She saw a young chempaka plant beginning to grow near the fence.

'I brough' ith frommthere. Yuh shud see ith bloom . . . enuf to fill whol' baskeths! Leth ith gro', I'll gibe yuh a cuttin'. Ith'll thriv' if yuh planth ith.'

Dakshayani looked at the womin in front of her. Rather ill-shaped now but someone who surged forth and flowed with such force! Try to stop this torrent with your foot, and it will be torn right off your ankle.

Kalyani's eyes were smouldering. Dakshayani's stayed locked on them for some time. Then she withdrew her gaze.

'Now, d'yuh feel yuh had enuf?' Kalyani asked.

'No. Why shud I gibe up?' Dakshayani laughed.

48

Dakshyani gently massaged some oil into Kalyani's outstretched legs. The veins stuck out on them, gnarled and prominent.

'Ith's surely sum . . .thin' . . . to geth a massage lik' thi's . . . *oru ithanne*!'

Kalyani stared at her legs which were relaxing unusually, as though they belonged to someone else.

'Doess yer bekk ache?'

Dakshayani asked.

'Yea, sumtim's.'

'Nee' to puth sum hoth compress's.'

Kalyani hummed in agreement.

At the moment, for no particular reason, Dakshayani wanted to tell Kalyani Kunhippennu's sthory. If this were fiction, then we would have had to wait for a proper time, an opportune moment, for her entry. In life, that is not necessary. If you feel like telling it, you tell it.

(And what am I to do when Kunhippennu does not appear on the scene despite five allotments?)

'Whe' I wen' dow'tthere I had a friend—Kunhippennu. Gooddwomin she wa'. Yuh know her sthory?'

Kalyani did not hide her unease at Kunhippennu's completely unscheduled entry. She was also somewhat irked at Dakshayani going all soft at the memory of some southie womin.

'Kunhippennu was froma reeallyppoor family. They wer' four girls. Ith is not lik' in thes' par's—habe four girls, an' yer lif' is gone, clean. Findin' mangalams fer four girls will dribe yuh crazy! There tha men don' nee' to habe a job—they nee' justh tha thingie bethween tha legs. Fer tha girl, ith's differ'nt—yuh hab to gibe gold and lan' and eberythin'. Eben if yuh habe to sell yer 'ouse! By tha thime her sisthers wer' marri'd, they solddaall thei' lan' till tha fence had to be built on tha bekk of thei' kitchin! They pawn'd tha 'ouse fer 'er mangalam—to a soldier. Usuall', ith's schoo'theach'rs there who geth soldiers for puruvans, so wasn' ith 'er gooddluckk? So 'er pipple did noth think muc'. In his 'ouse, there wer' his moth'r and an old'r broth'r.'

The floor of Nisha Talkies on which one could expect a shower of peanut shells anytime reappeared in Kalyani's memory. Somebody brought in the chairs with torn seats hurriedly. A screen unfurled in front of them. Kunhippennu, in her wedding finery leapt on it along with her soldier. In their background were some ten or twelve people who were unrecognizable. The screen's silvery glow cowered in the cinema hall by itself. (If you make people who are in thrall of Jodorowsky's aesthetics tell any story, you'd better be prepared for such a scene. Kalyani and Dakshayani may forgive me in the future for having applied such a self-devised technique).

By the time she entered the soldier's house, there were already some holes in the sari that Kunhippennu was wearing (which did not suit her at all). She stood in that house, afraid and nervous. No one told her what to do. Only after the din was over did she manage to get a grip on who all actually lived there.

Kunhippennu's permanent expression was one of perpetual worry: 'Oh my deayer Goddessu, whatever is haappenning?!' That expression did not leave her face that night when the soldier pounded her to a pulp as though she were a hard-husked *thettaambaral* nut. She woke up in the morning, got up, went to the bath shed, took a bath with the cool water, and turned up at the kitchen. In other words, it was like taking an insurance policy. That is, Kunhippennu herself was to never really lay her hands on the savings, ever; but she kept making payments. In the middle, all sorts of weighty events passed. All through, Kunhippennu lived through substantial existential crises.

Oh my Goddessu, my Devi, yis the laundry aall wettu agg-ain?

Oh my God, these len-tilsu haavu all gone baadu.

Oh my goodu Moth-er, this fish curry taistes so baadu. Entho pattiyatha? *Whaat haappenedu?*

Won'ddu the-yer be attu leastu four more peepple for tha speshyal lunchu on Chathayam day?

'The deuce taike youw! Whaat the fucku aare youw gooddu for!' was the compliment she received from her Soldier-Man. By the time his leave-period ended, she was trained well-enough to dissolve herself in this manner of offering praise. It was undoubtedly the antidote for all the aforementioned philosophical quandaries that passed through her mind. Women have that ability. They are not perfectionists. For example, say, they need *darbha* grass to complete a certain ritual. But if they can't find it and get stuck, they will complete the ritual with some commonplace hay, whatever.

The soldier's mother was a weird sort. Her husband had died when this son of hers was two; now that Kunhippennu had entered the house, her life had gathered a new aim and meaning.

The status she intended to upload about Kunhippennu read thus: 'The daiy this daaghter of ye wrinkleddu oldu villainn yenntered this house, ouwr baad lucku begaan!' When the soldier retired to his bedroom with Kunhippennu at night, this lady would follow them till the door and then spread out her mat an inch away from the closed door.

'The goldu and yeverythingg yis yinside, yis yit nottu? Do they paiy yany attunshun? No waiy! They aaru inn-erestedu yin oth-ar thinngsu . . .'

One day, unable to bear the anxiety about the gold, she went and knocked on the door. The soldier's roar resounded in the house; it blasted her, followed by her mat and pillow, right back into her room.

There was another character there, an *appaavi* of a brother-in-law, a real mild fellow. That was Chithrasenan. He lived quietly, strangely mollifying his surroundings. He had been jailed for political activism and his health had suffered. Kunhippennu entered that house at a time when he had started growing fonder of the past than the present.

49

That day, many moons back, during the rainy season when the people in their houses were trying to stop the rainwater leaking in through the roof with everything they had, from soap boxes to large vessels, the police arrived for the first time, looking for Chithrasenan. He escaped only because he wasn't at home then. Tandaserry, who the police had caught from Adoor that day, was killed in the police camp. What if Chithrasenan had been arrested that day? Human lives go topsy-turvy so easily! The life of that unthinking and insubstantial family of a mother and two sons was violently wrenched in another direction quite unexpectedly.

A distant uncle who was in the army had agreed to take Chithrasenan with him and make a soldier out of him. The training was a bit tough. But if he got through, the family's fortunes were secured for good. So many soldiers had helped their relatives this way! So many local ruffians had turned over a fresh leaf this way. Amma had wept and wailed trying to persuade Chithrasenan. He was the sort who would come and go as he pleased and run after random things. His mother was not pleased. Many a time, she would bark at those who came to call him away.

'You won'ddu gettu my son to maike koppu for you! Whaat to do yif the boy can'ddu sleep peaceu-fully at home-u? Aandu he yis keenu to go yeverywheyer sumthinggu yis drummed up-u!'

Chithrasenan was the youngest of the Party followers there, but certainly the most energetic and resourceful. The leadership found his willingness to obey more attractive than any of these qualities. He could see even in the darkest nights. He knew by heart all the tiny paths and by-lanes. Even if you stuff him in a sack, take him far, and leave him there, he would make his way back in no time. All the frontline leaders of the Party were underground at this time. They did not use their own names; they communicated with each other only when there was a dire emergency. They also had to change hideouts frequently. All this could be done only with the help of followers—and only the most trusted followers were relied upon. Chithrasenan was one such follower. There were also others—Unni Kurup and Sankara Pillai. But they were lacking in courage and would rather stay two feet away from danger anytime. Chithrasenan believed sincerely that this reticence was needed; it was foolish to get caught together in a moment of danger.

But Chithrasenan did not lead. Do not think that Unni Kurup and Sankara Pillai were under him. If he felt that Chithrasenan wasn't obliging enough, Unni Kurup would drop a stick or a torthu-towel—or deliberately leave something, as though he'd forgotten to take it—just to give a hint.

'Ayyo, I forgottu thaat, Chithraa. Caan you pleasu gett it?' When he responded to that request, Kurup would stretch himself and throw Pillai a meaningful glance. But Chithrasenan did not notice it. He did not think that it should be recorded and reflected on. So normal it seemed, like soil and cow dung.

'Isn't thaat some gooddu tendar coconuttu? Howwu to pluck yit withowt ye plucker?'

After fleeing someplace out of the fear of being recognized, when they settled down to relax and rest somewhere, Pillai's eyes would reach for the nearest coconut tree.

'Ha, is thissu nottu ouwr coconuttu plucker?' Kurup would throw his arm in a friendly way around Chithrasenan's shoulder and hug him. Chithrasenan would cut down the tender coconuts the best he could. Kurup and Pillai would glance at each other meaningfully. Chithrasenan belonged to an oppressed caste of coconut-pluckers. They had actually managed to get away with an affirmation of his caste-status.

'Howw longgu haas yit been since we yate at home . . . theyer yis a tree grow-ying in my tummy because yit haasn't seen fish curry for so longgu . . .' Unni Kurup frowned.

Unni Kurup's uncle had turned him out of the family. Their family was closely related to the rich feudal house of Thennilla—by *sambandham*-marriage connections as well. The Thennila-people were old feudal lords. Their word was the word of the desham. Unni Kurup who beat them up and called them all bastards was not welcome in the family anymore. Like everywhere, the disputes and scrapes around the harvesting, threshing and wages grew so much that soon, no particular reason was needed for things to flare up. Many wounds from these confrontations bled and remained unhealed. The theory that the peace of the land ended when the overlords began to receive violence in return for their violence began to gain ground. And many people had no doubt at all that all those who resisted repression were communist upstarts. But the communists were undeterred; they persisted. Old-style feudal threats were not working as well as before; the communists were the reason for that. They would escalate everything from one to many in a jiffy. Soon, people gathered on both sides to join the fray or to watch. Soon, there was fear about the police.

Chithrasenan did suspect much earlier that all the policemen who came to intervene in local goings-on were the stooges of the Thennilla. Their behaviour was such. What to expect from a policeman who addressed the senior man of the Thennilla family in such a craven way—as *angunne*, Your Lordship, or something close? The police would ravage the homes of those who were allegedly the enemies of the Thennila. Many policemen were experts at pulping the insides of human bodies without leaving a single mark outside. The victims would vomit blood later and die. You had to make sure that you didn't fall into their hands.

He had set out to catch some fish from the Ullannoor pond because Unni Kurup had been moaning about a tree growing in his tummy because he hadn't had fish curry for very long. The pond was being drained; the fish stuck in the mud were a-plenty. Usually, when ponds were drained, any villager could take some fish. Combine them with cooked tapioca and there, you have a good feast! But there was a problem here. Apparently, the pond and the fish were exclusively for the use of the Thennilla family.

Now, that wasn't right—one couldn't keep aside a whole pond and all the fish it in for just a few. Chithrasenan and Unni Kurup got into the pond.

But hardly had they gathered any fish in their basket, stones began to rain on them from the opposite side of the pond. And before they could turn, they were attacked. A whole desham, it seemed, had arrived at the pond-side, ready for battle. Chithrasenan and Kurup hit back some, and then ran. From Ullannoor, right up to the Kizhakkida paddy fields. When did the police arrive? How did some of them fall among the fish in the pond and wake into the freedom of a life beyond? How come two of those turned out to be expert pulp-makers of human insides—who left no external traces? How come the other two policemen fell into the Kizhakkida paddy fields? There was no time to think of answers to such questions. When Chithrasenan looked around, Unni Kurup and Sankara Pillai were nowhere to be seen. He did not also realize that he was running away for good from his very ordinariness. The next day, the Chief Minister declared that a place like Shooranad, where this confrontation happened, was not needed at all in the map of Kerala. He thus wrote off as insignificant a whole place and the human beings there, besides the large and small fish in that pond. Then it was a veritable hunt. The police spread all over like locusts. Twenty-five people were wanted. For killing policemen. They were not to be spared.

Kunhippennu shuddered. She felt uneasy sitting down in front of that tall, thin man twenty years her senior—it was

improper. So she stood up. She was scraping the coconut for
pounding a *chammandi*, and he was squeezing out the coconut
milk from the scrapings to be fried later for a curry. Her
nervousness amused him.

'Sittu down, Kunhippenne. Whaat would you then sayy yif
you heard the story of how the poleece caughtt me?'

Kunhippennu fell back on the seat of the coconut scraper.

Kalyani was sitting on the ground, legs stretched out, leaning
on a pillar, with her eyes closed. In Nisha Talkies, a man called
Paravur T.K. Narayana Pillai descended from the sky and hovering
there, declared, 'There's no place called Shooranad anymore'.
Kalyani heard it in a tone that resembles 'I hab no such daughther
an'more'. Below him, the police stomped into houses the size of
matchboxes huddled together. Women, children and older people
ran out, screaming. The screen swayed with the silvery sheen of
the small fry.

'An' thenn?'

Kalyani looked at Dakshayani.

50

'On an ordinary day, the police wouldn't have caught me,' said Chithrasenan. This land is the queen of winding, tricky little lanes. It would not submit so easily to policemen. He would not seek refuge in any house, even those of loved ones. It was common knowledge that this was the most dangerous thing to do. His mother and brother could be targeted too. Amma was smart enough to lock the house and leave for Alappuzha when their source of income had dried up and life became still; so that danger was averted. That very night, a group of people tore down the house. What you see now is the new house erected in its place. That was mostly the soldier's labour. Their mother had inherited the property from her mother. She could not bear to see it divided. She has often woken rudely from sleep, screaming—seeing a thorn fence dividing it.

The description of property inevitably made Kunhippennu rather uneasy. She knew that it was in a contrary relation to her. A memory from back home, of a fence that came right up to the steps of the kitchen, would scratch her hard on the back. So when Chithrasenan reached that part, she scraped the coconut hard so that the loud pa-RRa-pa-RRa noise would drown out the description.

When the police stormed into the Paikalil House, Bhargavy was bathing her infant in an areca palm sheath. When she saw them, she tilted the sheath to drain off the water and leapt up, holding her baby close to her chest.

'Whe-yer aare yo-ver pimbs, you fucking do-ughter of ye damned knaive? Kovaalan and Paramasivan?'

They wanted two men from the Paikalil family and would not leave without them.

'Don'd know, saar,' an ugly rattle rose up from Bhargavy's throat.

'*Ariyathilyo*? You don'd know?'

When the policeman lunged towards her, Bhargavy and the infant nearly fell. She screamed despite herself. The policeman suddenly pulled the baby off her arms. Bhargavy could not move for a second. Then her body just quivered like a leaf.

'Saare, givv me baack my baby,' she cried out.

'Lettu the dogs come he-yer furst.'

Her legs shook but she still ran behind the policeman who was striding towards the nearby pond with the baby. The faster she ran, the farther he seemed to get. The ground seemed to be falling away from her. The policeman squatted by the pond and plunged the baby's head into the water, nearly drowning it. Bhargavy almost went mad. The baby writhed and thrashed, bending like a bow in sheer agony. The pee rushed down between Bhargavy's legs.

'If he comes, I will bring him to you myself, saare, please don't harm my baby!' She shrieked and collapsed before the policeman. He lifted the child above the water level.

'Tell us, edi, whe-yer aare they?'

The policemen who stood around the pond threatened her.

'Yif you waand the child, you'd better tell quick.'

The cries of the mother and child grew feeble. At that moment, in a flash, the child was snatched from the policeman's hand and a hard kick landed on him. He crashed headlong into the water. Chithrasenan's foot was on his Adam's apple and he was pressed down under the water.

'I will kill you, motherfucker. Do you waand to go the saime way as the other two fellows? Do you?' He gnashed his teeth.

The policeman he held underfoot could not do much. But because Chithrasenan was a thin, not-too-healthy man, it was easy to overpower him. Before they reached the police camp, he had been beaten black and blue, softened almost like the *inja* bark pounded before a bath for a body-scrubber. Only half-conscious, he looked around for Bhargavy and the child. Before he slipped into the dark, his last thought was that if he ever returned, he should be greeted by the news that they were well.

Remembering those times, Chithrasenan told Kunhipennu: that was the happiest news. Not that after this mess, one of the accused in the Shooranad case, Sankaranarayanan Thampi, would fight the election from jail and become the Speaker of the Kerala State Assembly . . . Not that his own seventy-five-year sentence would be reduced to just seven years.

'*Ente Ponnammachi*, I can'd be-ar to he-ar aall thiss . . .' Kunhippennu cried. She was shaking. Her voice faltered. She did not even realize that she had wet herself.

Then, an interval opened up between Chithrasenan and the desham. That included the time in the police camp and in jail. In the years that slipped away from him, his younger brother joined the army, took two or three people to join with him, rebuilt the house; Unni Kurup and Sankara Pillai rose to leadership positions in the party. Chithrasenan forgot his age. His body had suffered and so he could no longer live an independent life. He stayed with his mother.

Chithrasenan was a good observer. He knew well the blood that ran in the Party's veins. By the time his frozen life began to flow again, the desham was prepared to repeat history. Twenty-five years later, he watched dispassionately sitting on the veranda of his house a new generation of Party workers turn radical, go underground, and try to do something for justice and equality. They were the Naxalites. This time police dared not step into his house after so many years, remembering his old case. Chithrasenan's cows grazed in the yard. The wind got caught in the bamboo he planted at its boundaries. The earth in his yard was perfectly cared for, without a single useless plant. Year after year, it bloomed madly. It sniffed at him.

The sign 'Interval' flashed in the rainwater-channel-like screen of the Nisha Talkies as Kalyani looked on.

'Hey, I hab a doubt,' Kalyani poked Dakshayani.

'Wha'?'

There were many little islets in Kunhippennu's story that Dakshayani knew little of. Her main informers were Kunhippennu and Nailsvendor's mother. But she tried to clear Kalyani's doubt.

'Why is ith thath thi' Unni Kurup an' all tha oth'rs who gott beathen bith Chitharasenan becam' big, why didn' he become anythin' at all?'

Dakshayani was really pleased.

'*Athenu* . . . Tha's tha real sthory I bant'd to tell yuh!'

51

[Letter from Soldier-Man's Mother to Soldier-Man, discreetly suggesting to him the prospect of a polyandrous three-cornered relationship between him, Chithrasenan, and Kunhippennu. In this precious primary source, she refers to a concept once common in that part of Kerala—*annazhikkal*, or the culture of care in fraternal polyandry, of brothers taking care of the same woman as joint-husbands. In this missive to her beloved son, the mother proposes the joint annazhikk-ing of Kunhippennu by her two sons.]

To be Readdu by my Dearestu Bo-yi, Amma writesu:

Makkale, hope you aare wellu the-yere? He-yer I aand Kunhippennu aare wellu, thaankgodu. He-yer tha rain thissu year yis verry little. It mustu be coldu the-yere still noww, *allyo*? Bringg Amma ye blaangket ne-stu ta-yime? Yif I cowver my legs with yit, my craamps will be *icchare* lessu. Tha one I haave haas now become threaddu-bayer. Youwar brether waas suffering tha whollu of lastu weeku, *mottham* of yit, from baick pa-yin annd leggu pa-yin. Ah, didn'd tha poleece beat him baadly baaicku then? Musstu haave caused much daamaige—*nalla hemadennam pattikaanum*! He haas haad lots of medicine buttu yit yis nottu yimproving. Daiy before yesterrdaiy he wentu to tha hospital at Mavelikkara. Yit yis ye little better nowwu. He caan'tu do muchu workku yin tha yaardu. Kunhippennu yis useless. She justu stands

215

the-yer aand gaipesu—whaat does she know, essceptu just sta-yer at peeple's mouths, *vaayinokkaanallathe*?

Thenn Auntu Pankili *Kochamma* of tha Paddeettil housu gottu knocked downu by ye vehikkil at tha y-east-sidu Kizhakke Mukku junction. Waas hospitalized aand staiyed in tha *aashoothri* for many daiys. I didn'tu go to see her. Ah, she's tha onne who picked tha buddsu off tha myagony trees near ouwar boundary-waall. She pulls aall tha smaall trees yin thissu yaardu through tha *mullu-veli* fence to her yaardu. Haaven't you noteeced? Tha tree's headd yis on tha other side-u olways! Thissu waas whaat she didd when we wentu to tha temble! *Enthavaayaalum*—yanywaiy, she willu be at home-u for some-u daiys. Ah, caan she be allowwed to maike so muchu wealthu?

Ah, thennu Raghavan kochaattan and Janu-echi from Pathaaram caime he-yer—they brought aan alliance—for youwar brether. The gerl yis a relashun of theirs. *Icheyi*, he yis nottu wellu, aafter youwar ta-yime who will *anathu* some warm waater for him to taike ye baath? Thingking of yit, thaat yis correct, no? Kunhippennu yis useless. Butt tha problem yis thaat whennu he brings ye wife-u, half tha prope-rrtty will be theirs. The gerl who maaries a sickku fellow yis nott coming to haave ye gooddu timeme! *Mone*, my son, haave we nott keptu this prope-rrtty inddaactu tillu nowwu? Without yit going to bits? I woulddu rather die thaan see yit divideddu. Thingking thaat yit may go to strange-rrs . . . I gett worried.

He seemsu ye little interestedu yin tha maa-riage aand yeverything, yit waasn'tu likeu thaat tillu nowwu. He justu waanteddu to taike ca-yer of thiss prope-rrtty. Now aafter you gottu maa-reedu he haass changedu. Thiss gerl Kunhippennu he-yer sitsu withu him aand they aare telling stories daiy aand nightu! He mustu haave wanted to gettu maa-reedu then.

Ouwar Unni Kurup haas boughtu tha paaddy fieldsu of tha Punchonil faamily. Nowwu you caan gettu to tha northu sideu roadu by crossing their yaardd. Evenu yif you don'ddu grow yany paddy they-er, you caan sell yit at a goodd price-u in tha future. Nowwu tha whole ye-rea northu of tha temble is theirs. Though Unni Kurup waas hangingk aroundd uselessly for some timeu, nowwu you can'd get yanything done he-yer withouttu him. He haas ye lottu of *pidi* in tha higher cercles! Yeveryone saiys, yit yis Parvathy Amma's graice! Yisn't yit ye faact thaat bothu brethers aare taiking care of aall her affa-yers—annazhi-kking her together, that is—aas two husbandds? Becose of tha joint-annazhikkal, nott yeven ye grainu of saandu gettsu ouwt of thaat faamily! Also, justu looku at Velu Pillai saar's housu? Waasn't yit his older brether—tha *chettacchaar*—who brought Ammini saar? They three aare fine together nowwu? Yit yis common ye-mong ouwar Nair casteu, no *poraika* yin yit, nothinggu to be ye-shamed of—don'd they ye-njoy tha standing from yit, the *ezhunnettam* of yit?

I haave heardu thaat yit waas likeu thaat amongk us too. Youwer fathere's sister was annazhi-kked together by two brethers, older aand younger! They stoppedu yit becaase of tha *parishkaaraam*, aall thaat reform aand yeverything. Whaat waas tha useu? Yeverythingu gottu cut up yinto smaall smaall plotsu, aand yeverybody staartedu livving sepprately! Tha vim n' tha vigour, tha *aekku* aand the *chelu* aare bothu gone! Whaatever, I won'd allow ouwar assetsu—ouwr *mothal*—to gettu divideddu aand scaatteredu. Yit yis haard-ye-earned by you my son, *ente mon*, suffering tha coldu aand tha sunn, aand eatin' tha *kolachoru*, tha killer's rice-u, yisn't yit?

Mone, you mustu keep yin mindu whaat Amma yis telling. Pleasu write baack soonu, *odane*. Thissu yis howwu thingsu aare. Thingku of youwer brether too. Peeple he-yer aare ol-ready whissperinggu, *poochum poochum*. Yif Velu Pillai

aand Unni Kurup caan do yit, why caan'd we? They were tha
janmi-laandlords he-yer, no? So yis yanything wrong withu
them? Yanyway, I-yam sikk aand tiredu of tha kicchen-
paripaalikkal. Even though ye bitt foolish, Kunhippennu issu
goodd for aall thaat. Thenn, mone, didn'd you saiy, whenn
we caime baack from tha bridu-seeing, thaat she yis nott
goodd to taike baack to tha aarmy withu you? Amma thought
of thaat, too. So if you aare aalrightu with your brether also
annazhi-kking Kunhippennu, do writeu soonu, *odane*!

Nothingku more to writeu. We aare conductting ye
para—wership yin youwer naime in tha temble. Thiss timeu
too, the-yer waas ye bumber taapioca haarvestu yin ouwer
yaardu, taapioca ayyarukali! Show yit ne-yar tha fireu aand
yit getsu cookedu, simbly faast! Haave got itt driedu for
vattal. We will fry tha vattal for you to taike baack. The-yer
yis nothing speshal aboutt Kunhippennu. Her oldu haag of
ye mather haad comeu laastu weeku aand I aaskedu her. She
saiddu, do aas you deemm fitt. So I didd nott insist on tha
goldd-demandu this timeu. Kunhippennu yis sitting here. I
am maiking her writeu thiss. Her haandwritingu yis goodd.
Thaat yis tha goodd thinggu ye-bout her.

Ennaa, lett me stopp. I-yam praaying for you, Mone.

Amma.

52

Kunhippennu stared out through the kitchen window; Chithrasenan was among the banana saplings, removing the dead ones. As she watched, the dull browns vanished from the garden and only the fresh green remained. A little while ago, she had gone over there with buttermilk made from sour curds thinned and flavoured with a mixture of crushed *kanthaari*-chilli, curry leaves, ginger, shallots and salt. Throwing down the machete, Chithrasenan had held his hand out for the jar. Instead of handing it to him, she had asked, 'Chithran Kochaatta, aare you also goingu to be annazhi-kking me?' He was not completely in the dark about the discussions going on, but this question rattled him a little. As for Kunhippennu, she was aware of such things. Such arrangements existed where she came from, too. No one had been ruined by them. Children have grown up quite normally in such families. Only that all the children would address as father the man who their mother had married formally. The family property would be intact. Quarrels and disputes would be rare. The peace of not expecting a new member will be palpable. Some people, were there, for sure, whose placid inner coves turned into raging seas at the prospect of a third presence. No one would know that, however. Kunhippennu too did not try to find out if a sea was raging inside her. She had no time for that. Or she deliberately decided not to.

'If you didn't like yit, you could've said thaat when you wrote yit, Kunhippenne?' Chithrasenan asked her.

She handed him the jar of buttermilk.

'Yanyway, lett us way-ite for his reply. I yaam not thaat insistent thaat I should also be annazhi-kking you.'

Chithrasenan looked at her.

'Yif he says no, then yit yis no. No one he-yere will force you. Will he say thaat?'

Kunhippennu wasn't sure. She had not felt indispensible to Soldier-Man's life. In the short time they were together, he did not speak much to her. They had been invited to some post-wedding feasts by relatives. She had eaten his leftovers each time. She did not know how, where, when to touch him—or if he would like it if she did. Once, her leg had almost touched his body when they were lying together in bed and it had almost made its way up—but she pulled it back quickly. That was because lying beside him was a bit like lying with the nation's military establishment in the form of a human body; to claim even an inch of it would have been unforgivable treason. It had merely arrived by her side to relax a bit and would soon depart. Kunhippennu was merely an impoverished little country it had conquered in between. It was her duty to feed, water and care for it. Its wish was her book of laws.

'Chithran Kochaatta, tha water's been *anath*-ed and warm.'

'Chithra Kochaatta, I can'd clean thiss *varaal*-fish.'

'Chithran Kochaatta, caan you peel thiss taapioca?'

'Chithran Kochaatta, caan you pleasu holdu thiss cowwu's leggu?'

'Kunhippenne, can'dd you we-yar some slipp-per-s? Why caarry so muchu water?'

'Kunhippenne, *dende*, here, taike *ichare* ash aand sme-yar it on this mushi aand varaal fish? Be ca-yerful, eh? Tha knife yis sharp.'

'Kunhippenne, don't get under the cow, she will kick you!'

The soldier's reply arrived three weeks later. Kunhippennu sat with Amma on the south-side veranda and opened the envelope.

Her heart had pounded hard when she heard that there was a letter. For some time, she wouldn't even touch it. She hung about the kitchen busying herself with non-existent chores. She simply could not hold in her hands anything she picked up. Just thinking of the letter made her want to run to the toilet for Numbers One and Two. There was no particular reason, but her eyes were welling. If only someone opened it and told her what news it bore; her insides were seething. She waited until her mother-in-law hollered, 'Oh nowwu I haave to fall at tha wench's feetu aand pleadd to gett her to readu it'.

The alphabets in the letter started swaying, escaping her eye. She felt a faint leap of faith within. In some line, at some turn of phrase, she would surely encounter the soldier laying a claim on her.

'*Okkathilla*! Nothingg doingg! Kunhippennu yis mine. Amme, you better mindu you-wer own businessu'—that was the sentence she desperately searched for as she dived into the letter. She swam frantically in the words, reading the letter aloud to Amma in a single breath.

'. . . aall other thingsu, you mayy think aand decide, Amma. I will come when I gett leave. You-wer son.'

Kunhippennu swallowed a catch and stopped reading.

She handed the letter back to Amma and rushed to the cowshed like she was swept by the wind. Flinging herself down on the seat inside, she pressed her forehead to the bamboo railing. The scent of the hay pushed up her nostrils.

'Aare you crying, Kunhippenne? Yif you don'd like yit, we won'd lettu them.' Kunhippennu looked up to see Chithrasenan. He looked quite serious, concerned.

She leapt up.

'Leave Amma. Whyaare you crying? Yis yit becos you aare sca-yered thaat I will also start annazhi-kking you?

Chithrasenan wanted to know. That's all he wanted to know.

Kunhippennu stayed tongue-tied for some time. She blew her nose and wiped it on the edge of her mundu.

'Tell me, Kunhippenne.'

Chithrasenan looked unsettled.

'To thingk . . . Thaat maan will olso be annazhi-kking me, Chithran Kochatta . . !'

She burst into tears.

53

A dry wind had been blowing since morning. Kunhippennu's lips were parched and chapped. It hurt to lick them. She lay down to sleep last night, yet did not catch any sleep; she woke at dawn but was still not awake. As usual, after a bath, she went to the kitchen. Buttermilk warmed with turmeric and dried chillies and garlic; flaming-red tuna curry; fried string beans; pickled baby mangoes; fried pappadam. That was enough.

Finishing up cooking, she set about cleaning the house. Then she went to the cowshed. After that she loitered about, not knowing what to do.

Soldier-Man's mother had summoned some people. They, and also Unni Kurup, Velu Pillai saar and Raghavan Kochaattan will come to the temple. Everyone was to meet there, at the temple, before the evening worship. They needed two tulsi garlands. Those who came home to visit afterwards would be given a glass of payasam. No other expenses. Chithrasenan, when he heard the plan, objected.

'My dog will come to youwer temble.'

The neighbours were stumped.

'Howwu thenn? Yowu don'd waant sammandham, tha maa-riyege?'

Amma beat her breast.

'I will jumbu in-du tha wellu aand die! I will nottu lettu you drinku waater!'

223

Such an incident had happened recently. But that was when the mother objected to older and younger brothers annazhi-kking the same woman. When the parties put the objection to vote and rejected it, she ran out and jumped into the well. This goodly deed was intended to merely cut off the family's water supply when the parties returned home after sealing the new annazhi-kking arrangement. The water level was low so the old crone didn't die. Just peed generously in there. The third day after the well was drained and water seeped back, the sammandham-marriage happened.

The present threat, however, was more serious. When the guests were busy deciding who among them was best fit to go down into the well, Kunhippennu was pacing the yard, yearning for some space in the netherworld to disappear into. What was there to return to in that house? What had happened? How did things get so muddled in a single night's time? How shameful!

After a seemingly endless time, Chithrasenan came looking for her.

'Kunhippenne, aaren't you taiking ye bath or washing?'

'I took ye bathu yin tha morningu, Chithran Kochatta.'

'Ah, *anganaano*? Yisyit? Yisn't this ye really good thing haappening? *Oru nalla kaaryam*?

Kunhippennu stared at him, utterly perplexed. What nalla kaaryam?

'I bought ye *chomalakkara* red-bordered mundu-*neryathu*. Taike ye bath, we-yar it. There will be no richuals. And even yif the-yere aare, yit will be at home. Olly those who come he-yere needd be present.'

At that moment, this vexed her. *Whaat kinddu of man this yis! Can he get yanything done straight? He shudd stoppu bugging people like this. No wonder the poleece gaive him ye good hiding.*

Kunhippennu pulled up a couple of buckets of water from the well and took a bath. A whole life was washed off by that water which flowed down her body hissing mildly. She draped the red-bordered mundu and felt pretty. The red blouse that had been tailored for her wedding which she had never worn was taken out—it fitted her well now. A handful of jasmine flowers twisted into a garland in her hair gave out the most intense scent they had ever shed in their entire life.

Chithrasenan's room was another world. There were a few old books there. A wooden bar on the wall to hang clothes on. The cotton mattress on the cot that smelt of sunlight. The room was airy. A black-coloured blanket was placed folded at the foot of the cot. In the open shelf, apart from several medicine-bottles, there were a few photos. It was clean; free of dust and cobwebs. Kunhippennu felt that this was really her room, and that she had entered entirely by mistake the other room that smelled of India all over, and which was so full of boxes, that it shrunk.

Kunhippennu sat near Chithrasenan. He was more than double her age. She quietly, steadily, licked the distrust off her mind. I entered this house with *this man*—she kept telling herself. Chithrasenan put his hand around her shoulder. His body shivered. And noticing that his arm crushed the flowers in her hair, he drew it back.

Why, I never felt strange talking with her until now, he flushed. There had never been an occasion all these years to sit close beside a woman. He was one of those men who thought it improper, even. Chithrasenan struggled with this decision now; it should not have not happened, perhaps? The thought that he might have to spend the rest of his days hiding from her struck him then; it scared him.

One day, not long after the soldier had brought home his bride, Chithrasenan woke up rudely from sleep. As was his usual wont when this happened, he got up and stepped out of his room. He opened the door and was about to go to the veranda when he heard a suppressed whimper and a sob, and a growl that followed it—he could make nothing of it. Then he heard a living human body being flung against the wall, held there. It was being pummelled hard. Only when he heard a sound, a gasping female voice, quite like that of a tabby cat which accidentally swallowed a fish, could he yank himself out of the feeling that he was in a lockup or a police camp. He stood rooted on the spot, unable to lower his raised foot, drenched in sweat, throat parched. Then, walking backwards like a dexterous thief, he closed the door of his room noiselessly, caught his breath finally, and fell face down on the cot. That day he realized it: he was not some dead and dried-up twig; he bore the drops of life that would grow if planted on the ground. Though he tried to wash that feeling off his hands many times from sheer self-deprecation, he could not look at anyone in the face for quite a few days.

'Why're you so qui-et Chithran Kochatta?' asked Kunhippennu. 'Whaat waas tha biggu fuss this yevening?' She smiled.

'There yis this truble with me, Kunhippenne. I olways proppose goodu things. But peeple nevver he-ar me out fully. They aare olways sum-whe-yer else. Thaat then leads to ye quarrel, aand fuss. No maatter how muchu of goodu I do, I olways gettu blamed.'

Chithrasenan used the chance to engage in some self-examination.

'Ah, yisn't thaat howu aall of your peeple aare?' Kunhippennu laughed.

The little imp, thought Chithrasenan . . . so she's heard all the stories and got to know of it all!

He looked at her, amused. *Where were you all these years!*

'Yif yit yis ta-yime for you to sleep, go, lie down,' he said.

'Yif yit yis ta-yime for you to sleep, Chithran Kochaatta, please sleep,' she said.

The song about that clever girl Maruthamkodi Ponnamma came to him.

Diddyou fin'thaat sickle, penne
Maruthamkodi Ponnamme?

Chithrasenan whispered, tickling Kunhippennu's ear-lobes.

Didn'd-yit-ggo yesterday
To haarvest aall the milletsu?

She held his hands and cracked his knuckles.

Whe-yer aare tha millets now,
O Maruthamkodi Ponnamme?

Chithrasenan rubbed her chin with his nose.

Waasn'tyit milled yesterday
Aand cookk-ed for tha porridge-u?

Kunhippennu gathered the salt-and-pepper beard on his face.

Whaat did you do wid' tha braan,
O Maruthamkodi Ponnamme?

He drew a circle around her navel.

Waasn't thaat braan thrown
th'y-other day
In-du tha hearth to boil tha milk?

She had begun to smoulder and burn.

Whaaddid you do wid'tha y-ashes,
Maruthamkodi Ponnamme?

Chithrasenan's laugh fell on her ears.

Weren't those tha ashes used
to rubb tha pooja-dishes-u?

Holding back the panting, she returned the laugh.

Where did thaat dish go, my girl,
Maruthamkodi Ponnamme?

Chithrasenan began to search in Kunhippennu's body.

Waasn'tu thaat the dissh-u stolen
By tha thief-u yesterday?

She laughed gaily.

Whe-yer is thaat thief-u gone,
O Maruthamkodi Ponnamme?

Chithrasenan hid in her.

Waasn' yit that very thief
Who raantotha forest yesterday?

Kunhippennu blindfolded herself and ventured through the path Chithrasenan had taken, fearless now.

Whaatdid you do to tha forest,

Maruthamkodi Ponnamme?
Chithrasenan asked, repeatedly.
I don'd know, I don'd know.
Kunhippennu laughed and cried and hugged his neck, feeling rich and poor at the same time. Though she closed her eyes, they continued to rain tears.

54

Thankappan's tailoring shop was in one of the two bazaar-rooms that Unni Kurup owned. In the other room, Chithrasenan and Thankappan sat next to each other facing some ten or eleven people. There was a very serious allegation about Thankappan and he had been told to vacate his shop soonest. True, he was one among them, a party worker. But his dalliances were simply not acceptable. This wasn't about one man's respectability or even about a few people; a whole movement was getting shamed.

But Thankappan was adamant.

'*Aaandu*, lookku he-yer. See, I yam running ye tailoring shop. Nottu tha State Secretariattu! Women aand gerlsu may come to gettu themselves measher-ed, or to gett sumthingg stitchedu. If they haave ye comblaintu, lettu them saiy. *Allathe*, othe-errsu who say I pinchedu their breast or bumm, lettu them come aand sitt he-yer daiy aand night! Tha hecck! *Sshedaa paade!*'

Those who heard the last sentences correctly hurriedly signalled to the others that they hadn't heard it at all. Thankappan was in a fury, nearly dancing with rage.

'Don'd use suchu laanguageu he-yer. Nott this *phaasha*, please.' Unni Kurup cautioned him.

'Whaat yis wronggu with thiss phaasha? Yisn't yit you who toldd yeveryone that I didd yit?'

Thankappan glared.

'*Eeyaal* shouldd nott say much esscuse . . . The-yer aare witnessess who saw you liftingg up tha chin of Ponnamma whenn she caime to youwar shopp! Waas thaat to measher her? Don'd thinku you caan do such things yin he-yer!' A young man in the group raised his voice. Unni Kurup told him to sit down, but he didn't.

'Whaat do you mean? Caan'd do yit *yinside* he-yer, or caan'd do yit yin thiss plaice?'

Thankappan asked, deciding to risk it all. The difference didn't look like much to the young fellow, and so he said, 'Cann'd do either.'

Thankappan pursed his lips.

'But thiss laand waas nottu givven to youwer mather whenn she waas sent he-yer to be hitchedd?'

The whole group, including the young man, was incensed. Chithrasenan too felt that Thankappan should not have used such pungent words. Thankappan, however, was still boiling with rage.

'Summ of us haave been suffering this for quite somme ta-yime now! Yif the-yer yis aan y-issue, call Kunjerukkan and Chaami— they aare lower yin society, *allyo*, they haave to sitt qui-yetly yin ye korner? Becos yit yis them, the-yer will be no quostians. I too waas thinking of sitting quietly. Butt whaat to do yif we aare provoked?'

Chithrasenan tried to restrain Thankappan.

'Lett us talk aafter they finish . . .' he suggested . . .

'*Enthonnu*? Whaat yis the-yer to he-ear? Aare you tryinggu to advisu me aafter you know thaat this per-sun haas been called he-yer? Aand thaat such aan yissue yis to be disgussed? Do these fellows haave no other jobbu?'

Chithrasenan was utterly flummoxed. He looked at Thankappan suspiciously.

'My dear brether Chithranna, how longg haave you been runningg insidu thiss . . . like ye dogg with ye burned legg? Aand whaat didd you gett for thaat? Why, aare you nott goodd to be givven ye posishun?'

Chithrasenan was not convinced. He had not been running all these years for ranks or fame. At each curve on the road, large groups of complete strangers had joined the race. He ran embracing them all. Men who once ran along with him had reached great heights by now. He had tried to dissolve into the stream as much as he could; he had lowered himself the best he could. Never had he felt any resentment that no water-pot had been held out to him even when everyone else was quenching their thirst. Chithrasenan's life was a vehicle that had lain motionless on the road since a very long time. Everything from tangles of vines to ants' nests could be found in it. It wasn't very long since it had started running again, and that too, quite unexpectedly. The wind swept off the wild growth and vines. The rain washed it; the sun dried it. That was plenty for him.

'Blaast yit!'

Thankappan shook his head in sheer frustration. 'My dear Chithranna, thaat is nott tha problem. Didd you know, aafter they caime to know thaat you aare annazhi-kking you-wer youngger brether's *pennpirannothi*, from he-yer to Dell[h]i, nobody has sleptt!'

Chithrasenan's mouth fell open in astonishment. What was the 'issue' in it? It was a common thing, sharing a wife. So many, including people like Unni Kurup, lived under exactly such a roof. How then could the trifling rambles of the humble Chithrasenan complicate the traffic on the highway?

Chithrasenan had not mentioned Unni Kurup on purpose. But Kurup flew into a temper at that. He spit out that vicious insulting word *kotti* for the lower caste Ezhava man, Chithrasenan.

'Thaat yis ye custom yin ouwar jaati! Nottu like-u sum kotti-sonofyeguns looking upp imitatingg high-yer caastes!

Chithrasenan was benumbed. Thankappan gnashed his teeth, snarled.

'Stopp tha bastaard taalkk!'

He could hardly utter a word after.

'Respetted Unni Kurup-addyem, pleasu, you don'd saiy! That's not so true . . .' The young fellow who had lashed out earlier at Thankappan grinned. 'Summ peeple haave olly tha haabitt of sitting upp the coconut tree an' looking down . . .' he mocked. That was a deadly caste-insult directed at the Ezhava men, who were once coconut-tree climbers.

Thankappan leapt up from where he sat and advanced towards Unni Kurup. 'Saiy thaat once more, you sonofyegun!'

The young man and some others jumped up ready to lay a hand on Thankappan. Chithrasenan rose from his seat and got in the middle.

He looked fondly at that young chap who had not even sprouted in his mother's belly at the time when he had got into the Ullannoor pond with Unni Kurup and Sankara Pillai. He was from the Paikalil house; Chithrasenan had nothing to tell him. He turned towards Unni Kurup.

'I won'd answer you now. Even earlier, I haaven't answered such laangugaeu with wordss. Justt tellingg you thaat the-yer yis nothing yin this thaat yany Kurup shouldd smokku his headd yeboutu. I thought thenn thaat Thankappan haad gone too faar. But now I feel yit waas too little! Nobody needu feel baadu thaat I yam he-yer. Lettu thingsu moovu.'

When he stepped out, Thankappan followed him. He kept hissing angrily like a snake. He was dripping with sweat.

'Chithranna, justu comme thiss waiy?' He called.

'I haad thought of vacatingg longgu time baack. Justu waantedu to see how faar yit will aall go. But they wendu too faar withu you, Chithranna,' he said.

'I yam nott disappointed,' Chithrasenan told him. None of this affected him. Nor did it prove that his former life was a mistake. All of it was there within him, with the full intensity of the old. That which was bound to be uprooted will be uprooted. What the sea must take, it will take. It was always like that. If one is swept away in that tide, let it be so. Let it become clean once again.

'How muchh we struggledd, Chithranna, thiss baad name waas unfa-yir.' Thankappan still could not stomach it. 'I haave hiredd two peeple to taike tha sewingg machinu to my house. I caan maike ye livving the-yer too.'

Thankappan stuffed the lengths of cloth in bags. Chithrasenan did not reply. When it was time to leave, he took down a small framed picture from the wall and gave it to Chithrasenan.

'Chithranna, you taike thiss. I haave ye big one in my housu.'

Chithrasenan took it.

When he reached, the house was scowling at him. Where did the lightness of the last few days vanish, he wondered. Seeing the soldier's trunk on the veranda, his surprise dispersed.

'He caime by evening. Where we-yer you? With Kurup-addyem?' Amma asked.

Kurup-addyem indeed! Respected Kurup! Chithrasenan was irked. When did she start calling him that?

'I waas nott with yany addyem,' he said, sounding cross. 'I waas att tha party offeece.'

He handed her the picture that Thankappan gave him.

'Keep yit yinside.'

Amma held up the photo to see. Then wiped it with the edge of her mundu. She lightly touched his forlorn face. Then touched the photo reverentially and brought it to her eyes.

'Whaat haappeneddu to you?'

She did not conceal her surprise.

'Yis thiss nott ouwar Narayana Guru Swamy? Verry gooddu. Lettu the-yer be ye piccher yin tha housu!'

55

When Kunhippennu was serving rice, soldier's mother went up to her and said:

'The boy haas been sufferinggu yin tha hottu aand coldu . . . you taike goodu ca-yer of him, penne?'

Kunhippennu agreed. She filled his plate with rice and pressed it down. Chose the largest piece of fried fish. Set the clay pot down, stirred the cooked tapioca with the wooden spoon and added some fresh coconut oil. She scooped out some into a half-plate. Ladled some of the thick buttermilk-moru-curry into a small bowl. And some fish curry into another. Waited for the soldier to wash his hands and come to the table.

'Amma, please tellu Chithran Kochaattan thaat yit yis taapioca aand fishu curry for dinner todaiy. He maiy nottu waant tha gru-el.'

She lowered her voice as she fried the pappadam and kept aside the warm salted cooked-rice-water. 'I willu taike ca-yer of thaat. You givv thiss fellow sumthing quicku.'

She hurried her off. She was highly dissatisfied seeing Chithrasenan flop down on the chair in the veranda as soon as he entered the house. What will the younger chap feel! Maybe he'll take it as a sign of displeasure at his arrival? That's no good. And not common, either. When the fellow who married the girl is present, he has a grain of greater claim on her. It is always wiser to accept that and carry on.

When she reached the veranda, Chithrasenan was not to be found. He was sitting behind the partition near the well, thinking.

'Whaat yis thiss, edaa?'

She went up to him and snapped.

'Whaat yis you-wer problem? He maiy gett tha wronggu ideya, eh?'

Only then did Chithrasenan become aware that his behaviour could be interpreted thus. He got up quickly, took a bath, and came in for dinner looking quite pleasant. Kunhippennu entered and exited in between, quick as lightning.

'The-yer yis verry goodd fishu curry. You y-eat tha rice-u todaiy.' She whispered to him, hurrying past.

She was to sleep that day in the room where the boxes were stacked. It was not open, like Chithrasenan's room. That night, something was going to colonize her body. But she was ready. She had already learned that you have to first master the slower moves before you perform the faster ones. Feet pressing down on the ground must be firm; the toe must take more force. The soldier realized that night that the distance from the Kunhippennu who he had ripped off himself and flung aside, to the Kunhippennu who was being annazhi-kked by Chithrasenan too, was much more than just a bridge connecting two shores. As he tried to struggle free from her, he told her, 'Yif I gettu ye transferr fromm Punjaab, I will taike you withu me once.'

Kunhippennu got up, shook her mundu and tied it back on her waist. Gathered up her hair and knotted it. Secured the hooks of her blouse easily even in the dark.

'Thaat waasn't whaat you toldu Amma whenn you caime for tha bride-seeingg?' She asked, sounding disinterested.

'Oh, thaat waas thenn. You too haave des-aire, no, *alliyo*? Yit caan haappen olly noww. The-yer is Amma noww to taike ca-yer of Chettachaar he-yer.'

Kunhippennu grunted mildly.

Chithrasenan too was sleepless in the next room. His ears did not let in the least sound from outside. Seeing a silent world turn around him, he was gripped with a sudden fear. He tried to get up, but could not. Feeling thirsty all of a sudden, he shouted loudly for Amma, still lying on his bed. His voice did not rise. The ways in which human beings can turn suddenly helpless are infinite. By the time we learn of their unique paths and forms, they are gone. The paths that lead into life are extremely narrow. The ones leading out are wide. They are more numerous, too. Chithrasenan thought as he lay there:

'A fever?' He began to worry.

By morning, he was actually feverish. Not seeing the man who was usually up at the crack of dawn to tend to the cows and the farm, the soldier himself went to his brother's room.

'Thoughttu thaat I didn'ddu see you, Kochaatta.'

Chithrasenan tried to get up but collapsed.

'Thiss yis high fever!' The soldier touched him.

'Aand how? Won'd come yin from tha farm? Willu you?'

He called Kunhippennu and ordered her to make some pepper coffee and then went off to his room to find some tablets. He returned.

'Don'd stepp on cowdungg when you-wer body yis bruised, ok?'

Chithrasenan nodded in agreement.

He noticed that the soldier has become somewhat skinny.

'Why aare you looking thin, edaa?'

'Oh Kochaatta, whaat yis the-yer butt runningg arounddu? *Alachil allyo*?

'Um.'

'Ah, lettu tha peereed of ser-veecu gett over.'

'Willu you gett ye transferr somewhe-yer else?'

'Nottu thiss yearu, I thinkku.'

'If you gettu, you mustu taike Kunhippennu aand show her yeverytthingu.'

'I haave toldu her. Nottu sure. *Okkuvonnu ariyathilla.*'
'Um.'
'Whaat yis she dooinggu the-yer? Whe-yer yis thaat coffee?'

Soldier was about to go look, when they heard Kunhippennu's loud cries from the yard behind the kitchen, '*Entammo* .. !' When the soldier ran up and Chithrasenan, who had mustered all his remaining strength, rushed there after him, Kunhippennu was trying to lift up Amma. She had collapsed there, spilling the milk pail she was bringing in. She seemed to be growing heavier by the moment and slipping out of her hands. Helpless, she laid Amma down carefully. Pulling Kunhippennu's right ear lobe and her hair close to her face with demoniac energy, she said, 'Don'd lett my child be aall yalone, Mole . . . my doughter . . .' That must have been the last sentence she was to utter on this earth. Kunhippennu was quite familiar with obscenities that ended in mole, e.g. daughter of a whore, daughter of a criminal. This rare non-obscene usage brought tears to her eyes.

Soldier returned to duty after the house began to revolve on a single axis, that of Kunhippennu. He believed that it was some premonition that made him come home on such a short break. So that he could be of help to his mother. But he was worried about life at home now. Chithrasenan, who spent most of his time outside the house, in his eyes, was a pathetic sight. He felt sorry seeing him pull the tapioca, cut the banana stem or grass. He was very angry when Kunhippennu failed to call him to meals at the right times and feed him properly.

'*Daande*, don'd show you-wer true colours. Thaat's my brether, don'd forgett. I haave maide ennuff prope-rrtty he-yer. Why caan'd you maike some goodd food for him?'

If she made some good food and approached Chithrasenan, he would start advising her. 'Kunhippenne, maike sure you taike good care of him . . . he should miss nothing . . . Amma yis no more, he should nott feel tha absence . . . he has to go to goodness knows whaat foreign laand.'

That annoyed her. 'No,' she would snap, 'I yam sitting he-yer aand y-eating upp yeverythingg!'

On the evening before the day of the soldier's departure, when Chithrasenan went into the kitchen, Kunhippennu was frying tapioca chips.

'Kunhippenne, yif he calls, you mustu go to tha aarmy, *ketto?*' he told her, softly.

'Didn'du Amma tellu me, don'd leave my childd y-alone?'

She drained the fries that were done. They made a *kilu-kilu* sound. She did not turn to look at him.

'Kunhippenne, I gaave you aan yimbossible promisu, no? Noww you should staiy he-yer withu Chettachaar.' Soldier said that softly, too.

'So whaat yabout Amma's sayingg, don'd leave my child y-alone?'

She closed the box without looking at him.

'Whe' I wen' there firsth thime, I didn' know thaat tha Kunhippennu who brough' tha milk wasn' justh tha a mere milk-sell'r womin! Which son did Ammachi mean whe' she said ". . . look afther my chil'!" Eben I feel suffocathed whe' I thin' abou' thaat! Ah, peopl' shud die sayin' wha' they're sayin' fully! Oh, wha' she saw, I wond'r—A sthrangeone-thaatwomin! *Bellaathor'thyaannappa!*'

Dakshayani looked at Kalyani, not concealing her astonishment.

'I too wud've thoug' thaat, Dachaani, if ith wer' befor'.' Kalyani replied, looking thoughtful.

'Nottjusth you an' me, all woul' thin' thath. Thath's becos we thin' thath if you love one man, you musth thin' all oth'rs bad! Rememb'r, my puruvan's amma cam' to tak' me bekk? She tol' me thi' then. Ith got int' my mind thennithsel'. I cann understhand Kunhippennu, I cann understhand'er eben if no other person in tha worldccan't. She'a human—she nee' not be a big womin, *balya pennu*, fer thath—she can well be a 'littl' womin'; a *kunhi-pennu*.'

Kalyani hit the nail on the head when she said that. Yes, Kunhippennu meant 'little woman'!

Dakshyani looked carefully into Kalyani's eyes.

56

Kalyani had thought that she would have to go to the hospital; turned out that she didn't have to. She was pulling the touch-me-not weeds outside when she suddenly knew that it was coming. Jumping up, she rushed inside, shouting, 'Call tha Mali now an' tha midwif'!' Her mother ran to Kaisumma's house. Noticing Kaisumma hurry this side, the cow also knew.

'Dakshyani, your friend didn't reach the hospital. Hurry, go to her! Make sure to get Kumb-echi; you are no use by yourself, remember. There's no suspense, it's a boy. He's going to be a big headache for Kalyani in the future. But there's nothing we can do about that. History sometimes flows away from a point only to come right back and rest on the same point. Things will repeat themselves at some turns of time. Versions of faces that we thought had disappeared forever from our lives will appear again. Leave them to their fate. Right now, just run to the midwife's house. Give Kalyani my wishes and tell her not to be afraid. From now, she won't have to face any major worry; just a sea of minor ones.'

The Mali swaddled the infant and showed it to Kalyani. She smiled weakly. Dakshayani took it out of the room. Kalyani, now freed of the burdens of mind and body, lay staring at the ceiling. The room smelled of wet bodies. Then, all of a sudden, she began to feel that the ceiling was slowly coming down, closer and closer to the ground. It was now barely a finger's height away from her. How will Dakshayani come in and lay the baby down beside her? She was afraid. If the ceiling came down, she would be the first to go *chappli*, crushed, pulped. The baby would go *ari-piri*, squashed and burst, like lizards' eggs broken. How to put it back together, then?

Which baby is Amma bringing?

'Kalyani, yuh can feedd tha babe now.'

'No, no, I won'! Thi' is nott my babe! Nott my kunhi!'

'Pha! Yuh dogspawn, then who's thi', yer fath'er?!'

Dakshayani ran in between mother and daughter.

'Kalyani, wha'sstthis? Isn' thi' yer babe?'

'No, no, I hab a babe-gir'! A *penkunnhi*! I rememb' well! She's bery red, bith a head full of curly hair! Whe' she cam' out, she ask'd, "Amma, is ith painin'?" "Neber min'," I tol' her! How di'tthath becum a boy-babe? Where's my mole, my girll?'

She was certain about it. It was a trivial thing, known to all those who have given birth in the desham. If it is a boy, the labour will be over soon. Boys bend their shoulders, hold their bellies back, fold their limbs, give a strong thrust with their heads, and are out in a jiffy. They lack patience, that's the thing. But you are in trouble if it is a girl. The mother will surely have a hard time. The girl is coy when she comes out. And she's full of compassion for her mother. Because she thinks a swift push might be painful for Amma, she taps the opening gently with her head, then withdraws, and tries again. Such patient folk have so often made people around them suffer! This is a similar situation. It is much better to get done with pain in a single, swift stroke. But because of their exaggerated compassion, female infants won't allow it.

'Wha'kkinddof *barthaanam*, Kalyani—wha'kkinddof talk? If ith wer' tha hospithal, yuh cud say thath. Bu' didn' yuh gibe birth righth'ere, befor' us? Tha Mali saw yuh come in leakin' an' pullin' inside here all tha bush an' brush. Will ith do fer yuh if she says?'

'No! No! I know, if ith wer' a boy, he'd push har', slash his wayout sayin', "eithe' me or Amma!" Ith will be ober in a singl' pain. If ith's a gir', she'll keep doubtin', "won' Amma be in pain?" Kumb-echi tol' me, Kaisumma tol' me—thath my kunhi cam' thath way? So it musth be a gir'! Where's she? *Atheduthu?*'

Dakshyani felt helpless. But she was now getting a grip over what was happening.

'Uyyentappa,' swore Kalyani's mother. 'Theres bee' no peace eber bith this wild beasth! NOTT my daughth'r! Leth'er be damn'd!'

'Don'ttccurse her now, yuh,' Dakshayani pleaded with her. 'We'll fin' yer mol, we'll searc' fer her,' she begged Kalyani. 'Bu' this one's throat is goin' to dryyup!'

Soaking a piece of twisted cloth in some boiled and cooled water, she wet the infant's parched mouth.

'Wha' to do now, *padachone*, goodd Go'! Isn' there a cure fer thi'?' Kaisumma exclaimed, worried.

'Don' worry, Kaisumma,' Dakshayani said. Whatever she knew of such cases urged her not to lose hope. Kalyani will calm down with post-birth care. When they start bathing her, rubbing the oil and washing it off with the hibiscus-paste, and when the bleeding stops. All of ninety nerves break during birthing. Healing each takes a day, and so to heal all, it takes the whole of three months. The wound inside takes longer to heal. For that, she will have to eat the chammandi of garlic, ginger, pepper and fried coconut pounded together. She will have to get back to a normal diet gradually. The milk will have to be pressed out. The frenzy inside the head won't subside if the milk stayed in the body. The woman and child needed care. The woman after birth is like someone through whom a thorny lump of wood had just passed. Slowly, everything will heal. But there were also women who never healed. Some of them are no longer alive. Some of the babies have gone, too. Dakshayani just could not bear to think of any of that.

'This will heal.'

She tried to convince herself.

In the days that followed, Kalyani refused to feed the child. Dakshayani's cow set aside deconstruction, philosophical crises, astrology and other such pastimes and quietly made milk. She realized that this was her role right now. Never mind. All thought faces the prospect of arrested development at some point in its history. Nothing to be sad about; the cow knows that.

Because Kaisumma was mostly in their house, Kalyani's mother could not escape there now. When the infant cried, she would curse Kalyani louder. If Dakshayani was around, she would take the infant in her arms and go sit near Kalyani. Generally, the scene was one of decay. The sky and the earth are decayed, claimed Kalyani. That's the thing about unease. It cares nothing for propriety. It just elbows its way into people's lives.

'Onc' yuh starth bathin', yuh'll feel betth'r.'

Dakshayani took the hot medicinal oil in her hands and began to rub it on Kalyani's body.

'Rub tha neckkapwards, hol' tha breasths togeth'r and flatth'n tha belly bith yer handds. Show me yer bum . . . ooh, ith's all so rough! Lemme rub tha oil well and pour tha hottwater! Leth's see if ith improv's . . . wha's yer puruvan goin' to say if he touc's . . .'

That was a mistake. Dakshayani just said that; like she would tell other women around who she cared after childbirth . . . she bit her tongue.

'Isn' ith time yuh sthopp'd thisstalk of puruvan-comin'-*barthaanam*, Dachaani?' Kalyani snapped.

'I saidtthath' bithou' thinkin' of yuh, lettithggo.'

Dakshayani poured the boiling-hot water gently on her joints. Her hands were reddened by the heat. Kalyani cursed her, saying that it was too hot.

'Yuh know tha ol' sthory?'

Dakshayani laid the baby next to Kalyani on the mat. She did not object.

Dakshayani said:

'There wa' a womin an' her puruvan longgthime bekk. He cudn' sthandtto suffer a day bithou' her—lovved her thath muc'.

'Thenn?'

'Ith wassthime fo' her to gibe birth; her fam'ly cam' to tak'
her hom'. He was makin' all sorths of *bairam* to sthopp her
frommggoin'.'

'Is 'e crazy?'

'Isn' summ crazy real nice, Kalyani?'

'Thenn?'

'They summ'ow push'd him awa' and thook her hom'. He
cudn' sthand or sith or walk. So ebery nighth 'e wud swim across
tha riber go to 'er. Ithwas a shame if anyon' saw. So he us'd to open
tha tiles of tha roof of tha room bhere she slepth'.'

'*Uyi*, fo' wha'?'

'Fo' nothin',justh to see tha lovvin' wife.'

'Oh, thathwway. Ok. An'thenn?'

'Anddmmydear, *entanne*, know wha'? On' dday when he
climb'd there an' moobed tha tiles, he saw her gibing birth.'

'Ooh, thath's faabbulous! An' thenn?'

'Seein' it, he got tha chills an' tha feber an' tha fathigue . . .
summ'ow, he manag'd not to fall—he gotddown and ranoff. Wen'
off hom' an' sthayed insid' quieth.'

'Musth habe seen ith really well, from tha top'.'

'Yes, he saw ith really well. But from thennon, he wass a
differenth man. "I won' see 'er," he sai'. "Don' bant 'er or tha babe."
Didn' bant them bekk.'

'Wassthere no one to knock'is teeth downn? Why didn' he
bant them?'

'Afther eberyon' made a big noise, he sai' to 'is moth'r.
"*Entamme*, I saw her gibing birth. Suc' a big babe comes ou'
through suc' a small hole! I was afrai'. How am I to sleep bith
her bithou' fear? Wha' if she swallo's me whol' through there? I
don'bbant her".'

'Uyyentappa! I thoughttsso!'

'Tha Ammachi took her son to a pond full of tha algae. She
toldd'im to drop a big sthone into ith.'

'An' thenn?'

'Tha algae moobed away from wher' he dropp'd tha sthone. Bu' he cudn' see tha openin'. Tha Ammachi tol' her son, "See, how big a sthone fell in ther', di' yuh see anythin' to mark ith? Womin's openin' is lik' thath. Justh rememb'r, wha' lookks bery small, is wha' geths bery big aftherwar's! Ith'll swallo' onl' whe' ith needs to. Wha'eber, yuh go an' get her bekk, mone'.'

'From bhere do yuh geth all thes' sthories?'

'Isn' thath why they don' allow men insid' bhere wimmin gibe birth?'

'Tru'. Poorrthings!! *Paavanagalaanappa!*'

'Ah, don' setthle thath! They becum poortthings whenn they nee' to!'

Kalyani turned her body towards the baby.

'I'll feed ith. Leth ith drin', huh?'

'Lett ith. Poortthing.'

Dakshayani laughed.

The infant touched Kalyani's right nipple with its lips.

57

There were many reasons why Cheyikkutty decided to bring Kalyani and the baby back soonest. One of the reasons she just felt; she couldn't really put her finger on it clearly (that turned out to be the most important reason, as will be revealed much later). The other main reason was the trouble Valyechi was giving her. Behind the door, near the well, by the window—she would hide and keep repeating: 'Bhere's my son?' She would just not let Cheyikkutty sleep. People's patience always wanes after a time. Maybe that's nothing for those who have passed. They are of course in the 'System Update' mode. The living are not like that. Their goals hang high above the steep ravines of life. Even if people dash towards them at full speed, they remain far away. And when you finally come close and raise your hand to pluck it, it flies away. Imagine, in the middle of all this, some people trying to settle accounts from their last birth! What could be worse! Cheyikkutty even suspected: is this a conspiracy between mother and son?

A third reason was Lakshmanan and Kamala. Lakshmanan in Nilambur and Kamala here, what was the use of such a life! Since Koppu-man was gone, Lakshmanan had to stay there to manage things. Kamala was eager to stay there with Lakshmanan in his one-room house. She was ready to do that just to hug him and hang around him all the time. Her aunt had taught her that 'family' meant her and her puruvan living together in his place of work. Cheyikkutty was not opposed to it. She was not among the women who tied male children to their waist-chains.

'Onc' they leav' yer breasth an' beggin to grab another' breasth, untie them. Don' tak' them on yer knee againn sayin' "my son, my son".' That's what she thought.

She had decided well in advance to tell Lakshmanan to take Kamala along.

Though they didn't mention it directly, Kalyani's house clearly struggled with want. What were they to get from that yard which had become tattered like a torn towel? Kalyani had just given birth. She was a woman who worked herself to the bone. This is the first; if the care was not adequate, she would become useless. Cheyikkutty knew that an unhealthy woman was like a house with broken rafters. The woman who had just given birth needs to be fed goat-head and liver and soup. She should be given the special post-birth medication. The infant should drink her milk, not her blood.

That was another reason.

So the Jeep that Cheyikkutty sent returned through the cashew grove a third time. Kalyani got out of the Jeep, holding the baby close to her chest. She shone like newly-shucked corn in the gentle sunshine. The light fell on her neck and cheek and scattered. The cows and house raised their heads and looked at her. Dakshayani's care shone on her body. Cheyikkutty took a good look and was satisfied.

'Nothbbadd. She looks brighth an' rosy. Tha trunk's shinin'.'

Kamala ran up and took the infant from her. Lakshmanan, who had arrived for the baby's naming ritual, was sitting on the veranda. Kamala spread a grass mat on the veranda.

''ere, lie downn, beddie-bed! Ooh wha' a cute litthle *kuttaappi*!'

She looked at Lakshmanan and laid the baby down. He bent down and held the baby's soft, spongy little foot between his fingers.

'Who'stthiss?' He asked, in a low voice. The infant kept flinging about its limbs. Lakshmanan did not want to stop holding the little one's leg. As he sat near it, touching it, something scalding, like steam, gathered inside him.

The yard was now overgrown with weeds. The well-side was slimy. The dry coconut-fronds and flowers were piled up under the trees and these were being eaten by termites. Much work awaited Kalyani. But the infant's cries and the nursing intervals pulled her into the house sure as a hook.

When Lakshmanan and Kamala left for Nilambur, Cheyikkutty, Kalyani and the baby were alone in the house. And not just that, both mother-in-law and daughter-in-law felt that their lives were now like over-pruned trees. The word is *taai-thadi*—'mother-trunk'. They were *taai-thadis* that loomed upward with no branches, really lonely. Of course, they did not know how to show their love for each other. When they quarrelled, they were quick to pick out each other as enemies. Kalyani thought that Cheyikkutty was a cagey old crone. Cheyikkutty would argue that Kalyani was a trollop who dragged her mundu all over the streets. And seeing that the other was completely unaffected by such invective, they would both calm down.

'Ith's becos I thin' of thi' babe . . . if not I'd habe brok'n yer head!'

'Ith's becos I thin' thi' shrew is ol' and wizen'd. Or I'd habe sai' words thath can'ttbbe rubb'd or scrap'd off tha skin.'

Both would walk away, gritting their teeth.

For example, just before supper-time, both of them would declare unwillingness to eat supper:

'To be dyin' bithou' eatin' an' drinkin'—di'sumoneof yers conk off in thiss'ouse??' Cheyikkutty would shout.

'If yuh die 'ere bithout eatin' an' drinkin', I can't gibe escusses. Yuh comin' to eat ornnot . . . ?' Kalyani would yell.

They would grit their teeth again. And know deep within that one would not eat any supper without the other.

Kalyani's life had narrowed down, but it still was a fast-flowing stream. It was the clots and clogs in the flow that chafed her most. Those impediments could turn her into a stagnant pond, she feared. Cheyikkutty could transform her unease into swirls of smoke at the dead of night. But Kalyani who could do nothing but lie flat and stare at the ceiling, had to find her own way.

'Kalyani, if yuh'r no' sleepin', come thisside,' called Cheyikkutty.

'Wha'? Yuh bant sum wat'r?'

She got up.

Cheyikkutty sat in the veranda looking like a smoking chimney.

'Uyyentappa, yuh tryin' to smother pipple bith smok'?' Kalyani was irritated. Cheyikkutty did not hear her grumbling.

'Wha's th's yuh'r doin', Amme, gulpin' downnall tha smok'? Thi' coughin' is goin' ttobbenoggoodd!'

Kalyani warned her.

'Ith tha weighth in my heartt!'

Cheyikkutty said. That was the first time she was admitting it to herself.

'*Uyi*! Yuh? Weighth?'

Kalyani was surprised. 'No one will beliebe . . . yu habe suc' a *thera*—so muchh spunk,' she said.

Though she said that tartly, she felt a great sympathy for the old woman. Cheyikkutty extinguished her beedi and glowered at her.

'There wassa womin lon' thime bekk—yuh hearddof 'er? She gabe birth to fourteen, an' all of them died.'

'No.'

Kalyani said.

'Thath womin wud dress up well an' lookk fine eben though all her chil'ren died. She knew tha Ramayanam by heart, tot'lly. Woul' read'ly talk bith anyon'. An' speak 'er mind anybhere. Wha' do pipple call thath kin' of womin?'

'*Ammoppa*!! Lik' yuh, Amma.'

'Lik' yuh saidnnow—*thera*-filled womin.'

'Oh.'

'Onedday tha Lorddof tha Land saw 'er walkin' through tha field. Tha womin who'd losth 'er chil'ren but wa' still walkin' abou' dress'd fancy an' arguin' an' eberythin'! "Call her here," he orde'd. She came, an' he stharte' questhionin' 'er. Thiswwomin is a disgrac' to tha land, he decide'. Thathtime she tol' him, "I habe much' sadness. I don' put ith on show. If I do thath, will I ge' bekk my chil'ren? Yuh bant to see the sadness inside me? So brin' 'ere a pot of paddy!"'

'Andd?'

Kalyani asked, impatient.

'She lay downn flath on tha groun' an' heap'd tha paddy on her chesth. Tha paddy puffed an' becam' rice puffs! Tha Lordd of tha Land was so scar'd! He sai', thisslland don'nneed thisskind of womin. Rub tha oil on her an' setther on fire! She burn'd insid' and outt and ran aroun' in agony.'

Kalyani sat down beside Cheyikkutty. She wanted to touch her ear lobes with the big piercings in them.

58

'Cheyiyaa . . . bhere's my son?'

Valyechi asked Cheyikkutty, who had come into the kitchen hearing a vessel fall on the floor. Time had been like a little calf running madly and merrily up and down the field, having broken its tether. Every script and syallbus had changed. Only Valyechi seemed stuck in the old syllabus. Cheyikkutty was sick and tired writing the answer to a question that was completely in tatters, reduced to a few threads. She lost her cool.

'*Ninte mon* is insid' thi' nose o' mine, huh! So wha'?'

Valyechi was standing near the hearth. She was all wet. Her mundu was stained with mud and moss. Her hair was still piled in a knot on top of her head.

Cheyikkutty had never spoken harshly to Valyechi, before or after her passing. Now she decided that such courtesy was not necessary. You can row as long as you have a canoe; but you can't guarantee that a canoe will be waiting for you at the riverside at all times—Cheyikkutty thought. She hadn't promised eternal courtesy, for sure. Indeed, if she had promised it, the rowing would have been weaker. The canoe would have sunk, even. Cheyikkutty was not prepared for that. She had been with the children until they could swim and row. That was good enough. Her *machunan* (brother-in-law) with whom she had lived—never had to scowl at her. She had been her father's favourite daughter. Those self-appraisal forms, she knew well. She didn't need a certificate from

Valyechi who had thrown away the life she had into the well. She did not need it anyway, to come on top. So she loosened her hair, tied it up again, went straight to the hearth, and made Valyechi move aside.

'Moobe asid' a bith . . . don' putt yer headd' into tha babe's foodd.'

Those who arrive from a dead and devitalized world will inevitably cast an eye on the tastes and aromas of the living world. If you eat the food that they eye, your tummy will swell even as you watch. The saliva in your mouth may start flowing. Your guts may overperform. Do not walk around outside in the evening carrying items of food. Some denizens of the unseen world will be probably on the prowl for food not included in the rations of the other world. If you are eating such food, better throw a little of it before the meal. Everyone knows this—just look how this woman is gadding about in the kitchen, now! Arrogance, for sure. All born out of the kindness shown to her— thinking that she is, after all, dead.

'I'm in tha berand', yuh come there . . . we can look fer yer son fromm'ere too? . . . Come ober 'ere.'

'I'll com', I'll com' . . . todayithself. I have a lot, plenty of things, to tell yuh . . . to listhen, yuh shud have thisssame spunk thenn.'

With that hint of a threat, she went down the kitchen steps and towards the well.

Kalyani had gone to the yard, down there. They are plucking coconuts; she's supervising. Her eye would not miss a single coconut-frond. It was the sight of the decrepit house-compound coming back to life again that made Cheyikkutty stay indoors.

'As lon' as she doesn' fin' anyon' to fighth . . . thath thongue of 'ers! Ooh! *Tadupporillappa*! There'snoperson 'oocanwardheroff!'

When she got out of the house, Cheyikkutty was filled with anxiety; she pressed her hand down on her breast. The little one always ran after her, though his grandmother tried her best to stop him. He was completely nuts. Even if Kalyani pulled out her entire tongue and it covered the whole wide yard, he wouldn't care. He was sucking the woman's blood, really. He was big for his age—around four or five now. But wouldn't let go of her breast. If she didn't nurse him, he'd throw a tantrum, dashing on the floor whatever he could lay his hands on or throwing it at anyone. Such mischief—it was hard to spare the rod. Kalyani would also not relent when he threw a fit. She would pull him down and give him a sound whipping. Cheyikkutty would slap her own head in alarm seeing mother and son fight like cats.

'I too habe rais'd four. Was there eber any sounddllik' thi'? Yer a moth'r, uh?'

'Yuh be quieth!' Kalyani would scream. 'Don'ttmmak' me tell tha sthory of yer chil'-raisin'!'

That would leave Cheyikkutty stumped.

'Bhere's Amma's ol' spirith?' Her daughters wondered.

'Whattwwas thath hubbub, edathyamme?' Nalini would occasionally try to claw at Kalyani. Usually, an exchange, similar to the one below, would happen:

'Whatt'ubbub?'

'*Alla*, ah—no, I though' yuh wer' beathin' up ou' Amma. Pleas' don' kill ou' Amma, uh? If yuh can'tlloo' afther 'er, justh sendd'er 'ere.'

'Is she a tiny babe fer me to carry 'er 'ere ? If yer lovve is oberflownin' so muc', yuh tak' 'er, huh!'

'Ah, indee'! Yuh can' whore aroun' if my Amma isn' there in tha 'ouse!'

'If I wan' to whore, thennIwwon' care eben if yer fath'r's aroun' tha 'ouse, yuh saadlloser!'

'Thath's how yer puruvan ranfferhis life!'

'Thath may be tru', he's got sum shame an' honor, yes . . . buttthen there are sum oth'r puruvans who won' go anybhere eben if tha wife's whorin' all tha tim'!'

'Who are yuh talkin' abou'?'

'Isn' there a chap who doesn'tddo anny workk an' has got in 'ere bith an eye on tha womin's koppu? Yes, I mea' thath bery fellow!'

'So, wha'? Becos yer no goo'! My man won' go an inch away fromm me. Yuh know?'

'Wha' so new abou'thath? Isn' ith commo' to fin' flies buzzin' aroun' shit?'

Well-chosen expletives would flow from Kalyani's mouth: xxxxxxx

This would provoke a piercing scream from Nalini. 'There's no one 'ere to ask afther me. Tha wench call'd me such names! I am nottallow'd to ask afther my Amma? No supprise if she beaths up Amma or even kills 'er in colddbblood! She's tha loosessort!'

After the entire tirade, she would wipe her nose and advance the hypothesis that Kalyani lacked a man to manage her.

'I'll do whateber's need'd fer tha'. Yuh go sthuff tha ghee in tha elephanth's bum.'

Kalyani would then fling the bucket into the depth of the well furiously, draw up some water and wash her feet. She would drink a few cheekfuls of water and then stride back into the house.

Cheyikkutty would look sadly towards Nalini's house. She's told that silly old bulb o' pus many times not to tangle with Kalyani. A daughter getting defeated is the same as a mother getting defeated.

'Kalyani, conthrol yer mouth!' She would suggest.

'Yuh cud habe saidd tha' whenn yer daught'r was leccherin' me ober there?'

Kalyani hit the ball high in the air.

Most mothers are run-out when their communication-routes with daughters fail.

What could Cheyikkutty do except fall silent?

'I canno' mathch up to thi' hussy! Wher' am I to run, my god!'

59

It rained non-stop the whole night. The downpour came right past the half-wall and soaked the wooden frame of the window. Water falling on the tiles flowed down the channel on the side of the roof and filled the aluminium bucket below. It bubbled up and overflowed. The rain washed each leaf in the cashew grove and fell on the earth. Cheyikkutty pulled a wooden chair into the veranda that smelled of rain and leaf. The rain glared at her.

'Cheyiyaa . . .'

Valyechi walked through the rain and stepped on the veranda. Even this heavy downpour had not washed off the moss and mud from her body. It made Cheyikkutty wonder.

'Ah, there yuh are. Not askin' me yeth, "Bhere's my son"?'

Cheyikkutty looked at her closely.

'Yuh thinkk ith is a joke, uh? Tha moth'r who asks "where's my son"?'

She sat down on the rain-soaked half-wall.

'Balyechi, I hab'nt tak'n any of thiss as a joke. Bu' there's summthin' yuh don' know. No matther how heart-rendin', how tear-jerkin', afther a thime, all thath is justh *yers*—yer thing alone, justh yers, yer alone. Howeber muc' yuh sing it, oth'rs won' feel tha'mmuch. Whenn yuh ask abou' yer son, I know tha way yer throa' falters. Bu' ith won' stickkin my throath.'

Valyechi smiled knowingly as though saying: this is exactly what I have been telling you all these years.

'Thath's wha' I said—yuh can onl' treath them differenthly. Habe yuh not tak'n from' my kunhi an' giben to yers?'

'Balyechi, yuh shudn' say thi' againn . . . I habe neber treat'd them differenthly. But our son justh cud not manag' to do summthings. Don' yuh blam' me fer thath.'

Cheyikkutty tried four or five times but the match would simply not light up. Valyechi touched tip of the beedi with her finger. Grains of fire shone on it now.

'Smok'upp,' she said. 'Whenndi' yuh starth thiss?'

'Afther Machunan lefth, balyechi. He wentin a big rainn lik' thiss, at midnighth . . . yuh rememb'r?'

Cheyikkutty's eyes darted to the cot on the inner veranda.

'How am I to remembe'? Wasn' I in tha well? I cud make out . . . him stridin' away at tha deadd of thath nighth, pasth Chonnamma's kottam. Wha' a wind blew thath nighth! I us'd to hear from' inside tha well tha nois' of him takin' off 'is towel an' shakin' it hard . . . I though', mebbe he'll come ober to tha well and lookk inside . . . bu' 'e neber did thath . . . . yuh madehhim hate me so muc', didn' yuh?'

After so many years, she was still tossed by the memory of someone she could never really embrace.

'I didn' mak' annyon' hate yuh. Don' mak' up thin's! Machunan saw me hug Narayanan to my chesth afther yuh lefth . . . He said, seein' thath was enuf . . . He was our Machunan, our cousin, don' forgeth . . . how we three grew up togeth'r laughin' an' playin'. . ? How cud I hate yuh? Weren' yuh his firsth womin? Who gabe him his gold'n boy, Narayanan?'

Valyechi let out a contempt-stained laugh.

'Why're tryin' to pull tha cloth ober my eyes, Cheyi? Wha' yuh goin' to geth fro' sayin' gooddtthin's abou' me? Yer thime is done too! Yuh're now a wizen'd ol' crone! Lookkit me, I'm sthill young, bith tha woun' of gibing birth sthill unheal'd! So wha'? Eben bekk then, Machunan didn' lik' me, yuh know thath. An' thath was becos of *yuh*.'

Valyechi stared hard at Cheyi. The wild and ancient fires of vengeance in that look seared Cheyi's inner refuges.

'Me? Wha' did I do?' Cheyikkutty's voice broke.

'Thath's it. Our fath'r Achootty baidyar pointhed to me an' toldd'im, gibe 'er tha cloth, marry 'er. He did. Go lie on her mat, saidd Achootty baidyar. He did. Go hugg 'er, do it, saidd Achootty baidyar. He did. Bu' whe' he did ith he alwa's scream'd, my Cheyi, ma Cheyi, ma darlin' Cheyi! Yer balyechi diedd righthtthen. Onl' my corpse fell in to tha well. Don'kknow how I press ith all down 'ere in my chesth . . !'

The rain fell thick and black on Valyechi's face. She cried, making ugly noises. She swallowed her words.

Cheyikkutty was stunned. She suddenly wanted to see Machunan, who had, one rainy midnight many years back, had sipped some hot rice gruel she gave him and went down the steps of the veranda to take a leak.

'Don' yuh see ith rainin'? Can' yuh justh do ith fro' tha sthep?'

'Why yuh sittin' there?'

'Uyi, wha' thissyer doin'? Don' fall in tha rainn?'

A bunch of memory-thorns pierced Cheyikkutty. Her eyes welled.

'I rememb'r onl' thath he wen' ober quic'ly to tha step o' the beranda and sath there . . . an' thath he fell face dow' . . . pipple sai' . . . Yuh sayin' . . . he walk'd pasth tha kottam? Yuh heardd? Was he sad? Yuh're sure?'

Cheyikkutty looked at Valyechi with feeling. Valyechi's eyes flashed.

'Hear 'er cooin' and fussin'! Goin' all sweeth!'

She was raging.

'Thath cad didn' bant to see me eben afther he diedd! Tha damn'd fellow isn' anybhere aroun' 'ere! Bhere did yuh hid' him? At Tirunelli? Take tha dearr pipple there, do tha rituals at thath themple, an' they'll neber come bekk! Thenn they can'ttccome, eber!'

'Yuh're wickedd, balyechi! Wickedd! Thath's a man who's pass'd . . . an' yuh still raging againsth him! Yes, he wen', an' has neber bee' bekk. An' goo'ness knows why, 'e doesn' come, eben in a dream! Mebbe thinkin', waitin' fer yer rage to end.'

Cheyikkutty was angry.

'Ha, thath's ith. One day whe' I cam' to tha cashew grobe to tak' a dump, I saw . . . yuh two . . . thwistin-thurnin', dancin' lik' serpenths! I was out of breath' runnin' inside, draggin' my big belly, fallin' on tha mat . . . do yuh know? Yuh thoughth I didn' see?'

Cheyikkutty wasn't surprised by that. She had noticed that evening, when she lay with him on top in the cashew grove, a glimmer of a shadow that went past her eyes, one which had a big belly. The memory of that shadow had haunted her for many years.

She thought of how after Lakshmanan was born, she made Narayanan, who had forgotten how to suckle, drink from her breast. Though her nipples were broken and bleeding and swollen when they got between his teeth, it felt like an effort to atone. The fault-finders know nothing of it. But there were some things even beyond this. It was better that Valyechi was told of it at least now.

Valyechi was growling, her thirst for revenge mounting. She clawed hard at the half-wall. Cheyikkutty noticed: the venom extended to the tip of her nails. A bluish tinge spread from their marks on the half-wall.

'Balyechi . . .'

Not taking her eyes off those bluish lines, Cheyikkutty called her.

'I understhand wha' yuh say. Thenn do hear thiss: yuh know thath Machunan had no greather god tha' our fath'r. It was justh lik' yuh saidd. If our fath'r tol' him to lie dow', he wud; if he saidd hug, he'd hug . . . Whenn he saidd to him, marry tha old'r gir', there was sumthin' our fath'r didn' know. Wha' yuh saw in tha cashew grobe was true . . . bu' ith wasn' tha firsth thime . . . if fath'r knew, do yuh think he wud've bant'd thiss? No, wud yuh have banted ith?'

Valyechi's eyes were fixed on Cheyikkutty.

'I alwayys say . . . to lovve summon' yuh don' habe to push anoth'r away . . . fer me, yuh and Machunan wer' alik' . . . both mine. An' I habe neber thought of yer son an' my son as two. Both mine . . . thath's ith.'

Cheyikkutty smiled lightly.

'Lookk. Lemme tell yuh so thath yuh fee' better. My son an' his womin aren' inntthis 'ouse anymor'. Yer son's womin an' 'er chil' are here.'

Valyechi's twisted smile did not vanish.

'Shrewd brainn yuh habe! I admith thath!'

'Balyechi, yuh're summone who wenth away fromm thisspplace. Don' try so hardd to get things done fer yer pipple who're sthill here . . . ith is shamefu'. Summ pipple pass away an' becom better. How come yuh're so badd?'

Cheyikkutty threw up her hands in dismay.

Valyechi got down from the half-wall. She was now more or less disarmed. The accounts of many years with Cheyikkutty seemed settled. Now there was no reason to come and wait at unearthly hours in the yard and near the windows. The living may ask, couldn't she have come earlier, ask, and satisfy herself? But even the living themselves don't do it that way, do they?

'Cheyiyaa . . .'

She called in a moist tone.

'Yes, balyechi?'

'I'm goin' to leave fer good . . .'

Cheyikkutty felt a terrible pain in her throat. Her only sibling. When she was taken out of the well, and finally borne out of the yard on the shoulders of the men of the family and Machunan himself, Cheyikkutty squirmed in the agony of knowing that they would never see each other again. But when she knew that she was in the well, it was a relief that she was near, like a neighbour, even if it was only to quarrel. Cheyikkutty sank under the weight of unbearable sorrow. Seeing her weep, Valyechi wept too.

'Neber mind, my dear . . .'

'Balyechi, will I see yuh agai'? I'm thinkin' of Machunan . . . I bant to see him too . . .

'Yuh try callin' . . . If you call, he will come . . . I can alsso see . . .'

Cheyikkutty looked at the dark softly and cooed coyly, "ey, lookk'ere, did yuh hea'? Bhere are yuh?'

'Wha's up 'ere, yuh two? Wresthlin' at tha dead of nighth in tha pourin' rain? Ah, so tha two sisthers habe madeppeace?'

Taking the towel off his shoulder and shaking it hard, Machunan came into the yard from beyond Chonnamma's kottam.

They both saw him come.

Not waiting for the rain to abate, Cheyikkutty quickly stepped into the yard along with Valyechi. They looked at him, looked at each other, and exchanged smiles.

'Yuh two walkkon,' he said. 'I'm righth behin'.'

Remembering something, Cheyikkutty turned.

'Lemme tell Kalyani an' . . .'

The rain fell on their faces.

'Ah, mebbe no' . . . I'll be sthill downn'ere, in thi' belly of tha earth.'

Clutching Valyechi's hand, Cheyikkutty climbed down into the well.

'Ah, ith's so slipp'ry, Valyechi . . .'

'Be car'ful . . .' Machunan stood up there, reminding.

'I'll come an' visith now an' thenn,' he said, leaning into the well.

'Alrighth,' said Cheyikkutty.

'Alrighth,' said Valyechi.

60

When Kumaran opened the door, he saw Kalyani's face. He was peeved.

'It's barely dawnn an' there she is, already draggin' tha nuisance!'

Counting this visit, this was the fourth time Kalyani had come seeking him. For sixty paise, K.K. Motors would cross the boundaries of the desham carrying her. Two libraries had come up in the two deshams; both were destinations crossed by K.K. Motors. People getting into the bus at either stop would ask for a 'Vaa'an-shaala' ticket. That's how Kalyani lands at Kumaran's doorstep. Kumaran is not interested in cleaning Kalyani's well. He has much more work these days.

And that was expected. Ooh, so much progress in the land these days! Instead of brawling in the toddy shop and temple festival ground, is it not better to deploy people's violent energies in the service of national reconstruction, as communists and Congress and Muslim League? Why not turn it into strategies to change the shape of the desham? To get rid of your political opponents and fill your corner of the desham with just your folk? Get this done with the call to thrash, batter, whip, wallop your enemies? That was what this progress was all about! Or, use subtler tactics. For instance, people may gather around a table to talk things through, but to *really* deal with your political differences, drop clumps of shaved hair, courtesy the barber's shop, in the opposite party's well!! Usually, it's the stubble. No matter how you clean the well, it will stay stuck to the rings of the well. When the water rises, it will float on it. If this is not available, a dog or a cat will be dedicated to the well. The wells seem to be in a competition to get dirty these days. Many wells, but only one Kumaran.

'I didn' come to sthay bith yuh an'bbe yer womin. Sinc' how long hab I bee'at yer bekk beggin' yuh to clea' tha well fer me?'

Kalyani was restraining herself utmost as she spoke.

'I tell yuh eac' thime, nothin's goin' to workk unthil tha rainn's ober? Alla, ah, thenn, why're yer so sthubborn? Is it tru' thath yuh push'd tha ol' womin int' thath well, lik' pipple are sayin'?'

She pressed down with great effort all that which boiled up within her.

'Tha rainn's ok . . . Didn' Abu'kka say thath we can drai' tha wat'r bith a motor?'

'Thath won' happ'n soo', Kalyani.'

Kumaran began to get pricey.

Kalyani lost it.

'Why thath? Don' I hab to drin' wat'r? There's a limith to pipple's pesshyence! If tha dawn dawns thomorrow, Kumaretta, yuh *will* be cleanin' my well! If yuh don', Kalyani will be bith 'er kunhi, sitthin' at yer doorsthep, justh yuh waith! Yuh don' know Kalyani!'

'Blasth'd womin!'

Kumarettan's brain was up in smoke.

In truth, Cheyikkutty's deed that day landed Kalyani in a terrible, dangerous mess. One may say that she escaped only because Abubacker rushed there quickly. Abubacker was a somewhat influential person in those parts. He was Kaisumma's older brother-in-law's son. Though barely at a sixty-paisa distance, Kalyani's and Koppu-man's deshams were independent republics. Nalini had protested aloud that Kalyani's paramours from back there were out to save her. She had issued advance warnings that Kalyani would kill Amma. But no one had listened. What now? When Nalini entered the second round of this mode of lamentation,

Lakshmanan who appeared from somewhere pulled her up by the arm, enlightened her consciousness with the following words:

'If yuh go on spitthin' out eberythin' thath comes to yer mouth, I'll sthrangl' yuh an' throw yuh in tha well, yuh daughther of a dog!!'

—and he got her to leave the house immediately. He also issued the gentle warning that if she ever spoke such rubbish, her puruvan would have both his legs broken and she would have to feed him his gruel every day. Though the cows whispered to each other, scandalized by the lack of political correctness in punishing the puruvan for the woman's words, Lakshmanan did not care. Seeing him striding about like the gods setting out in the *theyyam* ritual, Kamala began to feel weak and get the chills.

'Don' do, don' say annythingg, Lakshmanetta,' she pleaded, following him around.

'Go an' sith sumwhere quieth!' he roared. And she retreated, turning into stone as she reached the inner veranda.

Kalyani was sick of the drama. She had, of course, to pee and drink water. However, both the desham and the people there were ready to swallow her alive if she went out. Abubacker and Lakshmanan came into the bedroom after the rituals were over. They advised her to go back home. Abubacker had come in a Jeep. Kalyani could go back home in it. It would take time to clean the well. And besides, it wouldn't be proper for a young woman and a mere child to be staying all alone in that house. Wasn't Nalini's and Vanaja's presence and absence in the premises equally useless as far as Kalyani was concerned? Let things calm down like layers of leaves falling and settling, and she can come back. The cows can be taken to Kalyani's house. Or they can be sold. She'd have to come in between to keep an eye on the land. That's because some people may become more affectionate towards the orphaned land than their own.

'Leth tha cows come,' said Kalyani.

Some situations leave us tied up hand and foot. Right now, even the cow in the cowshed was better than Kalyani. Not all battlefields allow you to leap into them chest out. Brave warriors are not deathless. If you don't learn to slink off and retreat, your account may be closed before its time. So Kalyani did climb into the Jeep along with Abubacker. When it moved, Kalyani looked at the face of the desham that she could never ever be part of. Every time she tried to find a place in it, she had slipped back like someone trying to climb an areca palm with their body doused with oil. Each time she tried to sink her roots there, she was uprooted.

The three cows set off for Kalyani's desham in the mini-lorry. The oldest of them looked back at the house and sobbed. All three of them, after all, were eyewitnesses to the events of that night. When Cheyikkutty was descending into the well, the youngest of the three had wanted to waylay her, stop her. 'But none of this falls within the limits of our authority,' cautioned the older ones. 'All we have is a right to the knowledge that Cheyikkutty's hour had come. Make no moves on that basis of that right. Do not suppose that knowledge always empowers. It is knowledge that creates our greatest weaknesses.'

'That means?' The calf asked.

'In the olden days, our race too possessed much knowledge. We could speak human language. Some of our foremothers lived in the cowshed of a Brahmin.'

The older cow closed her eyes and began to tell the tale.

'Sensing that the brahmin's hour of death was near, she mentioned it to him. Each time the God of Death and Time, Kaalan, came, she would let the Brahmin know. The Brahmin would start praying to God Shiva, the Slayer of Death. Then Kaalan could come nowhere near. Kaalan's schedules began to go awry. Remember, the lack of coordination between different departments is not tolerated there. He is, obviously, a stickler for deadlines. What would happen if everyone decided to be so royally negligent? Kaalan was furious. He cursed us. We, who have so much knowledge, ended up and continue as four-legged creatures. All the things you know are not to be shared. The decorum that teaches you to keep some things to yourself is also a kind of knowledge. Just that some of us forget it again and again.'

The vehicle went over a pothole; the little calf got scared and hid under her mother's legs.

When Kalyani reached, her own house was steeped in a mighty silence. As she went back into the dark inside, she remembered Cheyikkutty, and for the first and last time, wept for her: 'But, but, my Amme, yuh wer' my home, my onnlly home' . . .'

61

There was a serious scuffle near the crossroad; it happened on the day Achooty Mash had a fall and sprained his back. Dakshayani had gone to meet Abubacker to ask if there was any chance of her getting a job at the plywood factory again. The loss of that job had affected her very badly. 'If I habe money, I can be worth sumthin' agai',' she told Abubacker. He wasn't very keen, but decided to take Dakshayani to meet Nambiar. If not here, then somewhere else, but meeting Nambiar was the only way. No one would dare refuse if Nambiar put in a word these days.

'Noth justh mine, Kalyani's sithuveshun is bad too.'

Dakshayani said that slowly, reluctantly, but looking at Abubacker with hope. With jobs, the two of them could still go together to political rallies and Nisha Talkies again. True—the cruel crushing wheels of society had rolled over their pasts and flattened them to the ground. So what? They had bounced back spunkier still. From now on, the actress Sarada's emotional outburst on the screen of Nisha Talkies: 'The husband's leftovers are not leftovers in the wife's eye, Chetaa, they are not leftovers!' would make them look at each other and lip-sync to their own line: '. . . they *are* leftovers in the wife's eye, Chetaa, they *are* leftovers!' When Balan told them, 'no nee' tto know wha' tha rally is abou', justh sthand in tha bekk', they will be able to shake their heads and say 'no, we're comin' onl' if we know wha' thi' is fer'.' The dawn can break only after the night. All this trouble now is the

mess that's to be expected when the night passes. It will pass.
Dakshayani was hopeful.

'Don'ddu worry, koche, aall thisu yis paartt of lifeu. The-yer
yis ye sayingg he-yer, about tha poo-ver nomaadd wimmin, the
kurathis. "Olly tha starving kurathi knows whe-yer to findd tha
thriving woodds". Sum haardshippu yis gooddu.'

Dakshayani often remembered Kunhippennu saying that, back
when she was struggling in Nailsvendor's house, not able to nail
herself anywhere there. And she reminded herself to tell Kalyani
this the next time they met. Dakshayani owed Kunhippennu some
debts she could never repay. This statement was one of those.

'If Kalyani gott a job, ith wud've bee' goodd . . .'

Abubacker had no objections about Kalyani.

'Bu' we canno' ask fer both of yuh now. Leth this requ'sth be
today's.' He said.

Dakshayani nodded, agreeing.

Kalyani's chances were weak. Because her uncles were
Congress people. Only Dakshayani was likely to be considered,
Abubacker let her know. Better be clear about things so that you
don't give false hope. Earlier, Dakshayani had just walked in there
and got a job. The factory was jointly owned by four or five people
and one of them was her brother Damu's friend. So being Damuettan's sister was her qualification. Now those four-five people
had no influence. Not just here, it was the same situation in the
cooperative society, the toddy shop and the glass factory. Things
have apparently become organized, controlled. Before, anyone
could enter or exit as they pleased; now there are some criteria
and it isn't a bad thing, Abubacker consoled himself. When it
came to appointing people, Nambiar's word was final. He might
ask, 'Yuh sur' she's bith us'? We don' habe to exp'cth no *koyappam*
or throuble from 'er?' Yes, that question may come. But it may
not, too.

'Yuh don' say muc' *barthamaanam* to him, alrighth? I will do
tha talkin'.'

Dakshayani thrilled in the anticipation of regaining the world which she had lost.

When they reached the crossroad, there was pushing and shoving going on under the flag mast. A crowd had collected. The red flag was stuck in the mud in a drainage channel nearby. Something flared up inside and singed Dakshayani's mind. The day she had fled Nailsvendor's house in the KSRTC big *aanavandi* bus rose up. She grew mellow in the memory of the red flags that had accompanied her on the roadside all the way to the railway station. Bending down, she pulled the flag out of the mud. Abubacker had got into the row. Dakshayani sat on the shop veranda until it was over and people had parted ways.

When Abubacker returned, brushing off the dirt from his body, Dakshayani held out the flag to him.

'Ith is muddi'd.'

'Neber min',' said Abubacker.

Balan said that after Nambiar began to lead the party, it had changed; it had a different feel. He already knew all about the clash when Abubacker mentioned it to him.

'Can'tmmanage any'more bithout' turnin'aroun' and givin' ith righth bekk to thei' faces . . .Fer sure, afther he took ober', we habe summore swagger!'

Achootty Mash rolled over on his cot with difficulty to face Balan, hearing him. He knew Nambiar from before. Nambiar's rise was rapid; his admirers grew by the day. He had a solution for any problem. Once you got to know him, you wouldn't think otherwise too. He was a crowd-puller. On the face of it, he seemed cool, quite placid. But he was everywhere.

'Justh hol' me, Balan,' Achootty Mash sat up and held his hand out to his son. His limbs were numb from not moving for a long time. Balan helped him sit up.

'Thath kin' of pipple are mor' bith them . . . nottbith us . . .' Achootty Mash would forget in between that he was no longer

Congress. That embarrassed Balan to no end. He had now to watch every word his father uttered.

'Yuh know sumthin'? EMS Nambutiripad, tha communisth, wa' speakin' at Payyanur. I wa' Congress, but I still wen' to hea' him speakk. Ooh tha crowddd! There wa' Shenoy, an' oth'rs too, as speak'rs. Nambiar wa' not so big thenn, but 'e wa' speakin' too. He came late', cam' afther setthling' sum labou' disputhe sumwhere. Yuh shud habe heardd tha applaus' whe' he climb'd up there! *Uyyentammo*! EMS had to stop speakin' fer a few minuthes! Really, ith's fromm then thath he becam' our leader 'ere.'

Achootty Mash emphasized the 'our' and looked at Balan. Balan did not say anything.

This was news to Abubacker. Someone shooting up so fast . . . no matter what great things he'd done . . . was no good, he thought.

'Why're lookin' at me lik' thath, *turu-turaa*?' asked Balan

'Pipple go an' see him fer thei' own bizness. Whe' he geths ith done fer them, won' they become clos' to him? Now, yuh too saw ith fith to see him fer Dakshayani? Tha's how pipple gro' big an' how the' are made big.'

Abubacker said that it wouldn't work unless he went; that's why he went. Achootty Mash was right. The applause is what mattered.

'An'way, ith's afther he came thath we began to gibe bekk lik' we gottith. Thass working fer us fer sure. Wha' nee's to be setthl'd bith blows shud be setthl'd bith blows!'

Balan turned to Achootty Mash. 'Enuf, lie dow'nnow. Yer bekk will swell up oth'rbise.'

'Bu' yuh really thin' there's nothin' wron' bith it, Bala?' Abubacker asked. 'Is ith okay thath we go round an' roun' justh one man?'

'Yuh say thath becos yuh don' know him yet.' Balan did not conceal his distaste.

'Yuh are from sumwhere else—came 'ere justh recenthly. We are all pipple from 'ere, *eeda thanna*. Yuh thin' thi' becos yuh don' know how sthuff wor's 'ere.'

Abubacker got up. The part of his life before he reached Kaisumma's house with his father from Mangalapuram was not included in his qualifying period. He had to prove himself as a true-blue local to be perceived as not horning in.

'Ther's lotts of pipple's sweath an' toil in setthin' up tha cooperative society . . . an' oth'r thin's too. Is ther' nothin' wron' in sthuffin' all of them bith yer own pipple? Thath's wha's throublin' me.' Achootty Mash aired his disquiet.

'How muc' of *yer* sweath an' toil, yuh tell me? An' eben if yer sweath is indee'there, it is all *our* sweath, of us all!! An' an'way, weren' yuh on tha oth'r side in those thimes?' Balan faced him spiritedly.

Abubacker stifled a laugh.

'Heardd?' Achootty Mash asked, 'Heardd him sthir things up?' He was angry. Huumph! Think of it! Having to convince this stripling of his loyalty! At his age! Indeed!

'Yuh lie there quiethy,' said Balan.

'Shud I come bith yuh?'

'No.'

Abubacker walked on.

62

Kalyani woke up hearing the cows shuffling uneasily in the cowshed in the middle of the night. The cowshed was a small one. The three cows she had brought from Koppu-man's house were also its residents now, besides her mother's cow. There were minor issues in the first few days between the local and the immigrants. Kalyani's mother's cow was somewhat more oriented towards worldly things, actually a committed materialist. She had great chemistry with Dakshayani's cows and prized her general knowledge—to lack that was to return to passive lying around and chewing the cud. When a vast yard lay open ahead of you, open and grassy, why crowd around the grass bucket? But the immigrants thought otherwise—whenever they had to pronounce an opinion, they referred to the Puranas. Whatever the topic may be, close your eyes solemnly, speak in a mystic tone, and your words would become authentic—so they believed. But the local declared there's no such thing as authenticity—and refused to be cowed down, shaking her horns and stomping on the ground.

'It is necessary at this point to alert Kalyani to the shadow that now creeps behind this cowshed. She needs to urgently shift the handle-less axe, the machete and the hoe from the corner of this cowshed to somewhere inside the house. There's a hammer lying under this heap of grass that went missing some time back, which Kalyani forgot about. We should tell her of it, too,' the local said local said, wobbling her nose.

'For what reason?' The immigrant cow asked, as though it were a trifle: 'That's their business—of human beings. We need to think of grass alone. It is not our concern what lies beneath the heap of grass. Such play of shadows is common near the houses of female humans who are young and without owners. Leave it to its natural course. In the Mahabharatha, the celestial damsel, the Apsara Panchachuda says some things about female human nature to Narada. Even remembering it makes you feel affronted.'

She shut her eyes and shook her head in disgust.

The local felt a rush of anger.

'I don't give a trifling blade of grass if it was Kalyani who willed this sneaky shadow-play or not. Before you came, I lived here alone. Four bulls have approached me till now. Though I was actually quite desperate, I thrust my horns at two of them and sent them packing. Haven't you heard—"The lazy bull bothers the cow"? I was bothered. I dismissed them summarily. Have been right here since; is there anything wrong with me? Did I lack visits from bulls? No! Another turned up the very next day! So leave aside this thing about 'natural course'. This is not it, for sure. This is not the time to shut your eyes and chomp up the Puranas to make mean insinuations!'

The immigrant cow now retched violently.

'Ayyoo . . . With whom has Kalyani lodged us? With a flighty *pumschali* who has exposed her buttocks to many capricious bulls who have lusted after multiple virgins? Ah! Woe is me!'

The local nearly laughed her head off.

'My dear friends, so you are very modern in such things. But allow me to say that your claim to modernity seems entwined with the most despicable traditionalism. Tell me just one thing. Was artificial insemination your choice, or was it foisted on you?'

The immigrants were now livid.

'Stop this nonsense!! Traditionalists have been, at all times, the most modern. What right do you have to question our fundamental right to receive superior semen to raise ourselves to the sublime state of the *veeraprasu*—The Valiant Procreatress? To keep away from risky bodily experimentation with sundry-motley *andan-adakodan* bulls?'

The local explained calmly. 'Who stopped you from becoming *veeraprasukkal*? I am just responding to the insult you flung at me. But I have two things to say. The first is important information. Next time they approach you with a syringe, remember it. The second is a sthory that is common around here. Just listen.'

The immigrants sank to the floor: ok, hell, say what you want and be over with it soonest.

'The Intensive Cattle Development Programme of the Kerala Government began in 1968 as part of the Intensive Cattle Development Project initiated by the Central government of India. Increasing the milk yield was a national policy goal. Hybrid cattle began to be introduced in India. Concerted efforts to develop animal husbandry in Kerala began during the First Five-Year Plan. It was then, in accordance with the Key Village Scheme, that arrangements for artificial insemination were first set up. So how were your progenitors getting things done? And your ancestral lineages before them? In Kerala, calling something "progress", after all, signifies the end of organic pleasures. No ideological differences about that. No difference between bovine and human either. Alright, let that be. You probably know that this semen stored is Jersey, Holstein. So what happens to our Thanku or Kunhappu? Middle finger in the mouth, right? The poor things! That so much is general knowledge. Now, the sthory. People here came to know of artificial insemination only rather recently. You all know of the practice of bringing the insemination centre to the cowshed instead of taking cows there. That's a recent one. Earlier, you had to go over there. There was a simpleton in these parts who was given the job of taking cows there. All the people saw was this: the cow went with him, it got pregnant. A newcomer around here who had just bought a cow heard of him and went to his house asking, "Isn't this the house

of the person who gets cows pregnant?" You can imagine the
rest. Maybe this story made up to make fun of outsiders—often
thought to be people who arrive here to break up local peace. Or
maybe the lesson of the sthory is, no matter how modern you
are, your letters always get delivered to the address of the old,
decrepit ways. As far as I am concerned, a bull is a bull. And a
syringe, a syringe. The truth is that you are all not very far from
that simpleton!

That's not the issue here. It was also not what I meant to say.
Do you know that the shadow that you saw creeping away from
here is that of a man who the police of Kannur, Kasaragod, and
Wayanad are searching for? Till now, he has clobbered six women
who lived alone on the head and raped them. Don't I have to tell
Kalyani of his visit? Or should I leave it to its 'natural course' and
chew the cud?'

The immigrants pondered the matter for some time.

'But really, not sure if we have the permission to interfere in
such matters. Our mandate is to lactate. This is the remit of the
dogs. You do not fall in that species, do you? Are you not a cow?'

The local stomped the ground.

'In some matters, I go beyond my jathi.'

She mooed the loudest she could, twisting her neck. And then
bellowed, '*Ambe, Ambe* . . .' her voice broke in two places.

'Kickin' dow' tha cowshe' eh?' Kalyani shoved open the
window and peered into the cowshed. 'Wha's yer probl'm, yuh
daughthe' of a dog?'

63

'Tha tapioca'll be abouth fivbe kilos, thath'll do?'

Kalyani asked as she scraped the coconut. After the tapioca was cooked to a creamy softness, the mustard seeds had to be crackled in hot coconut oil along with bits of chilli, crushed garlic and curry leaves. Then the cooked tapioca had to be added, and mixed well with the spices and leaves in the simmering oil. Fresh scraped coconut had to be added and everything sautéed well. It would be served on broad green *uppila* leaves to the men of the search squad. The jaggery-coffee was already boiling on the fire.

'Is this enuf, Kalyani-echi?' asked the youngest of the lot. 'Nottmmany of us, an'way? An', I've put tha uppila leabes 'ere. Yuh ca' do tha serbin' now.'

He's been going back and forth right in front of where Kalyani sat on the floor scraping the coconut, his leg almost going over her. She had to make way, holding back her body. It was irritating.

'If yuh've broughth tha leabes, then starth serbin' yerselves? Why shud I do ith fer yuh? Am I yer serbant?' She retorted.

The boy, a mere *chekkan*, a stripling that is, came close to her and whispered in her ear: 'If yuh don' bant to do *ith* fer me, tha's ok. Wha' if I do *ith* fer yuh?'

Kalyani flung the coconut shell she held forcefully at his leg and leapt up.

'Sonofadirtydog!! Firsth, lear' to piss prope'ly, bithout wettin' yer slipper, okay? Thenn come to do *ith* fer Kalyani!'

Balan and Abubacker ran up.

'Wha'? Wha'?'

'Nothin', he's dyin' to do *ith* fer me.'

Balan whacked the chekkan on the head and pushed him hard on his shoulders.

'If yer comin' bith tha squa' fer thi' kinddo'tthing, then don' ccome, uh? Oth'r pipple can'tt take responsib'l'ty! Thi' is not allow'd 'ere.'

'One man is goin' aroun' getthin' into 'ouses an' knockin' pipple dea' at nighth ; all these folk are nott closin' thei' eyes eben a bith, watchin' an' runnin' aroun'? An' wha' are yuh up to?'

Abubacker threw up his hands. 'Habe to habe sum grathitude? Some *mur'ma*?'

The whole desham was sleepless. Supper for the search squad was prepared in different homes each evening. All the men would make rounds with torches and knives and sticks. They were doing this on orders from above. The desham was all obedience. Fear was in everyone. Wariness of strangers lurking around at unreasonable hours was now almost a necessity. Groups of three or four men would go to each house to keep watch. The scared family was relieved by their presence. Every house and premise was under surveillance. Balan suggested that women who lived alone should sleep at the neighbours' homes. Let the cows and dogs remain. Many did not obey. Kalyani would shut the main door and pull a table near it. She would then stack some unbreakable pots and pans on it. If anyone pushed the door, the table would shake and the vessels would fall. The machete was under her pillow. Forgetting that her sister had taken Amma to live with her, she would shout now and then, 'Amme, you don' be getthin' ou' of tha 'ouse.' She would look anxiously at the fourth-standard student asleep beside her. She had seen that dream two or three times. The three-legged table and the vessels falling with a clatter. Her head being shattered even before she could rise from the bed. The nine-year-old running out, screaming, through the open door, with the shadow brandishing an axe in hot pursuit. Kalyani would jolt awake with a cry. By the time she noticed that the table and the vessels were intact, she would be soaked in sweat like she had taken a dip. If she did agree to go sleep somewhere else, she would have to be back early at dawn to milk the cows. The house was scarier then—what if it had hidden someone inside? Houses are places to which you can't return once you exit. Just like we don't believe in them, they too start disbelieving you, by and by. It was better to die with the house falling on the top of your head rather than live in a state of perpetual disbelief.

After the squads started making the rounds, the fear began to thin. There was the comforting sense of having someone within shouting distance. Though they did not pay her, Kalyani took over the job of cooking for them. Balan or Abubacker would bring the provisions. The fact that Bijumon was very fond of jaggery-coffee and creamy cooked tapioca, was also a strong incentive. He ate millet-flour upma for lunch at school every day. Kalyani knew how to make that, too. Nambiar had persuaded the school manager to let her join as one of the school noon-meal cooks. Though she couldn't go with Dakshayani to the plywood factory, life dragged her along too as it flew ahead. She did not care anymore that it dragged her through thorns or stones. Or that it cut her red and bruised her blue. If it was alright to go with the flow and if she didn't have to rack her brains over it, it was alright, wasn't it? But she was beginning to feel now that in general, she had a bad image. If not, would a mere stripling, who didn't even have a moustache, dare to hitch up his mundu and try to raise his leg over her again and again? But for now she had no other option but to ignore such things.

'Di' yuh hea'? Tha Taliparamba polic' achually caugh' him, they're sayin'.' Dakshayani told her. Kalyani felt sorry that the evening tapioca parties will cease now.

'So soo'?' She blurted that out without thinking.

The crowd, the bustle, the scents of tapioca getting cooked, the jaggery boiling . . . When these ended, Kalyani's life too would become still and stagnant.

'Why're yuh sad about thath?' Dakshayani was surprised. She also had something else to tell Kalyani. 'Yuh know? Damuettan saw tha pole-legg'd man, when he wen' bith tha squad!'

'Pole-legg'd man? Wha's thath?'

'No legs. Justh two bamboo poles! A man on thop, walkin' shak'ly.'

'*Uyi*! Ann'?'

'An' they all ranawway, screamin', wha' else?'

'Fer thath, do they belieb in crazy stories like tha pole-man? Wha's tha pole man to these pipple who don' belieb in God? And, ah, aren' they out to catc' tha Ripperr? So shud they runnawway all scar'd lik' thi'?'

'Ripperr is 'uman, no? Won' he listhen? Pole-man won' be lik' thath?'

'Listhen? Tha Ripperr?'

'Ah, an'way he's caugh'. Ith's finish'd.'

But before she reached home, Dakshayani had to turn and rush right back to Kalyani. Seeing Balan come up with the tapioca, she told him of what she'd heard. He gave her an earful.

'Yuh're goin' abou' sayin' half-bak'd things? Yes, they caught tha Ripperr and pu' him in tha lockup too. Bu'tthen ther' wasn' space enuf to lock up pipple from sum protesth-dharna. So they leth off eberyone who was in tha lockup. He escap'd an' kilt anoth'r womin yestherday too.'

'*Uyyente Muthappa* . . !' Dakshayani cried, evoking her favorite deity fervently.

Balan said sternly.

'Yes, yes, call him bery loudly. He's goin' to tha Muthappan's themple eachthime—afther he kilt tha womin. Tha polic' says, leth us searc' there now.'

'Who's goin' to belibe wha' tha polic' says now? They got him inside thei' fisth and then leth him go! Alla, wha' to say, puttin' in jail pipple goin' to tha protesth-*jaatha*, and letthin' out tha killin' man! Tha jaatha is a bigccrime' now? Whennddid *thath* happ'n?'

Dakshayani struggled to understand. Is the police getting fooled the same as people getting fooled? But much more than that, it was the news of the killer's proximity to Muthappan that left her deflated. Balan described how he came to pray at the Muthappan's Madappura after each murder. She stared blankly at Balan as though trying to process the news that someone closest to her had crossed over into the murky terrain of betrayal. 'At tha Muthappan's?' She repeated.

'Neber min'. He won' come eeda. We're all bee' aroun' here fer so lon'? There was nothin' to worry, achually. When they said, mak' a squad, we did ith, thath's all,' he comforted her.

Then he turned his head sharply and laughed.

'And becos we walk'd aroun' all nighth, we now know abou' lo's of pipple. Thath's a goodd thing!'

'*Uyi*, wha's thath fer?' Dakshayani did not understand.

'There are pipple here, uh, who don' sleep bhere they shud . . . and sum who change 'ouses at nighth! We won' do annytthing now. Tomorro' these chaps will come askin' fer sumthin'. Then leth's see. Leddthis geth ober. We'll stick tha posthers.'

That night the first attack on the desham happened, right under the nose of the night-watch squads.

64

Kunhappettan could remember nothing. Narayani-echi had a vague memory of seeing, half-asleep, a short form looming at her bedside. Because Kunhappettan was late to come home that night after shutting the shop, she had gone to bed late. All the windows and doors had been bolted from inside, too. When she saw the shadow beside her cot, she reckoned that it was Kunhappettan going to take a leak, or coming back after. There was no time to know more. Memories banged against something hard and were shattered. She quaked and shivered with every word. Her speech broke in many places, sometimes descending into a low hiss. The locals began to take relief: now that this fellow had laid his hands on Muthappan's realm, his days are numbered. His praying and making vows are all good, but no way will Muthappan, the Lord of this realm, forgive him! If you turn the yielding earth into an abyss, the Gods will not forgive you.

Though Kunhappettan and his womin escaped death, fear surged through the desham's veins. Someone was keeping them sleepless, getting past all the circles of protection. The looming image of an assassin with a weapon who may appear anywhere, anytime, made the entire desham shiver with fright. The locals began to look for magic wands to exorcise the evil. Iron bars were set on doors and windows. The squads went around houses warning people not to step out at night, whatever they may hear outside. Even policemen were afraid to leave their wives alone in their houses. Abubacker felt worried for Kalyani and Biju, who lived by themselves. But when he aired his fears a few times, Balan glared at him.

'There are many suchhouses lik' thath eeda, eh? Noth justh Kalyani's. Don' geth into a mess, eh?'

Abubacker shut up after that. Balan always drew a straight line and travelled scrupulously on it. His sense of the right and wrong was guided fully by orders from above. If the party ordered him to love, he would rend his heart and plunge into love. If it ordered him to hate, he would do that with the same intensity. Balan who used to be a staunch admirer of Nambiar, seemed to be slowly distancing himself now. Feudal posturing fetches you popularity, and that's really no big deal—this was what he thought now. He had also started declaring openly that political parties should not endorse positions just because they are popular. He was one among the many who held that view. But even in the middle of such disagreements and tensions, he and all the others gathered in cashew groves, teashops, and temple festival grounds to discuss how they could help the authorities to catch the killer. Some of the youngsters dreamed of felling him single-handedly. Because they did not really know what weapon he wielded, that part of the dream in which the villain is deprived of his tool couldn't be as colourful as it could have been. Except for that tiny snag, it was a perfectly enjoyable dream. These young men did not join the squads, though. Catching the Ripper, intervening in property disputes, facilitating love marriages—they believed that political parties should not get involved in such things. Local history tells us that many of these local-dreamer-notables later became political observers or theoreticians, who are of course, much needed.

Balan and his squad were supposed to watch the area stretching from Kundathil Ukkni's house to Govindettan's house. Kalyani's house was in another area, and was allotted to another squad. Abubacker was supposed to join it. But he had excused himself beforehand that day, being rather busy since morning. The police and the finger-print experts had come to Kunhapettan's house to record their statements and to look for finger prints. There had to be someone there to lend them a hand. Two or three capable people had to be sent to help out at the hospital, too.

This was the first time a police dog was setting foot on the desham. The desham opened its eyes wide and looked. There were dogs everywhere there. But the trees and soil and the humans of the desham were seeing one of this kind for the first time. First, she raised her front legs, fixed them on the back door of the jeep, and sharpened her ears. Then lifted her nose, sneezed away all the scents present in it and got ready to receive new ones. Scanning the premises with a single haughty look, she leapt out of the vehicle and trotted ahead briskly. The dogs who were standing around watching her, found it simply too much.

'Oh! Lookkit her nerbe!'

'Just an old police jeep, not an Impala car! And maybe she's in the police, but she no man, eh?'

One of these chaps was especially aroused; he lifted his leg under the electric post.

'Turnnaroun' an' show her tha mark und'r yer tail, eda. Don' leth her geth too gutsy!'

He barked to his friends and they obeyed.

But the police canine continued her work calmly, paying no attention. He realized that his mistake was to underestimate the females of his kind. When he also remembered that actually, these girls pay attention only to the tail and not to what's beneath them, the dog felt utterly undone. Sick of heart, he decided to set out on a long journey—that very instant.

After the police dog returned, Abubacker went back to the hospital. But he had not forgotten the evening meals to be served to the night-watch squads. He had to make arrangements.

The night-watch squads dived slowly into the darkness of the night. They, too, were afraid. Balan had given firm orders that no member of the squad was to get stranded during the patrolling. Before hiding somewhere, pay close attention to the surroundings.

'Don' go aroun' in circl's, okay? And don' play foolish games an' endupp in fronth of him an' bow yer headd to him,' He scolded the overenthusiastic.

Standing at the turn of the panchayat road, you can see Kalyani's house. The squad stood for some time near the road, looking at the house which was steeped in the dark.

'Leth's go there too. Why leabe ith afther comin' so far?' said Balan.

They entered the yard and began to search each corner. When they neared the cowshed, the cows woke up rudely. They peeked out.

'Oh, the squad.' The local said.

'Bodyguards.' The immigrant took relief.

When the group was about to leave through the other side of the yard circling the house, the chekkan at whom Kalyani had thrown the coconut shell crept up to Balan and poked him. Balan jumped.

'Wha's ith, eda?

He swallowed the question. 'Yuh're scarin' pipple?'

'Baletta, come 'ere. Lemme show yuh sumthin'.' The boy called him in a low voice.

Anxious, Balan and the rest of the group followed him. The boy pointed his torch at the stepping stone to Kalyani's house. The group peeled their eyes and leaned towards the sight.

'Wha'? Snak'?'

Someone asked. Balan too thought that something was coiled there, something light brown in colour. Rubbing his eyes and poking it with his staff, he could make out that it was not soft but quite solid and firm. What was it? The news that the Ripper had left an empty liquor bottle in the house where he murdered last flashed through Balan's mind. But this was not a bottle.

Chekkan took the stick and pushed the thing forward. Two or three torches now flashed and it was clearly visible now. Two sandals, yellowish brown in colour, of the type that nearly covered the whole foot.

A squeal of pretended surprise arose from the chekkan's throat. 'Men's sandals!'

65

'Oh, bu' sthill my dear . . . wha' an sthupid thin' to do!'

Dakshayani slapped her head in dismay. Kalyani had nothing to say. Admitting defeat for the first time in her life, she sat on the veranda, hand on chin, glum, bereft of words. The hens were pecking at the paddy left to dry in the yard, but she didn't care. Let them peck. Let them take away everything. Who cared!

It was from Dakshayani that she got a fair idea of the biggest blunder of her whole life.

'If yuh catc' tha creeper an' gibe ith a hardd shake, won' tha whol' plant also shak'? I wudn' feel so badd if ith wer' sumone else who mad' this blunderr . . . bu' ith's yuh!' Dakshayani said sharply.

Kalyani was at the brink of tears. 'Wha' to do now, Daachani?'

Dakshayani did not have much of an idea about what to do. It was Balan who described it to her in detail. He had instantly recognized whose sandals they were. There were after all not many in the desham who wore sandals of this sort. But because he did not favour a discussion in public, he had to close many mouths. He had warned the man earlier when he took rather too much interest in Kalyani. But he had not known that it was moving to such a climax. Not sure if even the youngest hairless chaps will give him any respect now. Anyway, it is a blow; one can't justify this sort of thing. But more importantly, what's going to happen to the relationship between the two families? And not to speak of the stories that will sprout and spread all over the ground in no time! Whatever, Dakshayani must have a word with Kalyani. One can see what's going on with her, but such things can't be allowed here. Kalyani was a wet piece of wood. Most vulnerable to termites. It's her responsibility to be careful.

Hearing that made the entire skin on Dakshayani's body crawl. She even peed a bit, so jittery she was. At first, she thought of not mentioning anything to Kalyani. Then she felt that it was unfair to push her into a public trial totally unprepared. Such things, you have to deal with all by yourself. Even your own shadow might cite a rule and appear there to testify against you. So wasn't it wiser to be prepared? That's why she went over to meet her. Kalyani had just returned home after the upma-cooking at the school. She served her a little from what she had brought back home in a bowl. The story of the sandal got stuck in Dakshayani's throat along with the millet-flour-upma. But she could not hold it back; so she laid it out before her somehow, hemming and hawing all the while. And listening to her side, Dakshayani had nothing to do but beat her own head in despair.

When she was a child, Kalyani had seen her mother pick up her oldest uncle's sandals and put them on the stepping stone to the house before shutting the main door at night; or throw an man's unused mundu on the clothesline behind the house. Sometimes she made Kalyani do it. She used to be perturbed by the sounds outside that seemingly no one else heard, and by the swirls of beedi-smoke that rose around there at night. Mother and daughter believed that none of it could cross the magic circle cast by the presence of those sandals. And nothing did come in. In a critical moment, our precious rules and principles, the stuff we badly want to apply in life, may not come handy at all. Our fate and that of others may be determined by the memory of a song heard long back and forgotten, or a story long dissolved in the memory. The machete may be ready under the pillow; but it may be the candle-stand that you grab. That's what happened to Kalyani in the sandals affair.

'An' now a fin' mess, no, Daachani?' She looked bleakly at Dakshayani.

'Don' yuh know tha pipple of thisplace? Will they leth yuh an' Bijumon be?' She did not conceal her worry.

'Wha' if I go telltthem?' Kalyani knew that she was asking an irrational question; she still asked.

'Yuh're daft or wha'? Dakshayani growled. 'Tell who? To all tha pipple 'ere? Alrighth, leth thath be—tell wha'? Thath Abu-kka didn' come, didn' come fer *thath*? Ah, thath's goin' to be clea'!'

'Bu'then he neber came. Isn' tha' tha truth?'

'Who wan's to know tha truth? Mosth pipple justh beliebe wha' they hear firsth. Nommatth'r how muc' yuh clearrup an' change afther, not eben half tha pipple will beliebe. So don' mak' thath missthake.'

That convinced Kalyani. But she still wanted to meet Abubacker soonest. She had a reason, at least, to offer and hold on to. He, however, may not even be aware of what was happening around him.

'Goo'nness knows wha' knott'd-up thing made yuh feel lik' doin' thath then!'

Suddenly, Kalyani felt that she would not have stooped so low if Bijumon was not with her. Swimming while you hold up someone who didn't know how to swim wasn't the same as swimming alone. Especially when he was someone who probably hadn't even thought of getting into the water. Dakshayani thought the same when she left; she was still uneasy. Shouldn't have done it. But there are indeed moments in which people give themselves up to be sacrificed. It is when they realize that their sacrifice was for nothing, that they freeze up forever. And if she never erred, Kalyani could not be human.

'She too's huma', *appa*, mebbe she thought of tha child . . .' Dakshayani calmed herself.

'So, how did things work out, finally?' The immigrant cow smirked, turning to the local.

'It is natural that a person errs.' The local replied coolly.

'You have no idea how important a symbol the sandal is. There's a story about that. But what's the use of telling you? You do it openly, in broad daylight!' The migrant cow crinkled her nose. And made sure that the calf wasn't paying attention. The local stopped chomping the hay and sharpened her ears.

'In the old days, when the Pandavas took turns with Panchali, they would leave their sandals outside the door. If the sandals were found outside Panchali's room, then it meant that she wasn't alone. Once, when Yudhishtira was with Panchali, Arjuna came into the room. He regretted that he did not notice the sandal outside the room. Later, it was found that a dog had dragged it away somewhere. Yudhishtira cursed the dog who had brought shame on him, that the species would forever do it in public. That's how the dogs began to do it in the open. This sandal is no simple object . . .'

The local laughed.

'You cowladies are impossible! Where are you going, I wonder, reeling off quote after quote? The story that I heard is quite different: that he cursed the dog that its pleasure would be interrupted always, like his had been. Whatever, humans make the curse true all the time. See two dogs come together, and their hands pick up the stone . . . but before that, a query. Before the curse, did dogs do it in secluded rooms? What about other animals? Why not *think* a little, sister?'

'As they say, "*samshayaatmaa vinashyati!*" Doubts are accursed! Your time is near. Do not think like this ever!' The immigrant cow turned her face away sharply.

'Never mind', said the local, quoting Voltaire in English: 'haven't you heard, "Think for yourself and let others enjoy the privilege of doing so" or something like that?'

The local bent her neck into the grass-bucket.

The ground seemed to be caving in at each step Abubacker took. But he did not bother to explain to anyone. When Kalyani came to see him, he met her quite normally.

'I shud've tol' yuh of ith befor', Abu-kka,' she said, remorsefully. 'I'll com' and tell them tha truth, an' bherever yuh bant.' She looked at him beseechingly.

'Yuh be sthill, Kalyani. Bhere yuh goin' to come an' say? Pipple will say thath they beliebed an' then will laug' at tha bekk. Lethithbbe. It's ober. Lethithggo.'

Though the sandals that appeared on Kalyani's stepping stone blighted Abubacker's political future forever, in his family, he was secure. Because these were the sandals that Kaisumma herself had brought Kalyani when she had requested her, and these were handed over to Kaisumma by none other than Abubacker's Ayisha, who told her, 'Yuh can gibe thi' to her, Elayumma—to put on tha sthepping-sthone. She ask'd yuh, didn' she? Thi' pair we don' need annymore—we got a new one.'

'If yuh bant, I'llggo spea' to tha Party pipple?' Ayisha asked Abubacker, feeling guilty.

'Wha'?'

'Is ith true? Thath yuh'll be senthout of tha party?'

'Nottpposs'ble to throw out summone lik' thath.'

Abubacker had a general idea of the complaints that had been raised against him; Balan had told him. He had actually seen it coming. But Kalyani's unexpected intervention sped up things a bit. Couldn't blame her for it, really. So easy to serve up a semblance of idealism and bravado! Life within is a different game. You can't predict how someone will behave in any particular circumstance. You can't judge someone on the basis of their prior history, assuming it to be completely transparent. And it is equally foolish to expect them to conform perfectly to the expectations of others. Humans are the masters of unpredictability.

Abubacker sat on the half-wall of the veranda of his house after a long time, unburdened by hurry, stretching his legs out.

Because he always used footwear that covered his feet, they were bright and unblemished. Seeing him still brooding, Ayisha was at a loss. She went closer to him and said, as though to console him, 'Insthead of tha fasshion sandal if onlly yuh'd worn tha orthinary rubb'r slipp'r? Will thi' troubl' habe happen'd?'

66

The police soon captured the Ripper but something happened so unexpectedly, the desham was numb and totally afflicted by uncertainty. Its tallest leader disappeared one fine day. The people's man, dynamic Nambiar, threw off the Party and strode away. People were disoriented as though dumped in the middle of the road at midnight. The desham felt like a post-wedding house from where the bride had run away.

How long can it stay that way? A blow on the head can't keep us down forever, Balan declared. There are many other things to care about. Protests are not relevant. They weren't necessary right now, either. But any weapon, if you let it idle for too long, will rust. Are people short of problems? For those who are busy trying to get people's problems resolved, where's the time to be idle? However, leaders should be clean. They should not secure their own interests behind the veil of public activism. For example, they should not enter houses where women live alone, leaving their shoes outside. A responsible public worker should maintain a clear distance from women. Even murder has a tiny bit of dignity. But getting caught in a *pennucase*, womincase, a sex-scandal, that is, will affect even your future generations. So what to say about a political movement? Balan's words were spiked amply with nails and thorns. Abubacker was a rising leader, he admitted. But he was not able to maintain purity in personal life.

And there is something even more serious. He belongs to a family that was settled in Mangalapuram for many years as merchants. They appeared here one fine morning and settled down. His antecedents must have been, therefore, thoroughly checked before he was allowed entry and granted responsibilities. That this was not done was indeed a mistake. If mistakes are noticed, then it behooves people and political movements to correct them immediately. Abubacker need not take up any critical responsibility for the time being. He need not air his opinions, either. But explanations are due from him regarding certain vital issues. These are listed below:

Kaisumma's house and the thirty cents of land on which it stands are the hard-earned fruit of the sweat and blood and tears of her husband who slaved in Saudi Arabia for many, many years. What right did Abubacker's father have over it? On what basis were Kaisumma and her daughter Nebisu evicted?

Nebisu is the daughter of Abubacker's senior uncle on his father's side—his *Vallippa*. Can Abubacker dissociate himself from the moral guilt of dispossessing her, a fatherless orphan, by marrying her off to some rogue from Mangalapuram and thus disfiguring her life?

When Nebisu returned after being divorced, did Abubacker have even have a chat with her bridegroom's family about returning her gold ornaments or paying her maintenance? Did he at least try to find out what happened?

Wouldn't it have been proper and dignified for Abubacker and his family to hand over the house and property to Kaisumma and Nebisu, and either move back to Mangalapuram, or buy some other land, build a new house, and settle there?

Does Abubacker feel no prick of conscience at all in making a senior lady and her daughter live in a cramped shed which was constructed before the house itself in order to secure the electricity connection?

Nebisu has been working in two houses as an *ayah* to the children there. Has Abubacker inquired how she was living in these places?

Now it is said that she is abroad with some man from Bombay (or a Bangladeshi, some say). She is reportedly taking care of his bedridden wife. Given that she has an income to be self-sufficient, what is the logic behind Abubacker's demand that a public subscription should be raised to build her a house?

When the list of local people with no land or house in their name was prepared, Kaisumma's name did not figure. How come it appeared in the higher committee's list?

Political positions need to be beyond friendships and relationships. Nothing should be in contradiction with the party's policies. Handing over welfare benefits to one's own people without adhering to rules and principles of justice is not right. Is it a good precedent to report against colleagues who point this out to the higher committee? Is it right to distrust them?

What is Abubacker's relationship with Kalyani?

Abubacker looked around calmly. All the faces in the room looked tightly wound-up—not a single one bore a relaxed expression. The ten questions scampered around the room, carrying many sub-questions by their teeth. How to begin—he had no idea. He was sure that the answers to many of these were simply no, no, no, yes, yes. But they expected more than one-word answers. An intelligent student knows the future the moment they see the question paper. Sometimes, intelligent questions, not answers, will be remembered. But Abubacker approached each question with utmost honesty. He was hurt, however, when he saw distrust cloud Balan's face. How easily human beings fall out! The closer you are, the more it hurt. It was their friendship— that went back to time he'd just settled down here after coming away from Mangalapuram—that had just hung itself on the upper storey of Achootty Mash's building. Right in the middle of the

R. Rajasree

circle of red-coloured chairs that lay on the veranda reached by the wooden staircase.

'I don'ttkknow if I can answer all thes' at one go.' Abubacker began in a low pitch. 'I don'ttkknow if yuh'll be sathisfied by ith. I'll say wha' I can. Tha resth yuh can ask tha *khatib*. Thenn yer doub's will be clear'd.'

Balan let him know that they had thought of meeting the khatib; he did not raise his eyes to Abubacker's face. Some of these questions can be answered by Abubacker, let them be dealt with first.

When he began saying that his father's business in Mangalapuram was also in sandals, there was a titter to be heard all around the circle. But it did not lighten the atmosphere. The heaviness hung about the place like salty breeze.

67

The khatib had gone out. He'd said that he'll come by on the way back. He didn't feel anything wrong in that. The khatib, after all, wasn't bigger than *Padachavan*, the Creator, Allah. He may have also thought that it was better to avoid all these men charging into the mosque. Even if we are to go there, who all are to go?' Balan asked them. Let everyone know how things are. Some things are like the goo of jackfruit. Won't kill you, but will bug you endlessly. Yes, coconut oil will loosen it. But you'll need to literally douse yourself with coconut oil, so much of it that the oil will giggle and slip down your body playfully! And then you have to work hard at washing it off. These are the places where you need problem-centred approaches. You need reason and logic there. Having a clear idea about the key issues that need the intervention of individuals, political movements, or deshams will be useful for another day, too.

The fire and smoke over letting Gopalan Mash's daughter go and live with the man she fell in love with, was yet to abate. That was an inter-caste thing. Actually, it was hoped that she could be shrewdly persuaded not to leave, but it was like a blow in the dark! Her father yelled that she received foreign aid! As if that wasn't enough, they conducted the wedding, fed the locals with cups of Horlicks, and took the bride away, right in front of his eyes.

'An' eben otherbise, wheneber yuh hea' thath two pipple are in luv, ith's *yer* thing to pus' tha two into a weddin'!' Gopalan Mash had bellowed. The barking and screaming in Mash's house was bad enough to make Balan and friends decide then and there that they should stop getting into this kind of scrape. After that, they were careful in dealing with such pickles.

'Ith shudn'bbe thath we summon'd yuh here . . . in tha end ...'
Balan told the khatib.

'No, *edo*. Won' ith be enuf if I com' here on my way bekk?'
The khatib frowned. 'Wha's thi'? Aren' we all huma'?'

'Justh to avoi' troubl' . . .' Balan looked mortified.

The khatib was a portly man, very calm, serene. He climbed the staircase with difficulty, panting. He looked at the group assembled there. Balan parked his bicycle and followed him. Abubacker got up and salaamed him. When he returned the salaam, there was perceptible amazement on his face. Drawing Abubacker into a corner, he asked, nervously, 'There's no *koyappam*, eh? No throubl'?'

'Wha' koyappam, khatibe? Ou' histhory is thath of guardin' all mosques fromm Pinarayi to Peringadi to sthop tha koyappam. Tho' ith is six'een yea's bekk, histhory is histhory, no? Pleas' sith dow',' Balan said, following the khatib and pulling a chair for him.

'Balan's bee' studyin' histhory bery nic'ly nowwadays,' Abubacker laughed.

'Thath's bery need'd. Habe to sthandup to those who'll turn againsth yuh tha nexth day?'

Balan's words did not have even a trace of warmth. He moved towards his chair.

Abubacker was wordless. He saw in a flash that even if acquitted, Balan's friendship will never be his again. He had presented his explanations, answering many of the ten questions. He had admitted that he had great guilt about Kaisumma and Nebisu. Each time he saw Kaisumma, his heart pounded with remorse—it was a human heart, after all. Her ear lobes on which so many little golden *alikkaths* fluttered once, are now bare and full of holes. She doesn't accept any clothes he bought her; just washes the old ones and wears them again. She says that she wants only what Nebisu brings her. She refuses all food cooked in his house. The shed has a hearth and a kerosene stove. She cooks there. When he passed by, Abubacker's heart would bleed seeing her clean some sardines, just four or five. She even refused the ghee rice Ayisha packed for her on Id.

'Whe' my girl is eathing tha leav'ngs of oth'rs, goo'ness knowssbhere, thi' won'ggo dow' my throat, dear,' she told Ayisha. Ayisha wept when she reported this.

When the Ripper trouble started, Abubacker had shifted her forcibly to the new house, despite his parents' strong objections.

'Remembe' *elappa*,' he said, remembering his uncle and reminding his father of his younger brother who had worked to his bone in Saudi to amass this property. 'All of thi' is elappa's hardd work.'

If Nebisu returns, Kaisumma will move back that instant; I won't let her be alone there in these awful times, Abubacker insisted. At first, Kaisumma resisted. She had surrendered to fate. She felt no vengefulness, she said. Nebisu's father was ordered by the Creator to work hard in a foreign land till his death. The knowledge that nothing that he earned was to be of use to her or their daughter, was now not as painful as it used to be.

Abubacker carried away Kaisumma's clothes-box and placed it in what used to be her room on the better side of the house. When she stepped into the room which she used to share with her husband, Kaisumma's eyes moistened. When Abubacker's Uppa said that the old part of the house, including the shed where Kaisumma lived, should be renovated and joined with the new house, Abubacker opposed his father. That may improve the house, but gradually, they would eject Kaisumma for sure.

'Wha'eber, leth her sthay here till all of thi' is ober.' He pronounced the final verdict. And Kaisumma stayed there. But Abubacker always felt that she was living on thorns. Whenever she saw him, she would ask, 'Di'tthey catc' him, kunhi?'

'Wha's tha hurry, Elayumma? Enuf to catchhim slow'y?'

'Alla, if he wer' caugh', I cud moobe bekk . . .'

'Eben if tha Ripperr's caugh', yuh musth sthay here . . .'

'No, kunhi. I'll die of a heaby heart . . .'

'I'll mak' sure no one here is rude to yuh.'

'No, kunhi, I justh bant to see my girl onc' . . . justh to libe bith 'er.'

Abubacker would smouldered in sheer helplessness.

For that, where was Nebisu now?

Whenever he remembered that they could have been fairer to her, he felt a rage towards his father. The uselessness of arguing with a man who could not be fair even towards his own children had been evident to him many times now. Though he had stopped talking to him except at unavoidable moments, Abubacker had stooped very low before his father for Nebisu. He couldn't remember when they had stopped talking. Abubacker believed that all fathers of that time were like this. These men treated their sons like pressure valves to let out the resentment and anger they felt towards the world for reasons unknown, which they could not openly vent otherwise. The result was that they raised an Opposition in the family-space, for no good reason at all. And when the children flew away to roost elsewhere, these fathers yearned fruitlessly to pull them back close. That was Abubacker's father. Because he had no influence at all on his father, Abubacker was powerless regarding Nebisu's marriage. Abubacker's father still believed that the bridegroom that some acquaintance of his back in Mangalapuram had brought for Nebisu was a perfect match. He was sceptical about the story of the talaq. She had surely jumped the fence because she couldn't bother to be quiet and obedient there. Weren't Kaisumma and her daughter living a life of ease, squandering the wealth that his younger brother was amassing in Saudi by dint of sweat and tears? Too much of food; all sorts of rich clothes. Baby-food made for Nebisu would even be shared with even the neighbour's girl, Kalyani. Ah, let that be. Do not spend too much on that which will eventually tear and stink. Don't coddle girls too much. What need do two women have for so much wealth, why do they have to manage it themselves?

Once Nebisu shifts to Mangalapuram, won't Kaisumma be by herself? That can't be allowed. Her husband has five brothers, counting me. Only Nebisu's father was gone. She's not to live as she likes, that's certain. This is the only way it can be. It's the right thing to do.

Abubacker knew that there were limits to how much one can fight in a generational clash. The old ones built their own world. That world moves according to their laws. Better than try to change it, walk away while staying close to its borders. It was not easy for Abubacker to control his father in the way Balan controlled his bedridden father. The truth was that he could not control anyone. Some people are like that. They may look as expansive as the sky. But their roots will stay shallow. It is the softwood that predominates in them, not the hardwood. The world will revolve around them only for a very short while, but they won't even notice that it has passed them by. Later, they will be mounted on walls and will figure in books, and from there, they will learn that life goes on as briskly as ever even without them. We remember them for the words they did not say, the decisions they did not take.

68

One share along with that of all the men in the family, but half of what a man gets: that's the law of Islam for women. True, all the wealth was earned by Nebisu's father. That everyone knows. 'But the law is like this: I have no more to say,' said the khatib. There is no lapse on the side of Abubacker's father on this matter. All of Nebisu's father's brothers have male children. Once they receive their shares, she gets nearly nothing. The property had now very many heirs. For Kaisumma and Nebisu to build a house, all of these heirs will have to sell their shares to raise the money. That's not even a possibility. Anyway, with so many heirs, the women will have only a few cents. That was useless.

'I can gibe up my shar', but thath too won' be enuf . . .' Abubacker said.

He had by then realized how the very things that he had himself started were now turning against him. He had made many miscalculations. He had tried to secure a house for Kaisumma because she was alone and destitute, but he hadn't foreseen that someone would question his intentions as she was his close relative. The tree there was a coconut tree, but he tried to climb it with a *talapp* rope harness fit for an areca palm!

The khatib said that it may be wiser not to sell the house.

'Bhere's she now? No news afther she wen' to Saudi?' The khatib looked at Abubacker.

'She'd firsth sai' tha' she's working in an ayurbedic hospithal. Thath we tri'd to fin'out. We *habe* to fin'out, we habe to! It wassafther thath' she lefth bith tha man. Befor' thath, she work'd in two 'ouses, they say.' Balan intervened forcefully.

Abubacker did not say anything to that. He knew that she had worked in two houses. When he had come down from Mangalapuram the first time, he had run into her in town. He could barely recognize her even when she came closer, calling him Abu-kka. She had taken a break in a journey and was waiting for the next bus. She had no time to come home for a visit. She looked frayed. Age had flopped on top of her.

'Do yuh nee' to do this, Nebisu?' When they sat on either side of the table in the teashop, he asked her.

'Thenn wha' am I to do, Abu-kka? Shudn' we libe sumhow? Umma too?' Her eyes welled.

'Wha' was reall' tha issue there, Nebisu, wha' happen'd?'

When he saw her tears fall into her tea, he changed the subject. *I need not know*, he decided. Irrespective of whether she left or they sent her out, the memories are likely to be pitiful. Why scratch it and infect further? Such search for truth was uncalled for.

'Whattdidd' yuh tell Elayumma? Doessshe know tha' yuh're a serbant in 'ouses?'

'Umma knows. There isn' muc' wor' there. Justh thakin' care of tha chil'ren. They are good pipple.'

Abubacker fell silent again.

'All thissis nothin', Abu-kka. Ith loo's sad onlly if yuh thin' of tha old thimes. Justh loo' at ith fro' now, an' ith mak's sens'. Umma keep's sayin', iffonly Uppa wer' alibe. Bu' Uppa's not alibe. Isn' thath tha truth? Isn' ith enuf to tak'upp frommtthere?'

Yes. That was the truth.

'Pleas' tell eberyon' there not to mak' my Umma sad.'

When they were going to leave, she held his hand.

'Um. Yes. I will. Bu' yuh musth lookkffer sum oth'r wor'.' Abubacker looked at her face. Nebisu smiled blandly.

'Cud yuh manag' to fin' me wor' bekk hom'?'

He heard that differently: if only you and your family had not shifted to the desham, we would have managed to somehow carry on with our lives in our home.

Seeing him fumble, she consoled him herself.

'Tha fam'ly I'm workin' fer is moobing thi' month. They saidd they'll fin' me work in an ayurbedic hospithal. Tell Umma I'll com' afther I get tha job.'

Before her bus moved, she leaned out and asked, 'Abu-kka, isn' Umma still in tha shed?' He looked away, pretending not to hear. *If the bus takes more time to leave, I will dissipate into the air like cotton candy*, he thought. He would remember later again and again with much contrition, that he felt immensely relieved when her bus disappeared from sight. In truth, he hadn't inquired about her after that. That was indeed a wrong. Not only that, everything they had done to do with Nebisu, including this intervention for her and her mother, was wrong. An air-mail that they received soon after said that she was living contentedly with a Bangladeshi family that she had met at the ayurveda hospital. Their little children were very fond of her. They come here regularly for ayurveda treatment, for the children's mother. She had been bedridden since many years. When he got to know of this, Abubacker's Uppa scolded Kaisumma very severely. But Abubacker paid no attention to his tirade. Let her find a life, let her live her life.

But though he knew so much, Abubacker could not correct the reference that she had gone to Saudi with some man she met at the ayurveda hospital. Even as he decided to strongly object to the slanderous allusions about Nebisu, he ended up doing the opposite. He agreed with every one of Balan's claims about her. That was another of his weaknesses. Making up his mind to say something and then, at the critical movement, covering it up, keeping it to himself. And instead, saying things he never wanted to. All that he had prepared in his mind to say would make funny faces at him.

The members of the group who were seated, began to rise one by one. No one can really solve any problem. They can, maybe, circle it, gawk at it. Or sharpen some needles to jab at it. And then brag that it was all settled. That's nothing new; there's nothing in it.

'Can tha khatib tell yer Uppa to do sumthin' . . . oh wha' a therrible law, *Appa!*'

Balan too rose.

'Mebbe *Padachon* meanth only thath tha men of tha deadd man's fam'ly shud lendd a han' to tha womin in managin' tha propperthy. But the' they keepp scratchin', claimin' thath tha *kitaab* says thath . . . Thi' is meanth to mak' sure thath tha womin don' becom miss'rable an' helpless . . . butthis is how pipple read ith now. Buttif he asks me, "isn' thi' our law?", I canno' say anythin' else. So there's real'y no lapse on hisside. Butthen if he vacathes tha 'ouse afther consultin' eberyone, then' goodd, tha'll be *Padachon*'s work.'

The khatib threw up his hands and started for the door as if making an escape. He hesitated for a few moments near the wooden staircase.

'Pleas' waith dow'sthairs? I'm comin'too. I'll tak' yuh bekk.'

When the khatib descended, Abubacker turned towards the rest of them.

'Yes, I thried to geth sum land or a house fer Elayumma from tha panchayath. If thin's go thi' way, she'll be tha firsth womin here to be homeless, an' thaths a shame! But ith is true. Thath time, Nambiar us'd to be bith us. Lik' in eberythin', I wen' and tol' him abou' thi' too. I'll admith to thath. Bu' afther he lefth, I hab'n't saidd a wordd abouth thi' to anyone. I don' know if anyone push'd ith afther. If thath benefith won' be giben becos they own sum land an' a house, I agree. Tha house shud be fer those who don' habe ith, nottffer tho' who habe. Thath's tha righth thin'. I habe no bizness complaining abou' Balan or anybody else fer sayin' thath. I haben' giben any complain' to anyone abouth tha'.

I still habe tha *taakkath* to geth fifthy pipple to come to any of our meethings. Why shud I then be envious of pipple who're bith me? Ann'tthen, tha thin' abou' tha sandal. My connecshun bith Kalyani is justh tha same as wha' any oth'r man here has bith her. Surely I don' habe tha' kin' of connecshun tha' nee'ds tha sandal on her doorsthepp. If yuh wan' to know how ith came ther', fin' out fer yerself.'

'Be careful!' The desham reminded its ranks. It is the government. Government-logic cannot hear common compassion. Kaisumma has no home, but the government can only hear her plea for one as the demand for a second house. Abubacker is ready to surrender his share for her, but according to the local progressives, he can only be the usurper of her assets. 'Put your heads into other people's affairs very carefully. Don't bite the stone and break the teeth.' It warned.

When he came down the staircase, Abubacker was shivering slightly. He reached out to hold the rope tied on one side for support, but it slipped off further away.

'Kunhi, I bant to go to tha N'laamittam Maqam. D'yuh habe tha thime?'

'Why so sudd'nly, Elayumma?'

'Lasth nighth I saw tha big snak' in a dream. When I wenth out to geth tha clothes laiddouut to dry, ther' ith was, creepin' on tha side. It had tha headdress too . . . I rann bekk sumhow and reach'd thisside. When I see this dream . . . I ushually go to ther'.'

Abubacker smiled. Water is still abundant and flowing in the Nilamittam Maqam even when it is a relentless drought elsewhere. It moistens the driest of depressions. Some of those who fought in the Battle of Badr rest there, in the coolness. Kaisumma needed to go there and convince the auliyas of some things. And also ask if her daughter was well. For her, the battle for her daughter was greatest battle for the truth.

'We'll go, Elayumma,' Abubacker agreed.

69

After the well was drained and cleaned, the water had climbed four rings. The wild growth in the rings and well-side had been cleared, too. But the yard, completely overgrown with weeds, wouldn't let Kalyani take a step in there.

'No, don'!' it said.

'Don' loo' in me!' the well bickered.

'Don' come near!' the cowshed wept.

'Go'wway.' The bamboos beyond Chonnamma's kottam grumbled.

Kalyani stood in the middle of it, looking glum.

'I'll clea' tha wild; I'll stir tha wat'r; brush offtha cobw'bs ; will tie ith tighth bith tha rope . . .' she told each one.

'I'm reall' sad, uh?' the house said, biting hard to keep its pain down.

'Kalyani . . .' When she opened it, the front door burst into a wail.

'Ah how . . . still, my friend—*entane* . . .'

The hearth burned slow.

'Don' yuh touchhuss!' The vessels clattered.

'Won' op'n!' The window stayed stuck.

She went into the bedroom and sat on the cot.

'Getthupp, go'way!' It protested. No one was letting Kalyani in. No one paid attention, though she had pushed her way in.

Now I am alien to them, she was convinced. But she cleaned up the whole house thoroughly, sprinkled water all over. Dusted, cleared the cobwebs. She scrubbed the vessels, washed them, and left them in the sun to dry. Washed all the clothing and cloth that was left outside, and burned the unusable. She searched for and found the dusty old machete from near the hearth. Tying a towel on her head, she stepped into the yard. The *tottavaadi* thorns bit and tore at her feet. The kara thorns poked her hard. The *unda* thorns pricked her skin and got inside it. Holding the thorns down, she pulled them off by the roots.

'Sprouthin' evils!'

When she parted the wild growth with the machete, the porcupine shook its thorns and dashed off. When she grabbed the wild bushes together and pulled hard, whole nests of ants came up with the roots. Removing the layers upon layers of fallen coconut fronds, she found four or five baby snakes. *Should I kill?* She thought for a moment or two. The old story of the snake flashed through her mind.

'Haben't yuh bee' giben yer own plac'? Why'ren' yuh ther', why com' make throuble fer humans?' She looked around.

'Wher's tha womin-snake gone? Pushin' out sum fifty critters eac' birth! Daive! Thissis tha plac' wher' my chil' is to play an' run abouth . . . Enuf. Yuh may die.'

Even a snake needs to show some sense of responsibility. She remembered how, while clearing Avukkar-kka's yard some time back, she had cut straight through a snake's head; the memory made her jump once. But now she broke the snakes' heads with the handle of the hoe pitilessly and buried them.

Near the Chonnamma kottam, the murikku tree lay on the ground, its back nearly broken by the weight of flowers. The chempakam was newly budding. The erinjhi was quietly in full bloom. There was infinite silence around the kottam. The grass was so tall, it reached one's calves. Careful not to make a racket, Kalyani cleaned the front side of the kottam and peered inside.

'Tha sthate of my courthyard!'

A red eye glowered near the window of the kottam.

'Tha weedds were coverin' my ankleth! Wha' am I to do?'

'Now yuh can leave yer hair down' an' wear tha red cloth an' go all abouth yer yardd. Habe clean'd ith.' Kalyani said, mildly.

'Wha' abouth tha milk-pungan, to eat?' The sound of a copper bowl falling rang there.

'Habebbrough' tha raw rice. Will make yuh sum tommor',' she consoled. The sound of the anklet grew distant.

'Tha poortthing,' thought Kalyani. 'Eben a god nee's lovve. Lethher go aroun' bith 'er hair loose . . .'

Walking up and down in the middle of the smouldering heap of dry leaves and poking them, Kalyani almost felt that she was acting a part in the *Harishchandran* movie. Like Harishchandra as the Chandala crematorium-keeper poking the burning pyres, she hummed tune of the song *'Aalmavidyaalayame . . .'* and dumped yet another set of memories into the burning waste heap.

The rope in the well was in tatters. She decided to get a new one the very next day; she lowered the bucket into the well. Cutting through the layers of water that had lain motionless since long, it hurtled down to the bottom. It then rose swiftly to the surface with the water. It went up and down again and again swiftly, breaking the water's surface repeatedly. The water hit and fell against the well's rings again and again. Frogs and worms and insects hiding in tiny holes were swept into the water and now thrashed about for dear life. Then Kalyani pulled up the overflowing bucket the highest it could go, and holding the rope's end in her left hand, let the bucket fall with full force. Well and water shuddered alike in the impact. Its rings completely drenched, the well fell into calm repose. Exhausted, Kalyani, soaking wet now, leaned on the partitioning beside the well and sat there quietly for some time.

After her bath, she lit the lamp and brought it to the veranda. There was some fuss in the beginning, but the hearth made friends with her again. Some memories came running at her when she cooked the tapioca. She gathered them up with the pieces of tapioca gone bitter from staying too long under the ground, dumped them under the clump of banana trees in the backyard, and went and sat next to the lit lamp on the veranda. The darkness flew up all around her and soon began to settle down. She did not feel like switching the light on. Fear was just one among the many chapters in her life. And besides, Biju was at Kaisumma's house. It was only for him that Kalyani had swallowed fear many a time. He loved to travel. Abubacker, Ayisha and Kaisumma were taking him with them to the Nilamuttam Maqam. Kaisumma was very fond of him. She made him unnakkaya and told him stories of how she had made it for Kalyani and Nebisu and divided it between them.

Kalyani had gone to Koppu-man's house many times, even before the Ripper problem. To clean the well, pluck the coconuts, gather the cashew nuts—she would return before Biju came home from school. But it was a place from which she had wanted to run, soonest. Despite that, now, within a day, most naturally, it became Kalyani's space. The house and yard and well and cowshed chatted with her as if she had been with them for many years. 'Is this really my home?' She even asked herself. But there was something—a single strand—that divided her from Koppu-man's house. Like a strand of hair caught in one's throat, it would not come, no matter how much you pulled it out. She stepped out and looked at the house which was standing quietly behind her.

'Tha paavam,' she said.

'An' wha' abouth me?'

The familiar voice, from the dark, seared Kalyani from within.

70

'Lookkwwho's here, *Appaa*!'

As Kalyani stood there astonished, Cheyyikkutty emerged into the light from the dark. She was dripping wet, but looked clean. Her hair looked as though a cow had licked it. Seeing a chempaka flower stuck in it, Kalyani was most amused. Her droopping breasts allowed Kalyani to see them through the wetness.

'Eesh! Nic' to see—both yer breasths can be pu' on yer shoulders now!'

'Beath ith, yuh daughther of a dog, an' stop preenin'.'

'Oh. Righth away! No leth up on tha tongue-lashin' eben on tha oth'r side?'

'Wher's my kunhi?'

'Whic'one? Narayanan or Lachmanan?'

'Yuh hussy! Yer kunhi. What's yer jumpin' up an' dow' bith him?'

'Alla, womin, lookks lik' yuh starthed to geth tha gall tha momemt yuh see me? Wha'dyuh bant?'

'Wha' I bant? D'yuh cookk anythin' fer me? Yuh come to take tha cashew an' coconut reg'larly, eh? Habe yuh any sham'?'

Uyi. Kalyani suddenly felt sorry. This was something Cheyikkutty did regularly. Coconut toddy, cooked rice, river fish curry in thick coconut gravy, chicken slow-fried with pepper, curry leaves and coconut bits for Achootty vaidyar. Creamy cooked tapioca lightly fried with crackled mustard, chilli bits, scraped

fresh coconut, crushed garlic and curry leaves with crab curry
for Machunan, kaara-appam and wholegrain rice payasam for
Valyechi. She would take it all to the south-side room, place it
inside, light the lamp and close the door. Then she would come
and sit silently on the veranda. Kalyani, in her time, would just
help to get everything ready for the cooking. Later, Kamala took
over the job of attending to these cravings. When the humans in
the house were mired in their own sorrows, those in the other
world must have come each year on the Vaavu new moon when
spirits are feasted, peeked into the south-side room, and returned
disappointed. As for Kalyani, she had just lived through a time in
which she could not even recall this inner-room-feast or the items
on its menu. So though she felt sorry, she did not yield.

'*Allappa*, didn' yer daughthers and yer son's womin—tha
cookin' ezpert—didn' they cookk anythin' fer yuh? Why com'
searchin' fer Kalyani sayin' thath?'

'Bu'tthen they aren' in thi' 'ouse? They aren' carryin' off tha
cashew an' tha coconuts?'

Cheyikkutty was angry. Drops of water scattered from
her chin.

'Uyyentappa, whattalotto' brighth cashew an' coconuts,'
she said.

Kalyani's hand was on her head. She had no reply to that.

Cheyikkutty lowered her pitch. 'All thi' koppu was yer
puruvan's fer sure, bu' . . .'

'Amma, I'll cookk fer yuh tomorro', eh?' Kalyani too lowered
her pitch.

'Why, is ith tha Vaavu day tomorro'?'

'Won' ith do if we thin' tha Vaavu's tomorro'?'

'Thath will do, uh?'

'Yea.'

The next day, the *etta* fish gaped with astonishment at the
dawn which walked up to it along with Kalyani.

'Amma's bery fon' of etta *meen*,' said Kalyani.

'Ith's bery bony, be carefu', watc' yer hand,' said Cheyikkutty from the kitchen steps, watching Kalyani fight a battle with the fish trying to clean it.

'Cut ith thowards tha head from tha side of tha bones.' She went towards Kalyani.

'Lik' thi'?' Kalyani asked, showing her the half-cut fish.

'Righth, lik' thath—now pull tha skin.'

The etta meen was soon boiling with a *kulu-kulu* sound in the earthen pot swathed in fiery red gravy. Holding Kamala in her mind, Kalyani flung a few garlic cloves into the hot coconut oil, swirled the pan, and poured it on the boiling curry. The house was filled with Cheyikkutty's food aromas.

'Yuh made onlly fer me? Oh wha' a lazy-bon's yuh are in tha kitchin! Nothin' fer Machunan an' Valyechi an' my Acchan?' Cheyikkutty complained.

'They'll come fer tha Vaavu, no? Will make fer them then. This is fer yuh, Amma, tha 'peshal food fer yuh fromme.'

Kalyani served the rice and the fish curry on the leaf. Then ladled the raw-rice payasam on another, and pushed it forward.

'Here, leth thathunger goawway.'

'Leth no one be hungry, Kalyani. Wha' bigge' merith is ther' oth'r than easin' sumone's hung'r?'

'Wha' abou' one's ownnhunger?'

'Wha' abouth thath? Of cour' ith is hunger too. Musth be eas'd. Tha house will be ruin'd if yuh go to bed hungry.'

'Tha's righth.'

Kalyani looked thoughtful. Then suddenly remembering something, she took out a pack of beedis from her waist-flap and put it on the floor.

'Here, yuh can tak' a puff. If yuh tak' ith dow' tha well, ith'll get wet.'

'I needdith at nighth only. Yuh keeppith sumwher' safe.'

'Tha womin ober there is pinin' fer milk-pungan . . . she's been askin' since last ebening . . . lemme take sum of thi' ther' fer her . . .'

Kalyani covered the pot with a leaf and went towards the kottam. When she returned, Cheyikkutty was not to be seen.

'Ah, righth, tha ol' womin sthill downs her prey an' go's off to sleep sumwher', no change, uh?'

When she was cleaning the kitchen, a familiar scent—but one which she had forgotten on the way—reached her nostrils. A rose-chempakam which had bloomed in the path towards the house was covered with blossoms. It seemed to be standing up with effort, its hand holding up its hip and saying, 'Kalyani, please gibe me a hand'. The *pichi* vine that climbed up on the roof too had flowered profusely and the scent and the flowers were jostling for space up there. In the Chonnamma kottam, the erinjhi tree was in full bloom, letting off its chilli fragrance. But cutting through all of these, came a scent that Kalyani alone knew. She caught the smell and followed it to the veranda. There was Lakshmanan, sitting on the half-wall. For a second, Kalyani stood rooted on the spot.

'Wha'sggoin' on?'

She heard his voice, like a small stone falling on the motionless water of a well. Though she dammed them with lighting speed, the tears overflowed the boundary of her eyes.

After some moments of silence, she returned the small talk.

'Wha'sggoin' on bith yuh?'

This time, Lakshmanan was silent.

'Nothin'' was actually the answer to both questions. They had nothing to give each other. And yet, their lives continued to flow.

'Yuh've eathen?'

'No.'

'Then go an' habe a bath.'

Lakshmanan went up to the well and looked in, pinning his hands on the partition wall. The water in the depths looked up at him lovingly. Somehow, he did not feel like drawing from it for his bath.

'How's our pond?'

'I neber go thath side,' she said.

'Lemme go an' tak' a bath ther'. Suchha a lon' time sinc' I had a bath in a pondd!'

The pond was stifled with weeds. The small round of clear water, confined to its very edge disappointed Lakshmanan. He took a dip within its immobility, limits, edges. Stretch out an arm and the weedy growth would tangle on it. How to swim when there's no space to even stand? He managed to take a bath without touching the slimy algae and came out. To get over the frustration caused by the water that flowed only vertically down his body in a tiny bathroom, he had to swim to the other side and back. He decided to clean up the pond. When he returned with his mind made up, Cheyikkutty's dishes awaited him.

'Amma saidd she banted to eath etta curry. Andd tha womin ober ther'—Chonnamma—ask'd fer rice payasam.'

He hummed as though it were the most normal thing.

'I justh came yestherday.'

'Kunhi?'

Lakshmanan raised his face. Kalyani felt as if a tiny finger had poked her breasts.

'He's ther'bbith Kaisumma now. He bants onlly her. Lik' me, whenn I was small. Andd then whenn my Amma, whenn she got angr' bith me . . .'

Lakshmanan hummed to that stream of talk, too.

He kept walking up and down the front yard of the house through the night. Kalyani sat on the stepping stone, watching him. His shadow seemed thinner now, she thought. The faint light and the wind shaking the trees mixed up their shadows. The bamboos at the boundary of Chonnamma's kottam sighed heavily.

71

'Can' yuh an' Kamala comm'bekk an' sthay here?'

Kalyani asked Lakshmanan. A faint light fell on Lakshmanan's face through the window opening towards the cowshed. Kalyani measured the distance from his forehead to chin with two fingers. The sweat flowing on Lakshmanan's back wetted the tips of her curls. His face was glowing, she noticed. He didn't look like that earlier. Till some hours back, his face was swollen like some sickly rheum had collected on it. His shoulders fell. Wherever her fingers touched, his body caved in. She felt very, very sad.

'Lie ober on yer face,' she told him.

He lay prone before her, like a baby. She ran four fingers firmly and swiftly from the top of his head to the lower tip of his spine. Like a dark cobwebby cloud had been pulled off his body, Lakshmanan emerged into the light. Words left him; his body shivered uncontrollably. He felt that his sagging skin was now being filled with fat and muscle. As he pressed his face on the pillow, he thought that he would become a big, fleshy fish if this filling continued. He felt the life-giving water break through the ridges and rush into all the hollows of his body to brim over their edges. His hair stood on end. He wanted to turn over and see her face. But she didn't let him. He wanted to move his hand; but Kalyani held it. He could not move his leg. It was almost like she had taken it away. The perspiration on his right temple seemed to have dried with her breath falling on it. Lakshmanan was for her

314

both the pond and the stepping-stone to the pond. She would dive into the pond from the stone and swim right back to it. And then sit down on the stone and smile at the ripples that her body had set off. A bland, colourless time was leaving Lakshmanan's body.

'Enuf, now turnn.' She whispered in his ear.

'Wha's thi'? Blekkmmagic?'

He stretched out, unwound, and looked at his rejuvenated body.

'Don'ttyuh see ith yeth, Lachuna?'

'Us'd to be "Narayanan's younge' brothe' Lachuna"—thath was nice!'

'Ith wa'. Bu' thath's not need'd an'more. Justh Lachunan.'

'Why? Did I get big?'

'Yes, yuh got big. Not thath ol' Lachunan I firsth meth, nottat all!'

'Yuh habe becom' big too? So shudn' I grow too, Not-Narayanan's womin, Kalyani?'

'Indee', yuh shud.'

Kalyani twisted the hair on his chest around her fingers. Kissed his nipples.

'Yuh an' Kamala com' an' libe here. Thath's betther,' she repeated.

'I habe thought of ith sumtime . . . thi' 'ouse won' lik' ith. And if yuh aren' here, ith won' feel lik' my house, so . . .'

Kalyani was silent.

'Kamala is bery good . . .' Lakshmanan's voice broke. 'Bithout her, my lif' wud be losth . . . lik' ith were lick'd by a dog. She keeps eberythin' in ord'r. Bery lovin', too. Bu' sumtimes yuh justh geth tir'd of ith. Lik' when sumone spen's all thei' thime coddlin' an' caressin' yuh . . . Onl' thath, oth'rbise she's bery nice . . . Buttwwha' abou' yuh?'

'Nothin' to say, Lachuna. I habe nothin' to be afraiddof, in my place an' here. Ith has all fall'n into plac'. No on' bants to eben gibe simpl' affecshun. Mebbe becos they're scar'd. So no both'r abou' thath too.'

Lakshmanan touched her eyes with his lips.

'Nebermin', we can' shuttup annyone's mouths? Leth them yak and yak. Nothin' goin' to happ'n justh fromm tha yakkin'?'

Kalyani measured the distance from his palm to shoulder quietly.

'Di' Amma tell yuh tha sthory of tha womin of tha Tharakke fam'ly? Eberyone in thi' plac' knows ith.'

Lakshmanan picked strands of Kalyani's hair from his neck and recalled the story to his mind.

'Thath womin had com' to libe here from sumwher'. She wasstha firsth womin in thes' parths to wear a nose-sthud—they say. Bery sthout womin; she sound'd lik' a man. Didn' heedd annyyone aroun'! She had fou' girls. Habe yuh seennthath ruin'd ol' house on tha way to tha bathin' stheps? They us'd to libe in tha bekk of ther'. No one dared to go thathsside durin' tha day. Buttat nighth ther'd be a crowd, lik' seeds poppin' from a pod! Ou' granddad tha baidyar wa' justh a chil' then. Pipple cam' fromm beyondd' tha riv'r . . .'

Kalyani pressed down her left elbow on the bed, raised herself up, and started listening.

'Fer wha'?'

'Fer sex, whattelse?'

'Uyyentappa, howccom'?'

'Thath I don' know. Bu' they weren' doin' any oth'r workkhere. If anyone dar'd to say sumthin' when she an' tha girls wentt'roundd, then tha sthory wa' sure to end righth ther'! Pipple here tried to geth rid of them but they wud nottggo. Not only they didn'tggo, all fou' girls got marrie'ttoo. Ther's a sthory tha' all fou' men were firsth tasthed by tha moth'r befor' . . . who knows?'

'Uyi . . . will suchtthings happ'n?' Kalyani whispered in his ear.

'Ammoppa! Tha sthories we bant to tell when a womin rows alone bith her fou' girls an' finally geths sumbhere!'

'Didssumone achually see any of thi'?'

'Really!' Lakshmanan laughed. 'If sumone haddereally seenn, wud they be abl' to talk lik' thath? Wudn' ther' be justh tha seein'? There'd be no sthories!'

'Anntthen?'

'Anntthen she libed fer sumtime lik' eberyon' anntthen she die'. Justh thath!'

Lakshmanan turned in the bed and hugged her. Trying to free her arms from his embrace, she murmured, laughing . . . 'Wha' if tha rum'ur wa' really thrue? Thath thing dow'thhere, ith doesn' geth worn out or sumthin' eh?'

As he was falling asleep, Lakshmanan retrieved the sthory's appendix from memory.

'Ou' Kumarettan is tha greath-gran'son of thath womin's youngesth daughther!'

'Which' Kumarettan? Tha one who digs wells?'

'Um,' Lakshmanan was now slipping into sleep. 'Ai, yes!'

Kalyani opened the databank of Koppu-man's desham. She knew that all this information was going to be quite useful to her. Knowledge of the histhory of the place (as distinct from History, or history) one was married into is as crucial as knowing the histhory of one's own place. The wimmin who knew both were valued everywhere. Those who didn't know any of this lore could wear jasmine garlands in their hair and gad about—and that was about all they could do.

When Lakshmanan fell asleep, she came out of the bedroom alone with a lit kerosene lamp. Feeling for the packet of beedis from above the door, she opened the door to the veranda. The cold wind chilled her lips. Cheyikkutty was sitting on the half-wall, cold and shivering.

'How longgssince habe I bee' waithin' here! Shud habe take' tha beedi thennithselff!'

Cheyikkutty was mad.

'Didn' I gibe ith to yuh thennithself?' Kalyani was not far behind.

Cheyikkutty took the beedi and caressed its tip. Its single eye began to glow. The curls of smoke enveloped Kalyani.

'He's sleepin'?'

Cheyikkutty asked suddenly. Kalyani looked away and hummed, unable to face her.

'Yuh are really a peculy'r womin . . . her inn'r-roomm-feasth! Rice fer me and . . . fer him . . uh! Don' mak' me say mor' . . .'

Cheyikkutty let out a series of puffs.

'Alla, Amme, wasn' ith yuh who toldd me thi' noonn thath one shudn' stharve annyone?'

Kalyani asked with extreme innocence.

'Uyyentamme!' Cheyikkutty slapped herself on the head. 'Oh, no one cann sthandd up to her! I justh' can'tbbe hurlin' in this bekk an' forth! Do wha' yuh pleas'! I gibe up!'

Kalyani let out a low laugh.

Finishing her beedi, Cheyikkutty got up.

'Yuh moobe thath side . . . lemme see my son.'

'Comm' . . .'

Kalyani moved away, took up the kerosene lamp, called Cheyikkutty, and went towards the bedroom. She followed, stepping on Kalyani's footsteps. Lakshmanan lay on his back, sleeping. The mundu had slipped from his waist; Kalyani pulled it up and covered him properly. Cheyikkutty's sunken eyes filled with tears.

'Leth him sleepp, my kunhi!'

She exited, quickly. Waited a few moments for Kalyani to come out into the veranda.

'Yuh're my home, know thath, my dear mole, my daughther!' she said in a faltering voice.

The wind scattered her voice and shadow.

72

'Bu'tthen yuh thinkk of me! Yuh aren' sad fer me? Plywoodd is a bery goo'tthingg! Bu'then if ith gets soak'd bith wat'er, wha's tha goodd of ith? If ith starths peelin', wha's tha goodd of ith? Ah, mah Ramendrran!'

Dakshayani banged her head on the half-wall's pillar.

'Itss' yuh who gabe thi' daughther of a dog tha drinkk who shuddbe kick'd, Goyinnetta!'

Kalyani looked out into the front yard and gritted her teeth. She held Dakshayani and got her to sit on the steps instead of the half-wall. Dakshayani sat there and moaned and wailed non-stop.

Govindettan stood there looking quite glum. Never ever had he faced such an awful mess. After all, it wasn't the first time that he had brought Dakshayani fresh coconut toddy. He wondered, quite fairly, whether something had happened to the toddy. This toddy hadn't yet reached the local toddy *shaap*. There was very little chance of an impurity. Maybe something had happened on top of the coconut tree itself? There had been a couple of incidents like that, earlier. Some super-bright fellows had tried to stop people from stealing the toddy from the tree-top. Once someone ground a piece of battery and mixed it in the toddy. The toddy thief did not last very long. The other trick was to mix dog poo. That's usually to stop someone's totally unmanageable drinking habits. Fresh poo is obtained by beating the dog. Then it is carefully mixed in the toddy. The poo does not have the technological sophistication to separate drinkers into severe and moderate. You'll vomit so hard, the breast milk you drank years back will come out of your mouth. And soon the very word 'toddy' will make you vomit. But this case seemed different. Dakshayani had simply lost her grip. The moment he handed her the toddy, she downed the whole bottle at one gulp and wiped her lips.

As Govindettan stood out there confused, Dakshayani, who had been sitting on the floor bounded up like a rubber ball and bounced all the way to him calling aloud, 'Ah my Goyinetta, Ah my Goyinetta'. She then flung her arms around his neck and hung there. She kissed his greyed whiskers and cheeks.

'Wha' a preththy cheek-a, Goyinnettan's cheek-a,' she sang in rhyme, pinching his cheeks hard. Govindettan who had lost his balance and was nearly falling, grabbed the young coconut tree behind him for support.

'Ahh . . . wha' yuh doin' . . . are yuh killin' tha ol' man, Daive!'

Kalyani jumped down from the veranda and rushed up. She dragged Dakshayani back and made her sit in a corner.

'Bulb o' pesthilenc'! Don' yuh dare moobe from here! Wha' tha hell ar yuh thinkin'?'

Dakshayani tore her hair and began to wail again.

'Bu'tthen lookit my lif! My Ramendrran! His singin'! Will I hearrhhis singin' agai'?'

'Wha'? Yer life is ober? When . . ?'

Kalyani yelled.

'Ramendrran? Ramendrran who?'

'I haddwwarn'd her righ'tthen!' Govindettan was angry. 'Whe' she gulp'd tha whol' pot down! Who thought thi'? My goo'lluck, Amma an' Damu wenttoff to sum weddin' earl' in tha mornin'.'

Kalyani fixed him in a stare.

'I don' clim' tha coconu'tree annymmore . . . I got tha boy to brin' down sum . . . frommnnow, won' gibe her any—thath's enuf!.'

Govindettan laid down his arms.

They both sat there guarding Dakshayani. Though she saw the whole drama, Dakshayani's cow lay calmly in the cowshed, chewing the cud. She occasionally sent a glance to the veranda.

'All this is very well. But if I am not untied and retied by evening, you'll have something to answer for. I'll be talking to you then.'

It jerked its head sharply, mooed, scared off the crow that had come to nit-pick, and slapped itself with its tail.

Kalyani had just returned from Koppu-man's house. On her way home after getting off the bus, she saw Biju and a bunch of his friends splashing in the pond with gusto. She had to have the rice gruel ready before he came home.

'Comin' fer tha *kanjhi*, eda?' She asked casually.

'No. I'll be bith Kaisumma today. We caugh' lott's of fish from tha pondd!'

'An' tha cows?'

'Ayisha-tha gabe them wat'r an' retied them.'

Peace, she thought. But she had barely gone two feet forward, when Biju called again, 'Amme, tha polic' is waithin' in tha house front . . .'

'Whattffer?'

'Sumone hungg'imself on tha cashe' tree.'

'*Eayyo*! Who?'

'Don'nno.'

She quickened her pace. If they had not cut down the body, maybe she could see. Just out of curiosity. He probably thought himself to be someone who belonged to this earth; now he's hanging helplessly from a tree branch. In the movies, she had seen only the feet. But she had never seen anyone like that ever in real life. Because this was the first time it happened in these parts. After this incident, people from faraway places came to the desham for this purpose. They visited God and offered thanks for all the efforts he'd made to solve their problems; they did not accuse God of neglect in matters that were beyond His capacity;

quietly, they hung their physical bodies like question marks on the branches of the lush cashew trees here. No one would touch the cashew nuts such trees bore; they would fall to the ground, sprout and grow, haughty and uncontrolled.

When Kalyani reached the spot, they were bringing down the body. An old man, just about five feet tall. They found a folded red lungi, a plastic cover, and a pair of rubber slippers under the tree. He had prepared it all, loosened up, and accepted the luxury of just a piece of rope. Kalyani went up to the corpse that was laid under the tree. He was apparently someone from far. Had been seen around here in the past couple of days. This was his intention, now it was clear.

Seeing his face, Kalyani grew very uneasy and thought, *leth no one hanggtthemsel's, Appa! Leth me go see Dakshayani now*, she decided. How much more of a relief it was to go see some living human beings out there, instead of poking one's head into the hearth like a kitchen-dweller of a cat (of course, if absolutely necessary, one might and will poke one's head in the hearth—that's another matter)! Kalyani thought that Dakshayani too hadn't cooked anything that day. Did she also go to see the man dead and hanging? When she got past the lane, she noticed that Dakshayani's house was in a tizzy; Dakshayani herself was raving and ranting. Govindettan was going about in circles, all confused.

Except her constant reference of 'My Ramendrran!' Kalyani could get a sense of the rest of her babbling.

When she calmed down a bit, Kalyani made Dakshayani lean on the wall, went into the kitchen and put some rice on the stove. When she returned, Dakshayani had once again begun to wail and beat her breast and recount her sorrows to Govindettan. The sorrows of her whole life. Experiences, good and bad. Kalyani listened for some time.

'Goyinnetta, yuh can go,' Kalyani said.

'Di' thath nailsvendo' ask abouth her aftherwwar's?' Govindettan asked.

Kalyani was vexed.

'Fer wha'? To roasth her or wha'?'

'Alla, I though' . . . mebbe thath's wha's stirrin' her up lik' thissnnow.'

'Yuh stop thinkin' big thinggs, ok? If she's gon'lloose now, she'll tighthen hersel' lat'r. Heardd?'

'Earli'r she was bery scar'd of turnin' int' a kitchin-corn'r womin. An' so she jump'd an' put her head und'r sum fellow from gooddnness knows bhere . . . ah, as if ther's no men in thes' parths . . . lik' they say, be too dainthy an' choosy, an' yuh landd in tha worm's ass.'

Govindettan walked away.

'Daachaani . . .'

Kalyani kneeled beside Dakshayani on the veranda.

'Wha's ith? My dear, I know yuh won' ge'lloose on justh sum toddy . . . Tell me, wha's ith?'

Dakshayani raised her head and looked at her. Her eyes were red, puffed-up, narrowed.

'Tha new perso' in thath 'ouse ther', yuh know thath . . . thath wa' Ramendrran,' she said.

Kalyani realized only a little while later that she was referring to the house in which Nailsvendor had lived when he came here first, the house where Dakshayani had entered as a new bride.

'Fer thath?'

Kalyani's voice never sounded as rough as now.

'Thath 'ouse is fer renth . . . pipple com' ther', they wenth away too . . . so why're yuh bellowin' lik'a cow fer thath?'

Dakshayani had no answer. But her throat was aching. She had gone there casually when they were whitewashing the walls of the house. Each stroke of the painters' brush picked out specific memories and erased them. When the workers cleaned the house and removed the waste, Dakshayani found an old hairclip of hers in the heap. A blue one, which she had bought from the market outside Muthappan's abode, the Madappura, before the wedding.

She held it in her hand for a while and then quietly put it back in the house again. She felt a strong desire to know how long it would live in that house with the new tenants. Must take it back after it had dipped and risen in many more lives. Must see how many colours it bore then.

'Who' yuh sai' libes ther' now?'

Kalyani frowned. The map of the land was so familiar to her, it unfolded in her palm. Right from childhood, she had known that learning through sight was more valued that learning from hearsay. She knew where, what, how.

Long time back, when they played together as children, sometimes, Kalyani would hold back Dakshayani who always ran like mad.

'Yuh musth run onlly on thi'sside of tha channel. If yuh bant, yuh canggo till tha Sheemakkonna tree ober ther'.'

'Why, isn' ith nice' to run tha'sside?'

'Yes, bu' ther's shit lyin' in two places tha'sside. One's from befor', tha oth'r's frommnnow . . . it loo's lik' . . .'

'Eee!'

'Bhey . . .'

The need to visiting the scene of crime as much as possible was dissolved in Kalyani's very blood. She has often hit back against people who used the epithet *tukkichi* to describe her (denigrating her intense commitment to fieldwork)—people who crouched in their comfortable, safe chairs hugging secondary material and ignoring primary sources—with the instantly-coined counter-epithet, *nakkichi* (lickass-wench). How to stay up-to-date about new people unless you hang around, she would ask.

For this reason, she was quite struck. How could she have missed this person Dakshayani was beating her breast about?

She repeated the question: 'Who's thi'?'

'He's a singin'mman, Ramendrran.'

'Singin'mman? Why is he sthayin' eeda?'

'Don'kknow . . .'

Kalyani saw something dart through the dry leaves. Its tail-end was pointed. It was not harmless.

'Yuh wentther' afther they whith'wash'd tha place?'

Dakshayani did not deny it.

'How did'yuh know thath he's a singin'mman?'

'Ther's an 'aaarmonium there. Yuh cannhhear when yuh pass thathway.'

Kalyani stood up slowly.

'Anddnnow tha fuss is goin' to starth, and pipple will say, yea we got her hairclip from thath house! Tha songg-an'-danc' aroun' a pair of sandals in my house hasn' end'd yeth . . . Wha' happen'd from ith? Kalyani gota baddnname. An' bith her, *opparam*, a poor man . . . Tha sthory of Kalyani becomin' badd got on tha bus to her puruvan's plac', payin' sixty paisa! Wha' if anyone says such thinggs abou' yuh? Nothin'. Bu' then can yuh standd firm lik' thath? Ah leth tha'ggo . . . wha's thi' sthory of Ramendrran?'

73

Winter Night's golden lamp
Flickers and dies,
On the boughs of the maakanadaa-tree
Night-birds close their eyes . . .

Ramachandran hummed as he walked by the river-bank where
the sand-miners were busy at work. What a feel! Dakshayani just
wanted to die. She had set off to the Madappura on an impulse.
The biggest loss she had felt when she got on a train to Kollam
with Nailsvendor was of this temple. No woman around there,
including Dakshayani, had the kind of devotion that impelled
them to go take a dip in the pond and pray daily. They sought
a helping hand, rather, through their prayers. When things
were really bad, when they tried to heave themselves out of the
holes into which they had fallen, they would hold out a hand to
God too, hoping for help. Gods do have some responsibilities
regarding human beings. Instead of immersing themselves in deep
meditation, they must pay attention to people struggling. They
must deliver at least one-tenth of that which the poor folk ask,
these folk who put their money into the offering-boxes outside
temples, a share of that they earn from toiling and sweating like
mules. And if any technical objection arises, then the minimum
would be a pat on the shoulder and a word of comfort: 'Don't
worry, everything will be done'. It's those gods who do not adhere

to this minimum, only them, who were sweetly cursed by a whole people at one time—through the unforgettable Malayalam cine-melody that began with an address to gods who do not open their eyes . . . '*Kannu turakkaatha daivangale . . .*'

That was a Thiruvappana festival day. It fell on a Sunday, so the crowd was big. Dakshayani managed to make her way out, but the bangle-stalls there seduced her after a long time. She picked up a spiral bangle; it reminded her of her own life's path. As she brooded on it, out of the blue, Ramachandran appeared in front of her for the very first time. He said that he came to the festival to see the God Muthappan appear to the people with his divine form invested in the body of an oracle; to see him touch and talk to people.

'Becos we are used to seein' ith we don' thinkkthath way.' Dakshayani revealed the chemistry between the God and the people. She owed Him a pretty large sum!

'Debt? To God?'

'Yess-uh! If sumthin' goes missin' in tha 'ouse, I vow to off'r a *payamgutti* feasth to him. When ith is foundd, I tell him, I'll pay yuh lat'r. Not justh me—tha kids 'ere also pray to Muthappan, "leth tha Saar an' Teach'r at schoo' be on leabe!" Thath's a debttoo.'

Ramachandran laughed.

'If you don't pay up, what if God gets mad at you?'

'We'll gibe fer sur', litthle by litthle . . . justh don' forgeth. If yuh do, Muthappan sendds a *naayi* to remin'.'

'Who?'

'Naayi . . . yuh southie pipple call ith *patti*, dog.'

'Oh!'

Dakshayani took him to where they were serving cooked lentils and coconut slices. It was all very new to him.

'They gibe rice at noon. I eath sumtimes.' She said. There was still time till noon.

Ramachandran did not buy anything from the stalls. Just went around, looking. She felt a little embarrassed to be buying bangles

when he stood watching. That's how she ended up walking to the
riverside ferry. He humming the tune, followed her there.

'D'yuh go to tha moobies?' She suddenly asked.

'That was my regular thing! There was a cinema theatre near
us. I saw all the new releases.' Ramachandran smiled.

'Kalyani an' I go to Nisha to see . . . Thath wassumm thripp
we us'dto do ebery Sundday noon! We saw all tha moobies thath
cam' ther'. Thennin tha middlle, we sthopp'd goin'.'

Ramachandran looked at her face with amused curiosity. It
was blooming and blooming.

'Wha' kin' of moobie do yuh lik'? Tha ones bith fighths an'all?'
Ramachandran said he liked movies with mellifluous
songs. He didn't care for the plot or anything. He just wanted
melodious songs!

He would get goose bumps before the song sequences began!

'I lik' all tha moobies with our *ankam* . . . maarshal arth-
warri'rs fighthin' bith swordds an'all. Thos' habe nic' singin' too.'

She began to count such movies on her fingers:

'*Aromalunni*.'

'Nine songs,' said Ramachandran.

'*Kannappanunni*.'

'Thirteen.'

'*Thumbolaarcha*.'

'Eight.'

'*Kadathanaattu Maakkam*.'

Nine!

'*Uyyente* daive!' Dakshayani nearly split in two with joy.
'How're yuh abl' to do thiss?'

By the pier on the river where the pleasure-boat was docked,
As I dozed under the Manivaaka tree,
Did you not come on a dream's gay chariot?
Did you not beckon with Love's honeyed banter?

Ramachandran sat on the ferry steps, humming.

'*Uyi*!' exclaimed Kalyani. '*Kadathanat Maakkam*!'

Dakshayani gazed ahead wistfully and in her mind, slowly turned into Maakkam, the mythical heroine. They were sitting near a sand-mining area. Like in the movie, she glided gracefully among the workers carrying the sand away—gold and diamonds glinted from every part of her body. It was such a grand contrast.

'*Uyish!*' She was triumphant.

Then, like in the movie, a canoe decorated with pearl-encrusted umbrellas and jasmine garlands strewn on it appeared on the river, slowly, nearing the river-dock with the music '*teyyaam, teyyathaam . . .*' in the background. Holding the hands of her handmaids, Dakshayani stepped into the canoe, looking utterly exotic and bewitching.

'Pleas' keepp an eye on my coconutt and gree' gram?'

Maakkam requested Ramachandran. When the canoe moved, she began to worry that Ramachandran might stop singing and leave by the time she returned. So she wrapped up the scene in a jiffy and jumped back ashore.

'Don'ggo.'

Ramachandran stopped humming and turned to her.

'What?'

'Nothin', sha' we go an' geth tha rice?'

They sat side by side at the long table. Rows of banana leaves were laid on it. She fought off the memory of sitting beside Nailsvendor at their wedding feast and eyed Ramachandran through the corner of her eye.

How well, how contented he looked when he ate his meal! Though there were just a few curries—sambar, cooked lentils and buttermilk.

Dakshayani got stuck to him like an iron nail on a magnet. *I am nottleavin' him*, she told herself.

'Alla, my dear . . .' Kalyani held her chin with her hand. 'To bhere are yuh runnin' . . .?'

Dakshayani could guess what Kalyani was thinking. Her thoughts were probably these:

Scar'd thath she may enddupp as a kitchin-corner womin, thi'one marri'd a nailsvendin'-fello' when he turn'ddupp here. When thath tie tighthened aroun' her nekk an' almosth kilt her, she pull'd ith off an' ran here. And ha'bbarely stharted to libe and breathe normall' when— ther'sshe's gone an' got sthuck on anoth'r. Thath too, a southie. An educath'd fello', ith seems.

'My dearesth Daachaani, I'll fall at yer feeth . . . will yuh pleas' listhen payshyan'ly to wha' I got to say?'

Dakshayani did not like that at all.

'Wha's bith yuh? Am I runnin' off bith 'im?'

Kalyani knew that if she indeed wanted to run off with someone, there were many hurdles to cross. Because she also knew that Dakshayani was still fixed on this long, pointed, thrust-out nail, and that the only way out for her was to fall off it, Kalyani was especially thoughtful.

But that was not the issue now. What about this character, Ramachandran?

'Ramendrran wasssingin' fer me eben yestherday. This aarmonium, ith is a big job. I tried.Whe' yuh press tha bars yuh got to geth tha' windd to come too, lighthly. Whe' yuh press, yuh forgeth to inflat', an' whe' yuh inflat' yuh forgeth to press . . . I gabe up!'

But then she covered her face with her hands and sobbed heartbreakingly.

'Bu'thhen I didn'kknow it wa' tha lasth time, Kalyani . . . why di'he hangg himselff?'

A split-second of silence, and Kalyani lost control.

'Hung 'imself! Indeeddd! Ith's yer ol'mman whos' hung'imself! Dearrie, I wenthther' befor' I camm'ere . . . I saw tha dea'bbody too. Tha's of an ol'mman, shortmman, lik' a squirrel! He's got no aarmoninum, he neber libed in thath house! Eben tha police know nothin'! Wher' on earth di' yuh fin' ou' all thi' sitthin' her'?'

'No. No. Ramendrran. Hisseyes are so sad, whe' he's singin' . . . ah, buttwwhy di' he do thi'?'

The thought of that singing throat stifled by the tightening rope, Dakshayani could hardly bear.

'Leth's go to tha Maamaanam templ' an' off'r tha coconuts, and see. Sumthin's got into yuh.'

Kalyani freed Dakshayani's hair from her hands and tied it up tightly behind her head. Ramachandran mirrored in the creases on her face.

But don't think that Dakshayani's story ends there. When the lives of others in the desham continued to turn regularly and remained boring and one-dimensional, Dakshayani's life was to be ever-renewed. Pregnant women with the fullest of bellies, singers with eyes sad and droopy, politicians insulted and ejected because of misunderstandings, runaway children, young women whose eyes were removed because others thought them dead . . . also all sorts of souls—from world leaders to cultural figures—who were successful in this world and who loved visiting their people . . . many such types visited Dakshayani every year at regular intervals. She dedicated herself to them completely on those days. Because it knew this, the desham declared a whole month less in Dakshayani's calendar.

74

'Ah! Thath'bboy's sumthin'! Lookit 'im, all alon' climbin' up in tha middl' of all tha polic'? He's wabin' tha flag . . . pipple are throwin' ston's fro' ther' . . . ther' . . . they're' showbin' him, only him . . . Oh, tha's justh a smallbboy . . .'

Biju dragged the chair closer and closer to the TV. Behind him, a melancholy silence had collected. On the screen, three mostly helpless minarets stood raising their hands towards the heavens.

The TV kept showing the boy who slipped past the police and climbed to the top of the minaret. Biju's eyes were fixed on the images of the minarets collapsing from one side.

'Abu-kka, how longg does ith tak' fer tha whol' thin' to fall downn?'

He asked, not taking his eyes off the screen. Abubacker knew that Biju was too young to fathom the depth of what was happening, but he was too stunned to say anything. The boy on the screen was around his age; he looked like a hero to him. When Abubacker felt that the stones and dust were piling on his feet, he pulled back his outstretched legs. Ayisha stood leaning on the door, both hands on her face. Inside the room, Kaisumma, trying hard to breathe, asked her what was on TV.

'Nothin', elayumma, yuh lie downn.'

She came near Abubacker slowly.

'Diddtthey swoop down onnith sudde'ly,' she asked.

'No, no. Eberyon' knew they'd breakkitth down.'

No one spoke for some time. Biju got bored of seeing the same images again and again.

'Will they habe oth'r programm's afther ith's brok'n downn totally, Abu-kka?' He looked at Abubacker impatiently. Abubacker stood up suddenly, went to the TV set, and switched it off.

'Yuh go home, Biju,' he said.

Biju was of the age when such a rebuff could have an impact. And the three boons that had followed Abubacker all his life— that what he thought to say would not fall from his mouth; that instead, something completely opposed would emerge from there; and that no one would be convinced of the rightfulness of his acts—also acted instantly.

Kalyani was surprised to see Biju return swiftly, like a stone from a sling.

'Wha's ith, eda?'

'Go fin' ou' fer yersel'!' He snapped.

'Wha'?'

She persisted seriously. Before he stepped out, tying on his head the towel that was hanging to dry on the clothesline, he muttered, 'Damn his TV! He's notttha onl' one here bith a TV!'

Kalyani felt a strange fear. Such fear she had known only during the nights of the Ripper hunt, when she watched a sleeping Biju, sleepless herself. She stood there, gazing at the path through which he had stomped out. Then she went to Kaisumma's house. Kaisumma had not returned to the shed; Nebisu had not returned. She could not go back there, anyway, as she was bedridden now. The two people who were bedridden in the desham were Kaisumma and Achootty Maash. Kalyani visited them often. They were the senior-most there; weather-beaten heads that had seen much sun and mist and rain. Who had known the childhood of the desham. Balan did not like Kalyani visiting much. He had instructed his wife not to let her too close. When her head appeared on the street outside, he would shoo his two daughters inside. Don't know what all she might say—that was his excuse. When Kalyani reached his front yard, he would step down there and ask, 'Wha'?' She knew that his aim was to stop her from entering. But she did not care. Whether she studied a lot or not in school, he was her teacher. A master—maash—is a national treasure of the desham. Balan could do nothing about that.

She would go near him and smear sandal-paste from the temple on his forehead.

'Tha's tha goddess' blessin''—Amma's sandal-pasthe. I've offer'd coc-nut oil at tha *kaavu*-themple in yer name . . . justh don'bbe afraidd'.'

The streak of sandal-paste marking would sneer at Balan long after Kalyani left. It made him angry.

Kalyani did not need permission to enter Kaisumma's room. She would feel sad when she went there.

'Kaisumma, d'yuh bant kara-appam? Madeinn ghee?'

No, she would shake her head. But Kalyani would anyway pull out the kara-appams moist with ghee from her waist-flap. When its scent spread in the room, Kaisumma would smile in the light of an old memory. On Vishu mornings, a little girl clad in nothing but a torthu-mundu around her waist, an imp who knew only to run and not walk, would hurry there, her untamed, unoiled hair flying, with a bronze bowl full of kara-appams. Little Nebisu would be waiting in the veranda for her.

'Gibe ith to Nebisu, kunhi,' Kaisumma would say. 'She really adoressith.' Kalyani could hear that even before she came close.

When she went over to Kaisumma's house that day, the house was totally silent; not even a leaf moved. For the first time, it stared at her as if she were a stranger. Kalyani saw that distance on Ayisha's face too.

'Wha's it, Ayisha-tha, sumthin' not righth?'

Ayisha did not reply. Kalyani peeped into Kaisumma's room. Abubacker contrived a smile, avoided her, and went off into the house.

'Nothi' . . . justh thath elayumma's condishun is ser'ous . . .'

Ayisha said that, but she did not make way for Kalyani. She looked pensive, leaning on the doorframe. A sharp, gnawing silence shrouded Kalyani. If it is word for word, you can win advancing your words. If it is blow for blow, you can advance too through blows. But if they have decided to hold themselves back, to embrace defeat, what is the use of competing with them?

'Elayumma is sleepin' . . .' Ayisha said. 'No on' hassslepth a wink 'ere lasth nighth.'

'Leth her sleepp. I'll come lat'r.'

Kalyani withdrew. She felt the distance between her home and Abubacker's grow too long to cover on foot.

That night, Kaisumma passed.

75

When she stepped on that boundary-marker built of boulders and soil, Kalyani's leg sank almost till her knee. That was a bandicoot's den. Kalyani did not feel at that moment that she should trap and drown the bandicoot who had apparently set his heart on burrowing his way to the end of the earth. Hugging the dried-up jackfruit tree at the boundary of her yard, she watched Kaisumma leave. Dakshayani was living at that moment in her calendar-less time. When Kaisumma passed by his house, Achootty Maash's Adam's apple became especially visible. The whole desham gathered on the panchayat road, saying farewell to her in silence. For a long time, Kalyani stood there, her arms tightly wrapped around the dead tree's trunk and her foot deep in the bandicoot's trench. Sometimes life spills on the floor but its contents may not spread and flow. Sometimes when you pick it up relieved that it didn't break, it will shatter into hundreds and hundreds of fragments; it will be lost forever. So no prediction is really possible about life. Till the moment it touches the tongue, nothing can be said about the taste of anything.

For days after Kaisumma's departure, Kalyani lived wordlessly. The house oppressed her, terribly. There's a limit to which cows or humans or kitchens can hold anyone close. To think that we are indispensible in any place is foolishness, given that no task or thing has ever revealed a preference for who is to do it or take it. And besides, Kalyani had never felt any belonging in her own house, ever. Kalyani was the girl who was dragged into its veranda, tied to the pillar there, tried, beaten, and finally pushed out into the yard. She needed a house from which to set out after her wedding—that was her only tie to it. This house was just the jackfruit bulb that bore and ejected her like a seed, or the bow which released her like an arrow, or the quiver that carried her temporarily. Each time she returned wounded, it was the war-tent that rejected the failed and wounded warrior. And so she had the feeling that her real roots lay in the house that she had long thought of as alien to her—Koppu-man's house. Suddenly she felt a rush of love for the handsome man who had left her such a house, removing himself from it. The day he left, he had come up to her and brushed off the dust from her hair. She was sure that he had looked at her that day with great gentle curiosity, with eyes that had been freshened and readied for all of his life's remaining sights.

'If onlly he cam'bbekk . . . If only I cud see him once mor' . . . he's a moth'rless chil' . . .' Something of that sort pulsed inside Kalyani. One day at noon, she pulled up Biju and went to Koppu-man's desham. Kalyani's going and coming was nothing new to her own desham. She always came back. Her roads touched two deshams.

Kalyani had already felt that she should take Biju away from here. He'd grown now, but hardly spoke with her these days. If they did speak, it would end in a quarrel. Quarrelling was Kalyani's field; even if the opponent was smashed, she would still twirl her tongue and hang back for some more.

Biju had been acquiring the tails and tips of a whole bunch of tales, meanwhile. He was also using them quite dexterously to defeat her. The thorn-tips of the conflict between mother and son sometimes extended outward as well. Though the next generation of cows tended by Kalyani and Dakshayani retained their legacy of thinking, their knowledge was shallow. All they knew was their mothers' prophecy that Biju would be Kalyani's biggest headache, nothing more. That is, they knew what histhory was, but not how it would work out in a particular conjuncture. And so they could not explain the cause-effect relationships that worked to firm up Biju's belief that Kalyani had returned to her house abandoning a good husband for her love of the Muslim.

'Bu'tthen, bu'tthen, my dear . . .' Kalyani lamented in front of Dakshayani on the day she left for Koppu-man's house.

Dakshayani was in the time when her calendar dropped a month. She was meeting the deceased communist leader and ex-Chief Minister of Kerala, E K Nayanar. He was of course, from their desham—a very interesting meeting for Dakshayani, but still she saw the seriousness of Kalyani's issue.

'I tol' Nayanar, whe' he cam' here, thath he shud tak' a decishun abou' tha mosque! Annywa' Biju musth inherit tha mosque sum day? Why's ith bein' kepth lik'thath? He an' his mosque! Letthim loo' afther ith! Nayanar sai'thath ith is bery hardd to be lookin' afther cashewnuts an' coconuts, so ith is betther to sellith. I saidd—no, yuh can' sell becos ith belon's to his fath'r . . . He shook my handd sayin' ooh Dakshayani, yuh know all thissowwell!'

Dakshayani held out her hand.

'Greath!'

Kalyani laughed, wiping her face with the edge of her mundu.

'I'll tak' sum thime to com' bekk. If only he'll putddownn his roots there! Yuh shud lookkafther yersel', don' go nea' tha well . . .'

Biju did not like Koppu-man's house. The house did not like him, either. When he tried to go inside it, it dropped a piece of tile on his head. It pricked him with thorns. Made the spiders lick him.

'Ith's *my* son, alrighth?'

Kalyani went near Chonnamma's kottam and said softly.

'Thath mebbe fer yuh. Fer me ith doesn' matther—amma, acchan, kunhi, nothin' matthers. If they try talkin' rubbish befor' me, I'll break thei' legs.'

She saw the sliver of red slip down the erinjhi tree and heard the sound of the anklet when the foot touched the ground.

A woman of two deshams is like someone with their feet in two canoes. Any moment, both may be lost. Whether in gain or loss, two is bigger than one.

'Yuh don' play too big, uh? I got to know yer virtue an' all.' Biju said.

'Wha' tha hell di' yuh gethtto know?'

'Don'mmake me say thath . . . A womin lik' yuh is a dissggrac' to pipple . . . Don' thin' tha' nobod' knows anythin'.'

'The' tellmme wha' yuh know, since yuh know so muchh! Yuh tellmme!'

'Haben' yet heardd wha' all pipple are talkin', though yer gaddin' up'n' dow' all tha thime?' I'm tha one thath hears, d'yuh know?'

'My goin' aroun' is my bizness. Yuh don'bbother abou'thath.'

'Fro'nnow on yuh habe to tell me when yuh go out. Yuh betther sthay insid' tha house.'

'Yuh sonofadog! Tryin'tto keepp me in line? Bith tha' body of yers thath grew big becos I brough' hom' foodd workin' on tha sthone and tha thorn? Who're yuh to conthro'mme, huh? I'll bash yuh to a pulp! Bigg'r pipple habe tried to conthrol Kalyani an' I didn' gibe a damn! And *yuh*, bant to try, really?'

'If yuh wan' to sthay here yuh can' don' any of thi'.'

'Sthay wher'? Don' do wha'?'

'Eeda. Thissplace. An' none of yer games, annyymore.'

'Pha! Yuh mis'rable starbin' gruel! Yuh'd betther be clea' abou' one thin'. Yuh habe nothin' eeda. Tha man of this 'ouse, eeda, is not yer father. Tha dogs tha' piss'd all tha sthories in yer ear in both plac's—go ask'em about yer father. Go tell'em to search' aroun' fer yer father an' geth his wealth fer yuh! Go, NOW!'

When Biju stormed off, Kalyani ran after him, wailing, cursing.

'Leththa serpenth geth yuh! I got wha' I deserbed fer raisin' yuh, yuh who wer' justh a mis'rable babeworm!'

Kalyani sat on the stepping stone to the house and blew her nose. She went over to the well and sobbed into it. The water lay motionless, nearly petrified.

'Kalyani, yuh can go,' said the house.

'Ith's noth yeth thime fer yuh to comm'ere. Don' scar' off tha baidyar an' Machunan an' Cheyi an' balyechi. Don'mmake Chonnamma angry. She won' brook suchtthings if she's in a rage. She'll justh plukk' an' throw! Yuh take tha chekkan an'ggo.'

Unable to find any peace, she went off to Chonnamma's at an unearthly hour.

The darkness was heavy in the kottam.

'Pleas' don' harm my boy becos I curs'd 'im whe' my heart was bburnin' . . .'

She tapped the fence lightly with a branch of the golden chempaka tree that touched the kottam.

A dying tongue of flame suddenly leapt up.

'Kalyani . . !'

A voice rose from the kottam.

She raised her disconsolate face.

'Do not count tha price of bearin' and rearin'. Thath's no goodd. Bearin' is a way to end yer sins. Helpin' in birth, too. Didn' Cheyi tell yuh tha sthory of tha'pothy—tha Bhagavathy—who end'd her sins by goin' from one birthin' chamber to another'? Yuh'd slepth off befor' she tol' all of ith? I'll tell yuh tha resth, wan'tto listhen?'

76

'Thi' was tha sthory of tha womin who show'd tha Lord of tha Land tha sorrow of losin' fourtheen chil'ren—thath kepth smoulderin' so much thath tha paddy put on her breath puffed up!'

'Don' leth thi' womin anybhere in tha Land! Wind 'er up in fourtheen drapes! Douse 'er bith oil! Seth'er on fire!'

The Lord of the Land hid his fear and bellowed. His minions wound her tightly in layer after layer of cloth, doused her with oil, set her on fire, and forced her to run. She was blown away like a torch in the wind. Swept into the river, she was caught in the swirling currents, and in the end, she sprouted and bloomed—and became an exquisite, rare flower. The wominflower's stem was blue and its petals were white, edged with the colour of fire. Its scent was that of cooked paddy.

When the Tantri of Kaalakkaat—that skilled Brahmin exorcist—got into the river to take a bath, he saw the wominflower floating by. A man who doesn't know that there can never be just a single bloom of a kind in the world can't be a Tantri. Seeing that there was no plant under the flower, he extended his hand.

'Hey, *Poo-pathy*, Half-Blossom, womin who becam' half-flow'r, will yuh sith in tha' worship-room quiethly? If so, com' bith me.'

Wominflower went along with the Tantri. She first agreed to share space with others at his home, but soon went back on her word. She refused to eat with them. She began to dislike her neighbours. Imagine, a womin who could recite the whole of the Ramayanam by heart, having to sit with fools—that's what she thought!

'Womin, hal'-flow'r, ge'mme tha' kindi jug,' the Tantri would command. No one dared disobey him in the worship-room. The prices he paid for his skills in magic were a whole lifetime (and the mother of his only daughter). The gods could not repay his losses. Though they were ready to do anything for him, the Tantri refused. So they did little things for him and stayed close—if Ganapathy pulled down for him the tender coconuts, the 'pothy—Bhagawathy—strung the flowers together for worship. Tantri, who could readily spot the reluctance on their faces, would ask firmly, 'Do you want to leave your seats? Or d'yuh bant tha offerin's of flow'rs and wat'r?'

But wominflower had had enough.

There was no way out. Though well-born, though learned, there was no escape from this slavish life.

When Kaalakkaatu Tantri was sitting in the worship-room, one day, his daughter, who had just given birth, went to the pond for a bath.

'Father,' she called. 'Tha babe's sleepin'. I'm goin' off fer a bath.'

It was then that the Gurukkal, the Master of the *kalari*, where young warriors were trained, brought the students' threads to be blessed. That was a time-consuming job. When Tantri took the threads and went inside with them, he heard the baby bawling. You can't put aside the kalari-threads and go off to do something else. That was not a good omen. The lives of the kalari-students, who will grow up to become the *chekons*—the warriors who guard the land—are in the hands of the Tantri and the residents of his worship-room.

'Hey, yuh new womin, Half-flow'r,' he called.

There was no answer. But the flame in the lamp before him leapt to life.

'Can' yuh show sum loyalthy? Comm'ere'?'

The Tantri was irked.

'Womin, justh sthop tha babe's wailin'.'

The flame in the lamp grew dim.

The baby's wails stopped.

When his daughter came in after her bath, the Tantri called her near and said: 'Tha babe wa' cryin' an' I tol' a womin to look. Now ther's no sound, yuh go an' see? I'm searin' insid', an' my manthras are failin'.'

A moment after she went in to check on the infant, he heard her heartrending cries. Flinging aside the mantras, he leapt up.

'Ah, daive! Woe!'

'Didn' yuh tellmme to sthop tha babe's wails? AnddI didd . . . ith won' cry agai' . . .'

'Pha! Evilspawn! Yuh sthop a babe's wails by killin' ith? Yuh who gabe birth fourteen thimes!'

Tantri abandoned the worship-room that very day. He sent away all the spirits he had housed there. He left the place with his daughter. Before leaving, he flung the flower back into the river. The flower now floated on, twisting and turning in the currents. It did not know why it did what it did. That's the thing about revenge and vengeance. It doesn't end where it began. It affects people who may have had to do nothing with it. Because the whole land knew the tragedy of Kaalakkaattu Tantri, the Poontottathu Tantri did not touch Half-Flower when he first saw her. He took her only when the Lord of the Land made a direct request.

'How will I believe you?' he asked her.

'I'll athone fer wha' I di'dd I really habe no bengeance . . . no unthouchability. . . I'll becom' a midwif' and go from birthin' room to birthin' room . . ,' Half-flower wept.

'I won' gibe yuh my word, Kalyani. Fer yer act an' yer word, yuh alone are tha witness. Kalyani, tha value of a word lasths onlly when ith is utter'd. Afther thath ith is justh usel'ss, mere husk! Hal'-flow'r who saidd she'll sthay subdu'd has beathen to death little babes even afther she made thath promise . . .onlly thath tha babes don' feel anny pain . . .iths justh like getthin' lighthly brush'd bith a cow's tail. If she doesn' feel thath tha honour she deserbes is not comin' she justh tears ith off tha groun'—ith may be justh a sprout or a mere sapling . . . She's borne fourtheen chil'ren, rememb' an' rais'd them . . . still . . . she's thath way!!'

Chonnamma paused. Then she continued:

'Kalyani, mothers donnott turn softh an' gibin' an' yieldin' justh becos they gibe birth. Theyccan be hardd and takin' and resistin'!! Don'ttyuh go softh inside now!! But then there's this: you can' think of gibing birth and bringin' up as things you do to gethsumthin' fer yerself, to gethsumthin' done, or sthop sumone from doin' sumthin' . . .'

The flame died. Kalyani too was steeped in darkness, along with the Chonnamma kottam. She groped her way back to the stone-step, breathless, panting—and sank down on it.

77

Let me remind you that I am permitted to follow Kalyani only up to this point, where she is sitting bowed and despondent, on the stone step of her house. For your sake, I have elbowed my way as much as I can into the life of Kalyani and Dakshayani, the sthory of which I undertook to tell under special circumstances. This was out of the belief that not just the person who lives a life, but also the person who undertakes to tell it, has a place in it. And this is because the two of them and the narrator roll together in the same life, like chicken pieces in biryani. As indicated earlier, if there was no permission to use their names, then this would have been quite different a narration. I must say that at least in parts of this narration, the fact that those two names stood on their own, without kinship-descriptors, was useful in overcoming a certain kind of guilt, akin to that that one feels after peeping into the bedrooms of older people (ah, don't glare—hearing, not just seeing, also qualifies for that guilty feeling). Also, there are many characters who popped up coincidently when the sthory of these two was being narrated. Their sthories were shared at different times by Kalyani and Dakshayani, and I collated them from their accounts. I have struggled to gather them up and hurry on, in order to keep pace with their swift-flowing lives.

Too many people sit on this *and* that side of the table trying to lecture me on all the toils and troubles that will waylay me on the road of life. It's possible that I may actually tumble down

I apo

into the hole they've dug inadvertently by just listening to them. For me, these sthories are the antidote to the venom that they injected as advice and threat. I have heard that seafarers about to drown leave a message in a bottle, cork it, and set it afloat before they finally go down under. My sthory-telling has a similar purpose. This is my request: those who get their hands on this narration someday should use it to counteract the social viper's venom—and yours too.

From now, I will be using the names Kalyani-echi and Dakshayani-echi instead of Kalyani and Dakshayani. One reason for doing so is that Biju is my classmate. I must indeed consider the indelicacy of calling his mother by her first name. I am returning the Power of Attorney granted to me earlier by Kalyani-echi for the free use of her first name. And because Kalyani-echi and Dakshayani-echi have declared that from now on, if they have something to say, they will say it themselves; and because I too also something to say here; and also because our sensibility has broadened enough to include Kalyani and Dakshayani (Oh no, *cche*! the two echis)—I am going to end this exercise of walking in someone else's slippers for the time being.

Where, Kalyani-echi, where?

'Kalyani-echiye. . . I am ending the sthory. How was it?'

'A whol' lottof fibs, bu' fun to listhen.'

'That is?'

'Alla, if yuh thin' ith is yersthory, *yuh sthart to meashur an' scratch ith*. Bu' if yuh thin' that ith is summone else's yuh can' listhennicel'! Isn' ithsso, Daachani?'

'Dakshayani-echi doesn' look happy, though. Why is that, Kalyani-echi?'

'How else to feellif yuh say thath she has one month less?'

'Ayyoo, didn't I say that because we can put it only that way?'

'Ah, thaths righthtoo. Bu' we can add wha' you hab'nt been able to say, if we bant to, righth?'

'Of course.'

'Ah, my dearr . . ?

'What's that coy smile, Kalyani-echi?'

'Go'wway, yuh imp.Tha coy smile is yer Amma's! Yer ol'womin's, huh!'

'Coyness isn't so bad! And Ammas are always coy? Kalyani-echi, you should not be speaking so apolitically. You have an image now. Don't throw it away.'

'Wha'd yuh say?'

'Apol-iti-cal.'

'*Poli* . . .? Breakkup? Bu' I didn' breakksumthin'up? Yea, didn' *poli* summin, nor did I agree to do thath . . ? *Polikkaannuettillallaa* . . .'

'Ayyo! I'm going to lie down and die! Kalyaniechi, "apolitical" has nothing to do with *polikkal* . . .'

'Ok, yer Acchan's tha coy one, will thathddo?'

'Ok. Yuh've become political now.'

'Thath'ss all? So easy tobbe poli . . .'

'Yes, that easy!'

78

'Did'yuh know, new pipple habe com to tha house bhere Daachani's nailsvendor libed?'

'No, who?'

'Wha', my dear? Yuh're neighbo's! Yuh shud know!'

'If I wander here and there, my Acchan and Amma will scold me.'

'Ah, ezzellen'! Sith at'ome, don'ggo an'bhere!'

'Who are new people there, Kalyani-echi?'

'Tha new ingineer fer our canaal they say. He an' his wif an' kunhi. Tha firsthingineer in our place! They ar' southies—*chettammaru*—thath girl is bery pretthy!'

'Really, that nice?'

'Yess! Lik' tha moobie starr Lissy!'

'Hey, you never liked Lissy, Kalyani-echi?'

'No'jjusth me, eben her man doesn' lik' her, I thin'.'

'Who doesn't like her?'

'Her puruvan, tha ingineer.'

'Oh. How come you know?'

'She's askin' how we know, Daachani, wha' to say?'

Dakshayani-echi opened her umbrella and stepped out into the rain. She turned towards us and said: 'Ther's no lines on her bekk, kunhi. Lon' time bekk, a womin tol' me tha' if a womin is lovved, she'll habe lines on her bekk, lik' a squirrel. Thath was when I'd gone to Kollam. Thath womin has com' to my 'ouse. Lemme go gibe her som' food. Meethin' her afther long!'

'I'm comin' too, don'ggo by yersel', lemme share yer umbrella!' Kalyani-echi ran after her in the rain.

The house where Dakshayani-echi's nailsvendor had lived was being repaired and extended. The flooring was now of red oxide. The windows had new bars. The kitchen now became much bigger and instead of a single well for five rented-out houses, it now had its own well. After the new tenants arrived, loud music could be heard from there. I could make out that it was from a tape recorder. One day when I came back from school, Amma was not yet back from work. I had time; usually, when Amma was late, I had the permission to hang around a neighbour's house till she came home. Usually I am at Ammini teacher's, at the back of our house. Her mother would feed me rice laddus and tea. When I got bored, I'd go out and walk around the yard. That day, I decided to gather my courage and go meet the new neighbours. Though the house appeared more mysterious the closer I got, I did not give up.

I had the memory of a movie, *Sandarbham*, in which our Malayalam cine-star Mammootty—though he dies in the end after falling from a building—is a good engineer. And on top of it we all knew that only those who aced math could become engineers. I am in a contrary relationship with math. My life is the reference for that. Any calculation, any method—if I do the sums, the answer will be wrong. If I got it right, it will go wrong when I copy it in the bottom of the sum. So I am full of respect for engineers, people whose calculations never goes wrong. It was with the same respect that I approached the math-experts in our class. And besides, to be an engineer's wife, you had to have a minimum qualification. I remembered the cine-star Lissy. Not much hope there, either, I alerted myself. When I stepped on their veranda, a baby's rattle was lying there, looking lonely and orphaned. The song which began '*Dreams, All of our dreams, let us share . . .'* was playing rather loudly. I suddenly realized there was also loud talk going on. Though I knew that pressing the calling bell was the decent thing to do, I could not help the urge to peep inside. I went around the house, bowing my head, towards the side of the room from where the song wafted. The tape recorder played there. Amma and Acchan had brought us up so well, with such clear, non-negotiable dos and don'ts! But I decided to set all that aside. They had left the window open, trusting the wire-netting covering it and the thin curtains.

Any thief will intermittently turn around to check if the world is interfering in their act. Once my own checking was done, I felt quite satisfied with my ability to be a law-breaker. The good-looking engineer was in the room. Since that was the first time I saw a man of his age without a shirt, it took me some time to notice the lady, Lissy-lookalike, sitting opposite him. Though her face wasn't clear, I noticed that she had wrapped a mundu around her body under her arms, covering her breasts. They were fighting furiously. The engineer rushed at her and delivered a forceful blow on her shoulder. I saw her lose balance and fall on the bed. The mundu came loose but she tightened it around her still lying there. I simply could not digest a woman famed by now for her beauty, snapping at her husband in a voice full of tears and anger. He advanced again, aiming a blow at her. I tried to sort out the stifling feeling in my head that came out of thinking that 'No, this shouldn't be this way'; just then their quarrel went up another level. Unexpected sights, even if they have nothing to do with your life, are capable of turning things upside down within you, just like momentous events.

Right then I saw the engineer plunge towards the bed and hold Lissy down by her neck. I froze and lost my voice. My mouth gaped open; I submitted myself passively to the sights that followed. In such moments, your sight and hearing multiply manifold. So I stood there like a machine that recorded many strange sights and sounds passively. The netting, curtains, and the song from the tape-recorder were now useless. I saw everything, including the strange guttural sound that rose from her throat when his mouth devoured her lips. Though I feared that the mundu that covered her might block my sight when his body crashed on hers, that did not happen. It fell calmly on the ground. When he raised his face, she whined. It is very distressing to watch a human being whine and yowl, but her broken screams actually comforted me. It was after quite a long time that I realized that this was because the sounds assured me that she was still alive. He thrust out his left hand and pressed it hard on her mouth and nose. I was sure that her breasts were in his right hand. I was half-petrified when I saw her legs thrash about on the bed. It was the same I who once seeing a similar murder scene in a movie, had ducked under the chair shutting my eyes and covering my ears, who was now watching it live from the window. *Run*, something urged, but something else that prompted me to stay overcame it. When I was shuddering, almost sure that Lissy was dead, I heard another thwack and a scream of pain. Gathering my wits, I peeped in again and saw something that just did not agree with all that had transpired till then: Lissy was being kissed by the engineer. Squashed between contradictions, I felt drained. When the row seemed to have ended, I took one last look. They were now lying together calmly in an embrace. I felt immensely relieved. Only then did I notice a cloth-cradle hanging in the corner of the room, rocking gently. As I sneaked away carefully from the window, my legs were numb. My upper body moved by itself through the air and dragged my legs away, I imagined. Managing somehow to get back to Ammini teacher's house, I turned to look at Lissy's and her engineer's house. The house was in the shade of large cashew trees, with huge boughs growing on all four sides. It frightened me. This was the incident that made me decide that (a) I will never marry an engineer, and (b) I will never see any of Lissy's movies again. Some decisions people take may have made you laugh. It's nothing, really. Don't some of our decisions make us, eventually, almost fall dead laughing? Just think of it that way.

'Wha' my dear, yer face lookin' sad?'

'Nothing, Kalyani-echi.'

'Nothin'?Thenwwhy?'

'Nothing. This life is a great wonder, isn't it?'

'*Ammoppa*! If yuh sthart libin' thinki' thath this life of yers—yers alone—is THA life, mebbe thath's tha big wonder. Becos we all justh walk'd togeth'r bith each oth'r, mebbe ith didn'sseem thath'way, uh?'

'Kalyani-echi, can we love someone even as we hurt them?'

'Oh my dear, isn' lovving ithssel' a big throuble? Wha 'ssthamatther?'

'Can someone share the same house with another without loving them or talking with them?'

'Fer sum time, yes. If fer a lon'ttime, only a husban' an' wife canddo thath. Yuh tell me, wha'swron'?'

'Nothing.'

'Yuh're grown allbig now.'

'Why do you say that, Kalyani-echi?'

'Nothing. My son's grown allbig too. I can'ttmmake ou' wha'ss in his mindd. He's not goin' to sthay in his fath'r's'ouse, or here.'

79

'Yuh're comin' to tha ingineer's'ouse?'

I leapt up from my seat hearing Kalyani-echi. The net-covered window and the sights behind it appeared before me again from months back. I had not thought of going there again. If I do, I thought, I was likely to go stand by that window again.

'What is happening?'

'Nothin'. We can see tha babe ther'? Comin'?'

It was Lissy who opened the door. I hid behind Kalyani-echi, overcome by an unknown fear. She had a pinkish face and had to hide the bluish scars on it with many smiles as she chatted with us. Almost like she was waiting for visitors, she served us tea and roasted peas sprinkled with pepper powder. I got a real shock when I found out that her name was indeed Lissy. It was around the time when I was discovering such supernatural abilities of mine. If I told a lie—it need not be a lie, just a statement about something I really didn't know of—it would come true, wondrously. How funny!

We found out that the 'Vinci-chan' she mentioned was the engineer. He is a very stubborn man, very set in his ways. An only son. He is staying away from his family home only because of this job. There was a great difference in economic status between his family and hers. And there were problems that came with it.

'Whaatever—if yoo don'ddu back-aanser, ther' ees no problem,' said Lissy. 'If yoo say any back-aanser then, oh Godu-

353

Karthaave, then yoo haave lost it. He may even beatte! But aafter thaat he will be derriblylovving. And if he haas two drinks, then *tekanju*, combleatly fine! But he is phayankara lovving to me, derriblylovving to me, eh? Vinci-chan will die for the faamily.'

She shook all over in her laughter.

We did not even smile.

'Wha'eber, don'gget beathen.'

Kalyani-echi said it aloud, and I, in my mind.

The baby looked exactly like Lissy. It crawled on the floor. A baby girl in a pink frock. I sat on the floor and touched her. My fingers felt her softness. Kalyani-echi and Lissy chatted as though they had known each other since many years.

'We yaar trying for a bo-iy,' she told Kalyani-echi. Kalyani-echi promised to get her the tender coconut offering from the temple of the Goddess at Idipeel, from the Theyyam there. If you drink the water from that coconut, you'll get pregnant soon and deliver easily. So many wimmin around here have experienced it.

When we came back, Kalyani-echi said that Lissy need not have acted so much. Her laughter was all hollow. You can know from sight if a woman laughs from within. Such women may not laugh outwardly.

'How old did she say the child was?' I asked Kalyani-echi.

'One, I though' she saidd.'

She looked at me.

'Then why did she talk of another child?'

'So thenn shud all pipple in tha land be an only-chil', lik' yuh? Tha two will justh go togeth'r . . . buth he hasn' let her body grow firm afther tha firsth one. He broughth her here afther justh a month.'

'Firming the body? What's that?'

'Ther's such a thingg as thath. . . accordin' to them pipple, they're atppeac' onl' if they habe a boy . . .'

Kalyaniechi suddenly slipped on a thought and slid down into some hole. *Becos ther's no man aroun' . . !*

I remembered how many times Biju used to say that.

'Wha's tha use of a moth'r lik' thiss?' he would say, 'Noth my moth'r, thath one! Is yer moth'r lik' thiss? Doe'sshe walk all ober tha place insthead of sitthin' at home? Has she made tha pipple talk? Pipple here are eben sayin' thath my fath'r is a Muslim.'

I did not take that seriously. I like mothers like Biju's mother, I longed to say.

But Kalyani-echi did not have the fortune to get a blessed coconut from the temple of Idipeel Amma, nor did Lissy have the luck to drink the sacred coconut water. Lissy's *appachan* got a telephone call from the Irrigation Project Office. The old man reached the desham by the morning train, crying that his son-in-law had told him on the phone that if he didn't take back his daughter and grandchild, he can look for them in the river. The engineer had locked the house and left, leaving the key with the house-owner. Lissy and the baby were in Ammini teacher's house. Lissy did not say a word. The old man kept sniveling and beating his breast. He apparently felt something bad was going to happen, something ominous, right after the wedding. My father, who had become more or less a local there, told them that he could help open the door if they needed to get something from inside the house.

'I haave nothing to taike from there, saare,' said Lissy, in a hoarse voice. She was holding her baby close. 'If this was a bbo-iychild, I wouldn't haave got even it.'

Watching Lissy weep, it seemed to me that the faamily was a place where horrors were neatly concealed. Later, when I heard that word, I would feel a sense of desperation, as though my head was stuck inside a pot. Before I cast suspicion on people gathered in faamiles that they have covered up much under golden-lace blankets, I have to turn my sharp eye towards my own home. That is, of course, the first faamily I knew and was a part of. Back then as a kid I used to dream of cute white mice scampering around me. They would come and nuzzle, hanging off the edges of my white bed-sheets. A horse-carriage, from the many Russian stories for children that I read, would arrive in the narrow bedroom of our rented house. The mice would soon turn into horses to be hitched to the carriage! The wheels of the carriage would land inside the bedroom with a juddering sound. But just then, I would wake up rudely, hearing faint squeaks—and find Acchan killing mice. My sleep broken, I would sit cross-legged on the bed and watch these murders. When I remembered that they were to become the horses for my carriage, I would weep.

'Now! Go back to sleep!' Only Acchan's command would send me back to bed.

On some days, I would not hear the wheels. But I could hear people making a huge ruckus. I was in an Arabian bazaar, fully lit. I would suddenly notice that no one was holding my finger and shriek from fear. When I jumped awake, I would see that I was in the middle of an ideal couple who chose the hour of midnight for their battles, so that the kid wouldn't know.

'Go to sleep at once, did you hear?'

When Acchan commanded sharply, I would turn to the other side of the bed and pretend to be asleep. My heart would be pounding hard. My throat would be dry. Even now, when a quarrel goes out of hand, I quake as though in a seizure. The faamily does not fear the emptiness of the desert like it fears a girl who has failed to walk the right steps.

He said that he had nothing to gain from a baby girl— Vinci-chan said—sobbed Lissy. The desham listened to her in sheer disbelief.

'Al'righth, didn' habe a boy. But why do pipple put'upp bith so muc', fer tha sak' of wha' starbin' gruel?' Kalyani-echi grumbled.

'I too habe a boy? He's alwa's quarrellin', quarrellin' wheneber he saw me! Wha' am I to do if he's sthart'd feelin' thath his moth'r's no goodd? If ith's Mangalapuram, the' letthithbbe Mangalapuram, letthim libe bher'eber. Ah, wha' else am I to say? Ith's a totall fib, tha whol' thin', no?'

If the sthories aren't about you, it is easy to make friends with them. Maybe that's why I loved Kalyani-echi's sthories and Biju hated them. But although he left for Mangalapuram, Biju's lived a good life. Kalyani-echi was happy about that.

Though I am one of the heirs to the legacy and the land of Kalyani-Dakshayanis, for some reason, it had not grown on me with the same intensity. How was the desham to accept someone did not smell herself, learn of her own scents? I became part of its histhory as the chief protagonist of the first wedding conducted there in an auditorium—that is, whose wedding wasn't in the front-yard of her own house. But only when my departure was imminent—after the ceremony and the feast—did the desham get etched into my heart, as truly and intensely mine. I wept really hard when I realized that all this dressing-up as a bride was really meant to cover up the bitter truth: that I was expected to leave behind forever the winding village paths, the mud-walls that slowly dissolve in the rain, the chirpy brightness of houses with playful calves, the heady aroma of the dosas growing crisp on hot stones, and the impenetrable mysteries of the cashew-groves. Meanwhile, unperturbed by the fear that its quiver would ever empty, the desham was nocking the next arrow on its bow.

80

Seeing the expression on Narayanamurthy's face, I could not help offering this explanation:

'Look, these stories I tell you are special. They are not dense and so tend to flow and spread fast. Perhaps faster than you think. They do much better and more thoroughly the work that you and your theories do. Except that their impacts are quite different and not what you would want. They refer to events that have already happened. They can't change their thrust—to suit your idea of the general good. Condemn them all you want, but they are under no obligation to hold up anything that is dead and fallen. But I am not trying to say that you are incapable. Just that you really can do nothing in my case.'

Narayanamurthy stood up. I could see that he was slightly put off.

'One can't really depend on individuals beyond a point in any deal. Making a deal on behalf of an institution like the family is quite different from making a deal from an individual's side. We may ignore an individual's inner emotions and preferences. But that's hardly possible when it comes to an institution. Because it is a collection of the inner emotions and preferences of a group of people. I am still talking about the family. That is my first concern. Your parents requested me to restore to them their daughter as she used to be. Your husband's demand was to give him back his obedient wife.'

Returning to his seat, Narayanamurthy picked up a pen and began to sketch some geometrical shapes on the paper in front of him. He then raised his eyes, held me in a decisive look, opened the flask, and poured himself a glass of hot water. I was silent. Though the details varied, I had heard these demands many times by now.

'I've listened carefully to all that you said just now and earlier. I can see how close these stories are to your life. There's no doubt that they really boost you up! If we had tried some other form of expression, not even one-fourth of your inner world would have opened up to me. The truth is that I feel lighter too. Like the high you get after a couple of drinks. I have nothing more to ask you. And you are right—as you said, this yields more than drawing. But drawings aren't so hard to interpret! And as in your stories—it is true—in the older times when joint families were the rule, it was the older women who advised girls. Nothing wrong in that, but it wouldn't be professional for sure. Whatever the old ladies think, they sing. Aren't these stories just that? Isn't it an exaggeration to say that they were used as an antidote for the venom we inflict?'

I could hear only the demands made by Vinayan and my own family in what he said. I was sorely irritated at having to belabour the point, such a simple point.

'Why didn't you tell them that nothing in this world exists in pristine form, as it used to be in the distant past, Doctor? Why didn't you tell him that "obedient" is a bad word?'

Narayanamurthy laughed.

'We part ways here. Why should I take your suggestion? I have a certain aim. If I need to reach it, I need to build some small dams here and there. I need to keep time from moving. Things change precisely because time is not static. But imagine it to be static. That you are your parents' little girl. Isn't it comforting? Remember how Cheyikkutty came to see your Kalyani freezing time, and how Machunan and Valyechi came to see her? If time is what wounds us, we must try to stop it from getting at us. Imagine those early days of your marriage; did you not feel for a brief moment at least that you are incomplete without him? Stop your clock at that moment. You'll be able to witness miracles.'

'But the clock can also be turned to other, later moments of our life too? Like, for instance, the one in which I was stranded at the railway station, not able to find three hundred rupees for a season ticket despite drawing a fairly decent salary?'

'Better not do that.'

'What if I turn it back to the moment in which we stood in the queue at the temple to make payments for puja, and when he added a caste-name to Acchan's name, just to let the others there hear?'

'Or maybe to the time when he made a friend call me and tell me that he just had a heart-attack and then hiding in his house, made the same friend shower abuse on me?'

'How can I not laugh?', said Narayanamurthy. 'Why is it that you cannot imagine your husband being in love with you like a teenager? If you can do that, the clock may be stopped there.'

'Why not stop the clock at the moment when my parents were bestowed the titles of 'Sir Cuntfur'—*mairan*-and *poori* 'Madame Cunt', respectively?'

'Better to not stop at these painful moments—and isn't it true that precisely those people who received such honours are waiting outside patiently, arguing for him, with no complaint at all?'

'Should we not turn the clock back to the time when we quarreled every single night throughout my pregnancy?'

'I am told that your husband and parents had suggested a way out of that then itself?'

'Yes. To switch off my mobile phone in those moments.'

'And did you do so?'

'No. I am an officer, I hold a responsible position. I have to attend phone calls even while at home. But how come this is a solution to the problem? What do you do to avoid a dog-bite? Tie up the dog or tie yourself up?'

'Better than going over and getting bitten, maybe one must tie oneself up sometimes.'

'Fine, let that be. But let me tell you something else. Some words come to me so vividly at times, so much so that I wonder if I didn't coin them myself, that I did not come across them in some movie or books. My biggest peeve these days is that I have to wrestle with these random words popping in my mind.'

'If it is obscenities popping in your mind when you stand in a house of God, then there is a discussion of it in Freud's case diary. What words are troubling you now?'

'I don't know if it is obscene. It is: "postmortem-table nights".'

'Ok, I get it. Let me ask you something in return? You don't have to answer this. Just keep the answer in your mind. Do you have any other relationships? You should not lie about this at least to yourself. Such a combination of words—postmortem-table nights—can't come from nowhere?'

I was incensed:

'I can do without the comfort that I have spent so much time with an expert in human psychology—but to think that I opened up with all these stories before someone utterly ignorant!! That is hard to bear.'

'Ok, leave it then. Let's not get into an argument over that. Especially after you are sick of recounting such things before too many people. Let's see how the accusation that you have changed can be dealt with.'

I said nothing. People will have lots to say. Each angle yields different understandings of what's right. When the world accuses someone of changing, do not forget that the same world has a role in making that person capable of changing. Maybe small, maybe big, but the world contributes, no doubt. You can blame those who change, and reject them too. Like Kalyani-echi says, you'll be blamed only if you act; the plough falls upon only the bull which can pull it. So I have no regrets about the tensions in my life and the decisions I took to ease them.

'You are not in a right state of mind,' said Narayanamurthy. 'Decisions taken by someone who isn't in the right state of mind will inevitably go wrong. So don't take any important decisions right now. Put them off for at least six months. I am going to tell everyone involved in this to make sure no upsets happen in this period. If nothing of that kind happens in this period, you should have no problems with continuing in this marriage? Your husband sat before me weeping, begging that he wanted his wife back. The family is everything for him. He said he was willing to forgive all your headstrong, willful acts. Please cooperate—please!'

'But what about my five lovers?'

'Sshe! Did I not tell you what I found when I analyzed his mind? If you ask, he'll say he never said such a thing. Because he has not really said it; just the thought was inside him.'

'I don't think this is going to get better. Have had to meet two of your friends earlier, and I felt the same then. Apologies, Doctor.'

'Let's try. We have six months, after all? Now, please smile, go out and tell your parents cheerfully, "Acchaa, Amme, Doctor wants to see you". You should tell your husband, too. There was a time when you used to call him sweetly, acknowledging his superiority—"Ettaa". Why did you stop? Do not start things that you cannot keep doing. That's going to be the biggest complaint you'll face in the future.'

I nodded and came out of the room. When I tried to coach my mind to think that these people waiting outside are near and dear to me, a great fatigue gripped me. I sank into the nearest sofa.

81

'Shall I bringg yuh sum tend'r coconut from Idippeel Amma's themple?'Kalyani-echi asked.

Dakshayani-echi observed that my belly had begun to fall.

'Tha veins in tha legs habe risen,' she said.

The agreement that there should be no conflicts during the good-behaviour period of six months was already broken. Sometimes I, sometimes Vinayan, broke it. Narayanamurthy had told Vinayan that if that happened, we should not go to him again for a resolution. I began to travel for my life. Because I was constantly accepted and rejected, soon, no one felt any novelty about my obsessive travelling. The desham had already mastered the art of marking such travel in the register of job-related transfers and saving its face. Right before my eyes, the desham transformed itself into something that stood back strategically from the daily life of its people. At least a few times it scared me, or gave up on me. This made me—and my generation—feel that the desham could not be trusted to remain solid enough for us to lean on. For us, it became a place to leave—like homes. The emptiness that this created was horrible. But not many realized the depth of this void. We were children who let go of the desham's fingers to run off into the high streets. For some reason, wherever we went, all those places appeared foreign to us.

'I canno' tak' care of both 'ouses, Appa, lik' in tha old thimes! Biju says we musth sell one. Thath house there I won' sell till I

die. Thi' is goin' to fall annyythime,bu' thissis my birthplace, no?'
Kalyani-echi lamented.

'Fer sum pipple, two places, two houses, two fath'rs, two
moth'rs. . . dubble of eberythin'. Fer oth's, wha'eber wassthere,
eben thath goes away!' Dakshayani-echi grumbled.

Though Dakshayani-echi had noted that my belly was falling,
there was still time according to the gynaecologist; bolstered by this
assurance, I went to the hospital. A pregnant woman coming alone
for the check-up at the gynaec's was a curiosity for onlookers but
I had got used to it, and now, learned how to feel good about it.
I was being taught—very crudely, directly—the different ways in
which people get excluded from spaces they consider their own. It
is certain that whether it helps me or not, all I can do is retain my
faith that things will change. What else would explain the fact that
though I had to leave the house and walk alone on the road in the
dead of night during my early pregnancy, I still lived normally with
Vinayan from the morning of the next day? That faith led me by my
nose on and on, kept alive the hope that things will change, change.

'Wha's thiss? Yuh're alon', uh?'

I turned; it was Biju. I didn't have a clue that he was back here;
I was surprised. The ferocious debates that used to happen between
him and Kalyani-echi had more or less subsided. They were
practicing and learning the art of keeping out of each other's way.

'The doctor says that the baby isn't moving as well as it should.
Asked me to eat something sweet; they'll examine me again after
that. Let me drink something.'

Biju looked at me closely.

'Yuh sith'ere. I'll go geth sumthin'.'

When he walked, I noticed that his right leg seemed to be
dragging a bit. I couldn't see because of his mundu. Did Kalyani-
echi tell me about it? Did I forget?

Biju brought me a glass of very sweet milk. I asked him what
was wrong with his leg. He showed me the bandage on his right
thigh. A motorbike accident. The silencer was searing hot and a

veritable Dhritharashtra. Like the old man embracing Bhima, it pinned him down tightly, searing his leg.

'My moth'r's curse really hiths!' he said.

'Lasth month I made a fuss, sayin' leth's sell fath'r's'ouse. Who's ther' to keep ith now? Amma has to do ith all, at thi'age? Anyway, ith end'd in baddwords, thi'wway an' thathwway. A *maapla* cam' to buy ith—all tha money's bith tha Muslim fello's these days, uh? Bu' he was scar'd whe' he saw tha Chonnamma kottam. Thath day Amma curs'd me to no endd! An' ther' ith sthruck—soon afther, tha bike wenttupsid'ddow'! My lukk, I'm not deadd!!'

I did not hide my amazement.

'That you've been to Mangalapuram is showing!'

'Onlly whennwwe go sum'bhere else will we know tha worth of ou'own birthplace! It keeps scratchin' yuh from tha bekk! No, won' gibeyuh peace.'

At that moment, a pond inside me began to shift. Pushing aside the weeds and slime, a tiny hand rose to the surface. The water rose around me on all four sides and I began to sway in the middle. My body was soaking wet below my waist. The mud-print of Biju's slipper could be seen in the pool collecting below.

'Don'wworry! I call'd hom'—eberybody's comin'. They'll leth yer man know?' Biju ran after me the best he could, pulling his leg behind him, comforting me.

I could see that pond. I couldn't see its depths, but the pond, the surface of which was a dark, blackish green, was coming with me. No, the water on which the flowers of the erinjhi, the wild chempakam, and the murikku fell and floated had collected inside me. It now brimmed over. The little hand was above the water's surface, its palm a tiny tight fist.

'Don't move—if you do, it will drown!'

I screamed helplessly.

Then I saw someone grab the hand and pull it up.

Everyone was in the room when I reached there. The unexpected arrival had jolted them all. Kallu, my little girl, just tall enough to reach below the cot, rolled her eyes and looked keenly at the new arrival. It wasn't very romantic to look at; Kallu actually seemed quite disturbed. Seeing a tiny red leg stick out through the bundle, she ran back to my mother's lap. I clambered on the cot from the wheelchair with some difficulty, Biju supporting me. Seeing him twist the urine bag at the foot of the cot made me feel strange. He tore a piece of paper from the newspaper on the table and wiped the floor here and there with his foot. I asked him what he was doing.

'Nothin', a few drops of blood, her'an'ther'.'

No one said anything.

'I'll go now an'bbebekk. Won' tha kunhi need a mosquitho-cober an' sheeths?'

Biju went out.

Vinayan reached the next morning.

He saw the infant and sat on the sofa. I did not check whether he was happy or not. The truth is that if the presence of another makes you uncomfortable even in your most vulnerable moment, when you need human presence the most, then it means that you can never really love that person. But usually, when that insight begins to dawn, many people simply hold it back and stop their minds from thinking anymore. In order to keep some things steady, other things have to be stopped.

'If olly you had checked the chart aand taiken tha right steps?' Vinayan asked, suddenly.'Olly one among my friends who followed it and made a plan haad ye different experience. They aall had a boy tha second time. Ah, how caan it be different? It's quarrelling aall the time, isn't it, *allyo*?'

Carefully, I tried to shift my body towards the baby. I had been thinking, lying in bed, that the windows of the room which were all closed should be opened. When Vinayan came near the window, I remembered Narayanamurthy.

'It's not true that you'll be calm only if you vent out everything you think,' he had said. 'It's better to keep some things to yourself rather than end up as an Abubacker who wants to say something, but says something else.'

'Who waas here?' Vinayan asked.

'Biju.'

'Who yis that matherfucker to get my baiby all these things? Lett me see him!'

There is nothing more unbearable in the world than intolerance. But I kept quiet.

'I haave been mad since I got to know, I don'dd need y-anny help from peeple like him!'

With the mercy one shows a dying creature, I smiled.

'He just bought it, that's all—it actually came from someone else. The erinjhi and the murikku and the paddy fields and the kottam can hardly bring the baby a mosquito-net umbrella and sheet! Anyway, please shut that door on your way out?'

82

My new friend and I lay there for some time, eyeing each other. Though swaddled quite tightly, she managed to stretch a hand and kick out a leg through the bundle.

'Wha's up?'I asked.

'Oh, it was quite hard coming out! And in the middle of it all, the pond I lay in suddenly got drained!! So it was simply not possible to lie on a banyan leaf and slide down here. Someone lifted me up.'

She stretched herself fully.

'That's alright. Wasn't bad at all. A great entry.' I consoled her.

'So you are my mother, right?'

'For the time being, yes.'

'The mess between the two of you . . . nearly drove me mad in there! I need some peace!'

'Will make sure you have some.'

'Ah, let that pass . . . how do I look? Like you thought?'

'You are so rosy!'

'How's this place, this . . .I mean, your neck of the woods?'

'What do you mean?'

'Clear. Does this place have a little scent of fish at noon and a little scent of man at night? Sure of that? If it's a no, then I am not game.'

She closed her eyes, folded her limbs, and became a reddish ball.

Then Kalyani-echi and Dakshayani-echi, came in carrying a big parcel, pushing open the lightly-closed door.

'Wha's goin' on, my dear!'

Kalyaniyechi came near and bent towards the baby.

'It's a girl, Kalyani-echi!'

'Girl is goldd! Goldd is tha wealth of tha land!'

'Leth tha land grow an' thribe! Leththa udders fill mor' an' mor'!'

Dakshayaniechi opened all the windows and the doors of the room.